DARLING JASMINE

Books by Bertrice Small

Leslie Family Saga (Cyra Hafisa)
- The Kadin
- Love Wild and Fair

The Border Chronicles
- A Dangerous Love
- The Border Lord's Bride
- The Captive Heart
- The Border Lord and Lady
- The Border Vixen
- Bond of Passion

O'Malley Family Saga
- Skye O'Malley
- All the Sweet Tomorrows
- This Heart of Mine
- A Love For All Time
- Lost Love Found
- Wild Jasmine

Wyndham Family Saga
- Blaze Wyndham
- Love, Remember Me

Skye's Legacy
- Darling Jasmine
- Bedazzled
- Besieged
- Intrigued
- Just Beyond Tomorrow
- Vixens

Friarsgate Inheritance
    Rosamund
    Until You
    Phillippa
    The Last Heiress
The Pleasure Channel
    Private Pleasures
    Forbidden Pleasures
    Sudden Pleasures
    Dangerous Pleasures
    Passionate Pleasures
    Guilty Pleasures
World of Hetar
    Lara
    A Distant Tomorrow
    The Twilight Lord
    The Sorceress of Belmair
    The Shadow Queen
    Crown of Destiny
The Silk Merchant's Daughters
    Bianca
    Francesca
    Lucianna
    Serena
Single Titles
    A Memory of Love
    A Moment in Time
    Adora
    Beloved
    Betrayed
    Deceived
    Enchantress Mine
    Hellion

The Dragon Lord's Daughters
The Duchess
The Innocent
The Love Slave
The Spitfire
To Love Again
Unconquered
Anthology Stories
    "Ecstasy" in Captivated
    "Mastering Lady Lucinda" in Fascinated
    "The Awakening" in Delighted
    "Zuleika and the Barbarian" in I Love Rogues

DARLING JASMINE

BERTRICE SMALL

Darling Jasmine

Copyright © 1997, 2022
All rights reserved.
This edition published 2022

Cover design by Elaine Tabol. Front cover image created by Tantor Media.

ISBN: 978-1-68068-360-8

The right of the author to be identified as the author of this work has been asserted in accordance with the Copyright, Designs, and Patents Act 1988.

The characters and events portrayed in this book are fictitious. Any similarity to real persons, living or dead, is coincidental and not intended by the author.

No part of this book may be reproduced or stored in a retrieval system, or transmitted in any form or by any means, electronic, mechanical, photocopying, recording or otherwise, without express written permission of the publisher.

This book is published on behalf of the author's estate by the Ethan Ellenberg Literary Agency.
Audiobook created and released by Tantor Media.

For Carol Stacy and Kathe Robin

Table of Contents

Queen's Malvern: *Twelfth Night, 1615* 1
Prologue...3
Chapter One 5
Chapter Two...19
Chapter Three 42
Chapter Four 60
Chapter Five..83

England: *Spring 1615* 107
Chapter Six..109
Chapter Seven 130
Chapter Eight......................................152
Chapter Nine 176
Chapter Ten 202
Chapter Eleven.....................................225
Chapter Twelve.....................................251

Scotland: *Autumn 1615–Autumn 1618* 271
Chapter Thirteen...................................273
Chapter Fourteen...................................291
Chapter Fifteen 314
Chapter Sixteen....................................337
Chapter Seventeen..................................360

Chapter Eighteen..................................381
Chapter Nineteen 402
Chapter Twenty 426

Queen's Malvern: *Midsummer's Eve 1623*..............449
Epilogue..451

About the Author................................455
About the Publisher.............................457

Queen's Malvern

Twelfth Night, 1615

Prologue

Adam de Marisco was dead. One moment he had been sitting at the highboard in the Great Hall of his home, surrounded by the many members of his family who were gathered to celebrate the holidays. Three of his stepsons and two of his stepdaughters, along with their families, grandchildren, and great-grandchildren packed the hall, which until a minute ago had been filled with laughter. *Adam's laughter.* Even at the advanced age of eighty-four, Adam de Marisco's laughter boomed loudly when he was amused. It was a particularly ribald jest spoken by his daughter-in-law, Valentina Burke, that had occasioned his latest bout of mirth.

Wiping his eyes, he had taken his wife's hand up in his and kissed it tenderly. Smiling out at them, he had said, "God bless you all, my dears!" Then his great leonine head had fallen forward upon his chest, and the hall was suddenly deathly silent.

She knew! Skye had, to her great shock, seen the lifelight fading rapidly from his blue eyes even as his lips had touched her skin. Almost immediately she thought, *Oh, Adam, my dearest, dearest love, how could you leave me like this?* And yet what a magnificent death it had been. He had not been ill, nor had he suffered, *and* he had left them with his blessing. It was so typical of Adam. His great heart had always been filled to overflowing with his love for them all. It was a merciful God that had taken him when he was surrounded by those whom he loved best.

"*Mama?*" Her daughter Deirdre Blakeley's voice quavered nearby.

Skye looked up, her eyes brimming with tears. *How can I cope with them at this moment,* she wondered. Yet who else was there? She knew she would not be allowed to mourn in peace until she had comforted them all, and assured them that everything was going to be fine despite the awful loss they had just endured. She loved her family, but would there ever come a time when they would look to themselves, and not to her? For a moment she was bitterly resentful, but swallowing back her own grief, she said, "It will be all right, Deirdre."

And then her children were surrounding her, offering her their love, their comfort, and support. But in Skye O'Malley's heart there was now an enormous empty place that could never, ever again be filled. Adam de Marisco was dead, and she was left alone to continue on without him.

Chapter One

Belle Fleurs
Winter 1615

"You simply cannot remain here alone, Mama," Willow, Lady Edwards, said in a firm tone that all of her children knew meant she would have her way in whatever matter she was discussing.

Skye O'Malley de Marisco stared out the window of her day room. The snow was falling lightly, but it had already covered Adam's grave site upon the hill. The snow, she thought, was better than that raw slash of dark earth. The snow softened everything.

"You are in your seventy fifth year, Mama," Willow continued.

"I have only just celebrated my seventy-fourth birthday last month, Willow," Skye said, her tone edgy with her irritation. She did not bother to turn her view from the landscape. It was growing dark. Soon she would not be able to see Adam's grave at all. Not until the dawn.

"A woman of your years cannot live by herself," Willow persisted.

"Why not?" her mother asked.

"*Why not?* Why not?" Willow blustered a moment, unprepared, although she knew she should have been, for the question. "Why, Mama, it simply isn't respectable for a matriarch of your age to live alone."

The light outside had faded completely now. Skye turned and faced her eldest daughter. "Go home, Willow," she said wearily. "I want you and all of your siblings to leave me in peace to mourn my husband of forty-two years. From the moment of Adam's death four nights ago you have not given me a moment's surcease. I need to be alone. I want to be alone. *Go home.*"

"But...but..." Willow began again, only to be silenced by a fierce look from her mother.

"I am not helpless, Willow. I have not yet lost my reason. I have absolutely no intention of closing up my home, displacing my servants, and moving myself in with *any* of my children. I intend remaining here at Queen's Malvern until I die. Is that quite clear?"

Daisy Kelly, Skye's faithful tiring woman, felt her mouth turning up in a small smile, but she withheld her laughter as she sat by the fire, mending the hem on one of her mistress's gowns. She was surprised at how little Mistress Willow seemed to know her mother if she actually believed Skye would come and live with her, or any of her other children. They might not be as young as they once were, Daisy ruefully admitted to herself as she squinted to see her stitches, but she and her lady were perfectly capable of looking out for themselves.

"But, Mama," Willow persisted, "Queen's Malvern no longer belongs to you. It belongs to the little duke of Lundy, Charles Frederick Stuart."

"Do you really believe that either my granddaughter, or the duke's guardian, the earl of Glenkirk, would dispossess me, Willow?" Skye snapped. "I think it is you who have lost her wits, and not I."

"Jemmie Leslie was back at court this autumn, Mama," Willow informed her mother. "He is very angry that he has not yet been able to track Jasmine down in France. It will be two years this spring since she fled him, taking the children with her."

Skye chuckled wickedly. "I do not know why he has been unable to find her," she said. "After all, Adam practically told him exactly where to look, but then, of course, I did send a messenger to warn her of her grandfather's lapse in judgment."

"Ohh, Mama, how could you?" Willow wailed. "You will make an enemy of the king should your interference with James Stuart's will become public knowledge! Was it not enough that you made an enemy of our good queen, Bess? Has age taught you no discretion?"

"My darling girl has made two marriages to please her family," Skye said in firm tones. "I hope that this time she will be able to make her own choice, Willow. No one, not even the king, should force Jasmine to the altar. It was foolish of James Stuart and his silly romantic queen to even try."

"But Jemmie Leslie loves Jasmine, Mama," Willow said softly.

"I know," Skye said, "but it is not all a certainty that Jasmine loves him. I shall go to France in the spring, and tell my granddaughter of her grandfather's death. Then we will see what she wants to do. Though I miss her, the choice must be hers to make."

"*You will go to France?*" Willow looked horrified.

"If you suggest that I am too ancient a crone to travel any longer," Skye told her daughter, "I shall surely smack you, Willow!" Her Kerry blue eyes glared at Lady Edwards.

"I was not thinking any such thing," Willow replied, although in truth she was.

"And when the snow stops you will leave," Skye said firmly. "You and *all* of your siblings. I need time to come to terms with the fact my dearest Adam has departed. *I must be alone.* I realize that you do not understand that Willow, but you must accept it."

Willow nodded, defeated, and, curtsying to her mother, left her apartments, making her way to the family hall where her brothers and sister awaited her.

"Well?" demanded the earl of Lynmouth, Robin Southwood, his lime green eyes twinkling. "Is Mama come to live with you in her dotage?"

"Oh, be silent, Robin!" Willow snapped. "I hate it when you are smug. Mama is most recalcitrant, as she always is when asked to be reasonable. I could get nowhere with her, as you fully expected, but I had to try. She wants us all to leave as soon as the snow stops."

"Should she be left alone?" Angel, countess of Lynmouth, worried.

"She absolutely insists upon it," Willow said sourly.

"I can understand that," said Deirdre, Lady Blackthorne, Skye's middle daughter. "Mama will show no weakness to anyone, even her children. Have any of you yet seen her cry? We must all go home as soon as we can, so she may mourn Adam in her own fashion."

Her siblings, and their mates, even Willow, nodded in agreement.

"'Tis not a strong storm," Padraic, Lord Burke, said. "'Twill be over by the morrow. We had best set our servants to packing."

"Mama says she is going to France to tell Jasmine herself," Willow informed them. "Sometime in the spring, she says."

"Has anyone sent to my mother and my father?" asked Sybilla, the countess of Kempe, a granddaughter of the de Mariscos.

"I dispatched a messenger the morning after," Robin Southwood told his niece. "I don't imagine he has reached Dun Broc yet with this weather, but in a few more days Velvet will know her father is dead."

"Poor Mama," Sybilla said softly, and her husband put a comforting arm about her shoulders.

"Aye, Velvet will be devastated," Murrough O'Flaherty said soberly. "She adored Adam. Hell! We all did now, didn't we? He was the one father we can all remember. None of mother's other husbands lived long enough though we may recall them slightly."

The others nodded solemnly.

"Adam was father to us all," Lord Burke said, "and a good father, too. We learned much from him."

"Do you think Mama can survive his loss?" Deirdre wondered.

"She will miss him greatly," Robin said quietly, "but I do not think Skye O'Malley is ready to give up the ghost yet, sister. She has survived the others well enough."

"But she was younger then," Willow noted.

"True," Robin agreed with his elder sibling, "but she is stronger now than she has ever been. We will leave our mother to mourn our father as she wishes to do. Then we will see."

"I wonder if she will wed again," Valentina Burke mused.

"*Never!*" Robin spoke emphatically. "Of that I am certain."

The snow had stopped the following morning as Skye O'Malley's children and other relations departed Queen's

Malvern. Each had bid the matriarch a fond farewell, and then clambered into their separate coaches to begin their journey home.

"Ye'll send for me if ye need me, sister, won't ye?" Conn O'Malley St. Michael, Lord Bliss, asked his elder sibling.

"If I need ye," Skye told him.

Conn shook his head. She was a proud woman, his sister, but he and his wife, Aidan, were near enough in case of emergency.

"*Cardiff Rose* will be ready when you need her, Mama," Murrough O'Flaherty said softly so only she might hear him.

Skye nodded and kissed her second born, and then his wife.

"God speed you safely home," she told them.

"I simply don't know what to say to you, Mama," Willow declared as she confronted her mother a final time.

"Farewell will do quite nicely, Willow," Skye replied, kissing her daughter upon the cheek. She turned to her son-in-law, James. "Godspeed, my lord. I do not envy you your trip."

"I sleep quite heavily upon the road," he replied with a twinkle in his eyes. "I do not hear anything."

"Thank God for that!" Skye said, and then she turned to her granddaughter, Sybilla. "Are you breeding again, Sibby?"

Sybilla chuckled. "Aye, madame, I fear I am, and 'twill make five. The babe will come in early June. Perhaps it will cheer Mama."

Skye nodded. "Take care of each other," she told Sybilla, and her husband, Tom Ashburne, the earl of Kempe.

Deirdre Burke was teary, but she struggled to maintain her composure as she bid her mother farewell.

"Now, Deirdre," Skye scolded the most fragile of her children, "you're just going home, and God knows you live near enough to see me whenever you like, but for mercy's sake give me a few days of peace."

Deirdre swallowed hard and nodded, as her husband, John, helped her into their coach.

"I don't like leaving you like this," Padraic Burke said.

"I need to be alone," Skye told her youngest son. "There is plenty of family nearby should I need them." She gave him a hug. "Yer like yer father. You don't think I can take care of myself, but I can, Padraic. Now let me be to mourn my Adam."

"Get into the coach, Padraic," his wife, Valentina, said in a firm tone. She kissed her mother-in-law's cheek, and gave her a wink.

The last to depart was the earl of Lynmouth and his family. Angel and her children had bid Skye good-bye. Now it came time for Robin Southwood to say adieu to his mother. "Will you consult with me, Mama, before you do anything rash?" he asked her wryly.

"Most likely not, Robin," she said, smiling at him.

"You're already plotting," he accused her.

She smiled mischievously. "How can you tell? It has been years since I did any serious plotting, Robin."

He laughed. "I remember the look, madame." Then he grew serious. "I am glad I was here this Twelfth Night instead of giving my fete in London. The damned thing has become outrageously expensive. I count it good fortune that I came to Queen's Malvern this year."

"I loved your father's fetes," Skye said, the memories rising to fill her heart. "Especially the Twelfth Night one. I can still see the queen's barge making its way up the river to Lynmouth House. Twelfth Night has always been special to me. I knew I carried you one Twelfth Night, Robin. And do you remember that Twelfth Night just a few years back when

Jasmine almost caused a scandal because Sybilla caught her in bed with Lord Leslie. And now Twelfth Night will always be etched in my memory with Adam's passing." She shivered, and drew her cloak about her shoulders. "I shall never enjoy the holiday again."

"Though I know you need your solitude," Robin said, "I dislike leaving you, madame." His arm was tight about her.

"I feel fragile at this moment, Robin," she admitted to him, "but it will pass. It did with your father, and it did with Niall."

But you had Adam to be your bulwark each time, Robin considered, but kept the thought to himself. "Tell me before you leave England," he said. "And tell that niece of mine to come home." He kissed her soft cheek, then hugged her hard.

"Godspeed, Robin," Skye said to her son, then stood watching as his coach made its way down the drive and around a bend, out of her sight.

"Yer a devious old woman," Daisy told her mistress as she helped her into the house. "You have no intention of telling him when yer leaving for France, do ye?"

Skye chuckled. "Of course not," she replied. "If I tell Robin, he will tell the earl of Glenkirk who will seek to follow me to Jasmine and the children. Nay, I'll not tell him a thing."

"He'll tell the earl anyway when he passes through London in a few days," Daisy said.

"Which is why I'll already be on my way to France," Skye answered her tiring woman. "They'll not use me to force my darling girl back to England. She'll not come unless she chooses to come."

"Oh, yer a wicked creature," Daisy said chortling, but then she grew serious. "How will ye mourn his lordship if ye go, my lady?"

"I do not have to remain at Queen's Malvern to mourn my Adam," Skye told her servant. "Adam is always with me no matter where I go."

"I'll begin packing this very day, m'lady," Daisy said, "and I'll pray for a calm sea when we cross to France."

"You do not have to come with me, Daisy. I can take a younger lass to serve me. I think Martha would do, do ye not?"

"I do not!" Daisy said indignantly. "Yer not going off without me this time, Mistress Skye. We're of an age, you and I. If you can travel, then so can I! Martha indeed! Why the chit is a slattern, and not fit to serve a child. Martha, humph," Daisy snorted. Then she bustled off to begin packing for their trip.

Skye had not yet removed her cloak. Pulling the hood up, she slipped from the house and, walking through the barely ankle-deep snow, made her way across the lawns and up the gentle hillock to her husband's grave. A small wooden cross marked the spot although later there would be a more impressive monument of stone. She stopped and stared down.

"Well, now, old man," she said softly, "and didn't you give us a Twelfth Night to remember. How could you leave me, Adam? Ahhh, I know 'twas not your fault." She sighed deeply. "They've all gone now. I don't know when I've been quite so irritated with Willow. Yes, yes, I know she means well, but you know how I dislike it when she tries to run my life. Three daughters. One who brays constantly like a donkey; the second, a dear mousekin; and the third, in Scotland. God's boots!"

A gentle wind ruffled the fur edging the cloak's hood, and a small smile touched the corners of Skye's mouth. "Now don't go trying to wheedle around me, Adam de Marisco," she said. "You know that I'm correct. Not one of my girls is a bit like me. Only Jasmine is like me, old man, and well you know it. I'll have to leave you for a while because I'm off to France to tell her of how you left us. She's enjoying her freedom, I can tell, but 'tis past time she came home with the children and settled down. She won't have an easy time with Lord Leslie until she makes her peace with him. You were right, old man. I should have insisted she come home long since instead of encouraging her in her rebellion. Ahhh, Adam, I can almost hear you laughing with my admission. I didn't often say you were wiser than I, but you were, my dearest."

Two days later, before the dawn had even begun to tint the eastern skies, Thistlewood, the de Marisco coachman, climbed up onto the box of his mistress's great traveling coach where his assistant already waited. "Well, me boy," he said, his breath coming in icy little puffs, "we're off for France we are. At least this day appears to be coming on fair, but Jesu, 'tis cold!" He settled himself and, turning, asked the younger man, "Are ye ready then?" And at his companion's nod, Thistlewood cracked his whip over the horses' heads. The coach lurched forward, moving slowly down the drive of Queen's Malvern toward the main road and southeast toward the coast.

In London the earl of Lynmouth found his friend, the earl of Glenkirk, at Whitehall Palace. "Are you in the mood to bring a wily vixen to heel, Jemmie?" he asked, a wicked smile upon his lips.

"You know where she is?" James Leslie replied, his tone cold.

"No, but if you are quick, I know how you may find her," Robin Southwood replied. Then he went on to explain that his stepfather had died, and Skye had said she would go to France to tell Jasmine.

"In the spring?" James Leslie said. "Then there is time."

"My mother said in the spring, but she is guileful as always. I would wager she'll be on the road now, racing for the coast, because she knows full well that on my way home I have come to London to tell you. I set two riders on my brother Murrough, who did not go straight home as he said, but rather has headed for Harwich according to information I received today. Mama will cross to Calais from there. You must get to Dover so you may intercept her and follow her to wherever my niece has hidden herself."

The earl of Glenkirk's green eyes narrowed in contemplation. Thanks to Robin Southwood, he was finally to catch up with the recalcitrant dowager marchioness of Westleigh, Jasmine de Marisco Lindley. A woman he had once believed himself in love with, but whom he had learned to hate these past twenty-one months since she had made him the laughingstock of the court by jilting him in the face of King James's order that they marry. Worse, she had taken the king's grandson, the late Prince Henry's infant, their child, with her. Yet the king had appointed Glenkirk the boy's legal guardian. But now for the first time in almost two years he had a serious chance of catching Jasmine, and this time, he instinctively knew he would catch her.

He had known she was in France all along, but the three times he had crossed the Channel to entrap her she was always gone, and her French relations always claimed no knowledge of her, shrugging in that particularly irritating Gallic way the French had. Yet his informants were his own relations who had married into France. They had played a very crafty cat and mouse game these many months, but somehow Jasmine always knew when he was coming, and was gone, with her children, before he could reach her. This time it would be different because no one knew he was coming. Because he would follow the old countess of Lundy right to Jasmine's door. *And then.* He smiled wolfishly.

"I take it," Robin Southwood said, "that you are pleased with my information, my lord."

"Aye," Glenkirk said.

"One thing, my lord," the earl of Lynmouth spoke in quiet, yet serious tones. "Charles Frederick Stuart is now the duke of Lundy, but Queen's Malvern is my mother's home, and has been for decades. You may take whatever vengeance you wish on my niece, Jasmine, but you will treat my mother with the dignity and respect to which she is entitled, *and you will not dispossess her.* If you render her any discourtesy, you will not have just me to contend with, my lord. Remember that BrocCairn is her son-in-law, and related to the king. And BrocCairn is Jasmine's stepfather as well. And do not forget Alcester, Kempe, and Lord Burke. They would be most unhappy should mama be discommoded in any way."

The earl of Glenkirk gave his friend a frosty smile. "I am more than well aware of Madame Skye's familial connections, Robin. I have no quarrel with your mother although I suspect she is more behind this than either of us knows. Besides, did you not know that Queen's Malvern belongs to her outright. It is not entailed upon the title."

"Of course!" Robin said. "She and Adam bought it years ago from the queen. Bess was always short of money. While it was a royal property she loaned it to them. The old queen sold it to my mother and stepfather when she couldn't pay her bills and needed the ready coin."

"So you need have to worry that your mother will come to live with you," Glenkirk mocked his friend.

"Live with me?" The earl of Lynmouth laughed. "My sister suggested to Mama that a widow of her many years should

not live alone and insisted Mama come to live with her. Need I tell you the outcome of that altercation, Jemmie? My mother has done what pleased her since birth and will continue to do so until the day she dies, but between us I am not certain that God above wants her back too soon."

Glenkirk laughed loudly. "You may be right," he said.

Robin Southwood took his leave of James Leslie and continued on with his family to his home at Lynmouth in Devon. There he found his man but an hour ahead of him.

"You was right, my lord," the servant said. *"Cardiff Rose* was docked at Harwich, and was scheduled to put out today with the tide for France. Yer mother was expected aboard her. I passed her coach two days ago on the road as I left, but they wouldn't recognize me now."

"Do you think James Leslie will find Jasmine this time?" Angel, the countess of Lynmouth, asked her husband.

"If he didn't dawdle he could have gotten to Dover and be in Calais before Mama," the earl considered. "Even with a fair wind it will take her at least overnight from Harwich. The Dover crossing is far shorter, my love." He patted her pretty hand.

"Why did Madame Skye not take that route then, Robin?" she inquired, curious.

"Because Mama would not want to come anywhere near London for fear of being recognized by someone, although there are few now at court who would know her. Still, she would not take the chance. She would risk the sea before she would risk being found out in her little deception. This time, however, she is doomed to failure."

"But surely Jemmie will not reveal himself to her until she is safely with Jasmine," Angel said.

"Nay, he will not," Robin agreed. "Actually, I am not certain what he will do, but I believe my niece has made an enemy of the man who is to be her husband. She will have to work hard to win him back."

"I think," Angel said, "that it is James Leslie who must put aside his pride and work hard to woo Jasmine, else their life together be a misery. Neither of them is easy."

Robin laughed. "You are a wise woman, sweetheart," he told her. "And, you are beginning to sound like my mother."

"Why, Robin, what a lovely compliment," Angel Southwood said, her eyes twinkling, her pretty mouth turned up in a smile.

He chuckled. "With any other woman I might believe her to be sarcastic, but not you, my love. You actually are pleased I have said you remind me of Mama."

Angel nodded. "She is a grand woman, Robin!"

"Aye," the earl of Lynmouth agreed. "She is a grand woman, but dear heaven she is no less troublesome in her old age than she was as a girl." He chortled again. "James Leslie is going to have his hands full with those two! I do not envy him his journey."

Chapter Two

James Leslie had left London with his servant, Fergus More, almost immediately. They had embarked from Dover as the earl of Lynmouth had suggested and were waiting upon the docks when *Cardiff Rose* put into Calais. Standing in the shadows they watched as the vessel was made fast, its gangway run up, the unloading done. Skye's great traveling coach had made the short journey lashed to the deck of the ship. Now it was carefully rolled off onto the land to the doors of a large warehouse. Immediately the doors were opened and sturdy horses brought forth to be harnessed to the vehicle. The activity in and about the coach held little interest for the earl of Glenkirk once it had begun. He watched the gangway, and eventually Madame Skye came forth, the captain of her ship escorting her to her coach, her servants following.

But only when she was settled in the conveyance, and her two coachmen up on their box, did the earl say quietly to his companion, "Time to mount up, Fergus. We dare not lose the old lady."

"There's only one way off the docks, my lord," Fergus replied. "Best we wait for her at the entry. Ye don't want anyone seeing us following her, and there's too many of her people here."

James Leslie nodded, and the two men discreetly led their mounts from the shadows and off the docks. Shortly afterward the coach rolled onto the street of the town, and the earl began his secret pursuit. From Calais they followed the road to Amiens, and then on to Paris. James Leslie was surprised at how intrepid a traveler his quarry was, considering her age. She lingered but a night at any inn, even in Paris, where he almost lost her, for she did not overnight at a public place, but rather at the home of one of her late husband's relations. Taking the chance that she would not depart before her usual hour the following day, he found a nearby inn where he and Fergus might get a hot meal and a bed.

"You was right," Fergus said the next morning as they again picked up the chase.

"She's no fool," the earl replied. "She's anxious to get there, but she knows she needs her rest, and so do her horses. There's no real need for haste although she's certainly not dallying."

From Paris to Fontainebleau to Montargis to Orléans to Blois.

"She is headed for Archambault," the earl said.

"We've been there before, and yer lady ain't been there," Fergus More noted. "Ye don't think the old lady knows she's being followed?"

"We've been too careful," James Leslie decided aloud.

But they passed by the gates to Archambault, and through the château's village. Finally, several miles from Archambault, the coach turned off on a narrow side road. James Leslie drew his horse to a stop. A light drizzle was falling, as it had been for the past few days. Silently he signaled with his hand for Fergus More to move forward carefully, so that their mounts were close together.

"This road can only go one place," he said softly. "To some sort of dwelling. We will wait and give Madame Skye time to reach her destination." He drew his cloak about him. It was damnably chilly.

"I saw a small inn back in the village," Fergus said hopefully.

The earl of Glenkirk shook his head. "Nay, I want no word of foreign strangers reaching this place until I have learned what is at the end of this little road. We'll wait here."

Fergus sighed.

They waited, and after a half an hour the earl deemed it safe for them to move down the narrow track. Several minutes later they rounded a bend, and before them was a small lake. Artfully set upon the shore so that it was surrounded by water on three sides was an exquisite little château. Built of flattened, rough-hewn blocks of reddish gray schist, the château had four polygonal towers crowned with dark slate roofs resembling witches' caps, one at each corner of the building. Access could only be gained through a tall, well-fortified chatelet, which was flanked by rounded corbeled towers that rose on each side of the entry arch. The earl stopped, enchanted by the beauty before him. He could see a garden on the fourth side of the chateau with low stone walls keeping out the forest that lay beyond. Even in deepest winter it was absolutely lovely.

"M'lord?" Fergus More spoke low.

James Leslie signaled silently for them to move forward. The horses' hooves echoed as they crossed the drawbridge and entered the courtyard, where the great traveling coach was now being unloaded. The servants looked curiously at the two travelers, but two stable lads hurried forward to take their horses, and the earl entered the building, his man behind him.

"Jesu!" Thistlewood, coming out of the stables where he and his assistant had been seeing to their own horses, said. "That looks like the earl of Glenkirk!"

"I thought we was being followed once or twice," said his companion, then staggered with the blow the coachman gave him.

"Ye daft lad! Why did ye not say something to me then?"

"I wasn't certain of it," the younger man replied, rubbing his head. "It wasn't until we left Paris, and this is a strange country."

Thistlewood shook his head wearily. Well, it wasn't his business anyway. His old mistress would take care of any trouble that came their way. She always had, and age hadn't slowed her down like it had the rest of them, he thought ruefully. "Let's go to the kitchens and get something warm to drink and some food," he told his assistant.

Adali saw James Leslie first as he stood in the hallway of the château directing the servants with the luggage. His smooth face indicated immediate surprise, which he quickly masked, but not before the earl had seen it.

James Leslie smiled wolfishly. "Tell your mistress I am here, Adali," he ordered the man. "Wait! On second thought take me to your lady. I cannot take the chance that she will evaporate before I have even seen her."

"Follow me, my lord," Jasmine's most trusted servant said.

The château had a small hall, to which Adali led the earl and his servant. It was a warm and cheerful room. Madame Skye was seated in a high-backed chair by one of the fireplaces, her boots by her side, a silver goblet in her hand, her stockinged feet to the blaze. Next to her Jasmine sat upon a stool, looking almost girlish, although she was now twenty-five, and the mother of four children. She was wearing her dark hair in a manner he could not remember seeing before. It was braided into a thick plait and twined with red ribbon. His gaze softened a moment, but then hardened with his resolve.

"The earl of Glenkirk, my princess," Adali said clearly.

Jasmine, dowager marchioness of Westleigh, jumped to her feet, turning to face him.

"*You!*" she spat angrily.

"Aye, madame, 'tis I," James Leslie said with understatement. "You have led me a fine chase, but 'tis over now."

"Get out of my house!" Jasmine shouted at him. "You have absolutely no jurisdiction over me. This is France, not England!"

"I beg to differ, madame. The king of England ordered our marriage two years ago, and the king currently treats with King Louis in the matter of a marriage between Prince Charles and the king's sister."

"King James seeks a Spanish match with the infanta, Doña Maria," Jasmine snapped. "Even here in my backwater I know that!"

"Would you like to argue the point with me, madame?" Glenkirk said. "You are the wife chosen for me by King James, and you will wed with me, madame. Remember, I am your children's guardian."

"You are Charles Frederick Stuart's guardian," Jasmine replied, "although I do not know why the king felt he needed a guardian at all."

"Nay, madame, I am guardian of *all* your children now," the earl said with devastating effect. "Your foolish and unruly behavior convinced the king that you were not fit to guide your bairns. I hold the future of not just Charles Frederick Stuart in my hands, but that of young Westleigh, Lady India, and Lady Fortune Lindley as well."

"You bastard!" Jasmine said furiously.

"Nay, madame," he replied mockingly. "My parents were betrothed for some months, and wed at least ten minutes before my birth."

Jasmine turned to her grandmother. "Madame, how could you bring him here? Is this why you have come? I shall never forgive you!"

"I did not bring him, my dearest girl," Skye said quietly.

"I followed your grandmother from the moment she arrived in Calais," the earl said.

"Robin?" Skye asked him.

He nodded. "He suspected you would not wait until spring," James Leslie said. "He sent two servants to follow Captain O'Flaherty's carriage, certain he would not go home but to Harwich instead."

Skye nodded, a small smile upon her lips. "Robert Southwood is indeed my son." She chuckled. "And he has his father's guile."

"If you did not bring *him* here to Belle Fleurs, Grandmama, then why have you come?" Jasmine inquired.

"Your grandfather is dead," came the immediate reply.

Jasmine gasped, and her eyes immediately filled with tears that flowed down her smooth cheeks. "Oh, Grandpapa," she half whispered. Then she turned on the earl of Glenkirk. "This is all your fault!" she cried. "If you had not hounded me from England, I should have had these last few months with him! Now, I shall never see him again, and it is all because of you, James Leslie! I hate you! *I hate you!*"

"Nay, madame," he said in icy tones. "Whatever you have lost is *your* fault, *not mine.* You did not have to disobey the king and run from me almost two years ago. A marriage was arranged between us. I loved you. I was willing to give you all the time you needed to mourn Prince Henry Stuart's death. I was not dragging you by force to the altar, Jasmine. You, however, took it upon yourself to gather up your children, and in direct defiance of King James's order, decamp from England. I knew you were in France. Three times I came, but I could not find you, for your relations hid you well. Now, however, the game is up. We will return to England, where you will wed me in a large and public ceremony, standing before that same court who have found such amusement in the April Fool you made of me those many months back."

"I will not!" she said angrily.

"Oh, but you will, madame," he answered her.

"I am a royal Mughal princess..." she began.

"Who cannot return home to India," he cut her off. "You have lived in Europe for ten years, Jasmine. You are an English gentlewoman now, and no longer an imperial Mughal. Your grandmother must have a few days' rest, then we shall begin the return journey to England. Do not attempt to escape me again, my darling Jasmine. Cadby needs its young master, and would you keep Rowan Lindley's son from his inheritance? And what of your daughters? I'll wager you have let them run with the peasants' children. None of them, I am certain, has begun any learning. They are English nobility, and you would do well to remember it!"

"I will kill you before I allow you control over my children," Jasmine snarled at him.

"Be silent, both of you!" Skye's voice suddenly cut into the conversation. "Adali, get Lord Leslie some wine, and then take his man to the kitchen for food. What is your name, Scotsman?"

"Fergus More, yer ladyship."

"Go with Adali, Fergus More. Your master is safe with me," Skye told him, and then, turning back to Jasmine, said, "I came to tell you of Adam's death, my darling girl, but I also came to tell you that it was time to resolve your difficulties with Glenkirk. Past time. While it was outrageous of the king to insist upon this match, I am beginning to believe it is a good idea. You cannot remain here at Belle Fleurs, isolated, and alone but for the children, and your servants. It is not good for you, and it is certainly not good for my great-grandchildren. Jemmie Leslie is right. Henry Lindley is the marquis of Westleigh as his father before him was. He is almost seven now, and I will wager his French is better than his English. He must go home to Cadby and learn to be its master, and an Englishman again. India will be eight next month, and Fortune is five. Do any of them know their letters? Or how to write? And what of the king's grandson, little Charles Frederick Stuart. He is the most royal of all your children, but what will his fate be if he does not return to England where he can gain his grandfather, the king's, favor? You must think of the children, Jasmine."

The younger woman gnawed at her lower lip, vexed. She knew her grandmother was correct, yet she struggled against herself. Glancing at James Leslie from beneath her wet lashes, she decided that he was still a very handsome man, but at this particular moment he looked very stern. It was a look she could not remember seeing on his face before.

"Just once," she said, "I should like the freedom to pick my own husband." Grumbling she continued. "My father chose Jamal Khan, and you and Grandfather chose Rowan Lindley. When do I get to choose?"

"Were you unhappy with either of your husbands, Jasmine?" Skye questioned her granddaughter.

"No," Jasmine admitted, "but you got to choose your husbands!"

"Dom O'Flaherty, my first husband, may he rot in hell, was my father's choice. Willow's father rescued me from slavery in Algiers and married me. Niall Burke was chosen for me by my uncle, the bishop, and we were wed by proxy without my knowledge. Fabron de Beaumont was the old queen's selection. Only Geoffrey Southwood and your grandfather were my decisions, Jasmine."

"And they were your happiest marriages," her granddaughter said. "I do not believe I will have six husbands, Grandmama. I want to make my own selection this time. I won't be coerced dammit!"

"Madame," the earl of Glenkirk said quietly, "you have no options but to obey your king as do I. To disobey is treason, as you well know, but should you choose such a dangerous option be advised that I shall return to England in several days' time with my four charges, the infant duke of Lundy, the marquis of Westleigh, and the ladies India and Fortune Lindley. If you wish to remain mother to your children, you will accompany us. If you do not, I shall see that you never see them again, for you shall be banned from King James's realm forever."

Jasmine's unusual turquoise-colored eyes widened with shock. *"You bastard!"* she hissed. "You would do that to me?"

He looked at her dispassionately. "I thought we had settled the matter of my birth, madame, and yes, I will obey the king."

She flung her goblet at his head, but ducking it he reached up to grasp her wrist in a firm hold. Slowly he forced her arm down, and back behind her, drawing her against him. Then, bending, he kissed her a fierce kiss, his lips hard, the embrace a clear declaration of war between them. Jasmine struggled, but could not break his hold on her, but when he released her a moment later, she reared back and slapped him with all her might. Then, turning about, she ran from the hall.

"Is it that you hate her or love her?" Skye asked him, curious.

James Leslie shook his dark head. "Once I loved her to distraction. When I arrived here today I thought I hated her. Now I don't know what I feel for her, Madame Skye. Why does she resist her fate so strongly?"

"Surely you have known since you first met her, my lord, that Jasmine is very proud, and absolutely determined to have her way in life," Skye answered him. "We both know that the king meant well for her when he ordered your marriage, and indeed it is an ideal solution for Jasmine. Even I am now willing to admit to it. You are an excellent candidate for her hand, as you are in high favor with King James, *and* you have your own wealth."

"I am astounded by this turn of events, madame," the earl of Glenkirk replied. "You were, if I am not mistaken, highly involved in Jasmine's departure from England almost two years ago."

"Indeed I was," Skye admitted, not one bit abashed. "But I only meant for her to have a little bit of time to compose herself and come to terms with her fate. Unfortunately the months became a year, and I swear to you that I meant to bring her home, but somehow I did not get around to it. I have a very large family, my lord, and they always seem to need one thing or another from me." She gave him a weak smile, and shrugged her elegant shoulders. "I am not as young as I once was. I regret I did not take action soon in this particular matter. Jasmine has, I fear, become quite independent of us all."

"Does she love her bairns enough to follow them?" he wondered.

"Whatever happens, my lord, do not weaken in your resolve," she told him. "I will help you to the best of my ability."

"You have not answered my question, madame," he replied.

"She loves her children, yes. Jasmine is a devoted mother," Skye replied, "but I will have all I can do to keep her from acting rashly again, my lord. In this endeavor, however, I will have the help of her servants. That trio have been with her since birth. They are used to all her moods and crochets. Her steward, Adali, has been a surrogate father to her. He will act in her best interest, and the two maidservants will follow suit. As for you, James Leslie, you would be well advised to loosen your curb rein a trifle. Highstrung thoroughbred mares do not respond well to it, or to the whip. As a woman who raises horses I possess expert knowledge, and you would do well to take advantage of my expertise in this matter." She struggled to her feet, thinking to herself that while she felt no older, and her mind still seemed to operate in relatively good order, her bones were old, and the rainy, dank weather was not helping at all. "Are you hungry, my lord? Surely you must be after traveling all day. I envy you your horses. That damned coach is a trial to ride in anymore, I can tell you."

He chuckled and, taking her arm, led her to the highboard, where the servants were even now setting out the evening meal. She had not bothered to put her boots back on, and walked in her stockinged feet. She lost none of her dignity for it, he thought. Adali appeared and settled the old woman in her chair.

"Where is your mistress?" the earl asked him.

"She has locked herself in her bedchamber and is swearing quite colorfully in at least three languages, my lord," came the calm reply. "Rohana and Toramalli are in her apartment. They will see she does not leave Belles Fleurs without your lordship."

"And the children?" He had seen neither hide nor hair of them since his arrival. "Where are the bairns, Adali?"

"In the nursery, my lord. Would you like to see them now or after you have eaten. They are already abed, however."

"Madame Skye and I will see them on the morrow, Adali," James Leslie replied.

"Shall I see a tray is taken up to my lady?" Adali asked.

"No," came the answer. "If your lady wishes to eat, then she must join us here at the highboard. She is not ill. Go and tell her we would welcome her company."

"Very good, my lord," Adali responded, his smooth light tan face bland as a pudding. He could but imagine what his mistress was going to say to such an invitation, but he was strangely comforted by the earl's firmness. Over the last months his lady had become more and more intractable and mulish. She had allowed her offspring to run wild. The three older ones spoke a mixture of Pidgin French and English to each other, and French to the servants. Jasmine had practically neglected them in her grief over Prince Henry's death. She lavished all of her attention upon his son, who turned two the previous September, and the lad was in danger of becoming very spoiled. It would be good for his lady to have a man in the house again, in her bed again. Now all they had to do was convince her of that fact.

He found his mistress now out of her bedchamber and directing her two maidservants in packing her trunks.

"We'll be gone before either he or my grandmother awaken in the morning, Adali," she said. "Is there something you can put in the wine tonight to assure them a sound sleep?"

Adali signaled the two maidservants to cease their activity. "You would leave your children, my lady?" he said quietly.

"Of course not!" she cried. "The children will come with us. Why would you think I would leave the children?"

"In your determination to have your own way, my princess, you would deliberately disobey the king of England and rob your four children of their inheritance? Such irrational behavior reminds me of your brother, Salim, now the Grande Mughal Jahangir," Adali said. His brown eyes surveyed her calmly. As a boy he had resembled his Indian mother. Now, a man in his late middle years, he favored his French father.

Jasmine was surprised by his words. Adali had been with her her entire life, and she thought of him as her best friend. Her anger diffused, she said, "Surely you do not suggest that I wed with the earl of Glenkirk?"

"He is a good match for you, my princess. A wealthy man who stands in high favor with King James. He is attractive, and you have already had the benefit of a night in his bed those many years ago. I do not seem to recall you considered him a poor lover then. He likes your children, and wants sons of his own. What more is there, my princess? Women of your high caste do not wed on whim, and without a powerful husband you can do nothing but sit and wait for death to come."

"Violent death has claimed both of my husbands, Adali," Jasmine responded. "And death reached out to claim Prince Henry, unexpectedly and in his prime. The earl of Glenkirk would do well to reconsider before wedding with such a woman as I. Perhaps my brother has cursed me from afar. Besides, James Leslie has no love for me any longer.

He marries me to please the king and for no other reason. Indeed from the look in his eye I would say he hates me, Adali."

"Then you should have no great feeling of loss if he dies violently as did Jamal Khan and Rowan Lindley," Adali reasoned with her, *"and* you will have obeyed the king, thus regaining his favor for yourself and your children. If your brother has indeed cursed you, my princess, and the men you give your heart to die, then surely Lord Leslie will feel the sting of the Mughal's malediction, too. It is an ideal way to rid yourself of your enemy, is it not?"

"You do not believe for a moment that I am cursed, do you, Adali?" Jasmine said irritably. "You are all against me now, even my grandmother. She will help the earl, which is why I must flee tonight else I shall never have another opportunity."

"Again you put your self-interest before that of your children," Adali scolded her roundly. "You have been alone too long, my princess. You must come back into the world again, and the children with you. I will not help you to run this time, and neither will Rohana or Toramalli. Besides, my daughter, where can you go if you leave Belle Fleurs? King James's lands will be forbidden, so you cannot go to England, Scotland, or your Irish estates. You have only managed to hide here in France with the aid of your relations; but when Madame Skye tells them 'Nay,' then France will be closed to you, too. Besides, there is already war in this land over religion. Soon it will not be safe at all. Where else is there for you? We both know you cannot return to India and your brother. There is no place for you except by your husband's side, my princess." The eunuch was firm of tone, and his look told Jasmine that for the first time in her life she had no other options but those very unpalatable ones presented to her. "Shall I tell his lordship you will be joining them at the highboard, my princess?" Adali gently pressed her.

She wanted to say no, but she was hungry. The idea of sneaking down into her own kitchens to steal food was intolerable. Besides, why should he drive her from her own table? James Leslie was arrogant beyond any man she had ever met, but God's nightshirt, he would not keep her from her supper. "I must change my gown," Jasmine said in regal Mughal tones. "Please tell my grandmother that I shall join her shortly." Dismissing Adali, she turned to her maidservants.

Adali restrained his delight that his mistress had decided to act in a reasonable fashion. It was, he knew, a temporary measure until Jasmine could come up with some other scheme to avoid doing her duty, but they would defuse that problem when it reared its head. Reentering the hall, he said, "My mistress will join you momentarily. She is changing her gown, my lord."

"Well done, Adali!" Skye complimented him. "Was she packing?"

The steward laughed. "Aye, madame, she was, but as I pointed out to her, she has no other place to hide. Her place is by her husband's side now not just for her own standing, but for the children's as well." Adali bowed, then began directing the serving of the evening meal.

James Leslie watched him with a speculative gaze.

"He is loyal to her first and foremost," Skye said quietly in answer to the unspoken question, "but he serves her best interests even when she disagrees with him. Treat her well, and he will be your most valuable ally, my lord. Remember, a powerful king trusted him."

The earl nodded, and then he saw her enter the hall. For a moment he almost forgot his anger, for she was every bit as beautiful as he had remembered her. Gowned in burgundy velvet, her black hair now dressed in the familiar chignon, she made her way to the table. James Leslie rose, bowing, kissing her hand, seating her by his side. Jasmine acknowledged him but briefly.

"How lovely you look, my darling girl," Skye said. "The picture of fashion, I vow."

"Have fashions not changed that much then these months?" Jasmine said lightly. "What a shame. I was anticipating having your Bonnie make me a brand new wardrobe, grandmama."

"You shall have whatever your heart desires, madame," the earl said. "As my bride you are entitled to a bridal wardrobe. My pockets are deep as you well know."

"If I wish new garments, my lord," Jasmine said in scathing tones, "I am more than able to pay for them. I am far wealthier than you are, sir. We had best discuss this now. The king may order us to wed, but until I agree to do so there will be no marriage between us. First there must be the legalities. While I will give you a reasonable dowry, my lord, the bulk of my wealth remains mine. Until you agree to that, you will not have me to wife." *There,* she thought, *that will set his proud Scots heart back a pace.*

"Of course, darling Jasmine," the earl said smoothly. "Your wealth remains your own. My own mother, and I am certain yours, too, had such arrangements in their marriage contracts. I would suggest we do it immediately, but I am not certain a contract drawn by a French advocate would be considered legitimate in England. I think, therefore, we must wait until we return to England."

"Until the papers are drawn to my satisfaction, and signed, my lord, there will be no formality between you and me," Jasmine replied.

"Naturally, madame," he returned.

Skye speared a haunch of rabbit and gnawed on it vigorously as she listened to her granddaughter and the earl of Glenkirk battle back and forth. James Leslie had obviously taken her advice, and was going gently with Jasmine, but Jasmine was not making it easy on the man. *Why she has decided he is her enemy, I do not know,* the matriarch thought to herself. *If I were twenty years younger I should be tempted to cast a lure for him myself were I a single woman.* Reaching across them, she tore herself off a piece of bread from the loaf.

"*I mean it,* James Leslie," Jasmine snapped.

"I am well aware of it, madame," he answered, his voice testy now.

"Then we might as well leave tomorrow for England," she decided.

"Nay, madame, we will leave Belle Fleurs in a week's time. Your grandmother needs the rest, having departed her own home almost immediately following your grandfather's demise. *And,* I believe it advisable that you and I become reacquainted on neutral ground."

"Indeed, sir? What is it you do not know about me that you need to know? I am beautiful. I am wealthy. I am royal. I have had two husbands, and a princely lover. I am the mother of four children, and I pleased you in bed those many years back. Is there more?"

"Aye," he answered her coldly, "you are all you say, madame, but I am curious to learn if beneath the prideful and cruel bitch you seem to have become, there is a vestige left of the charming woman I once knew, *darling Jasmine.*"

Skye choked on her wine, gasping and coughing at his words.

"Why you arrogant Scots bastard," Jasmine said angrily. "How dare you speak to me in such a fashion?" She was flushed with her ire.

"Nay, madame, the question is, how dare you speak to me with such disdain? I am to be your husband."

"When we return to England I shall petition the king to change his mind," Jasmine told him.

"And I shall implore him not to change his mind. He won't, you know. You will just irritate him if you try," James Leslie said. "The king doesn't like anyone, particularly a woman, impugning his divine right as the monarch. He has made a decision, and will not be denied. This is not about you, or about me, Jasmine. It is about the king's first-born grandchild, young Charles Frederick Stuart. The lad may have been born on the wrong side of the blanket, but the blanket is a royal one. Stuarts do not abandon their responsibilities."

"I do not need a husband to raise my children," Jasmine snapped.

"Nonetheless, the king has commanded that you have one," the earl rejoined. "At least the king knows I am honest and will not use his grandson for my own ends, as others might."

"Supercilious cad!" she sneered at him.

"Vicious vixen!" he snarled back.

"Beast!"

"Bitch!"

"*Cease!*" Startled they both looked to Skye, whose face was stern. "You are bickering like two spoiled children," she said. "You will stop it this instant!" Turning to Jasmine she continued. "The king has ordered you to marry this man. He is handsome, rich enough not to see you only for your fortune and as respectable as any widow might wish. *And I approve of him.* In this family that carries more weight than James Stuart's majesty. Therefore, you will marry the earl of Glenkirk, my darling girl. I wish the choice could be yours, but alas, it cannot under the circumstances. As for you, James Leslie..." She fixed her gaze upon him. "You will treat my granddaughter with dignity and respect when she is your wife. I hope you will come to love each other, for that is the best kind of marriage to make, but if you cannot, at least you will honor each other, and the Leslie name." She rose from her place at the highboard. "Now, I am an old woman, and I am exhausted with my travels. Adali!" Skye called to her granddaughter's steward. "Take me to my bedchamber before I expire with weariness!" She took his arm and walked from the hall with not another word to them.

James Leslie picked up his goblet and sipped the wine thoughtfully. "If you would like," he said quietly, "we could stay in France until the spring, renewing our acquaintance, madame. The sea is chancy at this time of year. We were fortunate in our recent crossing from England." His tone was almost conciliatory toward her.

"It might be better," Jasmine considered. "It would give the children a chance to know you, my lord; and I do not like the way my grandmother looks. Grandfather's death must have been a terrible shock to her. Then to leave Queen's Malvern to come to me at such a dreadful time of year for traveling. Perhaps in May?" she suggested.

"I thought April the first," he said softly.

"You cannot be serious," Jasmine said, remembering how she had tricked him almost two years back into leaving her alone until April first when, she had promised him, she would then set their wedding date. Instead, he had arrived at Queen's Malvern on that date to find she had departed with her children, and he had no idea to where.

"Be grateful, madame, that I do not fix our wedding date for that day," he replied somberly.

She was suddenly cold. "Do you hate me that much, my lord?" The sudden realization of his black mood assailed her. What had she done in running away from James Leslie? She had only wanted a little more time to herself. To mourn her sweet prince, and yet the king was so adamant that she marry the earl of Glenkirk. Still, had not he said he would give her more time? But how was she to understand that then?

"I do not know what I feel for you, madame," she heard him say to her. "Once I was overwhelmed by your beauty and your passion. I thought I loved you. Your arrogance, however, has made me see you in a new light. I am not certain if I can ever love you, but we must learn to get along for the sake of your children, and the children we will have together. Our home must be, I insist, a place of peace."

The words were out of her mouth before she could contain them. "We will have no children, James Leslie, except that they come from a love between us. I am not some finely bred mare to whom you have been brought to stud. I will wed you, and I will never bring shame to your name. I will manage your household, and stand by your side in all things, but I will have no child of yours unless it comes of our love."

"How very noble of you, madame," he replied scornfully. "You bore Westleigh three children, and yet your family arranged the marriage to keep you from the consequences of your wanton behavior. Did you truly love Rowan Lindley?"

"*Aye, I did!*" Then Jasmine laughed bitterly. "My wanton behavior, as you call it, resulted from your lust to possess me, my lord. I remember that Twelfth Night quite well. 'Twas you who approached me, *and aye,* I agreed to allow you to seduce me, for bereft of our mates we were both in need of comforting. Had not my stepsister, Sybilla, discovered us, and raised such a fuss, none would have been the wiser. You and I might have forgotten the entire incident, and gone our separate ways, as we did anyhow."

Reaching over, he grabbed her wrist in a hard grasp. "I would *never* have forgotten that chance encounter, madame!" he told her fiercely. "You were the most beautiful and the most exciting woman I had ever known; but I shall also not forget that you held me up to ridicule before the entire court by running off two years ago. Do you think, madame, that because you were born a royal Mughal princess that your pride is greater or more sensitive than mine? What do you really know of me, Jasmine?"

"Nothing," she admitted, gently loosening his grip on her arm.

"Well, I shall tell you," he said. "Long ago in the reign of King Malcolm and his saintly Queen Margaret, my ancestor, Angus Leslie, the laird of Glenkirk, wed with the queen's sister, Christina. The sisters were the daughters of the heir to England's king; but he died before King Edward, and it was their brother who was then to be king but that Harold Godwinson usurped his right, and then William the Norman conquered the land. The mother of these sisters was Agatha, a princess of Hungary. My great-grandfather, Charles Leslie, was born Karim, a prince of the Ottoman Empire. His father was Sultan Selim, his brother, Sultan Suleiman. My great-great-grandmother, Janet Leslie, was Sultan Selim's favorite wife. I have as much, if not more, royal blood in my veins, Jasmine Lindley, as you do."

She was astounded by his revelations, but she would not be moved. "Then we are indeed well matched even if none but us knows it, James Leslie," said Jasmine, rising from her place at the highboard. "The hour grows late, my lord," she said. "I will escort you to your chamber."

He followed her from the hall, noting the stiff line of her backbone as they went, wondering what further mischief she was plotting. Could he trust the old countess of Lundy now? Or was she merely lulling him into a false sense of security in order that Jasmine might escape him once again. Devious the old woman might be, he considered, but he had never heard it said that she was anything other than honest. He had to trust her. There was no option other than remaining awake all night watching, and for how long could he do that? Had he been a fool to allow Jasmine more time before their marriage? Was his desire for revenge overwhelming his common sense? Should he call the priest in on the morrow and marry her immediately, thereby putting an end to her headstrong foolishness? Then he shook his head at his own thoughts. Marriage, or no, if Jasmine de Marisco Lindley wanted to leave him again, she most certainly would. He had but two choices. Locking her away or winning back her friendship.

"You will find your servant awaiting you," Jasmine said as she stopped before an oak door. "Good night, my lord."

He took her hand up and kissed it. "Good night, madame," the earl of Glenkirk replied, then, turning, he entered the chamber.

Jasmine snatched her hand back and, whirling about, hurried off down the corridor. She could actually feel the imprint of his mouth upon her skin, and it was most discomfiting. This man she must wed, this man with whom she had spent an incredible night of passion almost ten years ago, was in reality a stranger to her. They had met again briefly at King James's court, but it was not an association she had encouraged. He was a dark-spirited man whom she did not in the least understand. She was even a little afraid of him, but she would never reveal that to anyone, least of all James Leslie. He was, she realized, a man she could not cajole or manipulate. He was as hard as flint.

She had offended him. Embarrassed him. Defied him. Yet he would obey the king and marry her in spite of it all. Jasmine shivered. This was a dangerous man, and unless she could find a way to soften him, her life would not be pleasant. Jasmine entered her own bedchamber, where her servants were waiting for her. Her grandmother would know what to do. On the morrow she would speak with that dear old lady, and Skye would guide her actions so she might find James Leslie's weakness, and touch his heart. *If indeed he even had a heart.*

Chapter Three

Jasmine awoke to hear the faint scratching of sleet upon the windows of her bedchamber. She could see the gray day beyond the slit in the half-drawn draperies. A cheerful fire burned in the fireplace, warming the room. She stretched herself beneath the fine lavender-scented linens and the down comforter that covered her. How lovely it was to lie here in the great oak bed her grandfather had long ago commissioned for this chamber. Jasmine loved this bed, with its eight-foot-high headboard of linenfold paneling and its four turned and carved posts. The hangings belonging to the bed were a natural-colored linen embroidered with a design of green silk. It was a wonderful refuge from the troubles of the world, but she had no troubles. *Oh, yes she did.*

Jasmine sat up suddenly. She most assuredly had troubles. They had arrived late yesterday in the person of James Leslie, the earl of Glenkirk. James Leslie, the man King James had made guardian of her four children. James Leslie, the man the king had ordered her to marry and from whom she had fled. Her temples began to throb, and she fell back against her pillows. She had to think. She had to speak with Skye. It was not going to be an easy day.

The door to her chamber opened, and her two maidservants entered. Rohana carried a small silver tray upon which sat a tea carafe, and a handleless round cup of blue-and-white porcelain. Bringing it to her mistress's bedside, Rohana set the tray down, uncorking the carafe as she did so. The aroma of the pale golden Assam wafted up faintly spicy from the two cloves that floated in the tea. Rohana poured half a cup and handed it to Jasmine, who first breathed deeply of the hot liquid, then sipped it gratefully, murmuring her pleasure as it warmed her innards.

Across the room Toramalli was choosing her mistress's garments of the day. A black velvet skirt and a bodice of silver-and-white brocade. The appropriate undergarments were laid out along with silk stockings, simple black velvet slippers, and jewelry. Rohana, meanwhile, was seeing to her lady's bath in the small inner chamber that Jasmine had designated as a bathing room when she came to Belle Fleurs. A pump had been installed in the room, and hot water was heated in a small fireplace to warm the water drawn from the pump.

Finishing her tea, Jasmine arose from her bed. She could already smell the night-blooming jasmine oil that was being poured into the bathwater by her servant. "Are the children awake?" she asked.

"They are already in the hall," Rohana said, helping her mistress from her chamber robe and into her tub.

"The nursemaids knew that Lord Leslie was here," Toramalli volunteered. "The children are dressed in fairly proper fashion."

Jasmine nodded, but said nothing further on the subject. "I cannot dally," she finally remarked. "I will seem a poor hostess if I am not downstairs shortly. Is my grandmother awake yet?"

"Madame Skye has elected to remain abed this morning," Toramalli said. "That ancient Daisy of hers came into the hall to tell Lord Leslie and to fetch something to eat for the old lady."

Jasmine bathed and dressed quickly. She could barely sit still while Rohana did her hair. Slipping a strand of fat pearls about her neck, she affixed large baroque pearls in her ears, and, jewels bobbing, she hurried from her chamber and down into the hall. Approaching the entry, she could hear her children's excited voices. She stopped a moment in the entry to observe the scene before her.

James Leslie, in black velvet, his short dark hair brushed straight back and just barely grazing his white linen neck ruff, sat in a high-backed chair by the fire. "Excellent, my young lord Henry," he said to the little marquis of Westleigh. "Your bow improves with each try. You shall not shame your late father, your mother, or me when you are presented to the king, and pledge him your fealty for yourself and for Cadby. Remember, a gentleman is first judged by the reputation that precedes him, and secondly by his manners."

"What of his purse?" Lady India Lindley demanded boldly.

James Leslie's mouth twitched as he repressed a smile. Then he said seriously, "That, my lady India, should be no one's business although there will be speculation aplenty when a handsome and interesting man as your brother will undoubtedly become one day arrives at court."

"Will you teach us to curtsy, my lord, as you teach Henry to bow?" India asked him.

"Your mother will see that your manners are polished before we return to England, my lady," the earl answered the little girl. "I will speak with her myself on the matter."

"Are you still to marry Mama?" Henry wondered.

"Aye," the earl said. "The king has commanded it."

"Do you love our mother?" India queried. "Our father loved our mother very much, and she he. I wish that Irisher had not killed our father, my lord. I miss him very much."

"I am surprised that you remember him, my lady India. You were very small when he died," the earl remarked.

"I remember a big golden man taking me up, kissing me, and tickling me," India said. "Henry does not remember him at all, being so new when our father was killed. Mama tells us stories of our father."

Suddenly Feathers, the family spaniel, barked sharply and scampered to the entry of the hall, leaping upon Jasmine's skirts until she picked the small dog up.

"Hush, you little brute," she gently scolded, and greeted them. "Good morrow, my darlings. I see you have already greeted our guest. Good morning, my lord." She moved into the hall to join them.

James Leslie rose, and, kissing her hand, said, "Good morning, madame. I trust that you slept well." He escorted her to the highboard, where the servants were beginning to lay out the morning meal. "Come, children. You may join your mother and me this morning."

Lady Fortune Lindley, who was four and a half years of age, tugged upon her mother's skirts, and when Jasmine looked down the child said, "Is this my father, Mama?"

Before Jasmine might answer, James Leslie said, "Nay, child. You have the same father as your brother and sister, but I *would* be a father to you if you will permit me. *To all of you.*"

"Do you have any little boys and girls of your own?" India questioned him.

"I did once," James Leslie said, and his face grew sad.

"*India!*" Her mother admonished her, but India spoke again.

"Where are they, my lord? Where are your little boys and girls? Will they come to play with us when you are our father, too?"

"My children, *ma petite,* are in heaven with their mother, and your papa," James Leslie told the little girl. "They have been gone a long time now. So long I cannot even remember their faces," he concluded sadly. Drawing out a chair, he seated Jasmine first, then her two little daughters. "In future, Henry, when you are allowed to take your meals at the highboard, you will seat your mother thusly," the earl told the boy, deftly changing the subject.

"Yes, sir," the lad replied.

Jasmine was astounded. It had dawned upon her almost immediately that her children were speaking English again not just to the earl of Glenkirk, but to each other as well. They were dressed respectably and had shoes upon their feet. They were, in fact, being very polite. She hadn't seen them like this in months.

"Their table manners will need improvement," the earl said to her in an aside, then he turned to admonish them gently to pass the bread to each other when they desired some and not to tear off a chunk and toss it down the table.

Jasmine had a strong desire to giggle at this, but she managed to refrain from it. In a sense it disturbed her that her children had taken so readily to James Leslie. She felt almost jealous. Yet on another level she knew it was better they like their stepfather, and he they, than have an antagonistic relationship. The little ones did not have to know how she and the earl felt about one another. James Leslie was obviously a good influence upon Henry, India, and Fortune, judging by what she had seen this morning. She had to admit, although she did so silently and reluctantly, that an authoritative male figure in her household was possibly not a bad thing for her children. Absently she fed the small dog in her lap a bit of ham, patting Feathers as he licked her fingers.

"He is quite spoiled, I see," the earl remarked.

"Rowan gave him to me when he was only a puppy. He was a birthday gift when I was eighteen," Jasmine replied. "Actually, my real gift that year was Maguire's Ford and its lands. I remember how angry my Uncle Padraic was that Rowan had obtained the grant for me. At the time I thought nothing of it. Now I, too, wish he hadn't gifted me with anything other than my precious Feathers." She scratched the dog's silky head, her beautiful face both thoughtful and somber.

"You have not been back to Ireland since?" he asked.

Jasmine shook her head. "Nay. The former lord's son, Rory Maguire, is my agent. There is both a Roman and Anglican church on my lands, and the people seem to manage to coexist peacefully. I raise horses there, or rather Rory does for me. I shall probably give the estate to Fortune one day, as she was born there. It would make a fine dower for her, don't you think?"

"Possibly," he agreed, then said, "We must talk, madame."

"Not before the children, I beg you, my lord," Jasmine replied. Her voice was soft, her glance pleading. "We seem to end up shouting at one another, and I do not want to do so before my little ones."

"Of course, madame," he answered her. "You are correct that the children should not be involved in our difficulties. I understand, but nonetheless we must talk, and at least for your children's sake resolve our differences." His green-gold eyes regarded her dispassionately.

She met his gaze directly. "Would it not be better if we renewed our acquaintanceship again, my lord, before we spoke on serious matters? And I would seek my grandmother's advice as well."

James Leslie swallowed a mouthful of egg poached in cream sauce and marsala wine and seasoned with peppercorns. It was a particularly tasty dish, and he wondered if the cook was Jasmine's, or belonged to the château. Wiping his mouth with his napkin, he said, "The last time you consulted with your grandmother regarding our future relationship, madame, you fled England. I am not certain her counsel is a wise one."

"The idea to go was not hers, but mine," Jasmine said quietly, "and she only allowed it because she thought I would return by summer's end. Please don't blame my grandmother for my actions. Besides, do you think me some mindless ninny that I cannot reason the consequences of my own actions? Please, sir, do not insult me."

"Your thought has merit," he told her. "Just how, madame, do you suggest we renew our familiarity with one another?" Although his voice was neutral, Jasmine thought the look he gave her both mocking and challenging. And was that a twinkle in his eye?

She struggled to maintain her equilibrium, determined not to show anger before her son and daughters, although she secretly longed to smack him. "I thought when you were finished eating," she began, "we might go and see Prince Henry's son, my lord." She would ignore his childish innuendo. It was not deserving of a reply.

The earl of Glenkirk swallowed back a chuckle. So, he could not get her to rise to his bait, eh? He realized how very little he really knew her. The idea of remaining in France and truly getting to know Jasmine was actually beginning to appeal to him. He swallowed a piece of ham, washing it down with a goblet of excellent cider, and said to her, "Is my youngest ward in good health, madame?"

"As all my children are, my lord," Jasmine answered. "I have kept my grandmother fully informed, and she in turn has kept the queen fully informed. I did not want Hal's parents fretting over his son, particularly given the distress the scandal involving Robert Carr and his wife is causing them now."

James Leslie was about to make a retort when his eye was caught by young Henry Lindley, already halfway down the hall. "My lord of Westleigh," he called to the boy. "Where are you going?"

Henry turned. "I have finished my meal, sir," he said.

"You have left the table without asking your mother's permission to be excused, sir," the earl said sternly. "Come back at once, and do so. In future I will expect that you remember this courtesy."

Henry Lindley returned to stand before the highboard. He bowed politely, saying to his mother, "Madame, may I now be excused from your board? The meal was most delicious."

"You are excused, Henry," Jasmine replied formally, nodding to her son. "Where are you going?"

"To the stables, madame. My pony needs attention."

"Take him an apple," Jasmine told her son with a smile.

"Thank you," Henry Lindley said, bowing again to his mother and then to Lord Leslie before running off.

India and Fortune were before the highboard now. "May we be excused too, Mama?" India spoke for them both.

Jasmine nodded. "Go and tell your great-grandmother that I will join her shortly."

"Yes, Mama," India said primly, and she and Fortune curtsied to the two adults.

"India," Jasmine said to her daughter, "you do not need my instruction in the art of curtsying. You and your sister do it quite perfectly." Then she smiled at her two little daughters, who, with delighted faces, tripped out of the hall.

"Your children love you," he noted.

Jasmine looked surprised. "Why would they not?" she wondered.

"Many mothers among our class are not maternal," he said. "They prefer spending their time at court and entertaining their own pursuits to mothering their bairns. That difficult task they leave to their servants, I fear," he replied.

"My mother did not," Jasmine said. "The mother who raised me was a Mughal princess, and while we had servants to serve us, never did Rugaiya Begum neglect me. I but follow her example and that of my other mother, Lady Gordon. One cannot expect one's children to grow into responsible men and women if one does not see to their education personally, my lord. While I have allowed my sons and daughters the freedom to run while here at Belle Fleurs, I will see that they are brought up properly so that they will not embarrass themselves when we return home to England. They are still, after all, quite small. I want them to enjoy their childhood years and not be overburdened with adult matters before their time." She arose from the highboard. "Shall we go and see little Charles Frederick, sir?"

He was impressed by her reasoning and her strong sense of responsibility toward her family. His memories of her were bound up in a single passionate night of love; of a stolen moment he had spied between her and Prince Henry Stuart at Whitehall several years back; of walks in her grandparents' snowy London garden when it was believed he might wed her stepsister, Sybilla. So much time had passed, and he really didn't know her at all, but he thought now that he wanted to know her. She was, after all, the woman he was to marry. James Leslie followed Jasmine to the nursery, where the king's grandson, Charles Frederick Stuart, was in residence.

The child was his father's image, all red-gold curls and wide blue eyes. He was garbed in a blue velvet dress trimmed in lace, and his face lit up at the sight of his mother. "Maaaaa!" he crowed, holding out fat, dimpled baby arms, and leaning from his nursemaid's careful embrace.

"Charlie-boy," Jasmine greeted her youngest son, and took him into her arms, kissing his fat cheek.

"Who he?" the wee boy demanded, pointing a finger at Lord Leslie, his eyes suddenly suspicious. "Who he, Ma?"

"*Who is he,*" Jasmine corrected the child. "This, my not so royal little Stuart, is Lord Leslie. Your grandfather, the king, has sent him to be my husband and your new papa. Please greet him as I have taught you, my son. Henry and your sisters have already shown Lord Leslie what fine manners they have. It is your turn."

The princely bastard looked James Leslie directly in the eye, and, holding out a small hand, said, "How d'do, sir." Then he smiled, showing his small pearly teeth, and the earl of Glenkirk saw Prince Henry Stuart all over again, and his heart contracted a moment.

Taking the little hand in his, he replied, "How do you do, my lord duke. I am honored to meet you at last."

"Play ball!" Charles Frederick Stuart said, squirming to escape his mother's arms and finally succeeding. He ran to fetch a small brightly colored wooden globe, looking hopefully up at the earl. "Play ball?" he repeated, his blue eyes bright.

Chuckling, James Leslie seated himself upon the floor, cross-legged. "Aye, laddie. We'll play ball," he replied grinning.

The little boy rolled the shiny orb across the floor to the earl, who stopped it neatly and rolled it back to him.

"I shall leave you to entertain each other," Jasmine said. "Grandmama will be waiting." She hurried from the nursery, leaving James Leslie to entertain her son. She had been surprised by his easy agreement to Charlie's request to play ball. She had been touched to see them both seated upon the floor rolling the round toy back and forth between them. James Leslie did indeed have a heart, at least where her children were concerned. Absently Jasmine stroked the silky head of the spaniel she had once again picked up. "What do you think, Feathers? Is this is a man we can live with?"

The dog looked up at her with soulful brown eyes.

Jasmine moved along the corridor of the upper hallway to her grandmother's bedchamber and, knocking, entered. Skye was comfortably ensconced in the large bed, her eyes closed. Daisy had just removed the breakfast tray. "Is she sleeping again?" Jasmine whispered.

"I am quite awake, darling girl," Skye said, opening her eyes, "and well rested. I always sleep well at Belle Fleurs."

"I wanted to put you in the master chamber last night, but Daisy told Adali no," Jasmine began, putting the dog down.

"And quite right, too!" came the reply. "I do not need to be reminded of your grandfather, Jasmine. He is always and forever in my heart. To sleep in that magnificent bed he commissioned built for us when we were wed would have undone me entirely. I have no memories of this room. Some of the children slept here, but I do not recall which of them. It was so long ago. Adam and I were happy here."

"I am so sorry, Grandmama," Jasmine said. "I did not say it last evening when you arrived. I was so stunned by your news, and then by Lord Leslie's arrival. I allowed my own problems to overwhelm me. I should have been at Queen's Malvern for you, Grandmama. I should have been there for Grandfather. Now I shall never see him again."

"Neither will I," Skye said softly. "Of all of them, I loved him best of all, darling girl, but don't ever say I said such a thing, for your aunts and uncles would be heartbroken."

"I understand," Jasmine said. "I loved my first husband, Jamal, and yet I loved Rowan Lindley better. No disrespect can be intended in such an admission." The younger woman climbed onto the bed next to the older. "What am I to do about Lord Leslie, Grandmama?" she asked. "Oh, I know I must wed him now, and this morning he has shown himself to be kind and patient with the children, but what am I to do about him? He really is most arrogant. Do you know he told me he is descended from an Ottoman sultan, and is as royal as I am? Is it true, I wonder?"

"I wondered about his lineage," Skye said, fascinated by her granddaughter's revelation. "A Scot without a doubt, but there is that slight, almost imperceptible slant to those green eyes of his. A tiny bit of Tartar in the blood. Interesting, indeed. Now what to do about him indeed, darling girl. Since you must wed him, you have no choice but to win him over, I think."

"Would the king not reconsider, Grandmama?" Jasmine wondered.

"Nay, he would not. James Stuart is every bit as intractable as his late cousin, Elizabeth Tudor, and the truth of the matter is that you must have another husband, Jasmine. I would have liked it if you could choose for yourself this time, but it is not to be. You must marry James Leslie, so the sooner you begin to soothe his ruffled feelings the better. I think I may have an idea," she chuckled.

"What?" Jasmine asked, curious in spite of herself.

"I think that you and the earl would do better without the encumbrance of an old lady and four children," Skye said. "In a week or two I shall take the children to visit their relations over at Archambault, and then we shall go on to Paris. By then the worst of winter will be over, and I shall return to England with my great-grandchildren. You and James will follow when you will. You will have all the time in the world that you need to become reacquainted. Then when you return to England to marry it will be a happy occasion. I would like you wed at Queen's Malvern, and I shall make my desire known to the earl."

"He wants us wed before the entire court," Jasmine said glumly.

"A wish hatched in the heat of anger," Skye replied. "If I say Queen's Malvern, he will acquiesce," she concluded with a smile.

Jasmine laughed at the arch tone in her grandmother's voice. "Even at your age, madame, no man will refuse you," she said. "God's blood, I wish I were more like you!"

"You are too much like me, I fear," Skye chuckled. "I hope you will attain a degree of wisdom far sooner than I did. I look back upon my life, with all its wildness and adventures, and I am amazed that I am here today to tell the tale, darling girl."

Jasmine looked up into her grandmother's face. "Don't ever leave me," she said quietly.

Skye patted the younger woman's hand comfortingly. "One day I will go," she said, "but not yet, darling girl; and even when this weary old body of mine has released its hold upon my soul I shall yet be with you, Jasmine. You will only have to remember me, and I will be there to whisper in your ear." Then she chuckled again. "There is one very good thing about your marriage to Lord Leslie," she told her granddaughter. "You shall not have to change your monogram. Lindley and Leslie both begin with L!"

Jasmine laughed in spite of herself. "You are extraordinary!" she said to Skye.

"Indeed I am," the older woman agreed. "And you are not the first to tell me so, darling girl. Oh, no! You are not the first."

"Shameless when she was young, and still shameless," said Skye's elderly tiring woman, Daisy Kelly. "Well, lady, are ye going to lie abed the whole day, or shall I prepare yer bath?"

"A bath, you old harridan," Skye told her servant and friend. Then she turned to Jasmine. "Where is himself?"

"In the nursery," Jasmine replied, "playing ball with Charlie. He is quite amazing with the children. I came into the hall this morning to find him teaching Henry a proper court bow, and both of the girls are taken with him, too. How many children did he have, and how did he lose them?" she wondered. "You know, grandmama, 'tis the only time I see him soften, with the children. He is hard otherwise."

"You cannot rely upon the children to soften him," Skye counseled wisely. "They will grow up and leave you together. If you have nothing to begin with, there will be nothing when the children are gone. Now as to James Leslie's history, I can remember this. He was wed to a cousin, a Gordon, I believe. There were two sons, and his wife was with child a third time when she took her lads and went visiting at a nearby religious house. The place was attacked by fanatics belonging to the Calvinist faith. They raped, slaughtered, and burned. The young countess and her sons were murdered along with the rest of the nuns. Although the king ordered a full investigation, and demanded the miscreants be caught and punished, none ever were. Naturally, James Leslie was very bitter about it. He still is, I suspect."

"And he has never remarried," Jasmine said thoughtfully.

"His family has certainly implored him to," Skye replied. "It has been fifteen years since his wife and children died. His sons would have been grown by now. 'Twas a terrible tragedy he suffered."

"Grandmama, when the king first ordered me to wed with the earl I remember that James Leslie told me he had come to Greenwood to ask your permission to court me after that tiny scandal we caused several days earlier. He said you sent him away because you had already arranged my marriage to Rowan. He said you told him it was best I not even know he had been there. Is that true, Grandmama?"

"Aye," Skye admitted without hesitation. "The earl does not lie."

Jasmine looked reflective, then she sighed. "I've been very foolish," she admitted. "I should not have run away."

"Do not distress yourself, my darling girl. You needed more time than it appeared James Leslie was willing to give you. Where you made your mistake was in staying away so long," her grandmother told her. "And I hold myself responsible for that. Instead of enjoying myself helping you to intrigue against the earl, I should have offered you wise counsel and insisted you return home. The deed is done, and now there is help for it. You must win James Leslie over if you are to have a happy marriage. To that end you will agree with my plan of action, Jasmine. Shall I take the children and wend my way home?"

"Stay at Belles Fleurs a bit, Grandmama, then we shall spring this little idea of yours upon the earl as if we had just thought of it," Jasmine said. "If he does not agree, we cannot do it, I fear."

"And he is apt to say nay if we spring it upon him too soon," Skye agreed. "We will, however, have to keep the little ones out of the way while they remain here. I know! We shall find them a tutor, and they shall begin their lessons. That way they will be well occupied while I help you to soften up the earl. Then, when he is susceptible, we shall gain his permission, and I shall take the children back to Queen's Malvern. Left alone, you may seduce the handsome devil, darling Jasmine, and once he is under your sweet spell you'll wed and live happily ever after," Skye finished triumphantly. "Ahhh, how such a strategy takes me back to my own youth!"

Little girl, little girl! Do not interfere so.

Skye stiffened. She had heard his voice! She had distinctly heard Adam's voice. *Or had she?*

"Grandmama?" Jasmine's look was a concerned one.

Skye shook off the eerie feeling. "'Tis nothing," she said, wondering if she was going mad. Then she pushed the sensation far into the back of her consciousness as, filled with new enthusiasm, she began to design in her head new schemes to help her favorite grandchild. Enchanting a man and stealing his heart was not all that difficult, and when a woman was as beautiful and as clever as Jasmine, why it would be almost too easy, the old lady considered. *A rival!* Yes, the earl of Glenkirk definitely needed a rival for Jasmine's affections. There was nothing like another man, eager and ready to woo, to make a prospective bridegroom even more anxious. Of course Jasmine could not know, for if James Leslie needed to fall in love with Jasmine again, so Jasmine needed to fall in love with James Leslie as well.

It would have to be a very handsome man, but a man who was perhaps a trifle shallow and nowhere near as principled as the earl. Her granddaughter was no fool, Skye knew, and would not be taken in by a less honorable man. And just to be absolutely certain Jasmine would not fall in love with the wrong man the rival should be married. Aye! *It was a brilliant plan!*

"Run along now, my darling girl," Skye told Jasmine. Then to Daisy, "Is that bath finally ready, or am I to wait until Michaelmas for it?" She shifted herself from the bed, waving Jasmine off as she did so. "God's boots! I had forgotten how damp this château gets in the winter. Put more wood on the fire, Daisy. I'm chilled to the bone."

"Can't go home soon enough for me," Daisy grumbled.

"'Twill be soon enough," her mistress promised. "I just have one or two little things to do, and then we'll be off."

"You've got that look in yer eye," Daisy said. "I haven't seen that look in twenty years, I haven't!"

"What look?" Skye feigned innocence.

"*That* look," Daisy replied. "His lordship wouldn't be pleased at all, he wouldn't. I always knew that once he was gone you'd be up to yer old tricks again, my lady. Now why can't ye settle back and enjoy the years left to ye with yer grandchildren and great-grandchildren?"

"I'll outlive you, you nosy old busybody," Skye said.

"Aye, ye probably will," Daisy agreed, "and when I'm gone there'll be none to keep ye in check."

"I want my bath," Skye snapped.

Daisy shook her head. "We're both too old for this," she said.

"Maybe you are, but I'm not," her mistress replied. "I'll not curl up my toes just because I'm an old woman, Daisy Kelly."

Daisy shook her head again. Perhaps she should have let that slovenly Martha come with her lady this time. Heaven only knew what mischief she was up to and how it would all end.

Chapter Four

"*Ma chérie!*" Alexandre de Saville, comte de Cher, greeted his sister-in-law with a kiss upon each of her cheeks. "I had not thought to see you again in this life, for I love Archambault and scarcely leave it; and for you it is the same with your beloved Queen's Malvern."

"Adam is dead," Skye said without further preamble, allowing the servants to take her fur-lined and trimmed wool cloak.

"Ahhh, *ma pauvre soeur*," the count said, his face collapsing with his sadness. "But he was not ill?"

"He was old, Alexandre," Skye replied. "Thirteen years older than you, and ten years older than me."

"When?" The count escorted his guest into a bright salon, where a warm fire burned, and seated her. Almost immediately a servant was at their elbow with wine.

"Twelfth Night," Skye answered him. "Nay, he was not ill, and he was in the midst of his family. One moment he was laughing at a jest, and the next he was gone. It was quite a shock for us all, and for Adam most of all, I imagine," she finished with a small touch of humor.

"'Twas a beautiful death as you describe it," the count said "God assoil my brother's good soul." He bowed his head a moment.

Skye sipped her wine, marveling at the delicacy of the vintage.

His silent prayer over, the count raised his silver head, and looked at his sister-in-law. "It was kind of you to bring us this news personally, but I imagine 'tis not your only reason for being in France. You have come to take Jasmine and her children back to England, have you not, *ma soeur?*"

Skye nodded. "'Tis past time, Alexandre." Then she went on to explain how Lord Leslie had followed her to Belle Fleurs. "Once he loved her, but now I do not know," she concluded. "At least he is fond of the children, and that is a beginning, I think."

"But not enough," the count observed wisely. "What will you do to help our beautiful Jasmine, *ma soeur,* for you will do something. Of that I am quite certain." He chuckled.

Skye laughed. "Am I so transparent in my old age then, Alexandre? You are correct, of course. I do want to help my darling girl. I thought if I can obtain Lord Leslie's permission, I would bring the children here for a visit, then take them to Paris, and finally home. This way my granddaughter, and her husband-to-be will be forced to renew their friendship and work out their difficulties. Perhaps after I am gone you will invite them to Archambault. A bit of time alone together, and who knows what may transpire."

"Ahhh, *l'amour,*" the count agreed. Then he said, "Of course you may bring Jasmine's children for a visit, *chérie.* Helene and I would be delighted to have you. We, too, are great-grandparents. Our grandson, Phillippe, the next comte de Cher, has a little son, Antoine, named after my father. He will enjoy his cousins from England."

"I was saddened to learn of your son's death," Skye said.

"These damned religious wars," Alexandre de Saville replied irritably. "My son, Adam, had nothing to do with any of it, and yet he fell victim to the madness on his way home from a visit to Nantes. His wife, Louise, succumbed of melancholy shortly afterward, poor girl. They had but one child. Phillippe is a good man, however. He married early, and sired Antoine, and his baby sister, Marie, and his wife is again with child. He and Jasmine are of an age. We will let him entertain her, and Lord Leslie, while Helene and I just sit back enjoying the young people. There are certain compensations to old age, *chérie*, eh?"

"Damned few," Skye replied, and she laughed. "Where is Helene?" I cannot return to Belle Fleurs without paying my respects."

"Come with me then, *chérie*, " the comte said. "I will take you to her. The damp weather makes her bones ache, and she keeps to her apartments."

"Where have you been, Grandmama?" Jasmine demanded of Skye on her return to the château. It had been a horrific week. She and James Leslie seemed to have nothing in common but her children, and could not seem to speak to one another unless one of them was involved. It did not bode well, and now Skye had disappeared, sending her granddaughter into a panic.

"I have been to Archambault," Skye said calmly. She handed her cloak to a servant and settled herself in a chair before the fire, sipping thirstily at the wine handed her. "Well, my lord, have you and Jasmine had a good day?" She beamed toothily at James Leslie, who was seated opposite her, glowering into the flames.

"It stopped raining long enough for us to take the children out into the gardens," the earl replied glumly.

"My brother-in-law, the comte de Cher, had the most delightful idea," Skye continued on breathlessly. "He has suggested that I bring the children to Archambault for a visit and leave you two alone to become reacquainted again without the distraction of your family. I hope you will let us go. His grandson, Phillippe, is Jasmine's contemporary, and has a little son a bit older than Charlie, and a tiny bit younger than Mistress Fortune. It would be so good for the children to get to know the French side of their family. Who knows! We may have a French princess for a queen one day."

"How far is Archambault?" the earl asked.

"But a few miles across the fields," Skye said brightly. "The comte, Alexandre de Saville, is Adam's half brother. His son, named for my husband, was killed, and so it is his grandson, Phillippe, who is his heir. They are a lovely family."

"How long a visit, madame?" the earl inquired.

"A week, or perhaps two," Skye ventured, refusing to acknowledge her granddaughter's outraged look.

"I will think on it, madame," James Leslie said.

"It is a ridiculous idea!" Jasmine burst out. "Why should it matter if my children know the de Saville children? Once we have returned to England it will not matter at all. Besides, Charlie is not quite weaned yet. I couldn't possibly let them go, Grandmama."

"The decision is not mine to make, my darling girl," Skye said with a nod in the earl's direction. "And as for little Charles Frederick, it is past time, Jasmine, that he was weaned. Why the lad will be three in the autumn. I never nursed any of my children for so long a time. As for your children, and the de Saville children, one never knows when one might need help from a relation. 'Tis better to know one's relations, even the distant ones, if possible. Alexandre de Saville is your great-uncle. His son, Phillippe, is your cousin. It could one day prove a valuable connection. Why I believe even Lord Leslie has relations here in France. Is that not so, sir?"

"Indeed, madame, it is. Two of my father's uncles wed Frenchwomen. Their families live near Fontainebleau, southeast of Paris. I am acquainted with both branches," the earl answered.

"There, you see!" Skye crowed. "The earl knows his French relatives." Her smile took them both in with its warmth.

"I do not want my children separated from me," Jasmine said stubbornly. Her look was definitely mutinous, her turquoise eyes angry. "I am their mother, and it is up to me what they do."

"Nay, madame, it is up to me as their legal guardian," James Leslie replied. "I think your bairns should go to Archambault to visit with their cousins. As for young Charlie, 'tis past time, madame, that he was separated from your tit. He's got teeth to chew his food, and you'll make a mother's boy out of him if you continue on as you have."

"Ohhhhhhh!" Now Jasmine looked truly affronted.

"My dears," Skye quickly spoke. "I do not want Alexandre's little suggestion to be the cause of dispute between you. Jasmine, my darling girl, be reasonable. The children have been cooped up here with you at Belle Fleurs for months. They need a change, and they need to be with other children of their own class. It will give them a chance to practice their manners and deportment before their return to England, when they must take their place in our society. You know that at one time or another they will go to court. Would you have them at a disadvantage? They will not thank you for it. Manners learned young are manners learned forever. Let them go to Archambault."

"Well," Jasmine amended, "'tis only a little way away."

"Aye," Skye purred in kindly tones, "and I shall be with them the whole time. I shall enjoy it, for it has been many years since I have visited with Adam's family. Ahhh, what fine times we had at Archambault when your grandfather and I were young and ripe!" She sighed gustily, and her hand went to her heart.

"Do not overplay your part, madame," the earl of Glenkirk murmured softly in her ear.

Skye's face never betrayed her surprise at his remark. *Well, well,* she thought, *he is brighter than I gave him credit for, is this earl of Glenkirk. Aye! I am doing the right thing in taking the children away, and forcing these two together to work out their problems.* She would discuss the Paris leg of their journey later on, but not now.

"Oh, very well," Jasmine decided, "but not for a week. It will take at least a week to make certain their clothing is in good repair, and to tutor them in their deportment."

"I agree with you, madame," James Leslie said with a small smile.

"You do?" Jasmine was somewhat surprised.

"We cannot always disagree," he replied, a twinkle in his eye.

"Perhaps not," she answered him, not certain what he exactly meant by the wry remark.

It was ten days before Jasmine was satisfied that her children were ready to leave for Archambault. She had kept her small staff busy washing, pressing, brushing their clothing until Skye had complained the nap would be worn off the fabrics altogether. The little trunks were packed neatly; the nursemaids given detailed instructions as to the children's care, and what to do in the event of this or that.

Finally, irritated, Skye snapped at her granddaughter, "I have raised seven children, my darling girl, and I will be with my great-grandchildren. *I know what to do.* We leave on the morrow, and I'll hear no more about it!"

The earl of Glenkirk repressed a small smile. Jasmine looked so worried. She was a good mother but far too obsessed with her offspring. He didn't doubt for a moment that this little trip to Archambault for Madame Skye and the children was all the old woman's idea. She had promised to help him, but he had not been certain he trusted her, especially after the last time. It would appear now, however, that his fears were groundless. She was whisking Jasmine's youngsters off so that he might be alone with their mother. He didn't know how she was going to do it, but he suspected that the children would not return to Belle Fleurs. He chuckled softly. What a holy terror Madame Skye was. He was glad to have her on his side this time.

In the morning, his arm about Jasmine, he watched as the grand old lady and the children departed Belle Fleurs. The rain had gone, and the day was bright and sunny. It was the end of February, and there was a definite hint of spring in the air. Jasmine sniffled, and he warned her softly, "Do not cry, madame, lest you distress the bairns. They are happy for this little adventure. Do not spoil it for them."

"I have never really been parted from them," she murmured low, attempting to disengage his arm, but he held her firmly.

"See how fine Henry, India, and Fortune look upon their ponies," he pointed out to her. "They sit their mounts well. Was it you who taught them, madame?"

"Aye," she said. "My father taught me when I was very small. In India women do not sit upon horses, but my mother had ridden with my father, and so he taught me. What freedom I had! I could hunt tiger and other beasts with my father and my brother, Salim. It was something my sisters were never allowed to do, if indeed they even considered such a thing." She waved after the pony cart containing Charles Frederick and his nursemaid.

He turned her gently to reenter the château. "How many sisters did you have, madame?" he inquired. "I have five sisters, and three brothers. Two of my brothers and three of my sisters live in Scotland. The others live in Italy."

"I was my father's youngest child. My siblings were grown when I was born," Jasmine told him. "I had three brothers, though two are dead, and three sisters."

"Why did you leave India?" he asked her bluntly.

"My eldest brother, Salim, now the Mughal emperor, Jahangir, had an incestuous lust for me. He murdered my first husband, a Kashmiri prince, in order to clear his path to my bed. My father was dying and knew that my foster mother would be unable to protect me once he was gone. So he sent me secretly to England, to my grandmother de Marisco, with whom he had had a tenuous sort of contact over the years." Jasmine laughed softly. "Before I left India my father learned that the priest who had been my tutor throughout my childhood was actually my cousin. My grandmother had sent him out to India to watch over me so she would always know if I was happy. Thank God for her!"

"And your brother never knew where you had gone?" he wondered.

"I do not believe so," Jasmine said. "It was a very clever plot my father devised. Salim thought I had gone to Kashmir to bury Jamal's heart in his homeland. My father did not die for two months following my departure from India. By the time Salim would have sent to my palace in the mountains it would have been late autumn, and the snows would be threatening. He could not possibly have learned that I was not in Kashmir until the following springtime, at which point I was safe in England. Salim knew little of my English mother. Even if he had unraveled the mystery of my whereabouts, what could he do?"

"Have you ever wished to return?" James Leslie said.

Jasmine thought a moment, then replied, "No. My early life in India was bound up with my father and brother, Salim, in a time when I was too innocent to understand his desires, and Jamal Khan, my first husband. My father and Jamal are gone. My brother has, hopefully, forgotten me at long last. My only regret is Rugaiya Begum, the mother who raised me. I was her only child. Now she has neither me nor the joy of my children, her grandchildren. For that alone I feel remorse. And for that reason I shall never forgive my brother Salim."

He could see the genuine pain in her eyes as she spoke the words, and James Leslie wanted to ease her sorrow. "Let us ask your cook to pack us a basket, and we shall go for a ride, madame. 'Tis a fine day, and I am certain that you know many a pretty trail hereabouts."

She was almost startled by his request, but January and most of February had been so wet and dreary. They had all been cooped up inside the château. Now with the children gone she was free to indulge herself in pleasure. She felt almost guilty, but then, shaking the feeling off, she replied, "Aye, 'tis a good day, my lord, for a ride!"

The cook, who thought Lord Leslie a very fine gentleman, packed the basket with a small chicken she had just roasted, a loaf of bread that had only been baked that morning, and was still warm; an earthenware dish of cold asparagus that had been marinated in white wine; a wedge of Brie cheese, two pears which she polished on her apron, and a goatskin of pale gold Archambault wine. The earl, watching her as she worked, took the finished basket from the cook and kissed her hand, bringing a flush to the good woman's cheeks. She watched them depart her kitchens, clutching at the honored hand, and looking upon it as if it would never be the same again.

Returning to the hall he found Jasmine waiting for him. To his surprise she had changed her clothes, and was garbed like a boy in breeches, cambric shirt, and a fur lined, sleeveless deerskin doublet with carved silver-and-horn buttons. James Leslie raised an eyebrow and suffered a moment of déjà vu. His own mother had once dressed as Jasmine was now garbed. "You ride astride," he finally said.

"I can ride sidesaddle when the occasion calls for it," she replied, "but I prefer riding astride as would you if you had ever tried balancing yourself in skirts upon a dancing horse, one leg thrown over the pommel of your saddle. 'Tis both uncomfortable, and discomfiting, my lord, not to mention unnatural. Surely you will not object?"

"Nay, madame," he quickly answered, seeing the light of battle dawning in her eyes. "In fact I agree with you."

She nodded and turned swiftly before he could see the amusement in her own glance. "Let us go then. It is fortunate you have your own mount, for I did not bring any but the coach horses with me from England. The stables at Archambault sent over a nice docile little black mare for me. She is pleasant to ride, but presents no challenges, I fear. If I had known I was to stay so long in France, I should have brought my own stallion."

"I am reassured that you did not," the earl said. "My own beast does not like the competition of another male animal about him."

"Then we shall have to keep separate stables, my lord," Jasmine said with a little laugh. "I do not intend giving up my horse for you."

"There is plenty of time to discuss such things, madame."

Jasmine turned, looking him straight in the eye. "There is no need for a discussion, my lord," she said firmly, and then she stepped out into the courtyard of the château, where the horses were waiting.

James Leslie had the urge to laugh aloud, but he wisely refrained from doing so. He was very uncertain of this beautiful woman who was to be his wife, but he was prudent to keep such thoughts to himself. Lady Lindley was strong-willed and would have to be handled carefully. He mounted his stallion and looked to her. "Lead on, madame," he said, making certain as he spoke that the hamper was firmly settled.

She led him through the gardens of the château along neatly raked gravel paths. He could see it was an orderly place, the flower beds mulched over with straw and uncluttered. The rose trees were well trimmed. A fountain tinkled merrily. A lily pond lay smooth, and uniced, in the sunlight. He could but imagine how lovely it would become in the spring and the summertime. Open on three sides, the garden was walled from the forest on the fourth. He could see a wicket gate in the stone as they approached it. Leaning down, Jasmine opened it.

"Close it behind you, my lord," she instructed him as she rode through.

Complying with her request, he followed her into the woods along a barely discernible, narrow path that wound and wound through the leafless trees of the forest. He glanced behind him and realized he could no longer see the château. He heard the sound of a stream tumbling over rocks, and then they were upon it, the horses picking their way across the unstable streambed. At one point he saw deer amid the trees. It seemed that they were in the deepest wood, then suddenly they exited onto a grassy hillside. Below them a vast vineyard spread itself out, and on a far hill was a magnificent château.

"That is Archambault," Jasmine said. "My great-grand-mère was once the comtesse de Cher. Her husband, however, was not my grandfather Adam's father. That was her first husband, John de Marisco, the lord of Lundy Island. Did you know that my grandfather was once seriously considered a pirate?" She laughed mischievously. "The old queen even put my grandmother in the tower at one time, for she believed that she was in league with him. My aunt Deirdre was born there."

"I wonder," the earl said with equal humor, "if the king is aware of your entire lineage, madame. Poor Jamie would be shocked."

"Perhaps he would not want you to wed me," Jasmine replied slyly.

"Alas, madame, were you one-eyed, and snaggle-toothed, the king would require our union, for you are the mother of his first grandchild."

"Then it is fortunate that I am not one-eyed and snaggle-toothed," Jasmine said drolly. She chuckled wickedly. "Would you wed me, my lord, if I were a hag and ugly as sin?"

"Aye, madame, I would, for I am the king's loyal man," James Leslie said. "The Leslies of Glenkirk have always been loyal to the Stuarts. It is our way."

"What if the king were wrong?" Jasmine teased him.

"Royal Stuarts are *never* wrong, madame," he told her.

"Divine right?" she mocked him.

"Aye, divine right," he answered. "Would your father have allowed any man or woman to question his decisions?"

"Not as emperor," she answered him, "but as a man my father was insatiably curious and always open to question. It was how he united a country and kept it united. Even in the matter of religion there was no right or wrong with Akbar. I was fortunate to be raised by such a man, for unlike my siblings, my father had time for me. Being the youngest of his offspring, and the child of his old age, there was always time for me. I was privileged, my lord, as few daughters are." She stopped her mare and looked down over the sleeping vineyards. "Shall we stop and eat here, sir? The sun is warm, and the view fair."

Agreeing, he dismounted, then lifted her from her own horse. While Jasmine spread a cloth she removed from her saddle pouch upon winter-dried grass, the earl took the basket from the pommel of his saddle where it had been hanging. They sat, and she spread the contents of the basket upon the cloth. He used his own knife to slice the bread, the cheese and the chicken into edible portions. There were two small silver goblets in the bottom of the basket, and Jasmine removed them, gracefully pouring the golden wine from the goatskin into them.

They ate, enjoying the food, but there was a paucity of sententious conversation between them. Jasmine gazed out over the vineyards below them and at the château on the hill beyond. James Leslie was equally quiet. His eyes wandered over the landscape, then to the woman who was his companion. She was, he thought, even more beautiful than she had been two years ago. But was there *anything* upon which they might build a meaningful relationship? He knew that they were capable of infuriating each other, but he did not want to spend the rest of his life with an angry woman. He had lusted after Jasmine once, and while he thought her capable of arousing his passions again, it was not enough. He wanted something more, and he would stake his life that she would want more too. *But what?* And how were they to find it?

"What is it you want?" he suddenly burst out.

Her face registered her surprise. "*Want?* What do you mean, my lord? I do not understand you. I believe I have everything anyone could want, and certainly a great deal more of it than most. I do not believe that I lack for anything, sir."

James Leslie shook his head. "Nay, Jasmine, 'tis not material possessions I question you about. I know you are a wealthy woman in your own right, but there are other things than one's tangible assets. Do you seek power, or amusement, additional wealth, *or love?* What do you really want that perhaps you do not have?"

"Ahhhhhh!" The light of understanding dawned in her beautiful and unusual turquoise-colored eyes. "*Love? I* had not thought if I should love again. The men I love die sudden deaths. Jamal and Rowan were murdered in their prime, and in both cases I was the direct cause of their deaths. Jamal's because my half brother coveted me; and Rowan's because my crown-appointed estate agent meant to kill me, and Rowan was in his way when the gun discharged. As for my poor Hal..." She sighed. "Henry Stuart should not have died before his time."

"But you were not responsible in any way for his death," the earl reminded Jasmine.

"Nonetheless he loved me, and he died," she responded.

"If you loved me, I should not fear death," James Leslie said.

Suddenly Jasmine smiled, and his heart jumped in his chest. "You seek some common ground upon which we may build a marital relationship, my lord, do you not?" And when he nodded in the affirmative, she continued. "Tell me, sir, did you love Isabelle Gordon, your deceased wife? Was she a pretty girl? Did you laugh together or cry together? How did she make you happy, my lord?"

He thought a moment, then said, "Bella was a pretty lass. She had long dark hair. Not the blue-black of yours, but rather a deep warm brown. I had been betrothed to her since my childhood, and we knew each other well. I believe I thought of her as I did my sisters. Then my father went off on an exploration of the New World and did not return. The king declared him dead, and I became the earl of Glenkirk. James Stuart insisted I marry immediately, ostensibly to get heirs on Bella so my line would not die out. In truth the king wanted my mother for his mistress. Declaring my father legally dead and forcing me into the position of head of my family was his way of making her presence at Glenkirk unnecessary. He ordered her to court."

"God's boots!" Jasmine burst out. "The king actually *lusted* after a woman? Why I thought him completely faithful to Queen Anne."

"Other than his passion for my mother he was. It began before he married the queen, but 'tis a long story, and I will not bore you with it, Jasmine. Suffice it to say my mother fled Scotland and has not been back since. She lives in the kingdom of Naples with my half brother, and two half sisters. My stepfather died two and a half years ago."

"And she did not choose to return?" How curious Jasmine thought.

"Nay she did not. She still fears James Stuart although I have assured her that he is a changed man from their youth. She says that cats do not change their stripes and that the climate of Naples agrees with her far more than that of Scotland. I think her memories of Scotland, however, are too sad for her to bear, whereas she and Lord Bothwell were happy all their years together in Naples."

"Were you happy with your Bella?" Jasmine queried him.

"Aye, I was. She was a good lass, a good mother, and a wife a man could be proud of, madame."

"You have not said if you loved her," Jasmine pressed.

"Aye, I did love her, but in a youthful and inexperienced way, I believe as I look back. We were comfortable together, and had she not died so tragic a death, I believe we would have been happy for the rest of our lives."

"'Tis how I loved my first husband," Jasmine said.

"But not how you loved the second?" he replied.

Jasmine smiled softly and munched silently on a piece of cheese for a long moment. "Nay," she finally admitted. "I loved Rowan Lindley in an entirely different way. It was as if we were one at times. You knew him, my lord. You knew the kind of man he was. Kind and generous. Loyal. A man who could laugh. That fate could snatch him from me, and from his children, is something I shall never understand."

"And yet you were able to love again," the earl said.

Jasmine smiled again. "Aye. But who could not love Henry Stuart? Everyone adored him. I did not seek his favor, you know. In fact I resisted him quite strongly, but he would not have it." She laughed with the memory. "Hal would have his way in the matter, and I have his son to remember him by. 'Tis a precious gift, and more than most royal mistresses gain."

"But that *gift* has forced you into the king's arena, madame," the earl noted. "Perhaps you should have been satisfied to take just jewelry and titles from Prince Henry."

Jasmine chuckled. "There is no man in England who could gift me with jewelry, sir, for the jewelry I possess far surpasses anything you have ever seen. Rowan knew it, which is why he gave me MacGuire's Ford. And Hal knew it, too. As for titles..." she shrugged. "I was born a royal Mughal princess. Only a queen's crown would impress me, and it could not be."

"So, madame, you possess lands, titles, gold, and jewelry in your own right, but still you must wed me. What can I give you that will make you happy, Jasmine?"

"Why do you care if I am happy or not, James Leslie?" she demanded of him. "The king has ordered us to wed, and wed we must whether I am happy or not happy. You have said you will obey James Stuart because the Leslies of Glenkirk have always been obedient to the royal Stuarts. What difference does it make if I am happy?"

The muscle in his jaw tightened. Jasmine Lindley could be the most irritating woman when she chose to be. Here he was holding out a rather large olive branch, and she was apparently refusing it. "Madame, I am not some monster who has been foisted upon you," he began, "nor are you being martyred to any cause by being wed to me. There are several ladies in England who would be but too glad to be my countess. Once even your own stepsister sought that honor."

"Do you wed me just because James Stuart orders you to, sir?" Jasmine asked him. "I do not like the idea that we must wed each other because of a royal command. When I was a young girl I accepted such a marriage, but it was my father's dictate, and not that of a stranger."

He swallowed the wine remaining in his cup, wishing that there was more, and sighed. "I cannot change what is, Jasmine," he said quietly. "When I arrived at Belle Fleurs several weeks ago I was very angry with you. I believe I was close to hating you, and I did, I will admit, seek revenge upon you for embarrassing me so publicly. Being with you, however, has caused my anger to drain away. I admire you. You are a woman of courage and determination. There are some men who might not appreciate such characteristics in a wife, but I do. I am not certain I can offer you love now or ever, nor can you promise me love; but I will respect you, and I can offer you companionship. You will not suffer as my wife, and I will be a good father to your children, I swear it on the souls of my own dead bairns."

"Will you force me to wed you before the court?" she asked.

He shook his head. "I am past vengeance, Jasmine. We can wed here at Belle Fleurs, or at Queen's Malvern. The choice is yours, I promise you, but please, madame, let it be soon. We cannot afford to incur the king's displeasure much longer."

"Is he angry at you, too?" She was surprised.

"Aye," he said with a little grin. "He said when the ram corners the ewe he should nae gie her freedom to choose her own pasture in her own time. Fortunately the Carr mess has kept him occupied, and he has not had too much time for me, but it would please him if we wed soon. He longs to see the little laddie, for he has not seen him since Charles Frederick was a wee bairn, and the boy is his grandson."

"Promise me you will not let them take him from me," Jasmine said. "That, I will admit to you, is my greatest fear. Once the queen told me how they took Hal from her, and she rarely ever saw him, and must beg permission from his governors when she wanted to be with him. I could not bear it if they took Charlie from me!" And her eyes filled with thick tears at the very thought.

He reached out and brushed the tears from her soft cheek. "They will not take him from *us,*" he promised her. "Henry Stuart was the heir, and the custom of farming the heir out an old one. 'Tis no longer done, thanks to the queen. Besides, darling Jasmine, your Charlie is but a royal bastard. He can never be heir to the throne. His importance is in his relationship to the king and the queen, not in his future."

"But what if they want him?" she persisted.

"What they want is to see the laddie and know him. I am his guardian because they know I am an honest man and will not use the boy to my advantage or to build my power base. Charlie will remain with his family. I promise you this, madame."

"I am afraid," she said softly.

He took her gloved hand in his big hand. "You must trust me, Jasmine. 'Tis a great leap of faith for you, I will admit, but I beg you to trust me." He could feel that her hand was cold beneath the leather. He attempted to warm it between his two hands.

A wind had sprung up, and the sun had now disappeared behind a hand of clouds. The promise of spring, earlier in the air, had entirely disappeared, and winter, it seemed, was returning.

"We had best go," she said, disengaging her hand from his, and standing up. She brushed the crumbs from her breeches and began packing up the basket and cloth.

"You will consider what we have spoken on this day?" he asked her.

"We will marry in the spring at Queen's Malvern," Jasmine told him with a small smile, "but not upon the first of April, my lord. 'Tis an infamous date for us, and I would begin our relationship on a more cheerful note. Would you not agree? I think perhaps the fifteenth of the month would be suitable. I do not like May. Marry in May, rue the day, 'tis said."

"You do not favor June?"

"Do you really wish us to try the king's patience that far?" she gently teased, as he helped her to mount her mare. She smiled down at him, her eyes twinkling. "Of course June is a lovely month, my lord."

"Did you not wed Westleigh in April?" he asked her, vaulting into his own saddle. Somehow the idea of marrying her in the month in which she had married another husband was irritating. Perhaps it was even the same day, thereby making it easier for her to remember. Even her monogram would remain the same. L for Lindley. L for Leslie.

"I married Rowan on April thirtieth, my lord," she replied, her tone just slightly frosty, "but it is obvious that you prefer June. So let it be June fifteenth. It will do just as well, I think."

The earl felt a momentary chagrin. He had behaved like a churl, and she had caught him at it and called his bluff. Now he would wait an additional two months, and the explanation given the king must be his. He swore softly beneath his breath, and, to his mortification, Jasmine giggled, or he thought she did. When he looked over at her face was a smooth mask of bland innocence.

She led him through the vineyards of Archambault and onto the carriage road from Paris that he had ridden over before. They cantered easily along the path until they came to the almost hidden way leading to Belle Fleurs. Now she spurred her mare into a gallop, and her hair, so neatly in its chignon, blew loose, flowing behind her. He urged his stallion onward, realizing they were to race home, and, as he drew even with the mare, she looked over at him and laughed. Pulling past her he reached the château's bridge before her and drew his beast up to await her, but she did not stop, and the mare raced by him into the courtyard of the castle.

Jasmine leapt down. *"I won!"* she bragged triumphantly.

"I thought the race ended at the bridge," he protested, dismounting.

"Why would you think that?" she demanded.

"Because it was the logical end of the course," he replied.

"Nonsense!" she mocked him, hurrying into the château, handing off her gloves to a servant. "A race ends at the door of the house. I thought everyone knew that."

"I didn't," he said, an edge to his voice.

"Why not?" she countered.

"Because you didn't tell me, madame!" he shouted.

"Have some wine," she offered. "It will calm your nerves, my lord. Gracious, it was only a little race."

He took the large goblet of fruity red wine and gulped half of it down. "Not telling me the rules is the same as cheating," he growled at her, his dark green eyes narrowing. "If you are to be the countess of Glenkirk, you must be honorable in all things."

"You are really a dreadful loser, my lord," Jasmine said. "It was a silent challenge, and to believe the race ended before it ended was just plain silly. You will have to be quicker than that if we are to have a satisfactory relationship, my lord."

"Are you *always* like this?" he groused.

"Like what?"

"Impossible! Totally, utterly impossible!" he roared.

"There is no need to shout, my lord," she told him. "I do not think it is particularly good for you. There is a little vein right there"—her finger reached out, and touched the side of his head—"that is throbbing fiercely. I must teach you a little trick one of my aunts taught me when I was a child that will help you to calm yourself. You sit perfectly still and clear your mind of all thoughts, then just breathe deeply in and blow the breath out. It is excellent for calming one's nerves. I used it myself on occasion."

He could feel the vein she touched beating a tattoo on the side of his head. There were but two ways to stop it and calm himself. He would either have to strangle her where she stood—and the thought at this very moment was deliciously tempting—or he would have to kiss her. He chose the latter.

Sweeping her into his arms his mouth found hers in a hard kiss. He crushed her against him, feeling her bosom, certainly fuller than it had been several years back before she had borne her children, push against him. He expected her to struggle, to give some expression of outrage. Instead Jasmine's lips softened against him, and she seemed to melt into his embrace, returning his harshness with a tender, sweet softness. He had meant to conquer her, but instead found himself the vanquished. He was astounded as he released his fierce hold on her, not just a little chagrined.

She stood straight, looking up at him, although if the truth had been known Jasmine's legs were as weak as a jelly. "'Twas either kiss or kill, was it not, my lord?" she taunted him wickedly.

He nodded, and, unable to think of any clever retort, said, "There was a time when you called me Jemmie, madame, and not always *my lord*. Do you think we can regain that place again?"

"You will never *tame* me, nor I you, Jemmie," she replied in answer. "'Twill be a terrible match, I fear." But Jasmine was smiling.

"Aye," he agreed, "it will, but there is no help for it. I am the king's loyal man and must obey. Still, a man might have a worse wife than you will be, darling Jasmine. As you are so fond of reminding me, you are rich, beautiful, royal, and clever," he gently teased.

"I have always been a good wife," she responded primly. "You will learn if you do not thwart me, I shall be loyal and bring no shame to your name, Jemmie Leslie."

"In other words, if I give you your own way, we will have no difficulties," he said, his eyes twinkling.

"Exactly!" Jasmine answered him brightly. "How fortunate I am to be marrying so perceptive a man."

Chapter Five

The weather turned again, and the early spring rains came. James Leslie and Jasmine Lindley kept mostly to the château, where they played cards and chess, and talked. Although they had been acquainted with each other, neither really knew the other. Skye had been correct in leaving them alone. When the children had been gone some ten days, the earl suggested that on the next day there was no rain they ride over the Archambault to visit Jasmine's relations and see how the youngsters were getting on with their cousins.

Jasmine flushed at the suggestion.

"What is the matter?" he asked her.

She laughed weakly. "I had almost forgotten about my children," Jasmine admitted, embarrassed. "It has been so lovely here with you, Jemmie, that I have come close to forgetting my responsibilities."

"You are the best of mothers," he reassured her. "No one would fault you for enjoying your time away from the children. When we return home to England we shall spend as little time at court as is possible that we may spend most of our time with our family."

"Will we live in Scotland?" she asked him. "My mother transplanted well there, but has always insisted upon her

English summers as she is wont to call them. Is Glenkirk beautiful, Jemmie?"

"Very beautiful," he said, "but we will only live there part of the year, Jasmine. Perhaps the autumn and winter months. Autumn is the best time in Scotland. The summers we will spend at Queen's Malvern, and Henry must go to Cadby then. In the spring we shall go to court so that James is not offended. I have overseen his empire's foreign trade for several years now, but I wish to resign that post now that we are to be wed. My own family has been heavily involved in trading for many, many years with our bankers, the Kira family. I do not know if your grandmother would consider it, but a merger of my interests with the O'Malley-Small trading company could profit us as all. That is something she and I must discuss."

Jasmine nodded. "It seems a sensible solution to all our domiciles, but I hope we shall not have to stay too long at court."

"Only to the extent it benefit us," he responded sagely. "We have the children to consider. Charlie is a duke, and Henry a marquis. Their sisters are heiresses, and will be prime on the marriage market one day." He reached out and took her hand in his, lifting it to kiss the inside of her wrist and her palm. "And we have *our* bairns to consider as well, darling Jasmine. Perhaps another earl, and a brother and sister or two?" He nibbled on her fingers seductively.

Jasmine colored becomingly. Of course there had to be children of this marriage, but until this moment she hadn't really thought a great deal about it. How long had it been since she had made love to a man? Her youngest child was two and a half years of age, and it had been several months before his birth when she and Henry Stuart had ceased their intimacies. It was almost three years, she realized, amazed.

She had grown used to life without a man. *Without a man in her bed.* Did she even remember how to play that game? The fire in the fireplace crackled and snapped, the flames dappling the walls with shadow, while outside the rain beat a light tattoo upon the windowpanes.

James Leslie saw the confusion passing over her features and realized the opportunity presenting itself to him. To his surprise, however, Jasmine pulled her hand away from him, distress written all over her beautiful face. Shaking her head at him, she ran from the hall. *So,* he thought, *she had felt it too.* She wasn't being coy, he realized, for Jasmine Lindley was a woman of experience; yet she felt a certain shyness with him that was astonishing given the passionate lover he recalled on that one wonderful night that they had shared those several years back.

He wondered if he should follow her and thought better of the idea. He considered if she had taken a lover while here in France and discarded the notion. The only lover Jasmine Lindley had ever allowed in her bed other than himself, and her husbands, had been Prince Henry Stuart. Then in a burst of clarity he saw the problem. Of course! It had to be! *There had been no man in her bed since the prince.* He laughed softly to himself. Jasmine, who disliked being at any sort of disadvantage, felt awkward about making love again. He was tempted to go to her and reassure her, but he knew that would be a mistake. He would have to court Jasmine as he had never courted any woman. He had not really courted Isabelle, for they had been promised in childhood, and it was a given that they would marry. It had not been necessary to court his late wife, and there had been none since her death he chose to court and marry.

It was an interesting concept, courting a woman, but court her he would have to in order to gain her trust and win his way into her bed, into her heart. What could he do that would please her? She lacked for nothing. James Leslie realized that he had absolutely no idea about how to court a woman who had everything. Had she been a simple lass, he would have wooed her with jewelry and other finery. She knew he liked her children, so there was no ingress there. What was he to do? And then he realized that he would have to seek advice from Madame Skye. He laughed aloud at the thought. Take advice from that beautiful and devious old woman? Aye! He would, for she knew Jasmine best, and was, if her reputation was to be believed, the most skilled and clever woman where the arts of love were concerned.

James Leslie poured himself another large goblet of red wine and settled himself by the fireplace, sipping the liquid nectar slowly. Tomorrow they would go to Archambault, and he knew that Jasmine would devote her time there to her children. He, however, would seek counsel from Madame Skye on how to win her granddaughter, and win Jasmine he would.

In the morning she behaved as if everything was exactly the same between them as it had been the day before. She came to the highboard dressed for riding, in green wool breeches, high leather boots, a cambric shirt, and her doeskin jerkin with the silver-and-horn buttons. She ate heartily, which both amused and delighted him. He liked a woman who enjoyed her food and did not toy daintily with her plate. His mother was such a woman. Jasmine never drank wine in the early morning. Her servants brought her a blue-and-white porcelain dish, pouring into it a fragrant hot liquid which she always drank with relish.

Curious, he asked her, "What is it you drink, Jasmine?"

"It is called tea," she told him. "Would you like to taste it, Jemmie? Adali, bring another saucer for the earl." She smiled at him. "We brew it with hot water, using the leaves of the tea plant. It is native to India. The leaves are cured or dried before use. It is a very pleasing drink. My mother and my aunts frequently put cloves or cardamom in the tea to add additional flavor to it."

Jasmine's steward placed a deep saucer before him and poured some of the tea into it from a pitcher. "This is black tea, my lord," he said. "The Chinese grow a green variety."

"It is more delicate," Jasmine said. "Our Indian tea is a most hearty brew. Taste it, Jemmie!"

He sipped at the hot liquid, finding the taste pleasant, but not particularly stimulating or exciting as wine, ale, or cider.

"I am thinking of suggesting to grandmother that we import tea into England," Jasmine told him. "The Dutch have been doing it for the past six years although they do not know how to market it and have not had a great success with it."

"The Dutch are excellent merchants," he replied.

"Indeed they are," she agreed, "but they still do not know how to sell tea. Tea is not spices or cloth that can be easily hawked to any housewife in the market. Tea must first be sold to the rich and the powerful. Only when they have taken it to their bosoms and made it a drink of the exclusive will the masses seek to have it."

Her analysis of the situation surprised him. He had always known that Jasmine was an intelligent woman, but he had put that particular brand of intelligence down to female common sense, but she was beyond that obviously. "You may be right, Jasmine," he said slowly. "Aye, I can see where having tea drunk by a select few would eventually make it modish, and very desirable to the general population."

She arose from the highboard. "We'll talk to Grandmama about it," she said. "Come, Jemmie, and let us be off. I have not seen my darlings in almost two weeks, and I am eager to be with them!"

They took the direct road to Archambault, arriving quickly, and Jasmine was out of her saddle almost immediately, sweeping her children, who were awaiting her upon the steps of the great château, into her all-encompassing embrace. On the top step Madame Skye stood with a distinguished gentleman the earl rightly guessed to be the comte de Cher. Alexandre de Saville shook James Leslie's hand and bade him welcome. The earl then kissed Madame Skye upon her pale cheeks.

"So, James Leslie," the old lady said, tucking her hand into his arm as they entered the château, "have you made any progress with my granddaughter?"

"We will wed on the fifteenth day of June," he replied.

"Ah, good! I am glad you have managed to bring Jasmine around to a more sensible frame of mind in this matter," Skye replied.

They entered an elegant salon, and he saw at once that they were alone.

"I need your advice, madame," the earl said, "and as we have privacy for the moment, perhaps it is the time to seek it."

She raised an elegant eyebrow. "You seek my advice? How interesting," Skye said, a small smile playing with the corners of her mouth. "Then, sirrah, you have decided that I am not your enemy?"

He chuckled. "I think you are a devious, wicked lady, madame, but I still need your advice; and no, I do not believe we are enemies, nor have we ever been."

They sat upon an upholstered settle, and he took her hand in his. "I believe that Jasmine has become shy in things of an *intimate* nature, Madame Skye. She is not comfortable once matters pass a certain point. It is not in her nature, I believe, to be cold."

"Hmmmmmmm," Skye said.

"I considered other reasons for her reluctance, but the only one I believe true is the fact she has not known a man since some time before wee Charlie's birth. I think she may feel at a disadvantage."

"God's boots!" Skye answered him. "What is the matter with the girl? You are handsome, and well made, and she has shared your bed on one occasion and not found you displeasing."

"We are being pushed into doing our duty," the earl replied. "I think I need to court her, Madame Skye, but how does one go about courting a woman with everything? What can I do, or say, or give her that she has not heard or received? My first wife and I were promised as bairns. I did not court Isabelle, but then we were both very young and used to one another. Our families had agreed to our marriage, and that was the way it was done in Scotland at that time."

Skye nodded. Now here was a small tangle that needed unknotting. She had not considered that Jasmine, once become sensible, would behave like a sheltered virgin, and her a woman with four children! It was simply ridiculous! "I will speak with my granddaughter," she said.

"Nay, madame, I beg you do not!" the earl implored her. "She would be mortified to learn that I knew her secret. Just instruct me in how to please her so that she will lose her shyness with me, and matters may progress naturally."

"God's blood!" Skye swore passionately. "What is the matter with you young men of today? In my day the men were bold! They swept a woman off her feet and into their arms without their permission. None of my daughters were like me, but this one granddaughter is. You will gain your goal with her by being audacious and gallant, and not by pussyfooting around."

"But Madame Skye..." he attempted to interrupt her.

"There are no *buts* where love is concerned, James Leslie," she told him sternly. "Do you know that Jasmine's grandfather seduced me the first time he met me? Like Jasmine I was mourning a loss and had been without a man, but Adam wanted me, and he took me." Her gaze softened with the memory. "I should have seen that he was the man for me then and there, but I outlived two more husbands before he realized that his first manly and fearless approach to me had been the way to my heart. We were fortunate, and in those days it seemed as if time went on forever." She was silent a moment, then sighed gustily before looking at him again. "Seize your opportunity, dammit! Give my granddaughter a taste of passion again. You cannot help but overcome her outrage with it." She chuckled wickedly. "I envy the girl, my lord, I do."

He raised the hand he had been gently holding to his lips and kissed it. "Thank you," he said.

She nodded, her Kerry blue eyes twinkling, yet wise. Then she said, "I believe that you and Jasmine should be together alone for a few more weeks, James Leslie. What would you think if I took the children on to visit Paris, and from there home to Queen's Malvern, where we will await you? It is already mid-March, and if I am to prepare for a wedding and notify the family, I cannot linger much longer in France. The children yet prove a distraction to their mother, so perhaps it is better they travel with their great-grandmother?"

"I tend to agree, madame," the earl said, restraining the chortle that threatened to burst forth from his throat. He had known that the old lady would not allow Jasmine's bairns to return to Belle Fleurs, but he had not been certain exactly how she would manage this feat. Madame Skye was absolutely brilliant in her tactics. "I will hire a goodly force of the comte's men to escort you first to Paris, then on to the coast. The roads are not all that safe, as you know, particularly now with another war threatening to break out."

"Aye, that is wise," Skye agreed. "I know Alexandre will be more than happy to give you the loan of some men-at-arms."

The door to the salon burst open, and Jasmine, looking agitated, entered the room. "What is this that Henry tells me, grandmama? That you are taking the children to Paris? I will not allow it!"

"Darling girl, do not be foolish," her grandmother soothed her. "Aye, we are off to Paris in a few days' time, and from there to England, where we will begin making preparations for your wedding, and notifying the family of your return. In the meantime, you and Lord Leslie will have more time to work out any little difficulties between you, and to know one another better. You are quite fortunate to have me relieve you of your responsibilities, even temporarily, Jasmine."

Jasmine glared at the earl. "And you agree with this plan?"

He considered placating her, but remembering Madame Skye's words he said, "Aye, I do, my dear. I realize that I am being selfish, but I very much want you to myself for the time being."

"*Oh?*" Her cheeks pinked slightly.

"You know that I adore your bairns, Jasmine, but 'tis I am marrying, and not the wee ones," he murmured, catching at her hand, and kissing it longingly. "This time alone is precious, and I will have it, my darling Jasmine!" *As I will have you.* The words were unspoken, but distinctly implied, and understood between them.

"So," Skye said briskly, "it is settled. Run back to the children and enjoy your day with them, darling girl. I must keep your betrothed with me a moment or two more to discuss certain arrangements about the wedding regarding his family."

Bemused Jasmine exited the salon.

"What arrangements?" he questioned her when the younger woman was gone.

Skye laughed. "There are none," she chuckled. "I just wanted Jasmine to consider what had happened without further distractions. 'Twas nicely done, my lord. You were forceful, yet loving. Continue on in that manner, and you will gain your objectives."

Eventually, he joined Jasmine and the children, all of whom were delighted to see him, and rushed at him, crying, *"Papa! Papa!"* He shook young Henry's hand and kissed the others warmly. The four youngsters were in excellent health and obviously having a wonderful time with their de Saville cousins.

"We're going home to England soon," Henry said.

"I know," the earl answered him. "Your mother and I will come shortly afterward, and be married at Queen's Malvern on the fifteenth day of June. Will you stand by my side as my witness, Henry?"

The boy marquis of Westleigh nodded enthusiastically. "Aye, Papa, I will, and gladly!" Then he sobered a bit. "Do you mind that we call you *Papa?* I know you are not yet wed to our mother, but..."

"I am pleased and honored that you would accept me in such a capacity, Henry," James Leslie answered.

"Will you teach me to use a sword properly?" Henry asked.

"We will begin this summer," the earl promised him.

The rest of the day sped by. They partook of a lavish meal with the comte de Cher and his wife, Helene. The comte's heir, Phillippe, his wife Marie-Claire, and the comte's two daughters, Gaby and Antoinette and their families were also there to meet the earl of Glenkirk.

"We know your cousins, the Leslie de Peyracs," Gaby said. "There is the possibility of a match between our two families."

"May it prove advantageous for both sides," the earl murmured politely. "My mother's uncle is, of course, long gone, but I am not particularly fond of his widow, the ancient dowager, Adele. She rules the roost, or so I am told."

Gaby nodded. "I know the old witch well, but 'tis one of her great-granddaughters who is to wed our middle son. They will live here in the Loire with us, and not at Château Petite."

The conversation continued on in such a vein. The comparison of families, local gossip, and curiosity as to when the wedding between Jasmine and the earl would take place. The de Savilles were filled with regret that it would not be celebrated at Belle Fleurs, but they understood, and wished the couple well. Finally their departure could be delayed no longer. Jasmine appeared close to tears.

"Do not distress the bairns, sweeting," the earl said softly.

"You are always telling me not to weep over my children," she snapped at him, but her melancholy was already gone.

"Let me know when you intend arriving," Skye said cheerfully. "'Twill be good to have you home again. Remember, your mother and your brothers will be arriving May first. How delighted my Velvet will be to see her grandchildren at long last!"

"I cannot help but think that you and Jemmie have somehow manipulated me, Grandmama," Jasmine muttered darkly.

"Why, darling girl, what a dreadful thought," Skye protested. "I am doing you a great favor. If you think it is easy for a woman of my years, yet in deepest mourning, to travel with four active children, then keep them and bring them yourself!"

"You would swoon if I agreed to such a thing," Jasmine teased her grandmother. "Nay, I do appreciate your kindness, but I will miss them." She hugged the older woman warmly.

"Get on with you, you clever vixen," her grandmother said. "I will see you in England, and do not dally too long with that delicious man you are to marry, although I should not blame you if you sampled a few of the honeymoon delights while still here in France. Spring is coming, Jasmine, and the sap is rising in all living things!"

She and the earl laughed at Skye's parting remark as they rode back to Belle Fleurs. "Can you imagine her in her youth?" Jasmine said.

"The thought is absolutely terrifying," he replied, grinning. Then, "Are you game for some chess this evening, madame?"

"After I have bathed," she said. "Do you not tire of being beaten, Jemmie?" She giggled mischievously and, kicking her mare into a canter, let him chase her back home. This time, however, he did not stop until his horse had reached the inner courtyard of the château, beating her by several lengths.

"Your stallion's legs are much longer than my mare's," she complained prettily. "Just wait until I have my great beast back under me. Only then will we be evenly matched."

"I already think us evenly matched," he said, lifting her down from her horse. Then he kissed her in a slow and leisurely fashion, letting his lips taste her mouth with outrageous sensuality. "You do not have to wait to return to England, Jasmine, to have this great beast beneath you," he murmured softly, nuzzling at a strand of hair that had come loose in their ride. His big hands remained still, molding her slender waist between his fingers.

Was she breathing? Aye, she was breathing, but barely. His hands were burning through the soft tanned deerskin of her jerkin, through the cambric of her shirt. His mouth on hers had been startling, but when he pushed at her hair with the tip of his nose her head had swum tipsily. She reached out to put her hands upon his shoulders, steadying herself against his bulk. "I think you go too quickly with me, Jemmie," she whispered breathlessly.

"And I think you go too slowly with me, Jasmine," he quickly countered. "We are neither of us children and know the path we are taking." A slow smile lit his features, crinkling the corners of his green eyes. "Let us make a wager on the outcome of tonight's chess match between us. Are you game?"

She nodded. His hands felt so strong on her flesh. "What hazard do you propose, sir?" She suddenly had the most incredible urge to be naked before him. And have him naked before her. What madness was this? She struggled to put the wicked images invading her mind aside.

"If I win," he said softly, "I will enter your bed this very night, my darling Jasmine." His gaze engaged hers.

"And if you lose?" she asked low.

"The stake is yours to choose," he replied.

"You will not enter my bed until we are wed." The words were out of her mouth before she even had time seriously to consider them. Why on earth had she said them, she wondered, feeling a sense of loss as his hands fell away from her waist. Did she really want to hold him off until the middle of June? It was too late to recant.

He chuckled. "Done, madame!" he said, leading her into the château. "I look forward to our match—and to after the match."

"For so mediocre a player you are overconfident, Jemmie," she said sharply. His attitude was mightily irritating.

"I do not intend losing tonight, Jasmine," he answered her. "The prize is too tempting and delectable a one to forfeit."

She pulled from his grasp and ran up the staircase to her bedchamber, ordering her servants to prepare her bath as she entered her quarters. Rohana and Toramalli hurried to do her bidding.

"You are disturbed," Adali noted. "What has upset you, mistress?"

"I have agreed to a chess match with Lord Leslie, and we have made a wager to make our game more interesting. I think I have been foolish, Adali, for I am not certain if I want to win."

The eunuch chuckled as he helped her to divest herself of her garments. "Tell me," he said, and then burst into laughter when she had finished. "Ahh, my princess, once long ago, when your father sought to bed your mother for the first time, he played a game of chess with her. It was in the royal city of Fatehpur-Sikri. Together your parents stood on a balcony. The courtyard below them was a chessboard of black-and-white marble squares. The pieces were live slaves, naked but for the jewels they wore, except, of course, the king and queen pieces, who were magnificently garbed and bejeweled."

"Did my mother win?" Jasmine asked Adali.

He shook his head. "Nay, she did not. The wager between them, however, was but a kiss. It was several nights later before your father gained his objective, and then only through the aid of the pillow book that Jodh Bai gave your mother."

Now it was Jasmine's turn to chuckle. "So history is about to repeat itself, Adali," she said.

"Are you certain you wish to lie with him now, my princess? I have seen your reluctance to accept this man."

"I must wed him, Adali," she replied, "and I find that I do like him. He loves the children, and they love him, *and* he would have me give him sons. The wedding date is set, and I suddenly find I do not wish to postpone the inevitable. When we were speaking just now in the courtyard, I had the most disturbing thoughts regarding James Leslie. I believe it is time to end my celibacy, Adali."

"You will have to be very clever, my princess," the trusted servant responded. "If Lord Leslie believes for one moment that you have allowed him to win the match, he will be most offended."

Jasmine smiled as he helped her into her waiting tub. "My father was the best chess player in all of India," she reminded Adali, "and he never once knew that I let myself lose more often than not, did he?"

Adali grinned. "Nay, my princess, the Mughal never knew that the student surpassed the master. You were adroit in your duplicity."

"I have not forgotten those skills," she assured him.

He left her to set up the chessboard in the hall.

Rohana and Toramalli bathed their mistress carefully, having been party to her conversation with Adali. Afterward, wrapped in a towel and seated by her fire, Jasmine thought drowsy thoughts as Rohana slowly brushed her long black hair, drawing the perfumed brush through the silken swath until it gleamed. She yawned. It had been a long day, and she suddenly realized she was tired. "Give me some wine before I collapse," she said to Toramalli. "The bath has rendered me weak."

"What will you wear?" Toramalli asked her as she brought her mistress the requested goblet of wine.

"A chamber robe, I think," came the reply.

The servingwoman nodded and, choosing a silk garment in a rich plum color, brought it to her mistress, who stood up and let her towel fall, holding out her arms to don the robe. It had long flowing sleeves and closed with a small gold frog just below Jasmine's breasts. Rohana then tied back her mistress's hair with a silver ribbon. Plum-and-silver silk slippers completed Lady Lindley's ensemble.

Finishing the wine which had revived her, Jasmine instructed her servants to prepare the bed with fresh linens. "The lovely lavender-scented ones we just obtained from the convent nearby," she said. Then she departed the bedchamber for the hall, where she found him awaiting her. She stared at his clothing. "A kilt?" she queried him.

"A Scotsman always wears his kilt into battle, Jasmine, and so I am prepared to go to war with you this evening over the chessboard."

His shirt was open at the neck. She could see the dark hair upon his chest. Her eyes strayed to his long, sturdy legs, which were covered in dark hair. His knees were shapely and rounded. Forcing her eyes away from his form Jasmine tried to quiet her thoughts. She was suddenly behaving like a bitch in heat. She felt both hot and cold at the same time. What had her grandmother said about spring, and sap rising? "You are, as usual, my lord, overconfident," she murmured with what she hoped was unconcerned disdain.

The laugh that rumbled forth from his broad chest was openly knowing. "I have the strongest desire," he told her, "to kiss that little mole of yours, darling Jasmine," and, before she could evade him, he did just that, pressing his mouth against the teasing little beauty mark nature had placed between her left nostril and her upper lip.

"You are too bold, sirrah!" she scolded him, pushing away. "Come, and let us begin our game." She seated herself in the tapestry-backed chair by the hall fire, motioning him to the seat opposite her. "You may begin," she told him.

He calmly moved a pawn in a familiar and quite typical opening move. Then his eyes met hers.

"'Tis hardly a challenging beginning," she mocked him, but her own move was quite similar to his.

The play now began in earnest. Jasmine kept up a taunting verbal assault as she played. Her tone was overbearing and overweening. She played hard, and he had not the slightest inkling that she was leading him carefully so that he could shortly capture her queen and win the match between them. She made a move, and then swore softly, reaching out to correct the apparently foolish maneuver, but he stopped her with his hand, shaking his head.

"But I did not mean it," she objected strongly. "I was distracted. Surely you will not hold me to such a play, Jemmie? 'Tis not fair!"

"You removed your hand from the piece," he said quietly.

"But I did not mean to, sir! I was distracted," she cried.

"If our positions were reversed, Jasmine, would you allow me to replay the move?" he demanded of her.

Her small white teeth worried her lower lip, and she did not answer him.

James Leslie reached out and, taking the black onyx piece belonging to him, silently completed the winning move, palming her ivory queen gravely. Jasmine leapt to her feet and, turning, attempted to make her escape. He was quicker, however, and his hard arm wrapped itself about her slender waist, drawing her back against him. "Nay, madame, you cannot go until you have paid your forfeit," he said softly, and his other hand firmly cupped one of her breasts. His warm breath in her ear sent a shiver up her spine. "Ya-sa-meen," he murmured the name she had been given at birth, "how I long to possess you again. I have never forgotten that night we shared so long, long ago." His thumb rubbed her nipple until it was stiff, and tingling.

"The servants..." she protested.

"Are too well trained by your Adali to enter the hall unless called," he told her even as he pushed the chess table aside with his big stockinged foot and drew her down upon the thick sheepskin rug before the fire. His elegant fingers fumbled a moment with the golden frog closure of her gown, finally releasing it so the plum-colored silk fell away, revealing her naked form to him. He stared at her, almost awed.

"How is it that after four bairns you still have the figure of an exciting young girl?" he wondered aloud. His fingertips caressed the generous swell of her bosom.

"I do not," came her soft reply. "My belly is no longer flat, and my breasts are much fuller than the last time we found ourselves in this situation. I have the body of a woman, Jemmie Leslie."

"To my eye you are the most beautiful creature I have ever seen," he assured her. His dark head bent to press a kiss upon her left breast. "I like your sweet titties," he said.

"You cannot continue to have me at such a disadvantage," she told him, her fingers unlacing his shirt, her hands pushing it from his shoulders. It fell about his waist. "What does a Scotsman wear beneath his kilt, Jemmie Leslie?" she teased him provocatively.

With a grin he stood, loosening the garment so that both it and his shirt fell about his ankles. "Only the badge of his manhood, madame," he answered her, stepping away from the discarded clothing.

"Take your stockings off," she ordered him. "I'll not make love to a man with a bare bottom and stockings on his feet." She kicked her slippers off as she spoke.

Chuckling, he complied with her request, finally joining her upon the sheepskin. "Do you remember the last time?" he asked her.

A small smile touched Jasmine's lips. "Aye," she said. "It was after my uncle's Twelfth Night gala. We seduced each other, and Sibby caught us and raised such a ruckus. My stepfather wanted us to wed to save my reputation. Poor Alec, caught between his two girls. One who wanted you desperately, or so Sybilla thought."

"And one who refused to wed me," he reminded her. "You said you would not be forced to the altar." He smiled at her wryly. "Yet now you are, and with the same man you refused those years back. I fell in love with you then. Did you know it?"

Jasmine shook her head. "Nay," she admitted, "I did not."

Bending, he brushed her lips with his. "Well, I did, my darling Jasmine. I fell in love with you then, but when I finally gathered up my courage to go to your grandparents, you were to wed with Rowan Lindley. I was too late. A laggard in love. That is why I cannot let you go now, Jasmine. *I will never let you go again!*"

"How fierce you sound," she told him, her hand stroking his handsome face. "Am I to have no say in this matter, Jemmie Leslie?"

"Only if you swear to belong to me forever," he replied, catching her hand in his, kissing each knuckle upon it, then turning it over to kiss her palm ardently. *"Swear!"* he growled at her.

In response Jasmine laughed softly. "Not yet, I think," she replied. "If I allow you to become too certain of me, Jemmie, then you will grow careless in your affections and actions toward me. Better I keep you dangling. At least until we plight our troth come summer." She retrieved her hand with a seductive smile.

"You are a bitch," he said, half-amused, half-angry.

"Aye," she drawled slowly. He lay by her, half-raised upon an elbow, looking into her fair face. Drawing his head down, she kissed him a deep, sweet kiss. "Would you have me be some simpering fool of a woman, my lord? Best you know what you are getting. Perhaps you will even change your mind and ask the king for release from this match."

"Nay, madame," he told her, looking into her turquoise-colored eyes. "I am no easier than you are. We are well matched, I believe." His head dipped, and, taking a nipple in his mouth, he began to suckle upon her while his hand kneaded her other breast.

The first strong tug on her flesh sent a frisson of pleasurable sensation through her body. It had been so long since she had been with a man that it almost seemed as if it were the first time. Jasmine drew in a deep breath and exhaled it, feeling the tingle all the way to her toes. Her fingers threaded themselves in his dark hair, pressing into his scalp. "Ummmmmmmm," she sighed, enjoying his attentions. The last time they had made love, the only time they had made love, she amended to herself, James Leslie had ended a period of celibacy in her life that began with the murder of her first husband, Prince Jamal Khan. Now he was ending another love drought for her. She wondered if her pleasure in him came from the cessation of her passionless state, or if he would indeed prove to be an excellent lover.

Releasing her nipple, the earl of Glenkirk began to lick at Jasmine's perfumed flesh. He encircled the nipples with his tongue, rousing them into tight little nibs. He laved the flesh between her two breasts, and then across her torso, blowing softly upon the glistening wetness he left behind. The natural fragrance of her body began to mix with the scent of her bath oil and but contributed to his arousal. He could feel her fingers digging into his head as her own sensual appetites were stirred and awakened.

Raising himself up, he kissed her mouth, feeling her lips soften and yield beneath his. Her tongue pushed into his mouth, demanding he caress it with his own. Their kisses melted one into another until there was no longer a beginning or an end. She loosed his hair, and her hands slid away from his head, caressing the graceful curve of his neck, feeling the prickles of sensation she encouraged in him beneath her fingertips. His broad, furred chest pressed down into the soft swell of her bosom. He groaned as Jasmine smoothed her hands down his long back, then cupped his hard buttocks for a brief moment.

He was hard and ready then, but she held him off. Repositioning herself just slightly, she reached down and began to caress him with such a delicate yet tantalizing touch that he almost spilled his seed, so filled with boiling lust was he at that moment. He groaned.

"Patience, my lord," she cautioned him. "A woman's passion is not so quickly raised as is a man's."

In response he pushed her hands away, for any more fondlings of his sensitive weapon, and he would be ruined. Rolling onto his side he squeezed her Venus mont gently, smiling, pleased, as she gasped with surprise. A single finger insinuated itself between the fleshy folds that hid her little pleasure pearl from public view. He found the jewel and began subtly to taunt the tiny nub until she was writhing.

My God, Jasmine thought in her last moment of clarity, *he certainly takes instruction well.* Explosion after explosion of sensation rolled over her burning body. She ached with both pleasure and hunger for more pleasure. Before she might peak, however, he stopped, and before she might protest, he pushed two fingers into her throbbing passage, going deep, his teeth sinking into her shoulder as his hand moved to awaken her further. *"Please!"* The word exploded from her tightly constricted throat.

He withdrew his hand from her, and, swinging over Jasmine's eager body, he drove himself into the wet hot receptacle she ottered him. The walls of her sheath enclosed themselves about his throbbing member, pulsing all around him in their ardor. He felt her legs wrapping themselves about his torso even as he sank deeper into her scalding flesh. "Ohh, wanton!" he groaned into the silken tangle of her black hair.

It had been so long! Jasmine could feel her heart pounding in her ears. He filled her full with his fierce passion, thrusting and withdrawing, thrusting and withdrawing until her head was spinning wildly. She pushed her hand into her mouth to stifle the cries that threatened to burst forth from her throat, but seeing it he tore the hand away, and her song of pleasure rang throughout the hall. "Jemmie! Jemmie! Oh God! Yes! Ohhhhhh!" She shuddered as she tumbled from her peak and down into the warm darkness of repletion.

He flooded her with his tribute, groaning with his satisfaction, as his lust burst, then finally drained away. Sprawled half-atop her, he breathed deeply the fragrance of her dark hair until he was finally able to raise himself and roll off her entirely. Reaching for her hand, he said, "Madame, you surpass my memories of you. I am mad for you, Jasmine! Tell me at least that you gained some measure of delight."

She laughed weakly. "My lord, I believe we have found something upon which we may agree. The passion between us bodes well for a happy marriage of sorts, I think."

"But there must be more between us, Jasmine," he said quietly.

"I know," she agreed, "but is this not a good beginning?"

"So you are willing now to do your duty as the king has ordered?" he teased her gently, nibbling upon her fingers.

"There, my lord, is another thing we have in common. We are both dutiful, and know our obligations to the crown and to our families," she replied. She pulled her hand from his, and then, grasping his hand, began sensuously to suck upon his fingers, one at a time, her eyes engaging his. Her mouth turning up in a small smile.

"Is there anything else, madame?" he murmured. Jesu! The wench was a witch. She had already drained him so deeply he thought little left of himself, yet her mouth, now tantalizing his fingers, was arousing him once more. He could already feel a stirring in his loins.

"We both like children and the simple life," she said.

"Aye," he agreed, "but they are *your* children, not mine."

"A situation easily remedied," Jasmine promised him. She released his hand and, standing, drew her chamber robe lightly about her. "Come, Jemmie Leslie. My bed will be warmer and more comfortable than this place before the fire. Now that I am of a mind to do my duty, you will find me very willing, my lord." Turning, she walked from the hall, pausing only a moment at the entry to beckon him to follow her.

The earl of Glenkirk rose, wrapped his kilt about himself and, gathering up the rest of his garments, trailed after her, a bemused smile upon his face.

ENGLAND

SPRING 1615

Chapter Six

They left Belle Fleurs, crossing the River Loire at Tours, and traveling up to Paris, where they rested for a few days at the de Saville town house, which was located in the Rue Soeur Celestine. Although Jasmine's coach accompanied them, she and James Leslie preferred riding their horses to being confined within the vehicle. A large baggage coach had accompanied them, containing not only the luggage, but Fergus More and Rohana, the two remaining servants. Madame Skye had departed for England two and a half weeks earlier, taking Adali and Toramalli with her, much to Daisy's great relief.

"Yer surely losing yer wits, my lady, when you volunteer to chaperone those four wild creatures back to England," she scolded Skye. "Do I not have all I can do just looking after you? You ain't getting any easier with age, and I ain't no lass anymore. I'm just an old widow woman like yerself."

Her mistress immediately reassured Daisy that Jasmine's two servants would be controlling the children. "They are only traveling with us, Daisy," she said. "Adali and Toramalli will handle everything."

"Well, I should hope so!" Daisy responded sharply.

Riding through the French countryside, Jemmie at her side, Jasmine remembered the exchange. She almost felt guilty that she had let her children go on ahead, thus allowing her this wonderful time with the man she was to marry. Beginning their journey, they had ridden a road through the vineyards along the Loire. The vines were replete with a new growth of bright green leaves, the tender tendrils reaching out for support. The vineyards eventually gave way to apple orchards in bloom, the air sweet with the delicate fragrance. The weather was perfect, and they rode beneath a canopy of blue skies with a warm sun on their shoulders.

The comte de Cher had supplied them with a large armed escort. He had arranged for their accommodation in small, clean inns, where the food was simple, but fresh and tasty, and the wines rich and fruity. It was almost a disappointment to arrive finally in Paris. Jasmine liked it little better than she liked London. Like that other city, the smells were rank from the garbage in the gutters, the crush of unwashed bodies in the streets, and the noise of discord that rarely seemed to die away. They visited Notre Dame and were admitted to the Louvre, where they saw the young king, Louis XIII, at dinner with his new queen, the Infanta Anne of Austria.

"Grandmama never liked Paris," Jasmine noted. "She says the French are an unpredictable people, prone to violence."

"She's right," the earl responded. "The Catholics and the Protestants are beginning to fight again. The queen mother, Marie de Medici, and her brother-in-law, Concini, are yet ruling in the king's name. Cardinal Mazarin is a man to be reckoned with, and there is a new, young cleric, Armand-Jean de Plessis de Richelieu, who, I suspect, will eventually be a power to contend with, on the horizon. France is not a safe place right now."

They stayed but two days, departing for the coast where *Cardiff Rose,* an O'Malley-Small trading company ship, awaited them. Boarding in the afternoon, James Leslie and Jasmine saw the coast of England the following morning, and remained on deck as the vessel swept around Margate Head on the incoming tide and into the wide estuary of the River Thames. The brisk May winds moved their transport up the waterway to London by the early evening. To their surprise they found Adali awaiting them with the de Marisco barge, which would ferry them to Greenwood House on the Strand.

"How on earth did you know when we would be arriving?" Jasmine asked her faithful retainer.

"I escorted your grandmother to Queen's Malvern, and then returned to London to await you, my lady. The captain of *Cardiff Rose* was instructed to tell me when he planned to depart, and how long it would take him to return to London. Lady de Marisco's factor in Paris notified her agent in London by pigeon when you left and when to expect you at Dover, my lady. The rest was quite simple," Adali concluded. Then he turned to the earl of Glenkirk. "Greetings, my lord. Your journey was a pleasant one, I hope." But before James Leslie could answer, Adali's sharp eye caught a movement, and he whirled about shouting, "Be careful of that coach, you barbarians! Has it traveled about England and France only to be destroyed by your carelessness? And go gently with the horses, or you will face my wrath." He turned back to Jasmine. "My princess, I think I must oversee this process else these louts ruin the carriage and frighten the animals. The barge will take you upriver to Greenwood. Toramalli returned to London with me and awaits you. All is in readiness for your arrival. There has already been a message from the king. He expects you at Whitehall in two days' time, and your uncle, the earl, is in residence at Lynmouth House, my lady." He bowed to them, and then, turning away, hurried off the vessel onto the docks, shouting instructions, and waving his arms.

Jasmine giggled. "He becomes more like an old woman with each passing year." she said, "but I could never do without him."

"Glenkirk Castle will certainly be surprised by him," the earl chuckled. "I like your Adali, darling Jasmine. He is devoted to you as am I. He is also intelligent and industrious, not to mention loyal."

"He has never forgotten that my mother, Lady Gordon, gave him the opportunity to advance himself, or that when she departed my father's realm my father entrusted my safety to him. He has been with me my entire life. I cannot imagine being without Adali."

They debarked *Cardiff Rose* and entered the barge, seating themselves within the little cabin, which had etched glass windows and a scarlet velvet bench with the painted red-and-gold designs upon the bench's oak back. The entry curtain was drawn back with a gold rope so they might see out as the Greenwood bargemen rowed them upriver to their destination. About them the twilight was deepening.

He put his arm about her, saying, "I cannot wait to pay our respects to the king and leave London so we may be wed. In the autumn I shall take you home to Scotland. We will hunt red deer on the heathered hillsides, and you will see the trees become banners of scarlet and gold with the arrival of the cold weather. And when the snows come, we will nestle together like two rabbits deep in their winter burrow, doing what rabbits do best," he finished mischievously, pulling her close and fondling her breasts as his lips brushed against her hair, her cheek, finally finding her lips.

She purred, molding herself against him with a contented sigh, her mouth ripe and yielding beneath his.

"Ummmmmm," she murmured. "Oh, Jemmie, you do bring out the wanton in me, I fear. Stop it this minute else the bargemen see and gossip."

In answer he reached out and, pulling at the door curtain tie, successfully obtained their privacy. Then, before she might offer a feeble protest, he knelt before her and, pushing her skirts up, lowered his dark head between her milky thighs. The touch of his tongue upon her sensitive flesh elicited a sharp gasp from Jasmine, particularly when he flicked his tongue rapidly back and forth over her tingling flesh. His elegant hands held her thighs apart firmly, but insistently.

"*Jemmmmmmie!*" she squeaked, struggling to keep her voice low so the bargemen would not hear her obvious pleasure. The tension was building within her nether regions. Her fingers kneaded his dark head frantically. "Ohhh, God!"

He raised his head, and his green-gold eyes were fierce. "*I want you! Here! Now!*" He twisted himself about so that he was seated once more, then he pulled her onto his lap, impaling her upon his manhood, which had somehow broken loose of the restraints of his clothing. With one quick thrust he filled her.

"Ohhhh, yessss!" she moaned, her head thrashing, feeling as if she was about to erupt with pleasure. They shouldn't be doing this *here*. Not with just a velvet curtain between them and four burly bargemen. "Ohhhhh, Jemmmie!" It was wicked. It was disgraceful. What if they were caught? *It was wonderful!* She rode him hungrily.

His head was spinning. *She was wanton.* She was delicious. He had never desired a woman like he desired Jasmine. *And now she was his!* He groaned and, unable to help himself, allowed his hot seed to water her hidden garden, even as she collapsed against him, her dark head falling onto his shoulder. His arms wound about her, holding her close, nuzzling at her perfumed hair. "You are irresistible, madame," he murmured low. "I came to France determined to punish you for your outrageous disobedience—hating you for making me a figure of ridicule—and within three months' time you enthrall me, and I am helpless to your charms once again. What is worse, I am content to be so, Jasmine. I believe that I have never stopped loving you." Gently he lifted her off his lap and set her next to him again.

Jasmine smoothed her skirts, her cheeks pink and burning. He was an incredible and daring lover she had discovered these past few weeks, but love? She could not lie to him, nor would he want it. "I have never had the time to fall in love with you," she said slowly.

"I know," he replied, "but I did fall in love with you that Twelfth Night so long ago at your uncle's fete. Alas, I was a laggard in revealing my emotions, even to myself, Jasmine. You married Rowan Lindley and went on with your life. I continued to love you in secret. When Rowan died, and Prince Henry claimed you for his own, you moved into a new relationship while I clutched my secret to my breast, never daring to believe that one day you would be mine. Now you are, and you will have a lifetime to learn to love me, darling Jasmine."

"And will I?" she asked him softly.

He turned her face to his with a gentle hand. His gaze was warm, and Jasmine was suddenly breathless. "Aye, madame," he answered her low. "You will learn to love me." Then he kissed her lips, and she felt as near to swooning as she had ever felt.

"Greenwood Landing!" a voice called out.

Instantly James Leslie leaned forward and drew back the curtain shielding them. "You made good time," he said to the head bargeman.

"Tide still be with us, my lord," was the answer, "and Gawd only knows how many times we've rowed up and down the old Thames."

The bargemen guided the boat up against the quay landing. It bumped the stone gently. When it had been made fast to the piling, James Leslie exited the little cabin, helping Jasmine, and they gained the shore, walking up the lawns to the house. A figure came forward to greet them, and, recognizing him, Jasmine ran forward into his embrace.

"Uncle Robin!" She lifted her heart-shaped face for a kiss.

Robert Southwood, the earl of Lynmouth, hugged his niece warmly, and kissed her cheek. "So, you impossible vixen, you have at last come home to us. The king is eager to see you, but not so eager to punish you now that he has seen his grandson, I think." Southwood escorted the couple up into the house.

"The king has seen Charles Frederick?" Jasmine was surprised.

"Mama stopped in London with the children when she arrived two weeks ago. She brought your offspring to court. The king was delighted and every bit as loving to your young marquis and his lady sisters as he was to his own blood. The children's manners were exquisite, and everyone was mightily impressed by them, Jasmine. Did you not know that Mama intended to visit Whitehall before she departed for Queen's Malvern? No," the Earl of Lynmouth answered his own question. "You obviously did not know. Mama is as clever as she ever was, I think. She has done you a great kindness, my dear, and taken the edge off of the king's anger. Things have not been going well for the king of late, and your very public disobedience has not helped his mood. Now, however, having seen little Charles Frederick, he is less testy. The boy is a delight, and charmed his royal grandfather completely."

Jasmine was silent, then she said. "All the children went to Queen's Malvern with Grandmama, didn't they, Uncle Robin?"

"Of course," he replied. "What made you ask such a question?"

"Jasmine fears that the king will take Charlie-boy away from her and give him to strangers to raise, even as he did with Prince Henry. The queen once warned Jasmine of such a thing. I do not believe that she will rest easily until the king assures her otherwise," the earl of Glenkirk told the earl of Lynmouth.

Robin Southwood looked thoughtful, and said, "I think that we must indeed get the king's word that Charles Frederick Stuart remains with his mother and stepfather. Aye! We need a royal guarantee."

"What have you heard?" Jasmine was pale with anticipation.

"Nothing, my dear," Robin Southwood hurried to reassure his niece, "but it is always wise not to put one's trust in kings, Jasmine. Their exalted status makes them believe that God sanctions their every move, and I do not think that it is always so. You did not, however, hear me say that. I am the king's loyal servant and would never question his divine right." He patted her shoulder, his lime green eyes twinkling.

She giggled, and the girlish sound did his heart good. "Uncle, you are really quite disrespectful of the king," she teased.

"Never, my dear," he replied. "You will remember that I grew up in a far more impressive court than this one is, and served a greater queen than this king. Like my father before me, I am the perfect courtier. However, I have only come up from Devon to welcome you home, Jasmine, and to smooth your way in two days' time when you must present yourself to James Stuart and make your abject apologies to him for your disobedience. After that I am gone, back to my sweet Angel and the children and our grandchildren. I no longer have a taste for this life, I fear. I think the king's little passions will be his downfall. First Carr, and now two new young men vie for his favor."

They found their way to the family hall and, seating themselves at the board, waited for the servants to serve them.

"The king was not always as he is now," James Leslie said. "I knew him from childhood. I think his age and time have conspired to make him behave foolishly."

"He never had a mistress like so many of his antecedents," Robin Southwood said. "He has always been faithful to the queen, but for his young men; and those only since he came to England."

"But he was not always faithful to the queen," Glenkirk said quietly, taking a deep draught of his wine.

Southwood was fascinated. "No?"

"The king once had a mistress." Jasmine said.

"My mother," Glenkirk answered. "It was a very long time ago. The king developed a passion for her, although she never encouraged him. He sent my father to Denmark to escort his new bride home to Scotland, and while my father was gone James Stuart forced my mother to his will. When my father finally learned of it, it destroyed their marriage, and Mama fled to Lord Bothwell for protection. It is a long story, and perhaps some time I shall tell you of it; but the king was not always the silly fellow he is now. He was ruthless, and cruel, and as tough as any soldier."

"Did the queen know?" Jasmine was curious.

"I don't know," James Leslie answered her. "I do not think so, for she was always very kind to me, and to my brothers and sisters. I don't think anyone knew but Lord Bothwell, my father, the king, and my mother's servant, Ellen. You must remember the strict way in which the king was raised, surrounded by overpious and overmoral men, who would have been horrified to learn that their king, their protégé, had coveted another man's wife and taken her despite her refusals."

"God's nightshirt!" the earl of Lynmouth said, using a favorite expletive of the late queen. "I should never have believed such a tale but that it is yours, Jemmie. Your mother married Bothwell, didn't she?"

"After my father's death," James Leslie said, "except that he wasn't dead. He went to the New World, and his ship was lost. He was presumed dead, but damned if he didn't turn up several years later at Glenkirk with a wild account of his adventures. By that time the king had had him declared dead, and Mama was remarried and living in Italy with Lord Bothwell and their three children. I convinced him to reveal himself to no one else but me. To remain dead for everyone's sake. Since he had no desire to resume his former life, he agreed. There was, it seemed, a beautiful young lady in the New World awaiting his return." The earl chuckled. "My father was ever the charmer."

"Is he still alive?" Jasmine wondered aloud.

"Aye! He married his lady-in-waiting, and has since fathered several more children," James Leslie told his audience.

"You will be completely at home in this family, I can see," Robin Southwood said. "My grandfather was a pirate. My sister, Willow, was fathered by a renegade Spaniard who lived in Algiers. And Jasmine is the daughter of an Indian emperor." He laughed. "We are not a quiet clan, but then neither, it would appear, are the Leslies of Glenkirk."

They had eaten as they talked. A simple meal of sliced salmon, roasted capon, new lettuce braised in white wine, baby peas, bread, and two cheeses: a soft Brie from France, and a sharp cheddar. Now the earl of Lynmouth arose to take his leave of Jasmine and Jemmie.

"I will leave you to yourselves tomorrow," he told them, "but I will come to escort you to Whitehall myself on the following day." He turned to his niece. "You must be prepared to humble yourself, Jasmine. You do understand that, don't you? The king is fully prepared to forgive you providing that you are properly contrite. The Mughal's daughter must masque herself behind the guise of a remorseful and apologetic dowager marchioness of Westleigh. Are you ready to do that?"

"Yes, Uncle," Jasmine said softly.

"Such docility, my dear," he teased her. "I am most impressed. Now behave that way with the king, and we will have no more difficulties." The earl of Lynmouth looked at James Leslie. "I would congratulate you on the success of your venture, sir, but I can see that you have fallen in love with her all over again and are as helpless as a babe before my niece's wiles. Try to appear in control of the situation before old king fool." He saluted them with an elegant bow and departed.

"Grandmama says he is much like his father," Jasmine observed when her favorite uncle had gone. She sipped at her wine and reached for a strawberry from the basket just placed upon the highboard. "Would you?" she teased him, biting into the berry, "like to continue our discussion of earlier? The one we began in the barge? Do you think anyone else ever made love while rowing upon the river, Jemmie?" She licked the juice of the ripe strawberry from her fingers.

"I suspect we were not original in our efforts there," he remarked dryly. He leaned over and licked the fruit juice from the corners of her mouth. "Ummmm, good," he observed, and took one of the berries for himself. Holding it by its green stem, he stroked the berry provocatively with his tongue, then, biting into it, he swiftly devoured it.

Jasmine reached out and caught his hand. Raising it to her lips, she slowly sucked each of his fingers free of the sweet juice, all the while holding him in thrall with her turquoise gaze. Rising from her seat she led him from the hall, but not before the earl of Glenkirk had reached out to capture the strawberry basket in his free hand. They moved from the main level of the house to its third floor, where the bedchambers were located. She led him into the large apartment that had once been her grandmother's. It consisted of a dayroom, a bedchamber, and a dressing room. Rohana came forward as they entered, but seeing the naked passion between her mistress and Lord Leslie, the servant quickly and discreetly withdrew even as the two lovers disappeared into the welcoming bedchamber.

Jasmine took the basket from him and set it upon the bedside table. Her fingers fumbled with the fastenings on his doublet, pulling it open, drawing it off, unlacing the shirt beneath, almost ripping at the fabric as she pulled it over his head. With a little cry she smoothed her hands over his furred chest, her fingers moving in excited little circles. Their earlier encounters had but whetted her appetite for him. His skin was warm beneath her fervid touch.

He matched her actions, undoing her bodice and loosening her skirt tapes so that the garment fell to the floor. Her breasts swelled dangerously over the top of her chemise. He bent his dark head and kissed the pulsating flesh. Then, impatient, he ripped the garment off of her, flinging the remnants of fabric across the room, even as she undid his breeches, drawing them down, letting them fall that he might step from them. She tore his drawers off as he had her chemise.

Their mouths meshed in a hot, humid kiss. Their bodies touched their full lengths as he pulled her against him. Crushed against his furred body, she whimpered deep in her throat, "Jemmie! Jemmie!" Her arms slipped about him, her hands slipped down his back to cup his taut buttocks. She kneaded the flesh with supple fingers, feeling his thighs press even tighter against hers, feeling his wiry, thick bush touching her velvety smooth Venus mont. She wrapped a single leg about his leg, forcing them into an even closer juxtaposition.

"Ohhh, bitch!" he groaned, taking her face between his hands and covering it with kisses. His warm lips moved across her mouth, her cheeks, her forehead, her eyelids. Their tongues intertwined in a lustful dance as his hands moved up to tangle themselves in her hair, pulling the pins from it so that it fell in an ebony swath about them. Now he was cupping the double moons of her bottom, forcing her to release her grip on his leg. Slowly he raised her, and then, equally slowly, he lowered her onto his hot raging lover's lance. "Bitch!" he half sobbed.

Jasmine wrapped her legs about his torso. Dear heaven! He was so hard that his deliberate entry had almost hurt her. Her head fell back, and at once he leaned forward, licking the slender column of her throat with a burning tongue.

She whimpered again as he moved across the chamber and carefully lowered her onto the edge of the bed. Fully braced, she unwound her legs from about him, and he pushed them back, allowing him greater access to her throbbing sheath. Her arms lay above her head, giving him total freedom of her breasts.

Reaching out with both hands he squeezed them hard, half-smiling at her cry of passion. Leaning forward, he began to tongue the nipples. Her breasts had always been her most vulnerable point. He teased them unmercifully, licking, nibbling, kissing, biting down on the sensitive nibs just enough to cause quick pain, which he immediately kissed away, all the while remaining buried deep within her sheath.

Jasmine could feel him throbbing within her. Her breasts felt swollen and tight, as if they were about to burst, but she knew even if such a thing were possible, she would still not obtain relief. She was afire with her own lust and almost maddened in her passion. *"Fuck me, dammit!"* she hissed at him. *"Fuck me!"*

He looked down into her face and laughed softly. "Tell me how much you desire me, darling Jasmine," he taunted her, then caught the hands that reached out, fingers curled to scratch him. He forced her arms back over her head again. *"Tell me!"* he growled. "Tell me, or I shall leave you. You may not love me, sweetheart, but by God, you shall desire me! *Tell me!"* His green-gold eyes blazed down at her.

"You desire me as much as I do you!" she retorted, and squeezed his manhood with the muscles of her sheath's walls. It was an old harem trick that all the women of her country used to pleasure their men.

"Say the words, Jasmine. Say that you lust after me!" he insisted, a spasm crossing his face as she tortured him.

"Say it!" Bending, he took a nipple into his mouth and began to suckle hard upon it.

She almost screamed. He was killing her. He claimed to love her, but he was killing her. Her whole body had begun to ache with her hunger to be satisfied. "I want you, Jemmie!" she half sobbed. *"I want you!* Now fuck me before you destroy me, you bastard!"

Almost at once he began to move within and upon her. The rhythm became faster and faster, until their combined passion exploded in a furious burst that left him breathless and her unconscious for a brief few moments. She soared so high with her pleasure that Jasmine thought she would never return to earth, and cared not, but of course, she eventually did. He lay half-sprawled upon her, his breathing rough and harsh, his heart hammering violently.

She couldn't move. She was replete with satisfaction and didn't want to move. Obviously neither did he. They lay there, and she dozed easily, relishing the pleasure they had just given each other. When finally he pulled himself to his feet, she asked him sleepily, "Did Rohana draw me a bath?"

James Leslie shook his head to clear it, and glanced across the bedchamber. There before the fire was her oaken tub. "Aye," he said.

Jasmine struggled to her feet. "I want to bathe," she told him. Bending, she drew off her stockings with their beribboned garters, and padded across the floor, climbing into the tub. "It's still warmish," she announced, and, taking up the flannel cloth and soap, began to wash herself, soaping everything he could see and everything he couldn't see.

He watched her, fascinated. He had just experienced the most passionate moment he had ever known. Their desire for each other had been such that they had both been close to violence. It had been damnably exciting. James Leslie had always been a conservative man. Responsibility had been thrust upon him at an early age by a less-than-restrained father and his beautiful, passionate mother, whose indiscreet affair had ended in self-imposed exile from Scotland. His sweet Isabelle had been a charming young wife, but there had never been any fire. He had not believed himself capable of fire until now. There was obviously more of his mother's nature in him than he had previously thought.

"Jemmie." She was standing in her tub now, the water sluicing down her lush body. She beckoned to him. "Let me bathe you, my lord."

In a half daze he stepped into the tub, standing patiently as she washed him, the flannel cloth and the soap moving swiftly up, and down his long frame, caressing his broad shoulders with a silken swish, sliding down his long legs as she half-knelt. He shuddered just slightly as her firm touch bathed the instrument of his sex, but if she noticed, Jasmine said nothing. Standing again, she rinsed him thoroughly.

"There!" she said, her tone pleased. "You're done. Let us get dry. You do me, and I'll do you." She handed him a towel, taking the other for herself and rubbing him vigorously. "Ohhh, that's so much better," she said when they had dried each other off. She dashed across the bedchamber to get into bed. "I haven't had a proper bath since we left Belle Fleurs. I hate being dirty, and those little sponge baths are never the same as a good tub of water."

"Don't you want a nightgown?" he asked her.

"Why? Do you want me to wear one, Jemmie? Come into bed, my lord, else you catch your death of cold." She motioned to the place beside her, holding the covers back in invitation.

He slid in beside her, and Jasmine immediately cuddled up against him. His big hand smoothed her long dark hair.

"I can't stop wanting you tonight," he finally admitted. "What magic is this, darling Jasmine, that you have spun about me like a spider's web?"

"God's blood," she swore softly, "my uncle is right. You are in love with me, James Leslie, but you mustn't be! This must be a marriage of convenience, and respect. It cannot be a love match!"

"Why not?" he demanded, looking down into her beautiful face.

"Because the men I love die! You know that, Jemmie!"

"We all die eventually, darling Jasmine. Why Madame Skye lost five husbands to death before she wed your grandfather and lived happily with him for over forty years." His arms tightened about her. "You are going to love me, sweetheart, and when you realize that you do, you are going to admit it to me." He kissed her worried brow. "Now go to sleep. Your lusty desires have exhausted me, and I need my rest if we are to enjoy another bout of Eros before the dawn."

"You are the insatiable one," she muttered, nestling contently.

He chuckled throatily.

They slept for several hours, and when Jasmine awoke she saw that the fire was burning as brightly as it had been when she had fallen into slumber. She lay upon her back and had obviously thrown the covers off. Feeling a fluttery movement, she glanced down, and saw that he had placed a destemmed strawberry in her navel, and was even now in the process of eating it. Placing a second berry where the first had been, he devoured it, too.

Jasmine giggled. "How long have you been using me as a plate for your fruit?" she asked him.

"I've eaten six berries so far," he admitted, grinning.

"'Tis my turn then," Jasmine said, sitting up. "Lie back, sir, and I shall begin." He had destemmed the remaining berries in the basket. She set one each upon his nipples, then ran a ribbon of strawberries down his chest to his navel, and from his navel to his groin. She outlined his dark bush in a half-moon of berries, then finished, she drew herself up and began to eat the fruits of her labor.

He forced himself to lie very, very still, even when her small teeth grazed his flesh, sending a tingle down his spine. He watched her, totally fascinated, as she picked at each berry delicately. His torso was soon covered in strawberry juice, which she licked from his flesh. Finally only the six berries half-circling his bush remained. Slowly, deliberately, she ate each one, and when she had finished, licking the juice up, she bent lower and took him into her mouth. Half-rampant already, he groaned with pleasure as her teeth delicately nibbled upon him, and her tongue sensuously teased at his hot flesh. And when he thought he would burst with desire, she released him briefly, climbing atop him to slowly, slowly, lower herself onto his hard manhood. Reaching out, he began to fondle her breasts with his hands as she moved on him, her little cries telling him of the pleasure she, too, was receiving.

Jasmine's head was spinning as she rode him. He was big and hard, and she couldn't seem to get enough of his passion. *This isn't love,* she insisted to herself. *This is lust. Nothing more than healthy lust.* She couldn't love him, for if she did, he would surely meet as bad an end as had Jamal, and Rowan, and her sweet prince, Hal. But, ohh, he was an incredible lover! "Jemmie! Jemmie!" she cried out to him, unable to restrain herself. Oh, God! It wasn't enough! *It wasn't!*

James Leslie saw the frustration and confusion upon her face and took immediate charge of the situation. Rolling her over onto her back he thrust hard and deep into her again, and again, and again. She needed him even if she couldn't admit it, and he knew it. *Oh, darling Jasmine,* he thought to himself, *you are falling in love with me even if you cannot yet admit it to yourself.*

Beneath him Jasmine writhed with total pleasure. There were stars exploding behind her closed eyelids and a building hot pleasure in her nether regions. Unable to help herself, she clawed fiercely at his broad shoulders as the spasms began to unleash themselves within her with a torrid violence that racked her very soul. She was crying out. Her teeth sank viciously into his shoulder, and then she and he exploded together in an incredible burst of raw passion. She could feel the heat of his juices almost burning her womb even as she tasted the blood in her mouth from his shoulder. Frantically, she licked the wound.

"Bitch!" he groaned, and his mouth descended upon hers in a fierce kiss that left her almost breathless, until he finally rolled off of her and lay panting upon his back. "My God," he at last managed to gasp. "What has happened between us? Is it always going to be so...so...so wild?" His heart was hammering against his ribs.

"I...I...don't know," she half sobbed. Dear heaven, it *had* been wild. She didn't understand this fierce desire between them. Jamal, her first husband, had been a gentle lover. Rowan Lindley, her second husband, had been passionate and tender, as had Prince Henry, when she had been his mistress. This was beyond anything she had ever known. It was a savage passion with each of them trying to gain a mastery over the other. Would it always be this way between them she wanted to know? Did they want it always to be this way? Could they survive if it remained this way? Jasmine just did not know.

He reached out and took her hand in his. "How can you not love me when our passion is so deep?" he asked her.

"I mustn't love you," she whispered. *"I mustn't!"*

"You do love me," he insisted. "I know you do!"

"I am afraid, Jemmie!"

He cradled her in the curve of his arm. "Why? And do not say it is because the men you love die, sweetheart."

"But they do, Jemmie," she said desperately. "Each time I have been given to a man, first by my father, and then by my grandparents, I have fallen in love, and I have been happy. All I have ever wanted was to love my husband and bear healthy children to love and raise. When Jamal was murdered I lost the child I was carrying. When Rowan was killed by that fanatic I was left with two children and was carrying a third. I almost died myself that time. And finally Henry Stuart. He should not have died! He should have lived to be England's king, but he did not. He loved me, and he died."

"The prince died of an illness contracted by swimming in the river when he was overheated from sport. It was unfortunate, but you cannot be held responsible for young Hal's death, Jasmine; and the fact that he was in love with you is inconsequential to the matter. As for your first husband, he was assassinated on the orders of your brother. The bullet that killed Rowan was meant for you, and not the marquis. Both incidents were lamentable. Jamal, Prince Henry, and Rowan Lindley were unlucky, but that is all there was to their deaths, Jasmine." He kissed the top of her head. "We are being married on June 15, sweetheart, and we are going to live a long and happy life together, darling Jasmine, because I will not have it any other way," the earl of Glenkirk concluded. "Now, tell me you love me, you impossible wench! I have certainly waited long enough to hear the words from your mouth."

"You are too sure of yourself, my lord," she replied.

"Jasmine!" His tone was threatening.

She looked up into his handsome face. "I do want a long and happy life together with you, James Leslie. *I do!*"

"Do you love me?" he persisted.

Jasmine nodded. "Yes, Jemmie, I love you," she told him, "and I always will."

Chapter Seven

Robert Carr, Viscount Rochester and earl of Somerset, was losing the king's favor, and he knew it. He was a desperate man. He had begun his career at court as a page. By twenty he was a groom of the bedchamber, having caught King James's eye when he broke his arm jousting. The following year the king gave the young man a tablet of solid gold set with diamonds. Three years later he was made a viscount. When his eye fell upon Frances Howard, the married countess of Essex, nothing would do but that he have her for his own wife.

Frances Howard had, at the age of fourteen, been literally forced to the altar by her family. She and Robert Devereaux, the earl of Essex, detested each other. She had dallied with Prince Henry before he had met Jasmine. Then she and Carr had fallen in love. There would be no divorce, however. Frances Howard demanded an annulment from her husband, claiming that he was impotent, not just with her, but with all women. It was a lie, of course, but the king and the archbishop looked the other way. The annulment was granted, and Frances married Robert Carr, who by this time had been created the earl of Somerset. She was sixteen, and he was twenty-six.

One of Robert Carr's friends, Sir Thomas Overbury, had objected quite vocally to the match between Frances

Howard and her intended. He had spoken out publicly, slandering the lady, whom he very much disliked, and had even appealed to the king to save Carr from Frances Howard. His efforts were useless, and shortly after the happy couple were united in marriage, Sir Thomas Overbury found himself arrested and imprisoned in the Tower of London. There he remained for the next few months cooling his heels until one morning his jailers found him dead in his cell. He had been poisoned.

An investigation was called for by the shocked king, and it was quite thorough. It was determined that Sir Thomas Overbury had ingested poisoned sweetmeats. It had taken some time to learn who had sent the deadly treats, but now the rumors were rife that they had come from the earl of Somerset's household. It could not be ascertained if either the earl of Somerset, or his countess, had ordered the sweetmeats supplied to Sir Thomas—the box had been given to a street urchin outside the Tower for delivery to Overbury, according to the yeoman of the guard who had received the gilt paper box. It was indeed quite possible that the messenger had himself been disposed of to avoid being found and used to identify the miscreant. But the gilt paper box was one that Frances Howard was known to favor when presenting gifts to friends. Indeed, its maker declared that he made the boxes *only* for her ladyship and no one else. And while it was indeed possible that someone had stolen one of the boxes, it was not thought probable. Still, neither the earl nor his countess had yet been charged in the matter because neither could be tied absolutely to the crime.

But Robert Carr was well aware he was losing James Stuart's favor. Since the Overbury scandal had broken, the king called upon him less, pointedly ignoring his old favorite. The royal and rheumy amber eyes were filled with interest when either of two young men came into his view these days. George Villiers, an unimportant little country nobody, was obviously fast gaining favor with his royal master. How this bumpkin had gained the sought-after position of royal cupbearer only last year was a mystery to Carr. Now he was appointed a gentleman of the bedchamber. Oh, he was handsome enough with his sparkling dark eyes and wavy chestnut hair, but Carr didn't trust the damned upstart.

And even worse was Piers St. Denis, the marquis of Hartsfield. With his ancient title he didn't appear to need the king's favor, and yet he was gaining it every bit as quickly as Villiers. St. Denis had great charm and amused the king more than any man in the court's memory. Where George Villiers had the face of an archangel, it was said; Piers St. Denis was spectacularly handsome, with perfect features. His nose was just the right length and as straight as a die. His blue eyes were evenly spaced. His mouth was big and narrow, and he had a single lock of honey-colored hair that insisted in falling into a single small curl upon his high forehead.

With both of these men intriguing and amusing the king, what chance was there for Robert Carr to regain his master's royal favor? Frances was not happy about the latest turn of events. She had expected that her husband would always have the royal favor. She had, after all, been born a Howard. Two of her cousins had been queens of England. Unsuccessful queens, to be sure, but they had been queens.

"How could you have been so stupid as to use one of my boxes?" she demanded of her spouse one night as they sat ensconced in their bed, the velvet curtains drawn to give them privacy. "Now the damned thing has been traced to us. What are we to do, Rob?"

"They cannot prove anything," he said. "Unless, of course, your hysteria gives us away, Frances. The box could have been stolen from your supply or from the boxmaker's shop. *No one can prove anything.*"

"What of the damned boy?" she demanded.

"I told you I strangled him when he returned for his coin. I threw his body in the river. He was just some nameless urchin, of no import to anyone. He was not missed, and if by chance he was, then it would be thought he fell victim to foul play as so many of these street brats do, or, perhaps, ran away to find his fortune. There is no one to trace those sweetmeats to us. We were careful, and we were clever. You made the treats, and I saw to their delivery. No one can trace them to us, Frances. Now cease your fretting," the earl of Somerset told his worried wife. "The matter of the box is just conjecture."

"The queen has barred me from her presence," Frances told him. "I am forbidden the royal apartments! *Me!* Frances Howard! I knew those apartments long before Queen Anne even came to England! It matters not, Rob, if they can prove we killed Overbury. *They know we did!* We are ruined, I tell you! *Ruined!*"

"It is but a temporary setback, Frances," he replied. "The king cannot do without me. Jamie Stuart is my friend."

"Why did you have to have Overbury sent to the Tower, Rob? God's blood, it was so public! Did I not say have the king appoint him to some minor position in Ireland, and then have him murdered there? We could have blamed it on the Irish! Now we will be blamed. I am surprised we haven't been arrested yet! 'Tis we who will end up in the Tower, Rob, and all because you would not listen to your wife!"

"The king loves me," Robert Carr said stubbornly.

"*Loves you?*" Frances, countess of Somerset, snorted with derision. "It is over, Rob. *Over!* He is besotted with both Villiers and St. Denis and concerned only with which one of them he desires more. You have broken the king's heart, Rob, and he will never forgive you. He will replace you, and he will forget you. And it need not have happened at all but that you would not listen to me!"

"Go to sleep, Frances, and cease your nagging," the earl snapped at his wife. "Tomorrow the earl of Glenkirk returns to court with the dowager marchioness of Westleigh. They are, I am told, to be married at last. I would not miss Jasmine Lindley's submission for anything!"

"Perhaps," his countess considered, "just perhaps such an occasion will divert the king, and he will forget about us."

"If he forgets about us," her husband said, "then we have lost his favor. Is that what you would like, Frances?"

"At least we would be alive," she retorted. "I don't want to end up on Tower Hill like my cousins, Anne and Catherine!"

"You worry too much," he laughed, but then the morning came and the earl found little to laugh at. When he and his wife arrived to join the day's activities, they were told to go home. They were not welcome at Whitehall any longer. They were to keep to their London house and await the king's decision as to their fate. Stunned, they retired, not even noticing the earl of Glenkirk's carriage as they passed it by in the road. Several days later the earl and countess of Somerset were arrested and lodged in the Tower.

"Was that not Frances Howard and her new husband?" Jasmine wondered aloud, leaning out the coach's window to view the departing vehicle.

"I would be very much surprised if it were," he answered her. "Robin tells me he is quite out of favor with this Overbury thing. Then, too, the king is newly besotted of two young men come to court recently. I'm certain after today we shall know everything there is to know about the whole situation. I cannot believe that Carr was so stupid as to poison an enemy and get caught; but then I always thought him a fool."

"Do I look all right?" she asked him for the third time since they had left the house.

He nodded, grinning. "Aye," he said shortly.

She had, she told him, attempted to dress modestly as befitted a penitent, but there was no way Jasmine could appear really contrite. She was too beautiful. Too elegant. Too much the Mughal's daughter. Yet she had tried. Her gown was subdued, of burgundy silk, and had a bell skirt. The waist was narrow, the sleeves had small slashes and puffs with black silk showing through; the stomacher was long and pointed, and decorated with black jets sewn in a geometric pattern, and matching the design on the bodice, which had a low square neckline. About her neck was a long rope of perfect black pearls, and from a shorter rope about her throat hung a large round ruby known as the Eye of Kali, which Jasmine had brought with her from India years earlier. Pear-shaped rubies hung from her ears. Her hair was fixed in its elegant chignon, and on her feet she wore black silk shoes ornamented with pink pearls. Her fingers were decorated with several rings, a black pearl, a ruby, and a large baroque pink pearl. She would be the envy of all the women who viewed her today, and the desire of all the men, James Leslie thought.

He had dressed himself in black and white, as much to complement her outfit as to appear serious himself. One of them had to look properly remorseful and apologetic for all the difficulty they had caused the king and his good intentions. As they moved along the hallway toward the chamber where the king was receiving that day, James Leslie could hear the hissing whispers of the courtiers as they passed by. "Courage, darling Jasmine," he murmured to her, patting the elegant hand on his heavy silk sleeve. "We are simply today's divertissement."

The king and queen sat on their thrones. James Stuart had aged. He was now forty-nine. The queen, a handsome woman, but certainly never considered pretty, was forty. She appeared very much the same to Jasmine as when she had last seen her. Neither the queen nor her husband had a great deal in common but their love of hunting, and their children. They led fairly separate lives, but were, nonetheless, devoted to each other. What was good for James pleased Anne, and vice versa. They had not been lovers for some time now, but they were very good friends.

James Stuart gazed dispassionately upon the newly arrived couple at the foot of his throne. The earl of Glenkirk bowed with an elegant flourish. The dowager marchioness of Westleigh made a deep curtsy, her sleek dark head slightly lowered, not looking at either of the royal couple as she dipped, and then rose gracefully. The room had grown very silent as the court strained to hear what would be said.

"So, madame, ye hae finally returned," the king began. His look was surprisingly mild. "I hae met yer whelps. Ye've done well wi them, madame. *All of them.* Our wee grandson is a braw laddie for one so young. Spoke French to me, he did." James Stuart chuckled. "And told me he could teach me to swear in Hindi. Now where would he have learned Hindi, I wonder?" The king cocked his head to one side questioningly.

"Most likely from my steward, Adali," Jasmine said softly. "Adali likes to remind Charlie-boy that he is the grandson of two kings."

"Aye," James Stuart agreed. "Our wee duke of Lundy hae much royal blood in his veins, *but he is English-born, madame.* Ye will remember that, won't ye?"

"Yes, Your Highness, I will remember it. I could hardly forget it," Jasmine replied. "His father will remain in my heart always."

For a brief moment the king looked sad. "Aye," he told her. "In all of our hearts. England lost a great king, but perhaps if I can live long enough, our bairn, Charles, will make a good king."

"Oh, Your Highness," Jasmine told the king, "I am certain Prince Charles will be of great credit to you and the queen." Then to everyone's surprise, even Glenkirk's, Jasmine flung herself before the king in a gesture of abasement, her burgundy silk skirts spread artfully about her. "Your Majesty," she said in her clear voice, "I beg that you forgive me my disobedience. The only excuse I can offer to you is that my heart was broken over Prince Henry's death, and I was not ready to go into another marriage so quickly. I am but a frail woman, Your Highness, and I have suffered much in my short life. I am ready now to do my duty, and marry the earl of Glenkirk, and I vow never to disobey Your Highness again." Jasmine bent low so that her head touched the tip of the king's shoe, and there she remained, waiting for him to speak.

The king was astounded, but he was also pleased. The young woman before him understood his total authority even if she had bridled against it. He had been very angry when she had fled England two years ago. But then two weeks ago he had seen his grandson, and the child had softened his heart toward Jasmine de Marisco Lindley. And now here was the very miscreant he had intended to punish but a short month ago, publicly humbling herself before his throne. James Stuart was mightily pleased and filled to overflowing with the milk of forgiveness.

"Get up, lassie," he said good-naturedly. "Help her, Jemmie." And when Jasmine stood before him once again, he continued, "It was a pretty apology and astutely delivered. Yer forgiven, madame."

"Thank you, Your Majesty," Jasmine replied simply, curtsying again.

"A woman, especially a beautiful woman such as yerself," the king said, "should hae a husband to guide her; but perhaps I was hasty when I chose for ye, madame. I realize now that I should hae given ye a choice of gentlemen from whom to choose a new lord and master. I shall gie it to ye now." James Stuart looked very pleased with himself.

Everyone else in the room looked astounded, including the queen herself. She glared furiously at her spouse, but he ignored her.

"Your Highness," Jasmine said quickly. "I am content to wed with Lord Leslie. We are old friends and have come to a complete understanding. Our wedding is planned for June 15 at my grandmother's home, Queen's Malvern."

"There will be nae wedding, madame, until ye hae made yer decision about a groom," the king said stubbornly.

"But I have!" Jasmine almost shouted.

"James!" the queen hissed at her husband.

He ignored her again, saying to Jasmine, "Yer a good lass, madame, and willing to do my bidding, I understand. Unlike many in this court, ye understand my divine right over my subjects. Two years ago I acted expeditiously, or so I thought, in my effort to protect both ye and my grandson. My rashness sent ye fleeing to France. While I know ye understand the reasons for my actions, I will now admit to having acted too swiftly in the matter. Therefore, I offer ye a choice of husbands, madame. Not only is the earl of Glenkirk a candidate for yer hand, but Piers St. Denis, the marquis of Hartsfield, will also present his suit to ye. I would offer ye my Steenie as well, but he tells me his heart is engaged elsewhere. So now, madame, ye hae two gentlemen from whom to make yer choice." He grinned at her, quite pleased with himself as if he had done something wonderful. "Ye'll find my Piers a delightful lad, and quite near yer own age, which Glenkirk is nae."

"Your Highness," Jasmine began, but the king waved her into silence, and the warning pressure of Jemmie's hand on her arm cautioned her to be quiet and make no more protest.

"Piers, my dearest laddie, where are ye? Come and meet the dowager marchioness of Westleigh," the king burbled, his tone almost coquettish.

A tall, fair young man stepped from the crowd of courtiers about the throne. He was dressed all in blue, and Jasmine would have sworn that the silk exactly matched the color of his blazing blue eyes. He was probably the most beautiful man she had ever seen, yet she was instantly repelled in the same way that she had been repelled by cobras in India. They, too, were beautiful, but dangerous. The marquis of Hartsfield bowed low before the king. "Sire," he said. The voice was pleasant enough.

"Make yer bow to Lady Lindley, Piers," the king girlishly encouraged the young man. "If ye please her, she may choose ye for her mate."

Hartsfield obeyed the king, giving him a quick smile as he did so. Then he turned to salute Jasmine. "Madame," he said.

"Now take her off, and chat wi her, Piers," the king instructed. "Glenkirk, ye stay by the queen, and gie yer rival a chance now. Ye've been wi the lady for several months in France now. Let my Piers hae his opportunity. Dinna fret, Jemmie Leslie, if she chooses my Piers, I'll gie a nice heiress to compensate ye." He chortled, well pleased with himself.

Masking his anger, James Leslie went to the queen's side, and, taking her hand, kissed it. "I am happy to see you looking so well, ma'am," he told her with a forced smile.

"You do not have to smile, Glenkirk," the queen said. "Having gotten what he thought he wanted, Jamie is now making a right mess of the situation, isn't he? I knew nothing about this, I assure you, else I would have talked him out of it. He will indulge his young men. Young George Villiers, whom I far prefer over Piers St. Denis, has lost his heart to Lady Katherine Manners, the earl of Rutland's daughter. He isn't good enough for her yet, but Jamie will see to it that he gets a title soon enough. Fortunately Villiers was clever enough to make his desire for Lady Manners known to the king else he should find himself another of poor Jasmine's suitors in this marriage-go-round."

"I should have married her in France," Glenkirk said irritably. "It was my first inclination, but she wanted her family about her, and I wanted her to be happy, ma'am."

"Ahhhh," the queen replied softly, "you love her, don't you?"

"I do," he admitted.

"And does she love you?"

"Aye, she does," he answered her. "I am the most fortunate man alive, ma'am. You do not think the king will force her to marry this marquis of Hartsfield? I have heard..." Glenkirk stopped, not knowing if he should reveal his knowledge of the gossip to Queen Anne.

"You have heard that Piers St. Denis and George Villiers have found favor with my husband," she responded. "It is true. You know that James is deeply passionate in his friendships, my lord. I do not mind at all, for it is easier to cope with these charming young men than it would be to cope with a *maîtresse en titre*. I was quite very relieved when your mother left Scotland. How is she these days?"

The earl of Glenkirk swallowed hard. So Queen Anne had known all along about her husband's youthful passion for his mother, yet she had said nothing. His respect suddenly grew for this woman, whom most considered silly and childish. "She is well, ma'am," he replied. "A widow, but content to remain in the kingdom of Naples. My younger brother and two sisters are there with her. She says she could not bear Scotland's climate after so many years in the warmth of Naples."

"How long has it been since you saw her?" the queen asked.

"I visited shortly after my wife and children were killed," he said quietly. "I needed her counsel then, but it has been many years since I beheld my mother's face."

"The Leslies of Glenkirk will be quite relieved that you are finally marrying again," the queen noted. "I assume you and Lady Lindley are already lovers. She is quite fecund, and you will undoubtedly have sons off her. Her children are delightful. Not simply fair of face and form, but bright and clever for such little creatures. Do they like you, James Leslie? It is important that you get on well with them."

"I believe we have already formed a comfortable attachment, ma'am," he replied. "They have taken to calling me *Papa*. Young Henry wants me to begin his lessons in swordsmanship this summer."

"That is to the good," the queen said approvingly. "You will be an excellent father to the young Lindleys and my grandson." She noticed that his eye was straying to Jasmine and the marquis of Hartsfield. "If she loves you, you need have no worry," Queen Anne told the earl of Glenkirk, but James Leslie could see Jasmine growing impatient, and his concern was not whether she could be suborned, but how soon it would be before she hit the marquis and caused a row.

Piers St. Denis had firmly eased Jasmine from before the king's throne, walking her across the room. "You are far more beautiful than I was led to believe," he said, "but then, of course, you know how beautiful you are. I know you have been told it many times, madame."

"Your compliment is accepted," she replied. "I am marrying the earl of Glenkirk on June 15. We love one another. I cannot imagine why the king, having insisted on this marriage, is now playing this coy game with us. I am furious!"

"The king seeks to please me," the marquis said, "especially now that the country bumpkin has dared to look above his station, and cast his net for the earl of Rutland's daughter. God's blood! Villiers doesn't even have a title. Rutland will hardly give his daughter to a backwater squire," Piers St. Denis sneered. "But, old king fool has promised his Steenie that he will make it all right, and the bumpkin bragged on it, so now the king must make it all right for me as well. Are you and Glenkirk lovers? You have the ripe and lush look of a woman who is very well loved. Ahh, you blush. How charming!"

"Why does the king call George Villiers *Steenie?*" Jasmine asked the marquis, ignoring his query by substituting one of her own.

"Have you met Villiers? Obviously not. Look over by the king's left hand. The young man with the face like an angel. Old king fool says he is reminded of St. Stephen when he looks at Villiers. Hence, Steenie, a diminutive of Stephen. It is sickening. Now, answer my question, beauty. Are you and Glenkirk lovers?"

"It is not your business," Jasmine replied tersely.

His fingers tightened upon her arm. "If you are to be my wife," he told her, "I need to know *everything* about you, my beauty."

"I am not going to be your wife," she said angrily. "Release my arm. You are bruising me, you brute!"

"Ahh, so you are lovers. Well, it matters not. You weren't a virgin anyway. Not with four children, and one of them a royal bastard," St. Denis said. "You are a passionate little bitch, aren't you, my beauty?"

"Let go of my arm," Jasmine replied. "If you do not, I shall scream, and cause a lovely scandal, placing you at center stage, my lord!"

He released her arm, laughing. "I do believe that you would," he told her. "When we are married I shall beat you if you misbehave."

Jasmine looked absolutely outraged. "A man who would raise his hand to a woman is no real man at all," she said. "Now, go find yourself some silly little heiress to wed. I am pledged to Lord Leslie." Then, turning on her heel, Jasmine hurriedly made her way across the room to where James Leslie stood by the queen. She curtsied low to Anne. "I am happy to see you again, ma'am," she said.

"You do not like the marquis of Hartsfield," the queen said bluntly.

"No, ma'am, I do not," Jasmine replied with equal frankness.

"Neither do I," Queen Anne answered.

"Will the king force me?" Jasmine asked.

Queen Anne shook her head in the negative. "Since Steenie has been promised that eventually he shall have

Rutland's heiress, Jamie feels he must give St. Denis a bride of equal value. This is really your own fault, my dear. If you had married Glenkirk when we expected you to marry him, you would not have been vulnerable now to St. Denis; but Jamie has a good heart, as you well know. He will not force you. He does mean the choice to be yours, but he will try to get you to approve his beautiful marquis in order to please St. Denis. I did not know he was going to meddle in this affair, or I should have convinced him otherwise. After all, our meddling after dear Henry's death, may God assoil his sweet soul, caused you to run away in the first place. I don't want you to run away with our little Charlie-boy again." She patted Jasmine's hand with her slender fingers. "It will be all right, my dear. I am certain of it. But you must not run off, and I shall charge you, Jemmie Leslie, with the responsibility for Lady Lindley."

Across the room the marquis of Hartsfield watched the exchange. He could not hear what was being said, but he would wager his name had come up in the intense discussion between the queen, and the beauty. "What do you think of her, Kipp?" he asked the man by his side.

"She'll want serious taming," his companion said, "but I imagine that you'll enjoy that, Piers," and he laughed.

Kipp St. Denis was the marquis's bastard half brother. The two men had been raised together; the bastard being taught complete and total obedience to his father's only legitimate heir. Kipp's mother had been the personal maid of the young marchioness of Hartsfield. Her mistress's betrothed husband had raped her a week before the wedding. She had been a virgin. After the wedding night, the previous marquis had insisted upon having the two women in his bed each night. He was a violent, amoral man. His bride, an orphan whose dowry consisted of the acreage adjoining his estates, loved her husband and was willing to do what he wanted. The estate was isolated, and there was no one to gossip but the servants, and they rarely did for fear of their master.

The half brothers had been born an hour apart, in the same bed, as the two women labored side by side. Had Kipp been the legitimate son, it was he who would have been the heir, as his was the first birth. Piers had joined him in the same cradle in the next hour, and they had been rarely separated since. Kipp was his mother's image while Piers was his father all over again. Both men, however, resembled their father in temperament. Despite the difference in their stations, the half brothers were completely loyal to one another, and there was no trace of jealousy between them. Kipp went where Piers went, serving his brother as secretary, valet, and general confidant.

"Ahh, Kipp, this is no ordinary mare to be tamed, but a finely bred creature who will take special handling," the marquis said. "Did you notice her breasts as they overflowed her gown's neckline? Little creamy love cones that were just begging to be caressed."

"If you want to win her over, you'll have to get rid of the earl of Glenkirk, Piers," his half brother said. "As long as he is here, you will have not the slightest chance with her. I heard her when you had her by your side. She is completely determined to wed him. And, brother, he is living in her house on the Strand with her—probably sharing her bed and giving her a good fucking every night. We don't want her with child—his child—do we? Tell the king, and he will see to the rest, I promise you. Does not old king fool love his darling boy, Piers?" Kipp St. Denis laughed suggestively.

"You are right," the marquis agreed. "I don't want to lose this chance. Lady Lindley is fabulously wealthy in her own right, and of even greater importance, she had the king's only grandson. A bastard like yourself, Kipp, but a royal bastard. Until little baby Charles gets himself a wife out of Spain, or France, and has a child of his own, the little duke of Lundy will remain his grandpapa's darling. To have control of that laddie is to have real power, Kipp! Villiers can have his whey-faced little heiress. I will have both a fortune and power over the king!"

"Only if you can convince Lady Lindley to marry you. I already see you cannot bully her. She is, the gossip tells me, a king's daughter herself; and her relatives are influential with the king. Her stepfather is his cousin, the earl of BrocCairn. Her uncles are the earl of Lynmouth and Lord Burke of Clearfields. Her grandmother is the old countess of Lundy herself. Why she locked horns with Gloriana, Bess Tudor, brother, and has not only outlived that queen, but survived to tell the tale. Lady de Marisco dotes upon this particular granddaughter, Piers, and the family does what she tells them. If you threaten Lady Lindley, they will gather about her to protect her, then reach out to destroy you for your impudence. It is a very large family. There's an aunt married to the earl of Alcester, and another who is Lord Blackthorne's wife. Jasmine Lindley is extremely well connected. You will have to charm her into marrying you, and you are quite capable of such an act."

"*I must have her!*" Piers St. Denis said fiercely. "She excites me as no other woman ever has. Her wealth, her beauty, *her royal bastard*. But even without the brat, I would desire her, Kipp."

"First the earl of Glenkirk," his half brother counseled. "If he remains too near Lady Lindley, you will have no chance at all. Look!" He pointed across the room. "The earl and Lady Lindley are departing even now. Quickly, Piers! You must see the king now!"

The marquis of Hartsfield moved gracefully across the room, blocking the earl of Glenkirk and Jasmine even as they turned away from bidding the king farewell. "Sire!" he said loudly. "If Lady Lindley is to give me a fair chance at courting her, I do not believe that Lord Leslie should be living in her house and sharing her bed, do you?"

"What's this?" said the king. "Jemmie, is it true? Yer at Greenwood wi Lady Lindley?"

"Aye, my lord," the earl of Glenkirk said tersely, casting an angry glance at the marquis of Hartsfield.

"Nah, nah, Jemmie, we canna hae that," the king replied.

"Sire, he may be my guest," the earl of Lynmouth said coming forward, and bowing low. "Jemmie and I are old friends."

"Excellent, excellent," said the king. "Ye'll stay wi Robin Southwood, Jemmie, eh? 'Tis a fair solution, is it nae?"

The earl of Glenkirk bowed to his king. "I will, of course, escort Jasmine home," he told James Stuart.

"And I shall come, too," the earl of Lynmouth said, "and we'll get you settled at Lynmouth House." His look warned both his niece and Lord Leslie to silence.

"Lynmouth's house is next to Lady Lindley's," murmured Kipp in his brother's ear. "Is that not a little too near?"

"If I speak further, I shall appear to whine," the marquis said low. "I will not debase myself with any further puling complaint."

"My lord," Jasmine said to St. Denis as they departed the room, "you are wasting your time, and will make a fool of yourself. Let matters rest as they are. The king will find you an heiress of your own if you ask him prettily, and I am certain you know how to beg, do you not?" She smiled sweetly at him as his handsome features darkened in anger.

But then Piers St. Denis laughed, sweeping the ire from his handsome face. "Ahh, madame, you but fascinate me with every word. I do not believe anyone has ever been able to infuriate me as you do. I shall not give up my pursuit of you. You are much too intriguing, and I vow I shall win you from Glenkirk."

"Never!" Jasmine said vehemently.

The marquis of Hartsfield took her arm, edging out the earl of Glenkirk, who fell angrily behind with the earl of Lynmouth. "Now, madame, do not be unruly with me. You will like me. Everyone likes me, except perhaps Villiers, but then I see him for what he really is when others do not. He is naught but an upstart. I am a most charming fellow as you will learn if you will but give me a chance."

Jasmine laughed in spite of herself. "My lord," she said quietly, regaining her composure, "this is a difficult situation in which we find ourselves. I must seem a shrew to you, but you must understand that I have known James Leslie for years. I have come to love him. Ours is an ideal match. My children adore him. I cannot be swayed even by your most prodigious charms. This is a futile quest upon which you embark, and, frankly, I am furious with the king for proposing it."

"You are adorable when you are angry," he purred.

"God's blood!" Jasmine swore.

Piers St. Denis chortled, his blazing blue eyes dancing devilishly. "Your little son swore in Hindi," he said. "Can you swear in Hindi, too? He was quite a delightful little fellow, your royal bastard."

"I can swear expertly in at least seven languages," she replied.

They had reached the courtyard, where their carriage was awaiting them. He helped her in, smiling toothily. "I shall call upon you tomorrow, madame," he said. "If the weather is fair, perhaps we shall lunch along the river somewhere. I will come in my barge." Slamming the door shut, he signaled the coachmen to depart, waving gaily at Jasmine, then turning about and saluting both earls as he made to retrace his steps back to the king, and the court.

"The bastard!" Glenkirk swore. "I came with Jasmine, and have no horse. How the hell am I supposed to get back to Greenwood?"

"In my coach," Robin said. "I didn't ride. Clever of Hartsfield to edge us out so neatly. I have noticed that he is not a man who likes to lose. He will drive Jasmine to distraction until you leave for mother's."

"We have made our peace with the king," Glenkirk snarled. "We will leave for Queen's Malvern as quickly as we can be packed up."

"Oh, no, Jemmie," Robin Southwood said quietly as they settled themselves in his coach. "The king has decided Jasmine is to have a choice of husbands. A bit after the fact, of course, but then timing has never been old king fool's strong point. He has offered up his favored minion for Jasmine's delectation. If you depart for Queen's Malvern, the king will be angry all over again, and Hartsfield will probably come after you. You have a bit over five weeks until your wedding day. You will remain here in London for four weeks, give or take a day. You will let Piers St. Denis play the eager suitor, and then Jasmine will announce her decision to marry you after all. Only then can you depart for mother's with the king's blessing, which you must have. The queen, as you well know, favors your marriage to Jasmine.

Now promise me, Glenkirk, that you will not be foolish, and you will follow my plan."

"Why do I want to punch our pretty marquis in the mouth?" growled Glenkirk.

"Because he is a slimey little turd," Robin Southwood replied.

"What the hell does Jamie see in him?"

"He's young, and very amusing, and clever. He panders to the king's affections; and right now James Stuart seems to need those two young men vying for his attention and his favor. He has never really recovered from Prince Henry's death, and Prince Charles is a dour little fellow, quite unlike his elder sibling. The king doubts he will ever make a good ruler, and is not shy about saying so. Charles, of course, is fiercely jealous of both Villiers and Hartsfield. He thinks they take his old dad's affections from him, but I wonder just how much affection the king has for his younger son. Now, Jemmie, you are going to behave yourself, aren't you?"

"I suspect I have no choice," grumbled the earl of Glenkirk.

Robin Southwood chuckled. "Well," he said wryly, "we could waylay Hartsfield in a dark alley and strangle him, I suppose."

"Now there's a fine thought!" James Leslie said enthusiastically.

"We will have to convince Jasmine to play along with our game," Lynmouth told his companion.

"You may have that privilege," Glenkirk said.

"You must back me up, Jemmie!" Lynmouth said. "My niece can be the very devil to reason with, as you well know."

"I'll back you up," Glenkirk agreed, "but if she's not of a mind to do it, heaven help us all."

"Damn, I wish mother were here," Robin Southwood said.

"Well, she isn't, and she'll have both our hides if we do not make this all come out right, Robin. I hope we're doing what Madame Skye would want us to do in the matter."

"There is nothing to keep us from sending her a communication as to what's going on," the earl of Lynmouth said. "She should know."

Glenkirk laughed. "Aye, so she should," he agreed. "She will not be afraid to take on this king. Divine Right means nothing to Madame Skye, does it, Robin?"

His companion chuckled. "Nay, Glenkirk, it never did, and I think Jasmine is more like my mother than anyone else I know."

"But Jasmine has always respected Divine Right," Glenkirk said.

"She won't when it interferes with her plans to marry you," the earl of Lynmouth said mischievously, "She has never stopped being the Mughal's daughter. May God have mercy on us all if the king does not cease his meddling in her life. There will be hell to pay for certain, and Hartsfield will learn to his regret that you cannot make our wild Jasmine do what she does not choose to do."

Chapter Eight

Richard Stokes, the earl of Bartram, was extremely worried. He had served the king ever since James had arrived in England, gaining his master's favor by his hard work and his sober habits. A protégé of Robert Cecil, the earl of Salisbury, son of Lord Burghley, who prior to his death had been the king's most trusted advisor, Lord Stokes was content to remain in the background doing his duty for the crown. Often it had meant long hours and very little time with his family, but his wife, Mary, had completely understood. Only on Sunday was Richard Stokes unavailable to his royal master. Sunday was the Lord's day, and he was a pious man. The earl of Bartram followed the commandment to remember the Sabbath and to keep it holy.

While openly espousing England's officially sanctioned church, Lord Stokes was secretly a Puritan. He did not hold with popery or the superstitious trumpery he believed tainted the Anglican Church. He firmly held that the church should be free of such tomfoolery. God's word was simple and direct, even as the church should be. The earl of Bartram did not approve of the dogma, the elegant ritual, and the businesslike organization of England's church. People should follow the Bible and its teachings as God had meant them to do, else he would not have had it all written down. Devout simplicity. That was what the true church should be about.

Richard Stokes, however, kept his faith to himself. Faith, he believed, was a very personal and a private thing. He did not like those men who publicly screeched and shouted their creed for all to hear in the market square, demanding that others follow them. Besides, Puritans who noisily trumpeted their beliefs too loudly for all the world to hear could find themselves the center of intense persecution. Even more than those misguided men and women who persisted in continuing to follow Roman Catholicism. A discreet faith, along with adherence to the official Church of England, was acceptable. King James too well remembered his own mother's difficulties in the matter of religion. It had cost him her company and caused him to live a basically cold, unemotional, and strict childhood devoid of either maternal warmth or any real loving affection.

Alas that Lady Mary Stokes, the earl's wife, was not as careful as her husband in the matter of religion. A devout woman, she had of late become an impassioned proselyte of their secret faith. In part Stokes blamed himself. His business kept him in London most of the year, and their children were all grown and married. The eldest of their daughters lived down in Cornwall, and the youngest had been wed up north into Yorkshire. Their only son and his wife lived on the family estates at Bartramhalt in Oxfordshire.

In service to the king from dawn until midnight most days, the earl understood how his wife, with nothing else to do, could become more deeply involved in their faith. Mary was a woman of high morals who did not believe in the frivolity exhibited by the royal lifestyle. She had no friends at court, and, without her family, she was lonely. Now she had suddenly devoted herself passionately to religion, certainly a worthwhile pursuit for a woman, but unfortunately his wife's enthusiastic zeal had come to the ears of the king. How this had happened the earl of Bartram could never learn, but James Stuart was not pleased by the knowledge.

"I dinna hold wi the Calvinists, Dickie," he said to the earl, having called him into his royal presence late one afternoon. "Were ye aware of yer wifie's nonconformism? The Calvinists dinna respect my divine rights, Dickie. Ye'll hae to beat Lady Mary and turn her from her heresy," James Stuart concluded. He turned to his two companions. "Is that not right, my sweet laddies." Then he smiled at them.

"With our children gone to their own homes, I fear my good lady is bored, Your Majesty," the earl said. "Mary means no harm."

"She doesna come to court," the king observed. "I canna remember the last time I saw her, Dickie. Does she hae all her wits about her?"

"She is a shy and retiring lady, Your Highness," the earl excused his wife, wishing that she were indeed addled so he might condone her behavior in that manner.

"Nae so timid, Dickie, that she could nae stand outside of Westminster handing out seditious tracts condemning our good church," the king said grimly.

The earl of Bartram paled. *"What?"* he managed to say. Mary had to have lost her wits to have done such a foolhardy thing.

"Are ye losing yer hearing then, Dickie?" The king did not look pleased at all.

"I shall certainly remonstrate with my wife..." he began, but he was cut short by the marquis of Hartsfield.

"Remonstrate, Stokes? Your wife stands on the edge of treason, and you, His Majesty's most trusted servant, and you want to *remonstrate* with her? You should beat the bitch

until she comes to her senses, my lord," the marquis of Hartsfield told the astounded man.

"Sir," the earl snapped angrily, "my wife is a good and decent woman. I have never had to resort to violence in managing her. She is a lady of reason. Since you have no wife, you are hardly an expert on the matter of spouses."

"Do you hold with her treason then?" the marquis said slyly.

"What treason?" the earl demanded, angered further, and drawn into indiscretion. "Where is there any treason in preferring a simpler form of worship, my lord St. Denis? Did not the old queen herself say that there is but one lord Jesus Christ, and the rest is all trifles?"

"You are familiar then with this *Puritanism*," St. Denis goaded the earl of Bartram further.

"I am a member of England's church," the earl said tersely, suddenly aware of the danger into which he was being so cleverly drawn.

"But yer wifie would appear not to be," the king noted. "Were ye aware of her heresy, Dickie?" James Stuart's amber eyes peered sharply at the earl.

The marquis of Hartsfield smiled toothily at the earl from just beyond the king's shoulder. Young Villiers, the king's other companion, however, looked just a trifle sympathetic toward the embattled Lord Stokes.

"Women are apt to be fickle, my lord," George Villiers murmured softly. "Has not our good queen gone round about you on occasion to obtain her own way?" He chuckled good-naturedly. "This matter has obviously caught Lord Stokes unawares. Allow him the latitude to straighten it out privately within his own house. As our good Piers has observed, the earl is and has always been your most loyal servant, sire."

The king turned and bestowed a loving smile upon the young man. "Ahhh, Steenie, ye hae such a good heart, does he nae, Piers."

"Aye, Yer Majesty," the marquis of Hartsfield answered sourly, forcing a smile. He didn't like Richard Stokes with his pious and hardworking ways. Stokes kept a tight rein on the king's expenditures and had recently convinced James not to bestow a small crown property near the marquis's estates upon Piers St. Denis, who had long coveted it. For that he would repay the earl of Bartram in kind when he got the chance, and he had almost succeeded this day had it not been for clever George Villiers and his faux sweetness. Villiers was as sweet as a rabid rat, had the truth been known, but he was a canny and resourceful fellow, damn him!

"Verra well, Dickie, go home and tell yer lady I will hae no more of her wickedness and revolutionary ways," the king said, dismissing the earl of Bartram, but not giving him the royal hand to kiss.

Richard Stokes bowed, throwing young George Villiers a grateful look and backing from the king's privy chamber. He now owed Villiers a favor, he knew, and he wondered what would be asked of him. Still, he was relieved to have escaped so easily. Obviously he had made an enemy of the marquis when the royal property he desired was denied him. Still, Lord Stokes thought, it was in the king's best interests he was working, and it had not been in James Stuart's best interests to lose the income from that property. Old Queen Bess had left the royal treasury full, but James, with his overgenerous ways, was fast emptying it, not to mention the queen's outrageous extravagances. Since Robert Cecil's death no one had really been able to keep the court's greed in check.

The earl of Bartram hurried from Whitehall Palace, calling for his coach as he entered the open courtyard. It was quickly brought, and the earl instructed his driver, "Home, Simmons, and take the fastest route!" Then he climbed into the vehicle, slamming the door shut behind him. His mind was awhirl. Mary had gone too far this time, and while he did not believe his life was in any danger, Richard Stokes knew he had no true friends among the king's courtiers. Ordinarily he would not have cared. His sole loyalty was to James Stuart. His value to his master was his strict honesty and his discretion. But these traits would mean next to nothing if someone like Piers St. Denis undermined the king's trust in him. He had just been saved today by the charming young George Villiers, and only because that young man desired a favor of Richard Stokes.

Villiers was an ambitious young man, the earl thought, who had already set his sights upon the earl of Rutland's heiress. The girl, according to the gossips, was besotted with George Villiers, silly chit. All she saw was his extraordinarily handsome face and form. She knew little of his character, or whether he was a godly man. Richard Stokes suspected not. The new co-favorite was charming, amusing, and polite to a fault—traits unusual in one his age. Perhaps he was every bit as good as he seemed, but Richard Stokes doubted it. Still, he would recommend to the king that Villiers be given a small peerage. The king would like that, especially as the suggestion would come from the earl of Bartram without royal prodding. He would claim to see promise in George Villiers, and perhaps there was promise in him. That should certainly repay the debt he owed Villiers for rescuing him today.

The earl's house was located in the village of Kew just outside the city. It was not on the river like the residences of so many of the rich and powerful. It was a simple brick structure standing three stories high, set in the center of a small park. The coach drove through the gates and down the drive, drawing up before the mansion's door. Richard Stokes exited his carriage and entered the house. "Fetch her ladyship to me at once," he told a footman, then went into his library, where a fire burned, taking the chill off the damp late-spring day. Pouring himself a small crystal goblet of wine to calm himself, he waited for his errant wife to make her appearance. When she finally entered the room he was reminded that she was still a pretty woman, despite the fact she was well past her prime.

"You are home early today, my dear," Lady Mary Stokes greeted her husband, and then her eye went to the goblet in his hand. "*Spirits,* Dickon?" she said with a slightly raised eyebrow. "Pastor Simon Goodfellowe says spirits are not godly."

"Our lord Jesus turned water into wine at the wedding in Cana of Galilee, Mary," the earl said sharply. "If wine was approved by our Lord, then how can Simon Goodfellowe disapprove?"

Lady Mary made a motion of smoothing down the dark blue silk of her gown. It was a simple garment adorned only by a white ruff of a collar. She wore no jewelry but her wedding ring. "You do not like Pastor Goodfellowe, Dickon, do you?" she replied.

"No, Mary, I do not. I find him narrow-minded, and mean-spirited, and I especially dislike him if it is he who has convinced you to stand outside of Westminster handing out religious tracts," the earl told his very startled wife. "What in God's name ever possessed you to do such a thing, wife? Have you lost your wits, madame?"

"The word must be spread, Dickon," she began, but he interrupted her harshly, his look dark and angry.

"You will cease your activities at once, madame! I absolutely forbid you to ever do such a thing again, and I forbid you to see this Simon Goodfellowe. He is a dangerous man, and will come to a bad end."

"But, Dickon..."

"The king is aware of your activities, madame. He considers them treasonous heresy. I have been in the royal service twenty years, and I came close to losing my place today because of you, madame. Only the intervention of that fawning puppy, George Villiers, saved me. Now I will owe him a service in return. If I owe a boon to people like Villiers, madame, I lose my authority and my usefulness to the king. How did you dare to involve yourself in such seditious activity?" the earl demanded of his wife.

"Ohh, Dickon," she replied, genuinely distressed. "I did not mean to cause you any trouble. I just want to spread our faith to others, for I love our Lord, and would have His church free of all popery. Do you not desire that, too?"

"Mary," he said, his tone softening a bit, and leading her to a settle where they now sat side by side, "you know I prefer a simpler faith, but I am no martyr. I can practice that faith quietly, thus satisfying my own conscience while appearing to follow the letter of the king's law. There is currently but one sanctioned church in England, and as loyal subjects of James Stuart we must give the outward appearance of being devout members of that church. How can I influence the king to moderate his stand in small ways toward the Puritans if I do not have his ear? I have forever been a loyal servant of England's monarch as you well know, beginning my service in the reign of Queen Bess. Your foolishness has today almost cost me the trust and respect I have built up over those years. The marquis of Hartsfield is my enemy because I convinced the king not to give him

Summerfield. Today he attempted to pull me down merely to gain his vengeance on me. He cares not for England or even for the king. He but seeks to advance himself in any manner he can, even pandering to a lonely and sad old man if he must. I have said more to you than I should have, but you will be discreet, I know, as you always are regarding our private conversations. Now, promise me, my dear, no more proselytizing."

"Oh, Dickon, I am so sorry. I did not realize what I was doing. I so wanted to help our dear Lord," Lady Mary told her husband.

"My dear," he said soothingly, "you are only a woman. You could not understand the seriousness of your actions. I am not content that we must hide our true faith, but if we are to triumph in the end for our God, then we must behave with sober modesty now. You will please our Lord best by being an obedient wife."

"I will have nothing further to do with Pastor Goodfellowe, husband," Lady Mary promised her husband.

"I will personally see the pastor is informed that you will no longer participate in his activities," the earl of Bartram replied.

"Dickon? I have the most wonderful idea of how you can be certain you regain the king's full trust and triumph over the marquis of Hartsfield. Did you not tell me he is to wed the dowager marchioness of Westleigh, who bore Prince Henry's bastard? What if you could convince the king to give you custody of that little boy? If he gave you his grandson to raise, then certainly you would be sure of his favor."

"Lady Lindley has been given her choice between the earl of Glenkirk and the marquis. She prefers the earl, for they have a past history, Mary. It is he who has custody of the little duke of Lundy. Piers St. Denis may woo Jasmine

Lindley until the cows come home, but he will not win her hand, although he believes himself to be quite irresistible."

"But if the king were to believe that the marquis will be offended by Lady Lindley's choosing the earl, he might want to give him a consolation of sorts, and custody of this little duke would surely be a fine prize. However, you might convince His Majesty that by giving the lad to a third, and neutral, party, he would be less likely to offend anyone; and of course, the marquis would have to have something, perhaps Summerfield, which he has sought all along?"

The earl of Bartram thought for several long moments. His wife's idea was a very clever one indeed. The boy, of course, would have an income of his own, which by rights would come to his guardian. *Other than ordinary expenses,* Richard Stokes thought, *I could return the balance of his income into the king's treasury, thereby offsetting the loss of Summerfield. In fact, the sum coming from the duke of Lundy would probably be far greater than that which came from Summerfield. And if the boy were raised in my house,* the earl considered, *I might influence the child toward the truer faith, and away from the Anglican Church.* But that would come later, and he would have to be cautious in that endeavor.

"My dear," he told his wife, "certainly God has spoken through you this day, and while Lady Lindley may object to the loss of her child, I shall point out to the king her unsuitability as a guardian for his grandson. Her previously unchaste life as Prince Henry's mistress, and her mixed blood, not to mention her own bastard birth, are more than enough to render her unfit despite her wealth and her powerful connections. The king can be made to see reason, I am sure. First, however, I must reassure him that I have put a stop to your ignorance and beg forgiveness for your misbehavior. Then, when Lady Lindley has made her choice known publicly, I shall make my move to gain custody of the duke. It will be good to have a child in the house again, will it not, my dear? He will keep you very busy, I have not a doubt." The earl chuckled. "I well remember Edward as a lad."

"Then I am forgiven?" she asked him.

"Aye, you are forgiven, Mary," he reassured her, his mind already moving ahead to consider the advantages guardianship of the royal bastard would bring him. He must continue, however, to remain in the background as he always had, for that was where his strength lay. In his discretion. He chuckled to himself, considering the obvious endeavor at revenge the marquis had attempted today. He hoped Summerfield would be enough to soothe the vain poppinjay when he lost the lady, her fortune, and the duke of Lundy. The earl of Bartram intended to see it was all he got, and, on Piers St. Denis's death, the property would revert to the crown. Richard Stokes would make certain of that.

As he chortled softly to himself, his antagonist was also considering his next move. He had already put the earl of Bartram from his mind, for he had more important matters to attend to, and little time in which to pursue his interests. Jasmine was proving to be a recalcitrant conquest. While he had succeeded in removing James Leslie from her house, that was all he had managed to do. She took great delight in appearing with the earl of Glenkirk each day at court; and while she allowed him to court her publicly, privately she avoided him. He could make no headway with her at all, and it was beginning to drive him to rashness.

At first he had sought her for her wealth, her royal bastard, her influential relations. The more he was with her, however, the more he realized that he desired her. He had never known such lust as he felt for Jasmine Lindley.

She intoxicated him with her lush form, the direct look she always gave him with those startling turquoise eyes, her creamy skin with its hint of palest gold. He dreamed of possessing her; and he would have her as no man ever had. His mind went to the hidden chamber he had in both his town house and his country home. He imagined her chained between the whipping posts, whimpering for mercy, as he thrashed her into submission. Would she respond best to the wide leather tawse, the thin bunch of birches, a whippy hazel switch, or his firm riding crop? Kipp, of course, would be there to help him, but he would not share Jasmine with his half brother. At least not until he tired of her if he ever did.

He considered that Jasmine, being a strong-minded woman, might also enjoy giving punishment as well as receiving it. If she did, he would teach her how to use the tawse and the rod. There was a definite art to it. One did not simply hack away at one's victim. The art of domination should be done with a mixture of sternness and tenderness. There was, the marquis of Hartsfield had discovered, pleasure in pain, although he knew that not everyone saw it his way. There were those who considered such things taboo and wicked. He licked his lips in anticipation of his conquest, and of hers.

But now that she had gotten over the shock of being told she had another suitor, Jasmine found the situation extremely amusing, especially as Jemmie had been forced to move in with her Uncle Robin. She would not even allow him to sneak back through the adjoining gardens at night to share her bed. "Only if I may entertain Piers St. Denis in the same manner," she teased the earl of Glenkirk.

But Glenkirk was not to be baited. "If you would like," he told her mischievously. "It will be the last opportunity you have to take a lover, madame, for once we are married, I shall serve all your needs quite well, I promise you. You will have no need for another man in your life, except for our sons." He took her hand in his, and turning the palm over raised it to his lips to kiss.

"Do not tempt me, Jemmie," she murmured, withdrawing her hand.

"Are you tempted?" he demanded, feeling a slight sting of jealousy. Surely she wouldn't! They had pledged themselves!

"Wellll," Jasmine considered, "he is outrageously handsome. I cannot help being curious as to what lies behind the charm."

"I have heard some rather unsavory rumors," the earl of Glenkirk replied stiffly. "From former lovers of St. Denis."

"Ohhhh? What kind of rumors?" Jasmine was fascinated.

"They are not the kind of things I want to repeat to you," he told her. "Let us just say he is deviant in his passion, Jasmine."

"Glenkirk," she said laughing, "I am twice married, not some swooning virgin. Does he enjoy entering a woman's portal of Sodom, or is he one of those pitiful creatures who must give pain in order to feel passion? Tell me this instant, or I shall ask him myself."

"You would!" he accused, and he laughed all the more. "Oh, very well, you vixen, it is the latter. He likes to whip his lovers, and he shares them with that villainous half brother of his."

"I thought him more self-assured than that," Jasmine replied thoughtfully, her laughter stilled for the moment. "How sad that he cannot obtain pleasure except by giving pain."

"Then you will continue to keep him at bay, madame," the earl said. "Perhaps we should end this charade pretense and tell the king we intend to keep our wedding day as we planned in France."

"Nay, not yet, Jemmie. The king must believe that I have given his marquis the benefit of the doubt, and that having done so, I prefer the choice he so wisely made for me two years ago. The queen is on our side and will manage the king nicely if I ask her, and so, I believe, is Villiers, although I think his attempt at friendship stems from the fact he considers my family connections useful to himself."

"You are brutally honest in your assessment of Villiers," the earl noted. "Have you no illusions left, darling Jasmine?"

She laughed again. "Few," she told him, "but understand that I hold no grudge against George Villiers for his behavior. He but seeks to advance himself, and there is nothing wrong that really, is there, Jemmie? We all seek something from the people with whom we come in contact in our lives. Youth is filled with enthusiasm, and Villiers is just a trifle obvious. He is not, however, as ingenuous as he would like everyone to believe. There is a calculating intelligence in those soulful dark eyes of his that he is not always able to conceal."

Now it was Glenkirk's turn to laugh. "You speak as if you were an ancient cronc, yet Villiers is little younger than you," he teased her. "He would, I think, be most distressed to learn you have seen through the carefully constructed facade he has erected and that even the king has not pierced."

"We shall not tell him then," Jasmine said.

"And the marquis of Hartsfield?" he persisted.

"What about him?" Her look was deceptively docile.

"You have not promised me you will keep him at bay," James Leslie reminded her.

"Nay, I have not," Jasmine told him, "and I will not. I am not your wife yet, Jemmie, and even when I am, I am quite competent to guide my own behavior, my lord, without your aid."

"No wonder your grandmother drove men to distraction," he grumbled at her. "You are obviously just like her."

"Am I?" she drawled at him. "Well, if I am, you had best beware, my Lord of Glenkirk. Madame Skye has outlived *all* of her husbands, *and her lovers, and* is still going strong!"

He wanted to laugh at her, but instead her words gave him pause. His mother had been such a woman as Jasmine and Madame Skye. He was used to independent women, but James Leslie did not know if he approved of them. Still, his Isabella had been a meek wife, and while he had been fond of her, she had never excited him or intrigued him as Jasmine did. While his intended bride might be determined to chart her own path through life, the earl of Glenkirk knew that she would never embarrass him or set herself against him to bring dishonor upon his family's name. She would never take the marquis as a lover although she might toy with him out of curiosity, and for her own amusement. *And he would have to let her lest he risk losing her forever.* "Be careful, darling Jasmine," he said softly to her.

She turned a dazzling smile upon him. "I will," she responded. Then she took pity upon him. "St. Denis is like a beautiful snake," she explained. "I am fascinated, but I am not foolish, Jemmie."

"He is quite determined to have you," the earl said.

"Then he is the fool," she replied. "The king has plainly said the decision is mine, and I made that decision in France." She leaned forward and brushed his lips with hers. "Go home, my lord. It is late, and I would seek my bed. Besides, poor Kipp St. Denis has been watching the house for hours now, and I am certain is quite exhausted. He will not leave until he is certain you are ensconced at Uncle Robin's for the night. He is a loyal dog to his brother."

"*St. Denis is having you watched?*" Glenkirk was astounded.

"He is very jealous," she chuckled, escorting him to the garden door. "Now kiss me, and let us give him something to report to his brother this night, Jemmie, my love." She slid her arms about him.

"Where is he?" the earl demanded.

"In the shadow of the wall that separates Greenwood from Lynmouth House," she told him. "*No!* Do not look! As long as he believes himself concealed, I know just where to find him. If you look, he will know we know where he is and will seek another hiding place I may not so easily discover." She gazed up at him seductively. "Don't you want to kiss me, Glenkirk? St. Denis would kill to kiss me," she taunted him.

Teasingly he nibbled at her lips. "You are ripe for bedding, madame," he murmured against her mouth. Then he kissed her a hard, swift kiss before turning on his heel without another word and leaving her.

Her hand went to her mouth. It felt bruised with his fierce kiss. She watched him depart, moving quickly down the lawn, and across the garden, and through the almost concealed door in the ivy. She remained for a moment after he was gone, her legs jelly, a growing ache in her nether regions. Since he had moved to her uncle's they had not made love even once. She realized now that she missed their shared passion just as much as he missed it. Damn the king! Damn Piers St. Denis! Damn everyone who stood in their way! It was over a month until their wedding day. Unless they could find a stolen moment before then, they would have to wait to be together once again. She didn't know if she could bear it. She had grown used to James Leslie in her bed.

Piers St. Denis, however, had grown quite annoyed with Jasmine's refusal to give serious consideration to his suit. He could never get her alone. Glenkirk was always with her but when she slept. Shortly she would announce her preference, and he knew it would be James Leslie, unless, of course, he could change her mind, but how could he when he was never alone with her? He complained to the king.

"I have not a chance with her with Glenkirk skulking about all the time," the marquis of Hartsfield said, his tone petulant. They were in the royal apartments.

"Gracious, St. Denis," taunted George Villiers, "do not say you are a laggard in love. I should not have thought it of you." His dark eyes danced mischievously. "The rumors are certainly otherwise," he finished with a grin.

Piers St. Denis threw the younger man a venomous look. "Your Majesty, I cannot court Lady Lindley if I must share her every waking minute with the earl of Glenkirk."

"My husband has said the choice is Jasmine's," the queen said, not even bothering to look up from her embroidery frame.

"But how, madame, can she make her choice if she does not know me?" the marquis of Hartsfield almost shouted, frustrated.

"Perhaps," the queen said giving him a mild stare, "she already has made her choice, my lord."

"Sire! You *promised* me a chance with Lady Lindley," Piers St. Denis almost whined. "You *must* do something!"

"I'll send Jemmie to Edinburgh," the king answered.

"*James!*" The queen's tone was pure irritation. She had only earlier spoken most severely to him about his foolishness in attempting to meddle in Jasmine's life again. Would he never learn?

"Now, Annie," the king said, "our Piers is justified in his complaints. Jemmie will nae let him near the lass. Let him go up to Edinburgh to begin the arrangements for our visit there sometime in the future, perhaps next year or the year after. When he returns Lady Lindley will be allowed to make her choice. 'Tis only fair."

"*She will not change her mind, Jamie,*" the queen said, annoyed with her husband's overindulgence of the marquis. "All you will do is outrage Glenkirk and possibly provoke Jasmine to some new rashness."

"I will speak wi them myself," the king said. "Our Piers must hae his fair chance wi the lady, Annie."

"Thank you, Your Highness!" the marquis said, kissing the king's hand with gratitude.

The king caught the hand in his and smiled at the young man. Then he ruffled Piers St. Denis's honey-colored hair. "Yer a braw laddie, Piers. How can she nae fall in love wi ye?"

"Well, it had best be settled now," the queen said briskly. "Steenie, go and fetch Lady Lindley and Lord Leslie to us, will you?" She caught Villiers's eye, and total understanding passed between them in that single moment. The queen liked George Villiers, and far preferred him as her husband's favorite to the marquis of Hartsfield, whom she hoped eventually to remove from the picture entirely.

George Villiers leapt up. "At once, Your Majesty," he said with an elegant bow, and was out the door before the king or St. Denis might protest on one pretext or another.

"There now," the queen said with a sweet smile. "Now, my dear St. Denis, you will be able to begin your courting more quickly."

George Villiers dashed through the palace, seeking either Jasmine, or James Leslie, not doubting that when he found one, he would find the other. Finally a young page mentioned he had seen the earl and his lady playing cards at some tables that had been set up in one of Whitehall's interconnecting galleries, with their stone and gold ceilings and wainscots of carved wood representing beautiful figures. Windows lined either side of these galleries, giving the impression that one was out-of-doors.

"'Tis the one overlooking the lawn and the river," the child called after George Villiers.

"What now?" Jasmine grumbled, slamming down what she was certain was a winning hand when Villiers found them.

"I'll tell you as we go along," Villiers answered them, ushering the pair from the gaming table and back along the corridors to the royal apartments, and he did.

"God's boots!" swore Glenkirk. "James did something similar years ago to my father. Sent him off when he wanted to create a bit of mischief." He went no farther than that, for he did not want George Villiers privy to his family's history. There were very few people left alive who knew that the earl's mother had once been James Stuart's secret passion.

"I will go home to Queen's Malvern," Jasmine said immediately.

"Nay, madame, you will not," the earl said. "You must remain and, even as you yourself have said, allow the king to believe you have seriously considered the marquis of Hartsfield as a suitor."

"If I can be of any help, Lady Lindley," Villiers said, "you have but to ask me. I have not just the king's favor, but the queen's as well," he told them proudly. "She gave him quite a scolding when he came up with this scheme to offer you a choice of husbands. I think she fears you will disappear again, taking young Charles Frederick Stuart with you, and that she will never see her grandson again."

Jasmine stopped dead in her tracks. "Sir," she said quietly, "I have twice run from my country—to save myself the first time and my children the second time. I will not be forced to flee ever again. England is my home, and it is my children's home. I will not allow anyone to take their birthright from them. You are quite free to repeat my words, if you so choose." Then she continued onward.

He ran to catch up with her. "Madame," he said in breathless tones, "I consider your words a confidence. I will not repeat them."

"We appreciate your friendship, Villiers," the earl told the young man, smoothing over Jasmine's rough edges. "You will understand Lady Lindley's irritation in this matter, I know."

"Aye, sir, I do," was the gracious reply.

They had reached the royal apartments and hurried through the doors that opened before them as they went. The queen looked up, smiling encouragingly as they entered. St. Denis, however, had a smirk upon his face that made Jasmine want to slap him. He was obviously quite pleased with himself. They made their obeisance to Their Majesties.

"I would hae ye go up to Edinburgh, Glenkirk," the king began. "I'll be wanting to make a visit next year, or the year after. I would know the climate of my welcome. Ye'll hae to speak wi the old bonnet lairds, the border lords, and of course, the leaders of the kirk. 'Tis an unofficial exploration ye'll be making for me, of course. And perhaps ye'll even hae time to visit yer own holding."

James Leslie smiled. "I'll be happy to go investigate the climate in the north for you, my lord," he said pleasantly. "I do not believe, however, that there will be time to go to Glenkirk and return to England by the fifteenth of June."

"Yer absence will gie our Piers his chance wi Lady Lindley," the king continued ingenuously. "Ye hae been taking all of her time, a wee birdlet tells me."

"When would you have me leave?" the earl asked.

"On the morrow," was the royal reply. "This is a private visit, Glenkirk. Ye'll nae hae any trappings of authority."

"Very wise," the earl agreed. "My man and I will travel faster alone and create no curiosity that way, sire. I shall, of course, convey your greetings to all I speak with so Scotland may know that you are thinking of her yet, even here in England."

"Verra good, Jemmie," the king said, relieved. He had feared an outburst from the earl, but as always James Leslie was behaving like the perfect royal servant; but then he always had, from the time he had replaced his father as earl of Glenkirk and taken responsibility for their clansmen and women. The king didn't know why he had been worried in the first place. The Leslies respected his divine right, and they had always done so. He didn't have to worry about their loyalty. His glance went to Jasmine, who was strangely silent. "Now ye'll hae time to get to know our Piers, madame," he said.

"As Your Majesty pleases," she replied, her look noncommittal. Jasmine made him very nervous. He had expected an outraged burst of anger form her that Glenkirk was to be sent off. His wife had made him see the error of his judgment in this matter, but a promise was a promise. He had promised Piers a chance with the beautiful and wealthy woman. "There is a masque tonight," he said weakly. "Ye'll come wi the marquis, madame."

"Alas, sire, I have a headache," she said sweetly, "and then, too, there would be no opportunity for me to create a costume. You know how famed my family are for their costumes."

"Could ye not wear the garb of yer native land, madame," the king persisted. "'Twould be exotic to our eye."

"Regretfully those garments are packed away at Queen's Malvern," Jasmine said.

"Oh," the king answered. He was disappointed. He well remembered Jasmine's appearance in a diamond-encrusted garment some years earlier.

"I can send to my grandmother, however," Jasmine amended, stemming any annoyance on the king's part. "There will be other masques quite soon, will there not be, madame?" Her query was aimed at the queen, who smiled conspiratorially and nodded in the affirmative.

"Indeed, Jamie, a salute to springtime, in two weeks," she told her spouse. "I'm certain Lady Lindley can arrange for a suitable costume by then, can you not, my dear."

"Certainly, Your Majesty," Jasmine promised.

"Then it is all settled," the queen continued brightly. "Now, you must go home, my dear, and treat your aching head. Should she not go this minute, Jamie? Poor darling!"

"What will ye treat yerself wi, madame?" the king asked, suspicious.

"Hot tea, sire, and Adali will massage my shoulders," Jasmine responded. "For me it is the sovereign cure. That, and a good night's rest, and I shall be in fine condition by morning, I am certain."

"Verra well, madame, then you are excused," he told her reluctantly.

Jasmine curtsied. The earl of Glenkirk bowed.

"Ye'll ride out at dawn," the king commanded James Leslie.

"I shall, sire," he replied and, taking Jasmine's arm, departed the royal apartments.

"There now, Piers," the king said as the pair disappeared. "I hae cleared yer way for ye, but it is ye who must woo and win the lady. I hae promised that the choice be hers, and I will keep that promise, for I am a man of my word."

"*I will win her, sire!*" the marquis of Hartsfield said firmly.

"*When cows fly,*" murmured George Villiers beneath his breath, but Queen Anne heard him and, unable to help herself, began to laugh, helpless to her mirth, which caused tears to roll down her somewhat plain face.

"Why, Annie," the king said, "I hae nae known ye to laugh so hard in many a year. What is it, my dearie? Will ye share yer jest wi us, eh?"

But the queen waved her hands helplessly at him, choking on her mirth as she did so. "'Twas j-j-just a t-th-thought, Jamie, and 'twould only be amusement to another female. "Or perhaps," she continued regaining control of herself, "'twould not be."

The king turned away to speak with the marquis again, and his wife shook her finger at Villiers, who grinned mischievously at her, then winked.

"You're a wicked laddie," she scolded him softly.

"Aye," he agreed complacently, and then, taking her hand up, George Villiers kissed it. "Your servant, Majesty," he said.

The queen smiled softly, a knowing light coming into her pale blue eyes. "You're a shrewd laddie," she told him. "I am glad that we understand each other, Steenie."

"I'll never hurt him, Majesty," was the answer.

"Then you will always have my friendship," said the queen quietly, "and we are of the same mind in *this* matter?"

"Aye, madame, we are," he told her, "but Lady Lindley is too much in love with the earl of Glenkirk to be swayed, never fear."

"St. Denis is ruthless," the queen warned, "and he is clever."

"I am more clever," George Villiers assured her.

Queen Anne looked at the beautiful young man with the face of an angel. "Why, Steenie," she told him thoughtfully. "I do believe that you are."

He sent her a radiant smile.

Chapter Nine

There was a faint scraping against the casement windows in Jasmine's bedchamber. A light wind ruffled the surface of the Thames. The moon silvered both the lawns and the river. Anyone looking up would have seen the shadowy figure of the man who had climbed the thick vine which grew up the brick side of the house. Clinging to his precarious ladder with one hand, he fumbled to open the casements and, meeting with success, swung himself over the sill and into the room. Walking over to the bed, he looked down upon the woman there.

It was the sound of the windows opening, and the thump of feet hitting the floor that had aroused and awakened her fully. Jasmine opened her eyes. "Jemmie!" she said, recognizing the silhouette looming over her. "Are you mad?"

"Aye," he told her. "Mad for you, darling Jasmine!" Sitting on the edge of the bed, he pulled his boots off, then, standing, began to remove his clothing. "Did you think I would go off to Edinburgh for the next month without coming to say a proper good-bye?" He slid naked beneath the sheets with her, taking her into his arms.

"But what of Kipp St. Denis, my faithful watchdog?" she demanded. "He will go running to his brother, and then the marquis will complain to the king, and then heaven only knows what will happen," she fretted.

"Kipp has gone home. I simply outwaited him. I then followed him back to his brother's house to make certain. Turnabout is fair play, after all, is it not, darling Jasmine?" He nuzzled her ear, inhaling the warm fragrance of her. "I even watched the lights go out all over St. Denis's house." He nibbled upon a perfectly shaped earlobe. "Only then did I come to you."

"Ohhh, Jemmie," she sighed, pressing her body against his. "I have been wild with longing for you, and now you are to leave me."

"But not until the morning, sweetheart. We have a few hours until then, and I intend that we make the most of them. It has been hellish not sharing your bed. I ache to have you as my wife."

"Promise me we will never have to come to court or involve ourselves with the Stuarts ever again," she said fiercely. "I do not like having my life manipulated by others, Jemmie. We will live in your Highlands forever, if we must, to escape the royal meddling. I know the king does not like his native land, and so is unlikely to chase after us."

He kissed her mouth in a leisurely fashion, tasting the familiar sweetness of her, his big hand cupping the back of her head. "We Scots are a contentious people, Jasmine. We are just as apt to murder our kings as obey them. Our lords, great and small, are an unruly lot. Jamie was always afraid of them, and rightly so, I think. If we live in Scotland, you will learn 'tis a turbulent and tumultuous land to which I have brought you, darling Jasmine. You will find, like your mother, that you will want some time in England each year. Our climate is unique, you will discover. Autumn is our best season." His hand slipped from her head to smooth down the length of her back, caressing her buttocks.

She purred with contentment, twisting herself about, and drawing his dark head down into the shadowed vale between her breasts. He rested there a moment, listening to the beating of her heart beneath his ear. Then, affixing his hands about her waist, he straddled her and, bending, began slowly to lick the flesh of her torso. The flat surface of his tongue moved all about the swell of her breasts, and beneath them. It blazed a trail across her chest, her shoulders, and up the slender column of her throat. Then, his head moving swiftly like a darting butterfly, he blew back the wetness, finally fastening his mouth about one of her nipples, which he at first suckled, and then gently bit.

"Beast," she murmured, and, raising her head up, nipped hard upon his muscled shoulder, her teeth dangerously close to drawing blood.

"Little bitch!" he groaned, his hands pinioning her down hard. Then he transferred his attentions to her other nipple, his fingers kneading the tender flesh of the first breast as he drew hard on the second. He half released her so that he might push his hand between her silk thighs, his fingers seeking. "Jesu, you're a hot little bitch. Wet, and hot, and very ready, darling Jasmine!"

She easily broke his light hold on her, her arms sliding about him. Her hands gently stroked him as she whispered hotly in his ear, "Fuck me now, Jemmie! I will die if you do not!"

"Not yet," he insisted. "I have barely begun to delight myself with your ripeness, sweetheart." A single finger found what it sought, and he began to tease at her most vulnerable spot, flicking the digit back and forth over the sensitive flesh, feeling it swell beneath the tender torture until she was gasping with pleasure.

Her fingers dug into his shoulders. *"Bastard!"* she hissed at him. "I want you! *I want you!*"

He laughed happily. "In time, darling Jasmine," he promised her, and then began to kiss her even as he pushed two fingers deeply into her sheath, moving them quickly back and forth until she drenched them with her love dew. "There, sweeting, that should take the edge off your hunger," he told her.

"I hate you," she half sobbed weakly, but he had eased her longing, and they both knew it.

"And I'm wild for you," he teased her. His lips met hers again, rendering her dizzy with the sweetness. "Each night I'm away from you I will remember tonight and all the other nights we have lain together making love to one another. I will count the days until we are married, and you are mine forever, Jasmine." He kissed her lips once more, and then her closed eyelids, the tip of her nose, her determined little chin. "Tell me you will hunger for me as much those long weeks we are apart."

"Yes, damn you!" she managed to gasp. What was happening to her? Usually she was equally in control of their lovemaking; but tonight he had taken firm charge, and she found she was utterly content to allow it. She wanted him to take her roughly, overwhelm her entirely, make her a slave to his masterful passion. She felt like a very young girl again.

Releasing his grip upon her, he slid down the length of her torso, leaving her breasts aching with longing to be touched by him again. Catching up her small, narrow foot in his big hand, he kissed it, suckling lightly upon each toe, his tongue tickling her high arch. His kisses trailed over her narrow ankle, up her shapely calf, across her dimpled knee and, sweeping over her silken thigh, moved across to her other leg. Then reversing the process, he worked his way back down to her left foot.

Pulling himself back up, he began to nibble lightly once more upon her ripe lips, while her fingers tangled in his dark hair. He nuzzled his face against her navel, rubbing his cheek against the satiny flesh. Every pulse in her body was throbbing with her desire. Lower and lower, he moved along her torso. Her vulva was swollen, and already pearlescent with her love juices. He licked at it, smiling to himself when she whimpered first, then swore at him furiously. Spreading her wide, he settled himself between her legs, gazing at her sex, which he revealed to his eyes, opening her nether lips with his thumbs to expose the tumescent core of her sex, throbbing beneath his hot look.

"God," he groaned, "you are so damned beautiful there!"

"Jemmie! You are killing me!" she cried out low.

Leaning forward, he licked several times about the coral shell of her, and then, fastening his mouth about the jewel of her sex, he sucked hard on it while her body arced wildly beneath him, almost dislodging him. His hands fastened about her hips, holding her still beneath the sweet assault.

Pleasure such as she had never known rolled over her in such wild excess that she thought she would surely die. Then, as suddenly as he had offered her this delight, he was mounting her swiftly and fiercely driving into her very womb, bringing yet another surge of pleasure so great that she could hear a violent roaring in her ears as her body began to convulse with a powerful orgasm the like of which she had never known. Her nails clawed at his back, and she moaned wildly.

He couldn't get enough of her. Over and over, and over again he thrust into her, unable to cease the furious motion of his loins. He groaned as she wrapped her legs about him, giving him greater access to the exquisite pleasure that their two bodies were capable of generating. Finally, when he thought relief was not attainable, his lance quivered wildly, then burst with such intensity that he thought he would never stop coming as his love juices poured into her womb, flooding it to overflowing. Exhausted, James Leslie collapsed upon his lover's pillowing bosom, sobbing with relief.

"Ahhh, you exotic witch," he finally managed to say, "you have come near to killing me, and I, you."

Jasmine managed a small chuckle. *"Wasn't it wonderful?"* she said, her arms going about him again.

"And now I must leave you for a month, more or less," he complained.

"Ride quickly," she encouraged him. "I do not know how long I can bear St. Denis's company, and holding him off will be both difficult and irritating. Thank God the queen is my friend!"

"If he so much as touches you," Glenkirk growled, lifting his head and staring into her turquoise eyes, "I shall make him this court's first eunuch. I hate the way the randy bastard looks at you, as if he were contemplating a delicious meal."

"He'll find himself poisoned if he attempts to take a bite out of me," Jasmine promised him. "I am yours, James Leslie. Body and soul, I am yours. I will have no other man as my husband. Now, get off of me, you great beast. I need to prepare love cloths so we may begin another sweet round of passion. I have hated being without you, and I need strong memories to last the next month."

"You are totally insatiable," he grinned at her.

"So are you," she shot back at him.

"Prepare the basin," he instructed her. "I'll need those memories too, darling Jasmine."

When she awoke long after sunrise the following morning, James Leslie was gone from her side, and she didn't even know when he had departed. On the pillow where his dark head had lain was a perfect half-open blood red rose. With a smile she lifted it and inhaled its fragrance, her mind awhirl with the memories they had made before the dawning. Those memories would have to sustain her in the weeks to come, Jasmine knew. The basin was gone from the bedside, and she realized that her servants, discreet as always, had already been there. Reaching out, she pulled on the bell cord to inform them she was awake and ready for her Assam tea.

Shortly Adali entered her bedchamber, the tray, with its blue-and-white porcelain cup and deep saucer, in hand. "Good morning, my princess," he said, setting the tray down. Taking the handleless cup up, he spilled some hot, fragrant tea into the saucer, and brought it over to her. "Your tea." He took the rose from her to put in a bud vase.

Jasmine sipped the beverage slowly. Then she said, "When did Lord Leslie leave, Adali?"

"Before first light, my lady. The skulking one had not yet returned to his post, nor has he come yet. I imagine his master will no longer require him to hide in the shadow of the garden wall now that the earl has departed for Scotland. He and Fergus More rode out just after dawn."

"And now begins the tiresome task of outwitting the marquis of Hartsfield while I pretend to consider his silly suit," Jasmine grumbled.

Adali made a disapproving motion with his mouth. "The gentleman has all the finesse of one of your father's fighting elephants," he observed. "A dangerous fellow, I sense."

"Aye," Jasmine told him. "Jemmie says he is deviant in his passions. I will have to be very careful about him."

"Surely, my princess, you will not allow yourself to be alone with him," Adali said, disturbed.

"I must at some point," Jasmine told him. "That is why he has had Jemmie sent away; so he may have time alone with me. He believes he can convince me to marry him. Of course all he wants is control over my wealth, and my not-so-royal Stuart son. Obviously he has a poor opinion of women, another mark against him in my books."

"You will want a bath," Adali said, dropping the distasteful subject of Piers St. Denis.

"Ummmm," Jasmine agreed. "I am deliciously battered, and replete with my lord's loving, Adali."

"Then you are truly content to wed with James Leslie next month? While I believe he is the proper husband for you, my princess, I should not want you unhappy. Not I who love you like a father and have raised you from an infant," Adali said, his brown eyes filled with tender emotion.

"I am content," Jasmine told him. "Thank you, dearest Adali. I would have you know that I love you every bit as much as I loved Akbar, whose royal seed gave me life."

He bowed low to her and, unable to say another word, hurried from the room, so overcome with emotion was he. Watching him go, Jasmine smiled. She could not imagine life without Adali by her side. He had always been there, with her and for her. He and her two maidservants. How would they adjust to life in the less civilized climes of Scotland? At least they would all be managing together as they always had, she considered with a small chuckle. Adali, Toramalli, and Rohana could make civilization anywhere.

Jasmine was just stepping from her bath when Adali entered her bedchamber, annoyance plainly written all over his light brown face. "The marquis of Hartsfield is here, my lady. Let me send him away for you. He has arrived in a most unseaworthy little bit of a barge, and says he wishes to take you on an outing today."

Jasmine burst out laughing. "He is attempting to be romantic, Adali," she giggled. "I shall go on his picnic, and as we are returning home I shall develop a cold, which ought to give me a few days relief from his company. Courting men don't like sickly women."

"Very well, my lady," Adali said. "When will you be ready to go, for he will surely ask me. An hour? Two?"

"Let us make it two hours, Adali. As he did not request the pleasure of my company beforehand, he can hardly expect me to be available upon his immediate arrival. Have a footman bring him some wine and biscuits, and then leave him alone to stew in the library."

Adali bowed and departed.

Dried, powdered, and wrapped in a chamber robe, Jasmine stretched out upon her bed and contemplated what she would wear on this outing. "Something girlish and countrified," she said to her maidservants.

"You have a lavender-blue silk gown with a wide lace collar," Rohana suggested.

"You could wear it with several petticoats and no farthingale," Toramalli said. "The neckline is very low, however."

"Hummm," Jasmine considered, thinking what fun it would be to tease St. Denis with a glimpse of what he could not ever have. She was very proud of her bosom, which, despite her four childbirths, was still firm and creamy. "Let me see it," she told Rohana.

Rohana brought forth the requested garment, laying it out for her mistress to contemplate. The gown was really quite simple. It was ankle-length, and its sleeves had slashes showing a fine creamy silk beneath. There was no decoration upon the bodice, which would be well covered by the beautiful lace, which formed a draped collar. The waist would be tied with a cream-colored silk *galant*.

"Yes," Jasmine said. "Do we have slippers to match?"

Toramalli shook her head. "Better you wear black with it, else you dirty them. You have a pair of new pantofles which will suit the occasion perfectly, my lady. What jewelry?"

"The pearl necklace with the pear-shaped pink diamond," Jasmine said mischievously. "He'll have a terrible time keeping his eyes off it, and yet will be desperate to appear disinterested in either my jewelry or my breasts." She grinned at her two servingwomen, who burst into laughter at her reasoning.

"You are as naughty as you were when you were a little girl and used to hide in the palace gardens from Adali," Rohana remarked.

For a moment a shadow passed over Jasmine's face. How simple her life had been then as the youngest child of the great Mughal emperor, Akbar. It all seemed so long ago, so very far away from her adopted land of England. "I suppose," she said, "that that little girl still resides somewhere within me, but don't ever tell the children, Rohana."

"They don't need to be told how to be naughty," Toramalli said. "It seems to be instinctive with them. I am amazed your old grandmother can control them, and yet she does."

Jasmine laughed. "Nothing is too big a challenge for Skye O'Malley," she told her servants. "They say I am like her. I love hearing it, of course, but I do not believe I have her greatness."

"You are young yet, my princess," Toramalli observed, "and you have the blood of conquerors in your veins from your father as well."

Exactly two hours after the marquis of Hartsfield had been announced, Jasmine descended the stairs of Greenwood House and entered the library, where he was impatiently awaiting her. She looked dewy fresh and deceptively innocent. Her beauty literally took his breath away. *He had to have her!*

She curtsied to him. "Good day, my lord."

He bowed, regaining his composure. "Madame. I thought perhaps you would enjoy stopping to lunch somewhere along the river."

"Adali told me. What a lovely idea, my lord. Shall we go?" Jasmine smiled pleasantly.

"Of course," he replied, hurrying to the door to open it for her. "I have a barge waiting."

They exited the house and walked down to the river, where, to the marquis of Hartsfield's surprise, another barge other than his own appeared to be awaiting them, as was Adali, garbed in narrow long white pants and a long white coat embroidered in gold thread and pearls that came to just below his knees. About his waist was a gold sash, into which was stuck a jeweled dagger. Upon his graying head Adali wore a small white turban. Jasmine had not seen him dressed this way in several years. She raised a dark quizzical eyebrow.

Adali bowed to her. "The marquis's barge was quite unsuitable, my princess," he said calmly. "I sent it away."

"But my basket of food was in the barge," Piers St. Denis protested, astounded by the servant's boldness.

"The contents of your basket would not have suited my mistress's palate, my lord. I have replaced your basket with one from our own kitchens," Adali replied, and then he helped Jasmine into her own barge.

When the marquis had entered the vessel and seated himself next to Jasmine, Adali also entered the barge and, with an imperious wave of his hand, signaled the bargemen to begin rowing.

"You are coming with us?" Piers St. Denis was becoming annoyed. Was he never to be alone with Jasmine?

"My mistress does not go off with strange men, my lord," Adali answered the marquis of Hartsfield. "It is my duty to protect her. Her father, the great Mughal Akbar, himself, placed her as an infant into my arms and gave me my instructions. I have never failed my mistress, nor will I ever fail her. I will be her protection until I die."

"You are a slave then?"

Adali shook his head in the negative. "I am a free man, my lord," he said stonily, his tone indicating his disapproval of someone who did not recognize either his authority or his social standing.

"I mean your mistress no harm, Adali," Piers St. Denis said in a conciliatory voice, attempting to use his great charm on Adali. "Certainly you must understand that."

"My mistress is a lady of rank, wealth, and extraordinary beauty, my lord. I am sure your intentions toward her are honorable. Nonetheless, it is my duty to be with her until she is remarried and put into the care of her husband. Then I will run her household even as I do now. I will continue to see to her safety and that of her children." He did not smile. His attitude was an implacable one. "Do not allow my presence to disturb you. I see and hear all but report nothing publicly." Then, turning his back to them, he remained standing outside the barge's open cabin door.

"I am surprised that you allow a servant to speak to anyone like that," the marquis grumbled irritably. Adali's bearing was very formidable. How the hell could he overwhelm Jasmine with passion if that damned creature was always there. Did Glenkirk have to put up with such an inconvenience? He doubted it.

"Adali is not truly a servant any longer," Jasmine told her suitor calmly. "He has always been a friend, and he is like a second father to me. I trust both his judgment and his instincts. He wants only what is best for me, my lord." And then she dropped the subject, smiling sweetly at him and saying, "Where have you planned for us to stop and eat? Isn't it a lovely day? There is no place in the world like England in the springtime, is there? Have you traveled? It seems I have been all over the world."

"I have never left England," he said stiffly. "Why would I? There is everything here that I could possibly want."

"Have you never been curious about other lands, and other people?" she asked him. "Until I left India, I had never been anywhere, but I did travel with my father's court, of course, across the vastness of our land. India is hot, however, and I preferred as I grew older to spend much of my time in Kashmir, at the palace my father gave to my mother. It was on a lake. The climate there was more temperate than that of Lahore, Fatahpur Sikri, or Agra. Such hot cities!"

"*Cities?*" he looked surprised. "I thought India a rather savage and barbaric land, madame. Your cities, naturally, could not rival London, or our other fine towns. They are made of mud and wattle, are they not? England must have been quite a revelation to you when you first arrived."

Jasmine could not believe her ears. Did he know nothing of the world outside of England? "India," she told him, "is a very ancient civilization, my lord. Our cities are far more urbane, in many instances, than your cities. While the poor live simply, as all the poor do no matter the country, our men of property do not. My father's palaces far outshine anything I have seen in England. In Agra my father's residence had walls nine feet thick, and 180 feet high. They were impossible to breach. There were soaring towers, and planted terraces with kiosks atop them. The walls had battlements, and breastworks, and places for archers. It was incredibly magnificent, and that was not even the best of his castles. Akbar built an entire city he called Fatahpur Sikri. It was all marble and sandstone, and so beautiful that just to look at it hurt one's heart.

"Why do you believe India is some backward place to be scorned? We have as many, if not more, artisans, merchants, and manufacturers than you do. Our land mass is enormous when compared to this little island kingdom of England. And in my father's land all faiths were welcomed. Such is not the case in England, or any of your *civilized* lands in Europe. Not only that, we have a great and glorious history which has been written down over the centuries, and can be found in the libraries of my father's palaces. And our music, painting, and literature is unparalleled!"

He was taken aback by her outburst. He had assumed that she had come to England to escape the barbarity of her native land. "If you loved India so," he said, "then why did you leave it?"

"Because," Jasmine said bluntly, "my half brother, Salim, who is now the Emperor Jahangir, wished to pursue an incestuous relationship with me, my lord. He murdered my first husband, Prince Jamal, the royal governor of Kashmir, in order to clear a path to my bed. My father was dying and knew he could no longer protect me from Salim. I was sent to England that my half brother be thwarted in his unnatural desires." She smiled sweetly at him as she had several times that morning. "Did you not know that? I would have assumed your interest in me would have engendered some curiosity in my personal history, my lord, but it has obviously not."

"My concern for you, madame, grows more as each minute passes, and I come to realize what a magnificent woman you truly are," the marquis declared. He was astounded by her frankness.

Adali made a sound that was very much like a sharp bark of laughter at St. Denis's words, but he did not turn around.

"You know nothing of me, sir," Jasmine said scathingly, "except what the king has told you. That I must have a husband because I am incapable, weak woman that I am, of running my own life, and raising my own children. That I am a wealthy woman. Wealthier even than the king himself. And I am certain that the king told you that I was beautiful, but until the day I returned to court with Glenkirk, my lord, that was all you had heard of me. You knew, of course, that I was Prince Henry's mistress, and had borne him a son; but you were not at court when I was here last. And since the king has offered you the opportunity to court me, you have not even bothered to learn anything of me other than what was previously told you. I do not find that particularly flattering, my lord. It would appear that you court me because of my wealth and the power you believe you will have as the stepfather of my not-so-royal Stuart son. You must be aware that I will not have you, yet you persist in this game. Why, my lord St. Denis? *Why?*"

"Everything you say is true, madame," he began, "but from the moment I laid eyes on you I knew that you must be my wife! I am consumed with desire for you! Yet you would not let me near you, and how was I to learn about you if I could not be with you? I would not base our marriage on gossip and innuendo, or worse, misinformation. Only you can tell me the true history of Jasmine Lindley."

"You had Jemmie sent away," she accused him.

"How else could I be allowed to spend time with you?" he asked her. "To have returned from France with you in tow was quite a coup for the earl; and to marry you will be but the final jewel in his crown. I, however, would pluck that jewel from him, madame, and wear it myself. There isn't a man alive, knowing the situation, who would fault me for it." He caught her hand and, raising it to his lips, kissed it ardently, turning it over to embrace both the palm and the inside of her wrist.

Jasmine snatched her hand back. "You presume, my lord!" she told him icily. The kiss had sent a shiver of distaste through her. There was something about him that reminded her of Salim, although there was absolutely no resemblance between her brother and the marquis.

"I will have you, Jasmine," he declared, his bright blue eyes glittering almost black. "You were meant to be my wife."

"I will be James Leslie's wife," she said quietly. "There is nothing you can say, or do, my lord, that will change my mind. However, if you wish to keep me amused while my Jemmie is away in Scotland, I shall be pleased to entertain your company, for I know it will make the king happy. Perhaps we can even decide upon a list of eligible maidens to present the king with when you finally accept that your quest of me is futile. From that list we will choose a bride for you. You had best take advantage of my suggestion, my lord. You are too complicated a man for the king. In the end he will choose Villiers for his favorite of favorites, and you will have no influence left with the royal Stuart. You have few friends, I suspect, and Villiers will certainly be content to see you fade into obscurity," she warned him.

"You are far too clever, and much too observant, I think," he told her. "Are you one of these intelligent women, then?"

"Aye, I am," Jasmine admitted.

Adali, who had been monitoring the conversation, now turned to the pair, saying, "There is a lovely grove of willows just around the next bend in the river. With your permission, my princess, I will direct the bargemen there."

Jasmine nodded.

"Do you read and write?" the marquis asked her.

"Aye. And I do mathematics. I know history, and I speak several languages quite fluently, my lord. I was taught by a very enlightened priest who came to my father's court for the express purpose of educating me. I was baptized in my infancy into the Christian faith. My foster mother followed Islam, as did my brothers. Two of my three sisters were members of the Hindu faith. I have told you that in my father's land all faiths were welcomed. My sisters were as well educated as I was except for poor Aram-Banu Begum. She is slow of wit, but a sweet girl."

Every time she spoke he was further amazed by her. She had said that he was complicated, but she was equally complex, he thought. "You, your brothers, and sisters, all had different mothers?"

Jasmine laughed, knowing even as he asked her he was shocked at what he already knew the answer would be. "Yes," she said. "It sounds quite licentious to you, doesn't it, my lord, but it is the custom in India for a man to have multiple wives and concubines. Of course, not all the men in India can afford more than one wife; but my father married for dynastic and political reasons. Many of his wives were the sisters and daughters of the men whom he conquered, or those who wished to forge alliances with him. My English mother was his fortieth wife, and, of course, he had a large zenana of favorites. I have often thought it quite unfair that men may have the privilege of many women, but women must be faithful to but one man at a time. What do you think, my lord?" Her turquoise blue eyes twinkled.

"I...I...I have not ever considered such a thing," he replied slowly. A man might have a wife, and a mistress, but God only knew that was enough trouble. *Forty wives?* The deceased emperor of India must have been a formidable man indeed.

She laughed gaily. *"You are shocked,"* she mocked him.

The barge slid up on the sandy riverbank before he might answer. Adali leapt out and, beckoning to his mistress, lifted her onto the shore. He left the marquis of Hartsfield to exit on his own. Two of the bargemen climbed from the elegant little vessel, carrying several baskets. Adali took a linen cloth from one of the baskets and spread it upon a patch of the grassy field, beneath a particularly large willow tree. He next set out the meal. A small chicken, roasted golden; a rabbit pie, still warm from the oven in its stone pie plate; half of a small country ham; fresh bread; a crock of sweet butter; a quarter wheel of hard yellow cheese; a small silver dish of runny French Brie; a bowl of fresh strawberries; and a carafe of wine. There were two silver plates, two Venetian goblets of crystal etched with silver butterflies, and the appropriate cutlery with silver blades and bone handles, and silver spoons.

"Have you food for yourself and the bargemen, Adali?" Jasmine inquired of him, setting her lavender skirts about her on the grass.

"Yes, my princess," he answered her, bowing.

"Then you may leave us to eat your own meal," Jasmine told him. "I believe that we may trust the marquis to behave himself, Adali."

"I will be within earshot," Adali responded, and moved away from them back to the barge, where the rowers awaited his further instructions.

"Will he always be with us?" Piers St. Denis asked her, sitting down.

"It will keep you from foolish misbehavior, I think," Jasmine teased him wickedly. "If I were forced to defend myself, I could harm you."

He laughed. Despite the fact she was the most irritating women he had ever met, she was also incredibly desirable. "Jasmine, for I intend even without your permission to call you by your name, if you will but give me a chance, you will find I am a most charming fellow. I should make you an excellent husband. I will manage your affairs every bit as well as Rowan Lindley managed them when he was married to you. Now, I'll have a bit of everything, for I am quite hungry, and your cook is obviously very good. Your Adali was right to send my poor basket away. It was much too common."

Now it was Jasmine's turn to laugh. She began preparing a plate for him as she spoke. "You may call me by my name, if you choose, my lord," she told him. "As for your managing my affairs, I had best tell you that I manage my own affairs. While I did, on occasion, ask Rowan for his advice, all decisions regarding my wealth abide in my hands. They will continue to remain in my charge." She handed him a full plate and, pouring a goblet of wine, passed it to him as well.

"Glenkirk has agreed to such a thing?"

"I should not have agreed to marry him had he not," Jasmine replied, putting two chicken wings, a slice of ham, and some bread and cheese on a plate for herself. "Is the wine good? It comes from the French branch of the family at Archambault in the Loire." She sipped at her own filled goblet appreciatively.

"You have French relations?"

"Aye." She gnawed on a chicken wing.

He grew silent, eating his food instinctively. This was not a simple woman, he thought again. She was educated. She was independent. She had traveled extensively. She had been the beloved of a prince who, had he lived, would have been England's next king. *She had his son. She was fabulously wealthy.* All of this far outweighed his other concerns, but he needed time to rethink his plan of attack. Jasmine was obviously not one bit afraid of the king's power, nor did she stand in awe of Piers St. Denis, the marquis of Hartsfield. How could he control her? What would frighten her into obeying him? How could he gain control over her wealth? Glenkirk was either a fool, or he had agreed to her wishes intending to get his hands on Jasmine's wealth after their marriage. *He needed time to think.*

When they had finished their meal there was nothing left to do but to return to Greenwood. He could hardly woo her on the riverbank with her bargemen and the disapproving Adali looking over his shoulder. As they progressed back down the river Jasmine began to sneeze. After a bit she started to sniffle. Her eyes grew heavy, and she was much less talkative than she had been when they had begun their journey to the picnic site.

"Are you ill?" he nervously ventured.

"I think I may be developing an ague, my lord," she said unhappily. Then she sneezed several times again. "It is so damp on the river, and it is still spring. Perhaps an outdoor luncheon was not such a good idea after all. Ahhhhhchooo!

Oh dear!" She fumbled for her handkerchief, shivering visibly as she did so, blowing her nose noisily.

"We are almost back to your home," he said, irritated. Good Lord! An ague! What if it was one of those fatal agues? What if she died, and he was held responsible! God's foot, how Villiers would laugh at his misfortune, all the while sympathizing with the king over her untimely demise. Then he should never get either Jasmine, her wealth, or the power to be had by being the little duke of Lundy's guardian. "Adali!" Piers St. Denis leaned forward, tugging at Adali's silk coat.

"My lord?" Adali had quickly turned about.

"Your mistress is ill, Adali. Have the rowers row more quickly. She should not be out in this damp air, I fear!"

Adali peered into the cabin, his face impassive. "Indeed, my lord, my mistress does appear flushed. An ague, I think." He turned away and ordered the bargemen to a faster pace.

Reaching the Greenwood quay, Adali immediately took charge, lifting Jasmine from her seat and carrying her up the lawn to the house. "The barge will take you wherever you wish to go, my lord," he called after the marquis, effectively dismissing him.

Piers St. Denis stopped dead in his tracks halfway up the lawn. Adali had put him in an untenable position. He could hardly run after Jasmine under the circumstances. He had been given only one choice. Turning about, he walked back down to the barge and climbed into it. "Whitehall," he said to the bargemen.

From the library windows she watched him depart, chuckling to herself, well pleased. "Carrying me into the house from the barge was a very nice touch, Adali," she praised him.

"I thought so too, my princess," Adali replied. "How long do you intend suffering with the ague?"

"I think several days at least, and then I shall allow the marquis a brief bedside visit," Jasmine replied.

"Do not be too clever," Adali warned her. "If the king does not believe his young friend has had enough time to court you, he is quite capable of postponing your wedding to Lord Leslie. I know that you do not want that, nor does your family."

"I do not like the marquis," Jasmine told him. "I told you that he reminded me of Salim, and now I realize why. Do you remember how my brother would say things as if they were absolute fact? *I will have you.* It was not just words for Salim. It was fact. He wanted me. He would have me. There wasn't the slightest doubt in his mind that what he wanted he would have. Piers St. Denis behaves exactly the same way. In the face of my open and avowed dislike of him; in the face of my impending marriage to the earl of Glenkirk; he is absolutely and utterly oblivious. *He will have me.* He truly believes he will, and it is irritating beyond all, Adali!

"Time I otherwise might have spent with Jemmie, I must now spend with the marquis. I did not wish to remain in London at all, but rather to go home to see my children, from whom I have been separated for many weeks now. I wanted to visit my grandfather's grave and bid him farewell. All the things I would otherwise occupy my time with, I cannot because I must remain here and allow that obviously greedy little royal sycophant to play at courting me. James Stuart is a meddlesome and sentimental old fool, but it is the last time he will interfere in my life, Adali! I have had enough!"

Adali could see that his lady was careening into a dangerous temper. He knew that he had to prevent it lest she unwittingly worsen the situation in which she now found herself. If only she had married the earl of Glenkirk two years ago, there would be no difficulty now. "Why do you not send for the children?" he suggested.

"What?" She looked surprised.

"We will send a message to your grandmother tomorrow requesting the children be brought to London. The marquis of Hartsfield should, I believe, be exposed to your offspring. After all, does he not seek to become their guardian and stepfather?" There was a twinkle in Adali's dark eyes. "Little Lord Henry and my Lady India will understand the situation if we tell them. They will like the marquis a little better than you do. As for my Lady Fortune, she will follow the lead of her elder siblings and be the naughtiest of them all. Taking it all in will be the youngest, Duke Charles. Recognizing his brother's and sisters' dislike of the marquis, he will reject him, too, when St. Denis, believing himself clever, approaches your son to win his favor. Little ones his age have very strong likes and dislikes, my princess."

"It is brilliant!" Jasmine cried. "And the king will be absolutely delighted to have some time with his grandson. Send a pigeon at first light, Adali!" Then she clapped her hands and laughed. "I cannot wait to see Piers St. Denis's face when he is set upon by my children!"

"I shall write the message to Madame Skye myself," Adali said. And he did, even before first light, slowly, painstakingly forming the tiny letters on the parchment. It was not necessary to inform the matriarch of the family of everything that had happened since Jasmine's return to England from France. Adali had already done that, for he always kept in communication with Skye when they were apart. She knew of the king's new foolishness, of Jasmine's irritation, of Glenkirk's trip to Scotland. Now using the code they had devised several years earlier, he told her that the children were needed to help their mother discourage her unwanted suitor. They must leave for London upon receipt of the message. Then, stuffing the tightly rolled parchment into its silver container, he affixed it around the leg of a Queen's Malvern pigeon and, going to the window, released the bird into the predawn sky. He watched as it turned for home, its wings beating strongly in the cool air.

For the next three days Piers St. Denis arrived at Greenwood, beribboned bouquet in hand, only to be turned away by Adali. His mistress, the formidable servant reported, was yet too ill to receive visitors. No, a leech had not been called. His mistress did not believe in leeches. Perhaps tomorrow she would be well enough to receive him. On the fourth day, just as the marquis was becoming irritable, Adali greeted him with a broad smile, saying that his mistress would be happy to see the marquis, but only for a few moments. Beckoning the visitor to follow him, he led him up the two flights of stairs to Jasmine's apartments.

As he followed Adali, Piers St. Denis's eyes flickered back and forth, catching glimpses of the rooms above the main level, for he had never been allowed upstairs before. An open door revealed a large library, but the other doors on the second level were closed to his sight. Greenwood was not a particularly large house, and he wondered at its location at the end of a row of homes belonging to the high and very mighty. Its furnishings were fine, but not ostentatious by any means. He might have even called it simple but that the tapestries, the carpets, and the silver were so obviously rich and of the finest quality. They had reached the third floor of the house, and Adali ushered him through the doors into Jasmine's apartment, through a dayroom, and directly into her bedchamber.

"My lord!" She held out her hands in welcome to him. Her dark hair was loose about her, and she wore a modest chamber robe with a round, high neckline. He was relieved to see she appeared recovered.

"You are well?" He kissed the two hands offered him, then, without being invited, sat upon the edge of her bed.

"I am weak yet, but the fever and chills have gone, I believe," Jasmine assured him, withdrawing her hands from his grip. "And I have received wonderful news from my dear grandmother. My children are coming to London to be with me!"

"*Your children?*" The marquis of Hartsfield did not look particularly pleased. "I thought your children lived in the country."

"Ohhh no, my lord! My children have always lived with me. I am not one of those mothers who but spawns her offspring, then leaves them entirely to the mercy of servants. Gracious no! My little ones are in the country because Grandmama brought them back from France so Jemmie and I might have a bit of time alone together; but now I want them back with me again, particularly as Jemmie is gone and I am so alone. Besides, you seek to be my husband, so you should really meet my children, don't you think? And, of course, the king will be absolutely delighted to see my little not-so-royal Stuart." She gave him a dazzling smile. "I do believe I am better just knowing my little ones are coming."

Piers St. Denis was not pleased. He had gotten rid of James Leslie so he might be alone with Jasmine, and the earl was gone a week now, and he had yet to be alone with her. Now her blasted brats were coming to take up her time, and when would he have his chance with her at all? This was something he could not complain to the king about, for the king was totally sentimental where family was concerned. He would be delighted to see his grandson and the other three little beasts as well. Aggravated as he was, he smiled back at her. "Of course I should meet the children," he said. "Aren't the two eldest old enough to be fostered out? As we are to spend our life at court, Jasmine, we should begin to consider your children's futures as well."

"I will not foster my children out, my lord," she said. "I consider it a nasty custom, giving one's offspring to other families to raise. My children are wealthy, titled, and of impeccable lineage. They will be considered quite eligible marriage partners when the time comes, and without being sent away into other households."

"I think, perhaps," Adali interrupted, "that we should conclude your visit, my lord. Agitation is not good for my lady, as I know you realize. You will be welcomed back tomorrow, however."

St. Denis rose from her bedside and bowed to Jasmine. "The queen sends you her regards," he told her. "I will be back tomorrow, madame. There is a masque at the end of the week, and I would escort you to it if you are well enough, and I hope that you are."

"We shall see," Jasmine murmured, falling back upon her pillows.

"Farewell then, my love," he replied.

"Farewell, my lord," she responded as he departed her chamber. *His love?* There was Salim's distant voice again, she thought, and shivered.

Chapter Ten

"Her Majesty, the queen," Adali said, ushering Queen Anne into Jasmine's dayroom.

Jasmine arose quickly from her chair by the fire and curtsied low. "You honor me, madame," she said.

"Let me look at you, child," the queen said, as the younger woman came forward. She took Jasmine's face between her thumb and her forefinger, turning it first this way, and then that. "As I thought," Queen Anne finally pronounced. "What a dreadful little fraud you are, my dear, but now you must cease your willfulness. I cannot help you if you will not help yourself. St. Denis has already begun to whine to the king that he has not enough time in which to court you. I have only just managed to prevent the king from doing something very foolish. You will have to let him dance attendance on you for the next few weeks, I'm afraid."

"If only the king…" Jasmine began.

"I know, I know," the queen soothed her. "If only my well-meaning Jamie had not interfered just as you and the earl of Glenkirk had come to a comfortable understanding. He's quite in love with you, you know. You do love him, don't you?"

Jasmine nodded.

"Let us sit down," the queen said, and turning to Adali, she continued, "Do bring us something nice to drink, Adali, won't you?"

Adali bowed. "Of course, Majesty."

They sat together by the fire, and the queen spoke once again. "Both Steenie and I are in agreement. We are your allies in this matter, my dear. And now another element has been added to the brew. The earl of Bartram has suggested to His Majesty that custody of little Charles Frederick Stuart be assigned to him."

"Who is he?" Jasmine asked.

"A protégé of Robert Cecil's who has worked in His Majesty's service for many years. He began his career in the reign of the late queen. He has recently lost favor with my husband thanks to the greed and the jealousy of Piers St. Denis and the foolishness of the countess of Bartram, who is obviously sillier than I am. He seems to believe if he can get the king to grant him the care and custody of our grandson, he will have been restored to our favor. Jamie, of course, has absolutely no intention of any such thing, but you know how softhearted he is. He cannot come right out and say no to poor Lord Stokes. While he will not return him to favor, and indeed will soon dispense with his services altogether, for the man has Puritan leanings; he is yet mindful of the many long and loyal years of service Richard Stokes has rendered the crown. He is seeking a kind way to retire him.

"In the meantime, however, Steenie and I thought we might use Lord Stokes ourselves in a rather clandestine manner, implying to St. Denis that the king is indeed considering transferring the guardianship of your son to Lord Stokes. The marquis will, of course, attempt to learn if it is true from the king, but Jamie will dither about until he has made up his mind how to rid himself of the earl of Bartram in a considerate manner. This will but add to the confusion. St. Denis will not have as much time to court you, which will relieve you of his company. Then, too, he will be desperately trying to decide which is more to his advantage: a rich wife or a powerful connection." The queen's laugh tinkled about the chamber, and she gratefully accepted a silver goblet of fruity wine from Adali. Sipping it, she declared, "You have the best cellar in London, my dear Jasmine! Well, what do you think of our little plot?"

Jasmine was not certain what she thought of the queen's intrigue. She was silent a long moment. Then she said, "I think that you and George Villiers may underestimate the marquis. I think he could be dangerous in certain circumstances. For the moment all he has to contend with is James Leslie, and he has managed to send him away; but if he believes someone else might gain custody of my son..." Jasmine grew silent again, a single finger tapping thoughtfully upon the arm of her chair.

"St. Denis? Dangerous?" Her laughter tinkled once more. "Oh, no, my dear. Piers St. Denis is simply an ambitious young man seeking to better himself, very much like our dear Steenie. In the end you will choose Glenkirk, and we will give him another heiress to wife with our royal blessing. He will then return to his holding and never be heard of again."

"He has suggested to me, madame, that he will remain at court after his marriage," Jasmine told the queen. "I believe Your Majesty's assessment of him to be correct in that he is ambitious. I think he is a man who desires power more than anything else."

"Do you? How interesting," the queen answered vaguely. She had said what she had come to say and, having emptied her mind, was now at a loss. She looked anxiously at Jasmine. "You will cooperate with us, my dear, won't you?

You will just slightly encourage St. Denis for a short time? Between us we can keep him quite confused."

"If it pleases you, madame, of course I will cooperate, for I wish for only one thing, to be James Leslie's wife," Jasmine replied.

"Oh, good!" The queen quaffed down the remainder of her wine, and, rising, said, "I must go now, my dear. I am happy to see you looking so well, and I shall, of course, expect you at my masque on Saturday night at Whitehall."

"Madame." Jasmine had arisen, too. "The children will be here in a few days from Queen's Malvern. I thought a good way of keeping St. Denis off guard was to introduce him to my little band of rebels."

"How deliciously ingenious." The queen chuckled. "I suspect that St. Denis will detest the competition of your offspring."

"Aye," Jasmine smiled. "He has already suggested that India and Henry are old enough to be fostered out. Of course, I told him I should not foster out my bairns to strangers."

"Unnatural monster!" the queen pronounced. "Of course not! You know how I feel about fostering children out. You were absolutely correct to say so." Then, kissing Jasmine's cheeks, Queen Anne departed Greenwood House to return to the palace.

Jasmine's next visitor was St. Denis, who once again came bearing a beribboned bouquet. She did what was expected of her. Burying her nose in the colorful flowers, she exclaimed over their lovely fragrance, thinking all the while that St. Denis lacked imagination. He always brought flowers but nothing else, which meant he was either without funds or mean-spirited. She suspected a combination of both.

"The queen has been to visit me," she said brightly. "She came to see how I was and to invite me to her masque on Saturday evening. Will you escort me, my lord?" She gave him a smile.

"What will you wear?" he asked her excitedly. "We must match our costumes, of course!"

"I cannot have a decent costume made in so short a time, my lord," Jasmine told him. "I shall wear a beautiful gown of royal blue silk instead. I shall leave the selection of a mask to carry to you, however. I want the most beautiful mask possible. We must outshine everyone else, eh, my lord?" She smiled again.

He could scarcely believe it. She was being most cooperative, and she was even asking him a small favor. "You shall have the finest mask in London," he promised her. And when he had left her and returned to his own house, he told his brother. "I believe she is beginning to weaken in her resolve to hate me, Kipp. She was so amenable toward me today. The queen had just left her, and I think she may have advised Jasmine to seriously consider my suit. I thought the queen was Villiers's ally, but perhaps I was mistaken. Who makes the best masks in London?"

"A fellow named Barrow, near St. James," Kipp replied.

"You must go to him and order two of his absolute best creations, Kipp. They must be ready for Saturday's masque at the palace," the marquis of Hartsfield said to his half brother.

"They will be horrifically expensive, especially considering how short a time you are allowing the craftsmen," Kipp answered him.

"He will not refuse the king's favorite," Piers St. Denis said with self-assurance. "Besides, when I have married

Jasmine Lindley I will be the wealthiest man in England," he concluded with a grin.

"*If you* wed her," Kipp cautioned him.

"*I will marry her!*" the marquis insisted. "And on our wedding night you and I will punish her for her arrogance, eh, Kipp?"

"How?" Kipp goaded his sibling.

"We will put her over the correction bar, her legs spread. Then I shall tawse her bottom until it is pink and shining. She will weep fiercely, I have not a doubt. And while I strap her, you will play with her beautiful breasts so that she is caught between pain and pleasure, which I have not a doubt she will soon learn to like. When I deem her ready, I shall have her, still bent over the bar."

"And will you share her, Piers, as you usually do with your women?" his brother asked.

"Not fully, not at first, not until I am bored with her; but I will permit you to take your pleasure within her mouth, Kipp. Together we will teach this proud beauty who is the master. And afterward, in a year or so, when she is well trained, and obedient, we shall allow her to learn this same art of domination we practice. Think of it, Kipp! We shall, the three of us, lure beautiful young maidens and handsome young men into our web of forbidden love. It will be wonderful!"

"I should have known you would have it all planned out," his half brother said admiringly.

The marquis of Hartsfield smiled. "Go and order the masks," he said. "And tell this Barrow fellow there will be an extra payment for his trouble. *But I want his best!*"

"Naturally," Kipp replied, and hurried off to do his brother's bidding.

Jasmine's gown for the queen's masque was a magnificent creation. Of royal blue silk, the skirt ankle-length, its undergown was of cloth of silver embroidered with sparkling tiny blue stones in a spiral design. The neckline of the gown was quite low and square, with a draped collar of delicate silver lace. The sleeves showed cloth of silver through their slashes, and silver lace cuffs accented her delicate wrists. Her shoes were matching blue silk with silver roses decorating them; and her hair was twisted into an elegant chignon, with a lovelock tied with a silver ribbon over her left ear. From her ears dripped sapphires, and about her neck was Jasmine's famous sapphire necklace.

The marquis of Hartsfield's mouth fell open in admiration when he saw her, his eyes fastening upon the necklace in particular. Wordless, he handed her her mask, an exquisite creation of silver and gold with white feathers.

"They are called the Stars of Kashmir," Jasmine told him, one hand going to her throat. "My first husband, Prince Jamal, gave them to me. The lake where I grew up, upon which our palace was located, is just this shade of blue. There was an additional stone found at the same time these were mined in Ceylon. It was a large teardrop shaped sapphire called the Wular Blue, after that same lake. We gave it to my father upon the celebration of his fiftieth year as emperor." Reaching out with her other hand, she took the mask from him. "It is lovely, my lord, and quite perfect with my gown, do you not agree?"

He nodded, his throat aching, his mind desperate to say something clever that would gain her approval. "You are the most beautiful woman I have ever seen," he finally managed to croak, realizing how mundane a thing it was he had just said. She knew she was beautiful, and had undoubtedly been told it a thousand times.

"How gallant you are, my lord," she responded graciously. Then, "We will take my barge, with your permission. It is more comfortable than any others in which I have traveled."

"Of course," he agreed, almost drowning in her smile. This was how he had imagined it would be. She with her blue-black hair, pale gold skin, and turquoise eyes. He, tawny-haired, fair-skinned and blue-eyed. They were perfect together! His costume of cream-colored silk, silver and gold, was an ideal foil for her royal blue and silver gown. They looked as if they belonged together, and they did! Taking her arm, he followed the ever-present Adali down to the quay, where the barge was awaiting them. Strangely, he did not mind the servant's company any longer. Adali, in his white clothing and turban, gave them a certain cachet that no one else at court had.

Whitehall was ablaze with lights. They joined the throngs of other courtiers entering the hall where Their Majesties sat. The queen, as always, was overdressed, but a charming and gracious hostess. The king slumped morosely on his throne. He hated his wife's fetes. He would remain for a brief time, then disappear with a few friends to drink whiskey and play at dice. The sight of Jasmine on the arm of the marquis of Hartsfield, however, brought a smile to his sad face, and he beckoned them forward to the foot of his throne. They made their obeisances, and, as she rose, Jasmine saw Prince Charles standing next to his father's chair.

"Ahh, Piers, ye hae brought Lady Lindley at last," the king enthused. "She's a rare beauty, is she nae?"

"Indeed, my liege," the marquis replied. "I am grateful to Your Majesty for this opportunity." St. Denis then bowed to the queen and nodded to the prince.

Jasmine smiled at Prince Charles. He was a small but dignified young man, who, until his brother's death, had stood very much in his shadow. "My lord," she said, "it is very good to see you once again." Then she curtsied low.

A tiny smile touched Charles Stuart's mouth. He was not a young man who showed his emotions, but he did remember his elder brother's mistress with fondness. It had been Jasmine who had taught him how to bandy words with his brilliant older sibling, how to win arguments with Henry, much to the elder's delight, for Henry Stuart had loved his little brother, although until Jasmine had explained her Hal's nature to young Charles, he had not believed it. The heir to England's throne was almost fifteen, and while he was considered prim by his father's court, he was quite fond of music and drama, as was his mother.

"I am h-happy t-to see you again, m-madame," he acknowledged Jasmine. The prince sometimes stuttered because he was basically shy.

"Thank you, Your Highness," Jasmine responded, curtsying prettily. Then she said, "Your namesake will be here in a few days, sir. May I bring the duke of Lundy to see his uncle?"

"Oh, yes, m-madame!" the young man said. "I did not see him when your g-grandmother b-brought him last. I have not seen him since he w-was a bairn."

"He is much like his father," she told the prince with a smile.

"I like children," the prince replied. "I w-would have a b-big family one d-day."

"You must choose the right wife," Jasmine told him.

"I hae an eye on the Spanish infanta," the king said.

"A French princess would be better," the queen murmured. "Jasmine, my dear, come and sit on a footstool by me while we watch the masque. St. Denis, you may stand behind me."

The masque that followed was a salute to springtime and the coming summer. It had not the imagination of the masques that Jasmine and Prince Henry had taken part in several years before. It was more music and dancing, with little story, although the costumes, as always, were lovely. Jasmine recognized none of the young people involved. *Times are changing,* she thought, *and I am getting older.* After the masque ended, there was dancing. The marquis of Hartsfield made to lead Jasmine out onto the floor, but Prince Charles stepped forward.

"The first dance is mine, I believe, my lord," the young man said. He did not stutter once.

"Of course, Your Highness," Piers St. Denis answered, stepping back and bowing to the royal prince.

Charles Stuart took Jasmine's hand, and they began to dance a stately country dance. "You are not going to marry him, are you, m-madame?" the prince asked.

"I most certainly am not going to marry him," Jasmine said. "Because your father is so insistent, I must play at letting him court me, but I detest Piers St. Denis, Your Highness, and I love Glenkirk."

"W-why did you run away then?" He twirled her gracefully.

"Like Your Highness, I am a king's child. I do not like being told what to do, and I had not finished mourning Hal. I was not ready to marry again. Not so soon. Now, however, it is different. Lord Leslie loved me even before I wed with my beloved Rowan Lindley. He loves me now, and I have come to love him. Try to love the girl you finally marry, Your Highness. It is so important to a woman to be loved." She dipped and, lifting her skirts, pranced three steps.

He lifted her lightly, swinging her about, and then replaced her on the floor, where they moved in the final elegant precise steps of the dance. "I d-do not like St. Denis. There is s-something unwholesome about him. And I like Villiers e-even less. He t-takes my father's attention from m-me. S-still, if I had to choose, I suppose Villiers is b-better. He is greedy, but h-harmless."

"I agree, Your Highness. You are very wise for a young man," she praised him. Then she curtsied deeply, the dance over.

He returned her to St. Denis, nodding curtly at the marquis. Piers St. Denis could hardly contain his excitement. The royal family treated Jasmine as if she were one of their own! It was not only the child, but its mother as well who would bring him power. With a broad smile he led her into the figure of the next dance.

He was, she thought, an excellent dancer. It made the evening more pleasant than she had anticipated. He suggested a small interlude after a time, fetching them chilled wine and leading her to a cushioned alcove in a window where they might sit and be restored.

"The king and his family hold you in high esteem," he told her approvingly. "You will, in time, wield a certain amount of power here at court because of your excellent connections."

"When I marry Glenkirk," she said, "I will not remain at court."

"Why do you persist in this fantasy that you will marry the earl of Glenkirk?" he demanded of her angrily. "I am the man you will marry, Jasmine. And we will make our life at court."

"My lord," she said patiently, "the choice is mine to make, as you well know. This evening is the fantasy, and it is yours, not mine!"

"I can delay your marriage indefinitely, Jasmine. The king will do it if I beg him. I can convince the king to change his mind and give you to me," the marquis threatened.

She laughed. There was nothing else for it but to laugh. It was either that, or she would scream. "The king is weak where his favorites are concerned, my lord, but he will never go back on a word so publicly given," Jasmine told him with complete candor.

In response he forced her back against the stone sill of the window and kissed her fiercely. One hand dived down the low front of her dress to capture a breast and squeeze it hard. His lips worked feverishly against hers. His tongue forced its way into her mouth.

Taken unawares, Jasmine struggled with herself a moment to maintain her calm and not panic. His kiss was abhorrent. She gagged on his tongue. The hand fumbling with her breast was repellent, and he was hurting her. She would be bruised. She bit down on his tongue, shoving him away from her at the same time, then slapping him hard.

"How dare you lay hands on me!" she hissed furiously.

He tried to pinion her again, but Jasmine, ready for him this time, shoved her knee hard into his groin. Hearing his gasp of both pain and surprise, she pushed him aside to escape from the windowed alcove. Grasping at the skirt of her gown, he momentarily restrained her, preventing her flight.

"*You will be mine!*" he half groaned, nausea sweeping over him from the pain she had inflicted on his private parts.

"*Let go of my gown, my lord,*" she said through gritted teeth. "What must I do to convince you that I do not welcome your suit? Must I kill you, my lord? I am fully capable of it, you know. I personally hanged Rowan Lindley's murderer in the very same hour as my husband's death." Jasmine's anger rose. "You repel me, my lord. I would just as soon slit your handsome throat as look at you! I will not play this game any longer! I will, under no circumstances, marry you, my lord St. Denis!" Then, with a determined hand, she smacked his grip away and moved off swiftly across the hall.

Reaching the area where the royal family was seated, she curtsied low to the king. Her color was very high. "My liege?" she said in a quiet, but firm voice obviously directed at James Stuart.

"Aye, lassie, what is it?" he asked her.

"My lord, I beg you, do not force me to wed with the marquis of Hartsfield," she said, sinking dramatically to her knees.

"Nah, nah, lassie, I said the choice was to be yers," the king replied, genuinely distressed by her flamboyant action.

"Then I beg you, accept my decision in the matter. Your Majesty was absolutely right two years ago when your chose James Leslie for my husband. I need a man to whom I can look up, and I do look up to the earl of Glenkirk. I need a man whom I can love, and who loves me. That man is the earl of Glenkirk. I have pledged myself to him before God Almighty; and having to endure the embraces of another man seeking to have me to wife under such circumstances makes me feel as if I am being dishonorable. Please, I plead with Your Majesty to accept my decision in this matter! I will not take any man for my husband but James Leslie, the earl of Glenkirk!

"I know how Your Majesty values the friendship of the marquis of Hartsfield. That is why I ask that you choose another suitable woman for his wife. If you love him, as I know you do, then find him a wife who will honor him and appreciate Your Majesty's kindness, *and* the marquis of Hartsfield as well. Unfortunately, that woman is not me. You have said that the choice of a husband is mine. I can say no more plainly than I have said that it is James Leslie whom I choose."

"God's foot," murmured George Villiers to the queen, "she has chanced all with a single throw of the dice! What incredible style!"

The king sat stupefied, not certain of what he should do. He had promised Jasmine the choice. He had promised Piers St. Denis the opportunity to court her; but here she was, troublesome lassie, refusing to cooperate once again. She had made it so publicly plain that she would not have St. Denis, poor sweet laddie, that he really couldn't force her to continue to accept the marquis's advances.

"Father?" Young Charles Stuart spoke softly to his sire. The king started. "Aye, my bairn, what is it?"

"While Lady Lindley has made her decision sooner than you would have wished, I think you knew she would choose Glenkirk in the end. The marquis is foolish if he believed otherwise, for in his heart he surely knew it also. Be gracious and generous, as only you know how, Father. I like Lady Lindley, and Hal loved her deeply. He would want you to give her this boon, and I know he liked Glenkirk."

"The boy is right," the queen interjected softly.

"Aye, my dear lord, he shows wisdom for one so young," Villiers said, ignoring the fierce, irritated look the prince shot him, which plainly said that he didn't need, or want, George Villiers's help. Villiers forced back the smile that threatened to crack his lips. Prince Charles was jealous of him, he well knew, but eventually he would win over the younger man. James Stuart was nearing the end of his life, but Charles Stuart would be England's next king. George Villiers intended to be on his good side when he inherited the throne.

The king heard them all. He looked at Jasmine, her royal blue skirts spread about her as she knelt before her, her dark head bowed. What a troublesome wench she was, he thought, but his son was right. Henry Stuart had adored her. He would want her happy, and if Glenkirk was the man to make her happy, then so be it. "Verra well, Lady Lindley," he grumbled at her. "Glenkirk it is, and God help the puir man wi such a headstrong lassie for his wife. Still, I suppose he knows what he is getting. But ye may nae go from court until he returns from Scotland. I want to see my grandson again before ye both return north." James Stuart held out his hand to Jasmine, and she kissed it gratefully.

"Thank you, Your Majesty," she said. *"Thank you!"*

"Steenie, help her up, for pity's sake, and dance wi her. Lady Manners won't mind as it is a royal command. I hae had enough for one night, and I'm going to bed."

"But my dearest, dearest lord!" The marquis of Hartsfield had finally regained himself, and stood before the king, woebegone.

"Dinna fret, Piers," the king said. "We'll find ye another nice lassie wi a good income."

"But I want Lady Lindley, sire!"

"Ye canna hae her, Piers. Now cease yer whining, laddie, and trust yer old da to make it right, eh?" He got to his feet. "Come and help me to my bed, Piers. I am exhausted wi all this fuss." He leaned heavily on the younger man.

"I'll go with you," the queen said, standing quickly, and offering the marquis a patently false sympathetic smile.

"I don't want to dance another step, Steenie," Jasmine told him. "Escort me to my barge. My servant is waiting." She took his arm as they walked through the crowded hall. A path opened before them, and the whispers, quite discernible, hummed all about them.

"Well, my dearie," Villiers said with a chortle as they were finally clear of the hall, "you have caused quite the most delicious scandal this night. What on earth made you do it? It was a dangerous ploy that very well might have gone against you."

"I don't like St. Denis to begin with," Jasmine told the king's young favorite, "but he attempted to make love to me, and I found it most distasteful. I knew then I could not play this game another moment until my Jemmie returned. Imagine keeping St. Denis completely at bay. The king did say, after all, that the choice was mine."

"And a damned good thing he did," Villiers noted. "Piers St. Denis appears to be totally obsessed with you, madame. I suspect he would have done almost anything to have you had the king not made the decision yours and yours alone."

"Thank you for your help, Steenie," Jasmine said as they gained the royal quay, and her barge was rowed quickly forward. "I do not forget my friends, nor does my family forget those who have rendered them a great kindness." She took Adali's outstretched hand and stepped down into her barge. "Hurry back to the king, my gentleman of the bedchamber, lest the dreadful St. Denis steal a march on you."

"Not while the queen is there," Villiers replied with a smile. He kissed her hand. "Good night, Lady Lindley. It was a fine match, excellently played. You have my admiration. Your skirts, spread so artfully about you, was indeed the crowning touch." He turned and walked away, chuckling.

Jasmine laughed as she took her seat and watched him go. A very clever young man as she had earlier noted. He missed nothing. "Adali," she said, "we are finally free of the marquis of Hartsfield!" And then she proceeded to tell her servant the details of her evening, unaware Adali had been in the hall and seen her pleading with the king.

"Shall we be able to return to Queen's Malvern then, my lady?" Adali asked her as he draped a cloak about her shoulders to keep the chill from the night river wind from her.

"The king has requested that I remain until Jemmie returns so he may see the duke of Lundy again," she replied.

"With your permission, my lady, I shall hire extra men-at-arms to patrol Greenwood and watch the house. The marquis of Hartsfield did not appear to me to be a particularly good loser. You have publicly repudiated him. He will, unless I miss my guess, be seeking revenge."

"It's just a few weeks, Adali, and then we shall be gone," Jasmine reassured him, "but it does no harm to be cautious. Hire the extra men to guard the house and the grounds."

"A few weeks and she will be gone, my lord," Piers St. Denis said to the king. "I beg you to change your mind and give her to me!"

"Nay, Piers love, I gie my word too publicly to take it back, and I dinna think I would anyhow. Lady Lindley is too sophisticated for ye. Leave her to Glenkirk. 'Tis better that way."

The marquis of Hartsfield pouted angrily, turning his handsome face from the king in a show of both defiance and bad manners.

"We'll find you a lovely young wife with a fortune," the queen promised him. "'Twill make up for your disappointment, I'm certain."

"No!" St. Denis said vehemently. "If you would make me happy, my dear lord, and if I cannot have Jasmine Lindley, then give me the duke of Lundy to nurture and protect. Then I will know that I have not lost your favor. Do not saddle me with some young innocent and send me away, I beg of you!" He caught up the king's hand and kissed it passionately.

"*What?* Ye want my grandson's custody, too?" the king said.

"*Too?*" Piers St. Denis repeated.

"Aye. Yer the second to ask me for the bairn. The earl of Bartram came to me just the other day with the same request, Piers."

"Surely you would not give the boy to *that* man, my dear lord?" Piers St. Denis felt his pique fading away as his sense of survival and strong ambition took center stage.

"He hae served me well," the king noted, "and 'twould be a fine retirement present *if* I decide to remove my grandson from his mother's care, and I hae not yet made that decision, my sweet laddie. Dinna fret now. I will gie ye something verra nice to make up for yer loss."

"What has St. Denis lost, my liege?" George Villiers asked, coming into the king's bedchamber.

"Lady Lindley," the king replied.

"Why, sire, he never had her in the first place," Villiers chuckled. "'Twas a question of a rather mangy cat looking at a beauteous queen."

The king chortled. He simply couldn't help it. The queen was also helpless to her mirth and giggled, to the marquis's discomfort.

"Yer a bad boy, Steenie, to tease poor Piers so," the king scolded him, halfheartedly. "He hae suffered a great loss."

"Aye, the loss of Lady Lindley's great fortune!" Villiers mocked his rival, grinning impudently.

The marquis of Hartsfield's hand went to his sword, and then it fell away. To fight in the royal presence was a treasonable offense. "I harbored a great affection for the fair Jasmine," he said stiffly.

"And a greater affection for her jewels, I'll wager," Villiers riposted. "When you danced with her tonight you looked not at her, but rather at that incredible necklace of sapphires she was wearing."

"You would not dare to speak to me outside of the king's hearing in such a manner," the marquis snarled, "for you know I should avenge my honor, which you are so easily sullying, Villiers."

"Come, then," George Villiers challenged, "and let us go outside, my lord. I shall be glad to fight you."

The king looked genuinely distressed, and the queen, **alarmed**

"I should not dirty my hands with the likes of you, Villiers. A marquis of Hartsfield does not do battle with a commoner of no standing, such as yourself." Then he bowed to the king. "With Your Majesty's permission I shall withdraw."

"Aye, go home and settle yer nerves, Piers, my darling," the king said. "I'll think on what ye hae asked me."

The king's gentlemen got him ready for bed, and when he was settled, and they had left the chamber, the queen came and sat by his bedside. "You will not give little Charles Frederick Stuart to Stokes, or St. Denis, will you, Jamie? He should stay with his mother."

"Aye, and I know it, Annie," the king told her. "Am I nae called the wisest fool in Christendom?"

"Then why did ye not tell St. Denis that?" she asked.

"Och, Annie, he would only sulk more and niggle at me over it. Ye were right. I should hae nae gien him the opportunity to court Lady Lindley, especially after she had agreed to wed wi Jemmie Leslie. I but raised his hopes, then I went and made it worse by sending Jemmie off to Scotland, which distressed Jasmine. He was seriously embarrassed this evening when Lady Lindley said so loudly and so publicly that she would nae hae him for her husband."

"He deserved it," the queen said. "I saw him from across the hall mauling her in an alcove. Jasmine was not pleased by his quite boorish attentions, Jamie."

"Ahh, so that is what set her off," the king observed. "Well, 'tis water 'neath the bridge now, Annie. Dinna fear. I dinna intend taking our grandson from his mam and Glenkirk. They will raise him well. Stokes is a fool with his talk of Lady Lindley's unchaste life; and my sweet Piers underestimates me in that he thinks I dinna realize that he wants our grandson to revenge himself on Jasmine. He also thinks the bairn will gie him power here at court and over us." The king laughed, and then he said, "Perhaps he foretold his own future tonight, Annie. I believe I am grown verra tired of being torn between him and Steenie. The latter is far more biddable, do ye nae think? He was wicked to tease Piers so unmercifully. Piers doesna hae a sense of humor where he, himself, is concerned."

"Then you *do* intend to send St. Denis away!" Queen Anne could scarcely keep the excitement from her voice.

James Stuart nodded. "I am growing old, Annie. I want an absence of strife in my life. 'Tis nae an easy thing to be a king. I hae no Parliament to irritate me right now. There is peace wi Spain and France. True, the Puritans and the Scots Presbyterians seek to cause me difficulty, but I believe I hae them well in hand. Bessie and her Frederick seem happy if her letters are to be believed. As for our bairn, Charles, eventually he may make England an king. Not the king our Henry would hae been, God rest his sweet soul, but we hae no other choice, Annie, do we?

"But there are those about me, as there are about all kings, who would make unreasonable demands. Bartram's time is over, and his usefulness to me finished. He must go wi my thanks, and something that will make it appear that he is nae out of favor, just pensioned off. There is nae doubt in my heart and mind that poor Sir Thomas Overbury was murdered, and more than likely the earl and countess of Somerset were behind it. He and his Frances will remain in the Tower and out of my sight for the present. Eventually I will pardon them, but they will be exiled from my court when that day comes. I dinna want to see either of them again."

The king sighed deeply, sadly. "Ahhh, Annie, I gie my Robbie so much and look how he hae betrayed me. I now see that Piers St. Denis is cut from the same cloth. He is blindly ambitious, and that, I realize, makes him dangerous. We'll find him a good wife, then he must go back to the country estate from whence he came. I need a more amenable laddie about me. Och, I know Steenie is ambitious, too, but his nature is sweeter and more obedient. When he hints at me for a wee something, I feel if I dinna gie it to him, he would still love his old da. He reminds me a wee bit of our puir Henry."

"Unlike St. Denis," the queen said meaningfully. "You're a wise old bird, Jamie, to give St. Denis an heiress bride and send him home. You'll have no peace until you do, particularly once Glenkirk returns from Scotland and marries Jasmine."

"Jemmie will nae stay at court. He hae told me that," the king said to his wife. "He says he'll spend the autumns and winters at Glenkirk and the spring and summers at his wife's home. There is the young marquis of Westleigh to consider. He needs to be on his holding at least part of the year. And Jemmie wants bairns of his own again."

"Aye," the queen replied. "His sons would be almost grown had they not died with their poor mother all those years back. Such a terrible thing, Jamie, and they never caught the murderers, did they?"

The king shook his head in the negative. "God knows them, Annie, and they will face his retribution one day, if they have not already done so. He will render a harsher judgment, I think, for those men who attacked a nunnery and burned it to the ground after having raped and murdered the women and children within. 'Twas a dreadful crime."

The royal couple were silent a moment, remembering James Leslie's sweet first wife, Isabella Gordon, and their two sons. Then the queen arose from her husband's bedside, leaning over to give him a tender kiss.

"Good night, my dear," she said. "God give you a good rest." She curtsied to him and backed from the bedchamber. "The king will sleep now," she told the gentleman of the bedchamber, who remained on duty for the night. "See he is not disturbed except for an emergency."

"Yes, Your Majesty," the gentleman said, opening the door to the king's apartments so the queen might pass through into her own apartment next door. "Good night, madame."

"Good night," replied the queen, not looking back as the door shut behind her.

"Young Villiers is waiting for Your Majesty," said Lady Hamilton, one of her ladies-in-waiting, coming forward to greet the queen. "I put him in your private closet, madame." She curtsied.

"Very good, Jane. I will see him first, then I wish to prepare for bed. It has been a very long day." The queen passed through the salon into the privacy of a small, paneled room, where George Villiers was awaiting her. Seated by the fire toasting his toes, he jumped quickly to his feet as she entered, and bowed. "Well, Steenie," the queen said with a small smile, "St. Denis may be on his way home before long. You will say nothing to the king, however, until it is an absolute fact. He is just as apt to change his mind as not, you know."

"The secret is safe with me," George Villiers replied, his heart racing with his impending victory. He would not disappoint the king as his rival had; or Robert Carr, either.

"If you behave yourself," the queen continued, "and I do mean you must be totally loyal to His Majesty, and a total model of decorum; you could be a viscount by Christmas, Steenie. And after that, who knows? The earl of Rutland and his daughter will be very pleased to see you advancing yourself, eh?" The queen smiled coyly.

"I would one day be greater than Rutland," George Villiers said. His dark eyes danced, and his handsome face bore an intense look.

Queen Anne laughed. "How bad you are, Steenie, for all you look like an angel. I suspect if you continue to play the game as well as you have so far, that one day you may indeed rise higher than the earl of Rutland. So high, in fact, that it will appear as if you did him a great favor to marry his daughter at all," the queen finished.

"Nay, madame, I should marry Kate one day even if she were not possessed of a great fortune," George Villiers declared.

"But how fortunate it is for you, my dear Steenie, that she is possessed of a great fortune," the queen remarked knowingly.

George Villiers grinned. "Aye, madame, it is, isn't it?"

And they both laughed.

Chapter Eleven

"She has refused me! Most publicly! I am a laughingstock at court, Kipp! The bitch must be punished for her temerity, and, by God, I will see her pain!" The marquis of Hartsfield tore off his coat, flinging it across the room, and taking the large silver goblet of wine his brother offered him, gulped it.

"You knew the chance that she would have you over Glenkirk was slight," Kipp St. Denis reminded his brother. "Oh, I know you said you would win, but dammit, Piers, you had to know there was next to no chance she would change her mind. You are no fool, brother. Now tell me what the king said."

"He said he would find me a rich young wife, or rather the queen said it. There's another bitch, Kipp. Hand in glove with Villiers, if I don't miss my guess."

"A wealthy wife, handpicked by the king, is no shabby gift, little brother," Kipp attempted to soothe his sibling. "Think of the fun we'll have with her, eh?"

Piers St. Denis gulped down the contents of his goblet and handed it to Kipp for a refill. "Fun with some wellborn, and no doubt pious, virgin? One night, and she'll be beaten, Kipp. Where is the fun in that? Jasmine Lindley would have been a challenge to break because she has fire, passion, and experience. No virgin can compete with such a woman."

"You cannot refuse the king's choice of a wife for you, Piers," his brother warned him. "Whoever she is she'll be good for getting your heir on, if nothing else. We will have plenty of other women to amuse ourselves with, as we always have."

"I asked the king for her son," the marquis of Hartsfield told his brother. "I told him if he wanted to make me happy, and I could not have Jasmine, I wanted her son to nurture."

"You are mad!" Kipp exclaimed, astounded by his sibling's boldness.

"Nay! If I have the boy, I have power over Jasmine even if she won't marry me. Her weakness is her children, Kipp. She will have to do what I want to protect her child even if she is Glenkirk's wife. I shall openly make the bitch my mistress and destroy that marriage she so desires. *And,* as guardian of the king's only grandchild, albeit born on the wrong side of the blanket, I will have a certain power over James Stuart, too." His bright blue eyes gleamed wickedly in anticipation of his victory.

"The king will never give you the duke of Lundy," Kipp said flatly. "Put it from your mind, Piers, or you will suffer another embarrassing disappointment, I fear."

"The earl of Bartram has asked for the boy, too," the marquis told his surprised brother.

"And did the king tell him no?" Kipp St. Denis refilled his brother's goblet a second time.

"The king has not made up his mind," the marquis replied, sipping thoughtfully now at his wine. "Perhaps we should help him to make up his mind, Kipp, and at the same time checkmate the Leslies of Glenkirk."

"How?" Kipp St. Denis was beginning to be interested in what his brother had to say. If it was possible to snatch a victory from his brother's defeat, why not?

"What if Bartram were murdered, and the suspicion for his demise fell upon James Leslie and his new wife?" the marquis said.

"You would take a leaf from Somerset's book then?" his brother said thoughtfully. "It would have to be very well thought out, Piers."

"Aye, of course," was the reply, "but do you like my idea? Do you think it possible, Kipp? We could remove both possible guardians for the duke of Lundy in one stroke!"

"That still does not mean that the king would give you the boy," the practical Kipp said.

"Who else is there, brother? *Who else?*" the marquis exulted.

"Lady Lindley's grandmother, the old countess of Lundy," Kipp said. "She is the matriarch of her family. One of her sons is the earl of Lynmouth, another Lord Burke of Clearfields. Her son-in-law, the earl of BrocCairn, is the king's own cousin. The king likes that fierce old woman because she flatters him. He could give the child to her or any of her children."

"She would not live to see the boy grown," the marquis said. "She is already past her time, and as for her children, the king already has their love and loyalty. He does not need to do anything for them, but he does need to do something for me to recompense me for my public humiliation and my great disappointment."

"I wonder if you do not think yourself of more importance to the king than you really are, Piers," his brother considered. "Villiers, your great rival, charms the king with his sweetness and good nature. You, on the other hand, behave like a spoilt child each time you do not get your own way. Up until now the king has chosen to overlook your infantile behavior, but how long will his goodness last? He is not so big a fool as many would believe.

"When Bartram advised against giving you a Crown property, what did you do? You sulked and whined until the king was forced into offering you something of greater value, in this case, a chance to win the hand of Lady Lindley, in order to silence you. He should not have done it, but he didn't know what else to do to make you content again, so he gave both you and Villiers an opportunity.

"Your rival had the good sense to turn the king's offer down graciously, declaring his heart engaged somewhere else, then coyly admitting his passion for the very wealthy Lady Katherine Manners. You, Piers, had no such good sense. Now, having failed to gain the prize offered, you have once again gone into a fit of the sulks. The king will certainly tire of your behavior, especially in light of Villiers's sunnier disposition, brother."

"Villiers is a low-born opportunist," the marquis declared, angrily.

"Perhaps," Kipp replied, "but he has great charm, and the king to my eye is fast falling beneath his spell."

"Another reason for us to move quickly," Piers St. Denis asserted. "If I am indeed losing the king's interest, then I had best strike while I have yet the chance of getting what I want. Once I have the duke of Lundy in my possession, let Villiers have the king's attention all to himself. It will no longer matter to me, Kipp. Perhaps I shall cultivate Prince Charles. He is furiously jealous of Villiers, you know, and he is the future, not old king fool. That's it! I shall help to forge a bond between the young Charles and his royal uncle. When the elder becomes king, both shall thank me for it!"

"Now there is a better reason for obtaining custody of the boy," Kipp said. "His mother is not really important, but the lad! He is real power, little brother!"

"We are in agreement then?"

"Aye!"

"Then let us consider how best to murder the earl of Bartram, while placing the blame on the Leslies of Glenkirk, Kipp."

"Lady Lindley should be advised that the earl of Bartram is seeking to take her child from her," Kipp suggested.

"Yesss!" the marquis enthused, "and either she or Glenkirk, or possibly both of them, should face down Bartram publicly. Then when he is found dead under suspicious circumstances, the suspicion will naturally fall upon the Leslies of Glenkirk. The king shall be encouraged to remove his grandson from such unwholesome people, and *voilà! I win!* Even if Glenkirk and Jasmine are not charged with the death of Richard Stokes, the suspicion alone should do them in even as it did in Somerset and his vindictive wife."

"It will take clever planning. How much time do we have?" Kipp asked him. "When is Glenkirk due back from Scotland?"

Piers St. Denis thought a moment. "I don't really know, but he has been gone almost three weeks now. Perhaps in another ten days or more he should return. He was sent on a fool's errand, after all."

"I shall inquire about the court," Kipp said. "Discreetly, of course. You will say nothing further about the duke of Lundy lest suspicion in this crime fall on you, Piers. You do understand that, don't you? You cannot brag, even to Villiers, that you will obtain custody of the king's grandson.

No one knows but the king, I imagine, and no one else must know."

Adali had more than doubled the guards watching over Greenwood House and its parklike grounds. Would there ever come a time when his mistress was completely safe, he wondered? Perhaps this Scotland would offer the sanctuary that they sought. He prayed it would be so.

The children had arrived from Queen's Malvern, and but for the absence of James Leslie, Jasmine was happy again. Her two eldest children were much like their father in features, although they both had her dark hair. India, however, had Rowan's golden eyes, while Henry's eyes were her own turquoise. It was her second daughter, Fortune, who seemed to be the swan in the duck's nest. Fortune had bright red-gold hair, which Skye claimed had been the color of her own grandmother's hair. As the child had Skye's blue-green eyes, Jasmine had to assume her coloring came from her Celtic ancestors; and indeed she was very much like the children who had played in MacGuire's Ford, the village on Jasmine's Irish estates, and little like her elder siblings.

As for baby Charles Frederick Stuart, he was every bit a Stuart, with his auburn curls and amber eyes so like his grandfather's, the king's. Almost three, he visited the court with his brother and sisters dressed in a satin suit of orange tawny with wide collar of delicate Irish lace. He carried a miniature sword with a gold hilt decorated with tiny emeralds and topaz that had been made just for him. Sweeping off his soft-brimmed hat with its three white plumes, he bowed to the king and queen while his proud mama looked on, well pleased by her smallest child's exquisite manners. Manners, Jasmine knew, she had not instilled in her baby. She silently thanked her grandmother.

Behind the tiny duke of Lundy, who by virtue of his seniority in rank led his siblings, came Henry Lindley, marquis of Westleigh; followed by his sisters, Lady India and Lady Fortune Lindley. The young marquis was dressed like his little brother, but his suit was turquoise blue satin, his custom-made sword studded with diamonds and aquamarines. His sisters were garbed in gowns of pink silk and lavender silk. As their elder brother bowed, they curtsied deeply, rising slowly and very gracefully to the silent approval of the queen and the court ladies, considered matrons.

"We are pleased to see ye once again, my dears," the king said in kindly tones. Then he beckoned to his grandson. "Come here to me, Charlie-boy," he said, and when the little boy had clambered within reach of his grandfather, James Stuart lifted him onto his lap, and reaching out drew his son, Prince Charles, into the child's view. "This is yer uncle," he told Jasmine's smallest son. "Ye are named for him. He is Charles, too. One day, when I am dead, Charlie-boy, this Charles will be yer king, and ye must be loyal to him. Yer a Stuart, laddie, and we Stuarts may fight among ourselves, but we are always loyal to each other in the end."

"Aye, sire," the little boy responded. Then he said to the young prince. "Why you look at me?"

"Because you look so much like your father, Charlie-boy. Your father was my big brother, like Henry is your big brother," the prince said. His eyes were filled with tears.

Charles Frederick Stuart, the duke of Lundy, reached up with a small hand and brushed a tear from Prince Charles's cheek. "No cry," he said in his baby voice. "No cry, Unca."

The king pulled out a silk handkerchief and blew his own nose, while those nearest the throne who had heard the full exchange sniffled audibly. The queen struggled to hold back her own tears.

"Play ball?" The child looked hopefully up again at his uncle.

Then to the amazement of those in the hall, Prince Charles smiled, a rare occurrence indeed and, lifting the child from his father's lap, took him by the hand. "Aye, I like to play ball," he said. "Let's go out into the court, my lord duke." He looked to the nearest footman. "Fetch us a ball, man," he said, and then hand in hand the two Charles Stuarts walked from the hall, chatting as if they had always known each other quite well.

"He's a braw little laddie, madame," the king said to Jasmine. "All yer bairns are fine laddies and lassies."

"I thank Your Majesty for your kindness to my children, and in particular for the favor you have shown the duke of Lundy," Jasmine said genuinely. Then she curtsied to the royal couple and, with her three older children, withdrew from the royal presence.

"Nicely done, my dearie," George Villiers said, coming up to them shortly thereafter. "You've raised some fine kits for such a wily vixen," he said with a mischievous grin.

Jasmine laughed and introduced her children to Villiers. "The gentleman will soon reign as the king's sole favorite," she told them afterward. "It cannot hurt to have his friendship, but he warned he is not as sweetly simple as he would like you to believe."

"He has no title," her eldest son noted.

"He will eventually," Jasmine said. "The king will reward him lavishly, and young Villiers has his eyes on an heiress of excellent family. He will have to be of equal rank with her father, or even higher before she is allowed to marry him, but he will be, I have not a doubt."

"He is very beautiful," Lady India Lindley said.

"Handsome," her mother corrected. "A man is handsome, a woman beautiful, my poppet."

India shook her head. "He is past handsome, Mama. *He is beautiful!* I am an heiress, and I would marry him without a title if he would but ask me." She looked admiringly after George Villiers.

"I do not like his eyes," Lady Fortune Lindley said.

"Why not?" Jasmine asked her younger daughter, curious. It was, she thought, a rather interesting observation for a little girl.

"They are like your black pearls, Mama. They reflect the light, but I can see nothing in them," Fortune remarked.

"You are such a fool, Fortune!" India mocked her. "I think his dark eyes, like a velvet night, filled with stars."

"Gracious!" Jasmine note. "You are a very romantic child, India. I think I am going to have to keep a sharp eye on you from now on, miss!" She found her two young daughters' observations on George Villiers interesting. While she found him amusing, and certainly useful, she tended to agree with her younger daughter, but then Rowan's posthumous daughter had always been sensible from her birth, she considered thoughtfully. India, on the other hand, had a streak of willful wildness very much like Jasmine's brother, who was now the Grand Mughal of India. It was to be hoped that she would outgrow such tendencies.

Prince Charles asked that his small nephew be allowed to stay in his apartments at court with him for a few days. It would have been ungracious of Jasmine to refuse, and Charlie-boy was most anxious to remain with this newfound uncle of his. Adali personally delivered a trunk of the child's clothing to the royal apartments. The prince, serious in his religious devotions, began teaching his nephew his prayers and his letters. The little child, who had a quick mind, was an excellent student, much to his royal uncle's great pleasure.

"It is like your father's court in that the courtiers scramble for the king's attention and favor," Adali wisely observed. "I suppose all royal courts are alike, my lady. Our littlest child fits in quite well, and is very much at ease with his princely uncle."

"Both of his grandfathers are kings," Jasmine observed, "and both of his uncles are or will be kings. If my not-so-royal Stuart had been born his father's heir, he would have been a king one day."

"He will have far less grief in his life being a duke," Adali said with a small smile, and his mistress laughed.

"How can you be so happy when I have been away?" James Leslie said, entering the room and surprising them both.

"Jemmie!" Jasmine squealed, and flung herself into his arms. "You're back! Ohh, now we can leave London, and go home to Queen's Malvern! Hooray! Hooray!" Then she kissed him hard, molding her body against his. "Did you miss me, my lord?" she murmured softly, nuzzling against the side of his neck. It was damp, and he had the aroma of horses about him, but beneath it she could scent James Leslie, her Jemmie.

She felt wonderful in his arms. God, he had missed her! He tipped her face up to his, saying, "Another kiss, madame. I am weary with longing for you." Then his mouth descended on hers, tasting the softness of her lips, her perfume, the night-blooming jasmine, enveloping him in its seductive scent. She yielded so sweetly in his arms, and, when he finally released her, his head faintly spinning, he grinned happily. "May I take it then that you have missed me, madame?"

She nodded. "And I have sent the marquis of Hartsfield packing, Jemmie! Most publicly, too. He will not come near me again, I vow."

"*The king?*" His tone was just slightly concerned.

"Ohh, the king understood perfectly once I explained it to him," Jasmine replied breezily. "And the children are all here! Charlie-boy has been at court with Prince Charles, who has taken a great liking to our little laddie; and Henry, India, and Fortune have made very good impressions on everyone. Why I've had a number of very serious inquiries regarding marriage for them; but now we can go home!"

The earl of Glenkirk turned to Adali. "What should I know?" he asked the household steward. "Or rather, what hasn't she told me?"

"Jemmie!" Jasmine looked somewhat aggrieved.

Adali grinned, then chuckled. "Actually, my lord, it is just as she has said. You were scarcely gone when the marquis was on our doorstep. He came to take my mistress on an outing. Naturally I accompanied them. Then my good lady caught a chill out on the river that turned into an ague, and could not see the marquis for several days."

Glenkirk snickered. What a clever wench Jasmine was.

"Then the queen had a masque," Jasmine took up the tale, "and the marquis aroused my ire by luring me into an alcove, and putting his hands all over me as if he owned me! I was forced to take drastic action, Jemmie."

The earl of Glenkirk winced, imagining the action she had taken to disengage her unwanted suitor. "Did you geld him forever?"

"Only temporarily," Jasmine replied. "I went immediately to the king and asked him to release me from St. Denis's unwanted attentions."

"She knelt," Adali told the earl. "She prostrated herself before Their Majesties, her skirts spread all about her. It was quite dramatic, my lord, and the king was very moved. Even I could see it from my place at the back of the hall."

"Jasmine!" James Leslie didn't know whether to be angry or not.

"Well, it wasn't fair!" Jasmine declared. "I'm in love with one man, and planning to wed him in just another two weeks, and I'm saddled with an unwanted suitor, Jemmie, who leers at me constantly and paws at me like a stableboy with a dairymaid. I've had enough of everyone telling me what to do! When I leave London I'm never coming back again! I hate the court with all its pretentions! And I don't enjoy most of the people who inhabit the court either. I didn't like my father's court, and I like this one little better, Jemmie. I just want to be your wife and a mother to my children. And, of course, I want to involve myself in Grandma's trading company. We must bring tea to England, and make it popular as the Spanish have done with chocolate, which I think a nasty drink. And there are the horses being raised at MacGuire's Ford to consider. And there is your own Glenkirk Castle to be looked after, too. We have so much to do together, Jemmie, and there can be no time for court and all its attendant silliness. And somewhere along the way we must have several bairns of our own," she finished.

"Aye," he agreed with her. "We must indeed have several bairns, madame. I am glad you have remembered that wifely duty amid all your wonderful plans for importing tea and raising horses," he chuckled.

"Ohh, Jemmie, the bairns come first, I swear it!" she promised.

"Good!" he replied. "Now, Adali, I want a hot bath and a good dinner, and I want to see the children. Then, madame, it will be an early night for us," he finished meaningfully.

"The children first, my lord," Adali said wisely. He knew that once the bath and the dinner came, there would be no time for anything but passion between Jasmine and James Leslie. Bowing, he hurried off to gather up Henry, India, and Fortune, who were delighted to learn that the earl of Glenkirk had returned from his trip to Scotland.

Racing ahead of Adali, they dashed into the library, where their mother and the earl were awaiting them. "Papa! Papa!" they squealed, flinging themselves at him simultaneously. Laughing, the earl bent down, and gathered them into his embrace. "So, my wee trio of rascals, you are glad to see me, are you?" he said with a broad smile. "Well, I've missed you, too!"

"We've been to court, Papa!" Henry said. "Charlie-boy led us in, and the king greeted us personally. He looks so sad, but I like him. And I bowed, just like you taught me!"

"And the girls curtsied beautifully," Jasmine said, making certain that her daughters did not feel left out.

"Did you bring us a present from Scotland, Papa?" India asked.

"Papa was on the king's business, greedy one," Henry said. "There is no time for presents when a man is on king's business."

"Oh?" The earl feigned surprise. "Then you do not want the gift I have brought you, Henry?"

"You really brought us gifts?" Henry Lindley's face was all boyish excitement. "What did you bring us?"

"A fine dirk for you, Henry, and silver thistle necklaces for my lasses," the earl said, producing the items from his pocket.

"Nothing for me?" Jasmine teased him.

"I will give you your gift in private later," James Leslie said, his green-gold eyes meeting her turquoise ones. Then he carefully fastened a thistle necklace first about India's neck, and then Fortune's. "See, lassies, each thistle has a tiny amethyst for a flower head."

"I will keep my necklace always," Fortune said adoringly as she looked up at the man who was to be her father.

He gave her a little hug and kissed her cheek gently.

"You chose well," India noted. "I like jewelry, Papa."

"Most ladies do, I have found," he replied, giving her a hug and a kiss, too. His eye then went to Henry Lindley, who was delightedly examining the small silver dagger with the carved bone handle.

The boy looked up. "'Tis a fine weapon, sir," he said slowly. "Will you show me how to use it? And you won't forget my fencing lessons?"

"We shall begin them when we reach Queen's Malvern," the earl said. "And this winter, when we are at Glenkirk, you shall have lessons every day except Sunday, Henry."

"Come along now, children," Adali said. "Your papa has ridden far and is tired. He wants a bath, his supper, and his bed. Bid your parents a good evening." He shepherded them from the library.

"How good you are to them," Jasmine said. "It makes me love you all the more, Jemmie Leslie. I shall give you fine sons, for you are a man who obviously loves children."

"I have a painted ball for Charlie-boy I found in a street stall in Edinburgh," he responded. Then, reaching out, he pulled her into his lap as he sat down by the fire. "I missed you," he told her simply, "and I agree that there is really no need for us to come to London again. Will you truly be happy if you don't, Jasmine? I love you so deeply that the very thought of your unhappiness gives me pain, my wild lassie." He nuzzled the top of her dark head.

Safe. The word popped unbidden into her head. She was safe at last, Jasmine realized. But then she had been safe with Rowan until his life had been snuffed out by a madman. She had lost two husbands to violence, and a young lover to an unnecessary and premature death. Surely this time it would be all right. Had not her own grandmother lost five husbands before she married Adam de Marisco? *It would be all right.* "You stink of horses, and now so do I," she said, sliding from his lap. "Adali certainly must have your bath ready, or at least being prepared."

"I don't have to go back to Lynmouth House then?" he teased.

"I will never be separated from you again, Jemmie Leslie," she told him and, taking him by the hand, led him upstairs to her own apartments, where the large old iron-bound oak tub had been set up before the fire in the dayroom. "I shall maid you, sir," she told him, and began pulling his boots off, then his damp, knit woolen stockings.

"And I you," he replied, seating her and drawing her shoes from her narrow, high-arched feet.

Jasmine stood and removed his doublet and his shirt. He removed her bodice and her chemise, pulling her against him for a brief moment to feel the softness of her breasts against his darkly furred chest. Drawing away reluctantly, Jasmine unbuttoned his breeches and slid them over his narrow hips, past his shapely calves to his ankles. He stepped from the garment and kicked it away. Then he undid the tapes of her skirt first and the several petticoats she wore beneath it, lifting her from them when they puddled about her ankles. Naked now but for her stockings, Jasmine pulled his drawers off, and he kicked them too across the chamber. Kneeling, he slipped her garters down her legs, then rolled her silk stockings off, sliding them from her feet as she lifted each one in turn.

He pressed his face against her smooth belly, his breathing very ragged. Then, standing, he took her face between his two hands, and said, "I can't wait, darling Jasmine. I must take the edge off my appetite for you. It has been the longest month of my life!"

"Mine also," she told him, reaching out to caress him. He was rock hard and practically throbbing with his desire. Jasmine drew him down to the floor between the fireplace and the tub. Lying upon her back, she opened herself to him in sweet invitation, reaching out to draw him into her embrace.

With a groan he pushed himself into her, finding to his delight that she was hot, and wet, and very, very welcoming. "Ahhh, God!" he moaned thickly as his manhood slid deep, and she wrapped her legs about him, encouraging him onward. His hunger for her seemed to increase rather than ease as they found the passionate rhythm of love together.

Jasmine sighed deeply as the thick column of flesh delved into the deepest recesses of her very being. She took her pleasure of him shamelessly; the walls of her sheath tightening and releasing him, causing him to cry out with unabashed delight as she gave back every bit as much as she took. Her fingers dug strongly into the muscles of his back, her nails lightly raking him.

"It's too much," he half sobbed, and exploded his tribute within her, but Jasmine was with him, already soaring and utterly replete with her own satisfaction as their lips met in a scorching kiss.

They lay side by side afterward upon the carpet, the fire cracking practically atop them, fingers entwined. Speaking in soft voices, they both agreed that they were utterly shameless, then they laughed together, happy and perfectly pleased with themselves.

"Now we really do need a bath," Jasmine murmured. Her thighs were smeared with his love juices, which had been extremely copious. If it had ever occurred to her that James Leslie might have been unfaithful to her while he was away, that thought was quickly dispelled by the evidence of her eyes and the abundance of his creamy passion.

He somehow managed to get to his feet, drawing her up with him. "I have never had such desire for a woman as I do for you, darling Jasmine," he told her candidly. "I am not even certain being your husband will rid me of my hunger for you."

Jasmine climbed into the tub and beckoned him to join her. "You flatter me, Jemmie Leslie," she said. "I am just a woman."

The earl of Glenkirk laughed. "You will never be *just* a woman, my darling Jasmine," he told her. "Now, madame, wash my back like a good wife should, and afterward I shall reward you for your efforts."

Jasmine giggled. "I am not your wife yet, my lord. I should far prefer to be rewarded like a good mistress would. Mistresses, I am told, have more fun than wives."

"Not in my house," he riposted wickedly.

Adali entered the apartment in the company of Rohana and Toramalli. He bore a silver basin of perfumed water, and an armful of small white linen cloths, which he took into the bedchamber. The maidservants carried trays of food, which they placed upon a rectangular table.

"Ohhh," Jasmine sniffed. "That smells delicious. What have you brought us?" She scrambled from the tub to be dried by Rohana.

"Cook has sent up a variety of foods, m'lady," Rohana told her, toweling Jasmine, then powdering her. "She thought m'lord would enjoy a hearty supper as he had ridden far today according to Fergus More, who is in the kitchens eating now." She helped Jasmine into a cream-colored chamber robe. Then she moved on to help Toramalli who was drying a slightly embarrassed Lord Leslie, who could not quite get used to being attended at his bath by pretty women.

Jasmine began lifting the lids upon the dishes. There was a dish of cold, raw oysters in cracked ice, and seawater; a thick rich stew of rabbit in a winey brown gravy with scallions, sliced carrots, and new peas; a roasted capon; a medium-sized trout, steamed in white wine, and set upon a bed of cress; a small ham; a bowl of new lettuce from the kitchen garden; fresh bread warm from the oven; a crock of sweet butter; a quarter wheel of Brie already runny upon its silver platter; and, finally, a bowl of tiny new strawberries with a pitcher of clotted Devon cream. She hummed approval. "Tell Mrs. Davis her menu is well appreciated, Adali," Jasmine said.

"Will you want me to serve?" he inquired politely.

"Yes," she surprised him. "Send for the footmen to empty the tub, and have it put away. Then we will eat."

The servingmen came, each carrying two buckets, and the tub was quickly emptied, then stored away, the drain in its side being carefully replaced. Rohana and Toramalli set up the table before the dayroom fire, and Adali quickly served his master and his mistress both food and wine. He then withdrew with the women. James Leslie ate with a good appetite, as did Jasmine. She filled his goblet several times with wine, and soon between the heat of the fire, the excellent meal, and the long day's ride, he began to nod.

"Come," she said to him, rising. "You need to sleep, my dear lord," and she led him to the bedchamber where he fell into bed, asleep almost before his head touched the pillows. With an indulgent smile Jasmine banked the fire, tucked the coverlet about him, and climbed into the bed next to James Leslie, snuggling against him even as his arm instinctively reached out to enfold her in his embrace.

When the earl of Glenkirk awoke, it was already past sunrise, and Jasmine was dressed. Adali handed him a saucer of steaming tea, and, to his great surprise, he found it most refreshing. As Jasmine's servant helped him to dress, Jasmine chattered at him happily.

"We must go to court this morning and bid the king and queen farewell, Jemmie. Then, tomorrow, we can begin our journey to Queen's Malvern. The servants are already packing, and I am taking the staff home with us since I will never again return to London. Grandmama will find places for them, I know, and I will not leave them here after all their years of faithful service to the family. Greenwood House will be closed up. Perhaps I shall even sell it as it will be mine one day."

"If you sell it," the earl observed, "then your family, who do like to come up to London, will have no place to stay, Jasmine."

"Let them stay at Lynmouth House," she responded.

"Would you wish your Aunt Willow on your Uncle Robin?" he teased her. "What if they both needed to be in town at the same time?"

She thought a moment, then laughed. "Oh, very well, Jemmie, but I'm closing the house, and if someone needs to use it, let them open it, and pay the cost. I'm only leaving the gatekeeper and his wife, to look after it, and see the park is maintained. Now, hurry, and dress, my lord!"

"I'm hungry again," he complained. "I will go nowhere, madame, until I have been fed again."

"Toramalli, find some food for Lord Leslie," Jasmine ordered; and when it came, she ate with every bit as good an appetite as he did.

Their carriage drew up before the door of Greenwood House, and the earl of Glenkirk and Jasmine rode the distance to Whitehall. They were dressed richly but conservatively. The earl in dark green silk breeches, cream and gold showing through the slashes on his doublet. Jasmine in a gown of apple green and gold brocade with a creamy wide lace collar; a necklace of topaz and gold about her throat.

The king's face lit up with pleasure as they entered the hall. "Jemmie!" he called to them. "Yer back safe, I see."

The earl of Glenkirk bowed low to the king as Jasmine curtsied.

"I am, my liege, and happy to tell you that Scotland eagerly awaits a visit from James Stuart," James Leslie said. "Now, Your Majesty, I come to take my leave of you, and Her Majesty. I have a wedding to attend in several days, and must return to Queen's Malvern before the old countess of Lundy sends out a search party for me."

The king nodded. "Lady Lindley hae made quite clear to us that her choice of a husband is ye, Jemmie, and nae other. Is that nae so, madame?" His amber eyes were twinkling.

"Yes, my liege," Jasmine said meekly.

"Hah!" The king barked. "Ye were nae so mild-mannered, and humble just a day or more back when ye said it, and broke puir Piers St. Denis's heart, madame. Now I must find him a prize to equal ye, and I dinna know what I hae to offer the puir laddie."

"It is true," the earl of Glenkirk interposed before Jasmine might say anything to get herself in trouble, "that my bride is a jewel beyond price; nonetheless *anything* Your Majesty would choose for the marquis of Hartsfield would surely more than equal Jasmine's hand, coming as it will from Your Majesty."

The faintest smile touched the king's lips at James Leslie's words. He knew when he was being cajoled, and yet the earl's words, so publicly spoken, would force his darling Piers to accept whatever James Stuart offered him to assuage his disappointment over Jasmine. He nodded at the earl, murmuring, "Nicely done, Jemmie. I'll miss ye." Then he continued for the consumption of his court. "We will be sorry to see ye both go, but we understand that ye must leave us."

"We are both Your Majesty's loyal servants, and will come should you need us," the earl of Glenkirk promised the king.

"Aye, aye!" The king arose. "Come wi me, Jemmie Leslie. I want a more detailed report from ye in private." He looked at Jasmine. "'Twill gie ye time, madame, to say yer good-byes to yer friends, eh?"

Jasmine curtsied again. "Thank you, Your Majesty," she said.

"I will return for you when I am done," the earl told Jasmine. "Try and stay out of trouble, darling Jasmine, while I am with His Majesty, eh?" He blew her a kiss with his fingertips and followed after the king, who was making his way from the hall.

The queen had overheard, and laughed softly. "He knows you well, doesn't he, my dear? I think you should have a very interesting marriage if you can survive each other."

"I shall miss Your Majesty," she said quietly. "You are the only friend I have at court to say good-bye to, madame."

"What? Am I not your friend?" George Villiers demanded, pretending to be greatly aggrieved. He stood in the space between both the king's throne, and the queen's throne.

Now it was Jasmine's turn to laugh. "Oh, Steenie, of course you are my friend, too. I would have enjoyed watching you climb to great heights, but if I promise sometimes to write to you, will you write me back and tell me of all your triumphs?" She gave him her hand. "Once, I am told, my Uncle Conn was called the handsomest man at court. I believe, sir, that you now possess his mantle. He was not, however, as circumspect as I suspect you are. The queen had to marry him off to keep him out of trouble."

George Villiers took the elegant hand offered him, noting as he did the beautiful rings upon her fingers, each worth, he would wager, a king's ransom. He kissed the slender hand, then said, "You may trust that I am your friend, madame, and if you are kind enough to take the time to write to me, I shall most certainly correspond with you, telling you all the lovely gossip you will miss by running off to live in the country. Will you really spend winters in Scotland?"

She nodded. "Aye."

"Do you like rain and mist?" he wondered aloud.

"Why?" she asked.

"Because, I am told, there is much mist in Scotland, and it does rain a great deal. Is that not so, Majesty?" He turned to the queen.

Queen Anne nodded. "You get used to it," she said.

"What a charming scene," a voice next to them suddenly sneered.

Jasmine, recognizing the marquis of Hartsfield, did not bother to turn about. Her eyes, however, filled with anger.

"Good day to you, Your Majesty," Piers St. Denis said, pointedly ignoring George Villiers.

"Good day, my lord," the queen responded politely, but she wondered what he wanted. Probably to cause some trouble, she thought. He really was a bad loser.

"And where has your lover gone, madame?" The voice was cutting.

"My lord is with the king, although that should be no business of yours, my lord," Jasmine responded, still not bothering to look at him.

"Undoubtedly the king is telling him that your little bastard is to be given away to be raised by someone more *suitable* than yourself," the marquis said cuttingly. "I, myself, have asked for the child, and would make him an excellent guardian, madame, for I should raise him here at court with his grandparents, and his uncle to influence him, and to be about him. Not remove him into the wilds of Scotland, where he will undoubtedly grow up like a barbarian and not a prince's son."

Jasmine grew pale, and she finally turned about to look into Piers St. Denis's handsome face. "*Suitable?* You consider yourself fit to raise *my* son? *You?* A man who cannot, I have been informed, obtain pleasure from a woman unless you abuse her? I would kill you, or anyone else who attempted to remove my son, or any of my children from my care!" Jasmine snarled. "You, my lord, are not fit to raise *any* child!"

The marquis of Hartsfield had flushed when she had publicly revealed what he considered his secret vice, but before he could retaliate, the queen's voice spoke with certain knowledge.

"Jasmine, my dear, do not listen to him. The king is not giving *any* of your children to Piers St. Denis. He is more than well aware of the marquis's foibles and frailties." She put a hand out to comfort the younger woman. Then she turned an angry eye on the marquis. "Sir, you overstep your position!"

Piers St. Denis was astounded by the rebuke, and but angered further, and yet the queen had played into his hands if she had known it. "If not me, madame," he said, "then perhaps it is the earl of Bartram who shall have the lad. I have, myself, heard him importune the king over the boy's custody." He looked again at Jasmine. "Lord Stokes believes you unchaste, madame. He says a woman of mixed blood should not be allowed to raise a Christian prince's son, no matter which side of the blanket he was born on. He even questions your heritage, for were you not born to your father when your mother was yet wed to the earl of BrocCairn, Lady Lindley? That would make you a bastard, too, wouldn't it?"

She hit him; and the exquisite, large, oval-shaped Golconda diamond that she wore on the middle finger of her right hand cut the marquis of Hartsfield's face from the corner of his right eye to the right hand corner of his mouth. "I am a trueborn princess of India, my lord," she told the bleeding man in icy, even tones that never rose beyond a conversational pitch. "'Tis you, I fear, who are the bastard! And I say again to you, and *anyone* else who is interested, that I will kill any man who attempts to steal my children, *any of my children,* away from me. I am their mother. I am their guardian, and there is none fitter than I to raise them!" Now it was she who smiled at the marquis of

Hartsfield. "I fear, my lord, that you will never again be as handsome as you were before you accosted and slandered me this day. What a pity." Then Jasmine turned, curtsied to the queen, and began to make her way from the hall. Her heart was pounding with her anger. How dare James Stuart once again attempt to interfere in her life! She did not hear the queen calling after her, but instead her eye lit upon the earl of Bartram, who was just entering the hall, his normally reclusive wife upon his arm.

Jasmine blocked their entry. "How dare you attempt to steal my son from me, my lord!" she almost shouted at him. "Well, neither you, or your mealy-mouthed Puritan wife shall have him!" Then she pushed past the couple, departing the hall.

Behind her the countess of Bartram fainted, so frightened was she by the turquoise-eyed virago who had just confronted her. She would later swear hellfire had leapt from Jasmine's eyes. Her husband struggled to keep his spouse from collapsing upon the floor, but Mary Stokes was not quite the slip of a girl she had once been.

Queen Anne wanted to laugh, and she could see that Steenie did, too, but they somehow managed to control themselves. She handed the bleeding marquis of Hartsfield her own handkerchief. His doublet was already ruined. "You will live, my lord," she said dryly.

"I want her arrested!" he cried, petulantly.

"No," the queen said in implacable tones. "You deliberately told her something that was not true, my lord. You did it to cause trouble and for no other reason. You are angry that she has refused you in favor of James Leslie, but how could you not have known her feelings even when my dearest husband was foolish enough to offer ye a chance with her. Steenie knew, and was wise enough to avoid the confrontation, but not you. Your greed, not just for Lady Lindley's wealth, but for the power you thought controlling her children would bring you, has instead brought you the disaster you so richly deserve. You no longer have my friendship, my lord. *And,* I will be certain to tell the king of your penchant for wickedness. I will advise my husband not to entrust you with any young girl of good family, my lord. God only knows what would happen to her in your care! Now, he gone from my sight!"

George Villiers manfully struggled to maintain his composure as he watched the marquis of Hartsfield slink from the hall. *I have won!* he thought gleefully, *and I hardly had to do a thing. What a fool St. Denis is to have destroyed himself. Granted, he would never have won the hand of Jasmine Lindley, but he might have come out of this with a rich wife, the simpleminded gudgeon. Now he will have nothing for all his trouble—and I didn't have to do a thing to accomplish this end!* A small chuckle escaped him.

"Restrain yourself, Steenie," the queen said quietly. "Smugness does not become you, sir."

"Yes, Majesty," George Villiers replied meekly, but his heart was soaring with his victory.

Chapter Twelve

"Did I not warn you to silence, little brother?" Kipp St. Denis scolded the marquis of Hartsfield. "You have lost Queen Anne's favor, and now will probably lose the king's as well. You have gained nothing from this sojourn at court, which has cost us so dearly. The world was within your grasp, Piers, and you flung it away for the mere chance to torment Lady Lindley because she preferred another husband to you. Father always said you were a childish fool."

"It was our father who squandered almost all our resources, leaving our mother to die in virtual penury," Piers St. Denis snarled. "Besides, not all is lost. I can still beg the king's forgiveness. I have become quite the expert at begging, Kipp. And remember, we have not yet put the rest of our plan into action."

"You have lost the game," Kipp replied. "The duke of Lundy will remain with the earl and countess of Glenkirk."

"Not if it is believed they have murdered Lord Stokes," the marquis said softly. "And Jasmine has played right into our hands, Kipp, by publicly declaring she would kill anyone who tried to take her children from her care. If Stokes is found dead, she will be the first one who is considered the murderer, and Lord Leslie, too, will be named her accomplice. The child will be removed from their care, and they will certainly end up with Somerset and his shrewish wife in the Tower."

"Even if you can attain this goal, there is no guarantee that you will be given the duke of Lundy, particularly now that the queen has made clear her dislike of you, Piers. Attempt to mend your fences with the king so you may gain something out of this before we must leave court. Snatch a small victory from this defeat."

"*I will have the child!* You should have seen the smug look on that upstart Villiers's face, Kipp. I could have easily killed him had the queen not been there! I must have the child, Kipp. His income will save us. You know how little money there is left. I don't want to leave court and return to Hartsfield Hall. I hate the damned country! I want to be here, in the center of the universe, where there is so much excitement happening. To be at court is to be alive, Kipp!"

"We haven't the money to remain indefinitely, Piers," his brother reminded him. "If you don't get an heiress bride out of this, we are ruined! This was why we originally came to court. That you caught the king's eye was a gift from God. You need a rich wife to restore Hartsfield Hall *and* to remain at court. Without one we are lost; and the king is your only hope to obtain that wealthy wife. You are angry, and you want revenge upon the earl of Glenkirk and Jasmine Lindley. I understand, and perhaps one day you will gain your revenge, *but now is not the time.*"

"You have been watching the earl of Bartram, Kipp," the marquis said as if his elder brother had not spoken at all. "Is he out at night? That would, of course, be the best time to waylay him. We shall do it ourselves, so there be no witnesses."

"There is no time to plan such a crime, Piers," Kipp said in a final attempt to dissuade his sibling. "Certainly now that the earl of Glenkirk has returned from Scotland, he will be taking Lady Lindley to her grandmother's home in Worcestershire for their wedding."

"We will kill the earl of Bartram tonight," the Marquis of Hartsfield said calmly. "Glenkirk and his bitch will still be here tonight."

There would be no convincing his brother otherwise, Kipp St. Denis knew. The plan was surely flawed, but Piers would follow the course set, and Kipp could not refuse to help him. It would be up to him to make certain that the marquis of Hartsfield was never tied to the crime about to be committed, so that the king would award his previous favorite a rich maiden to marry, and they could be saved. Kipp did not believe for a moment that they would obtain custody of the little duke of Lundy. The queen had more influence with her husband than the young men surrounding James Stuart thought. That had been his brother's error. He had refused to see it, and had made an enemy of Queen Anne in the process. George Villiers, however, had seen how the land lay and used his knowledge wisely. Kipp well knew how arrogant and thoughtless Piers could be. Eventually the marquis would see there was no future for him at court. Then they could go home, taking the wealthy bride with them.

The king had just arisen the following morning and, having peed in the silver vessel held out by one of his gentlemen of the bedchamber for that purpose, was greeted with the news that the earl of Bartram had been found murdered outside his own gates that morning. James Stuart was deeply shocked and demanded an immediate explanation. He was told that no one knew.

"How was he killed?" the king asked.

"A knife, my liege, expertly placed between his ribs to pierce his heart," was the answer. "The gatekeeper swears he heard no cry."

"Who is responsible?" was the next royal query.

"It is not known, sire."

"What was he doing outside of his own gates, then?" the king wondered. "It was night, I assume."

"Lady Mary says he received a message, handwritten, just before they were to retire. The earl said he had some quick business to attend and should be back shortly. He told his wife to go to bed, which, being a dutiful woman, she did. When she awoke this morning she saw that her husband had not returned and sent to the gatekeeper to ask if he had seen his lordship. The gatekeeper remembered letting Lord Stokes out and watching him walk down the roadway around a bend. He saw nothing and heard nothing. He had fallen asleep awaiting his master's return. After being questioned by his mistress, the gatekeeper went back outside and, passing through the gate, walked down the road. He found Lord Stokes dead just around the bend in the pathway," was the explanation.

"And where is the note that drew the earl of Bartram from the safety of his house?" the king said. "Where is it?"

"It cannot be found, Your Majesty. Lady Mary does recall that he did not toss the missive in the fire. She thinks he tucked it in his pocket, but she is not certain. It was not, however, in his pocket."

"It would appear," the king said, "that Dickie hae an enemy, eh, gentlemen? Now, who should want the puir man dead?"

"Lady Lindley said she would kill any man who took her children from her, my lord," the king's page piped up. "I heard her say it!"

There was a general murmuring about the king's bedchamber as his gentlemen helped their lord to dress. "Aye!" "I heard it, too!"

"Everyone at court heard it," the king said with a chuckle. "She hae a fierce temper, Jasmine Lindley, but I dinna believe she was the person who lured puir Dickie to his death. She hae no reason, laddies."

"The rumor was you were giving the duke of Lundy to the earl of Bartram to raise, my liege," a gentleman said.

"The rumor was a false one," the king told them. "When she left the hall she stormed into my privy chamber and demanded to know if it were so. I reassured her that it was nae so, and she need hae nae fear. Her bairns were hers to raise as long as they respected my royal authority. I hae finished my business wi Glenkirk by then, and so I instructed him to take her home, marry her, and gie her a few sons to keep her busy," the king concluded with a small chuckle.

"Besides," George Villiers said, "Lady Lindley is a slender woman, and does not, I suspect, have much strength. How could she divert poor Stokes long enough to murder him with a knife? She might have wounded him, but the report is that the knife was skillfully placed to cause instant death. What woman would know such a trick, gentlemen?"

"She is a foreigner," one gentleman said. "And what about that turbaned servant of hers? He looks to me to be a dangerous fellow."

"Lady Lindley is an Englishwoman no matter where she was born," the king said. "I am England's king, and yet, sirs, I am Scots-born. As for her servant, Adali, while he is devoted to her, he is nae a murderer. He is a eunuch, gentlemen, and we know a gelded man is nae a savage, but rather sweet, like a lass. Nah, nah, laddies, 'twas nae Adali."

"Then who was it?"

"Perhaps we should look for whoever had something to gain from Lord Stokes's death," Villiers suggested. "Or someone who thought he might gain if the earl of Bartram were no longer here."

"Steenie," the king said, "ye must go and speak wi poor Dickie's widow and see if she can shed any light on this matter."

But George Villiers could learn nothing from Mary Stokes that would aid them in their investigation of the murder. The poor woman had convinced herself, aided by the clergyman who was with her, that it was Jasmine Lindley who was responsible for Richard Stokes's death. The king's favorite carefully explained to the half-hysterical widow that the king was convinced it was not Jasmine, and told her the reasons why.

"Lady Lindley had no reason to harm your husband, madame," he concluded. "She had no quarrel with him."

"S-she threatened my Dickon because the king was to give us the duke of Lundy to raise decently," Lady Mary wept.

"The king told Lady Lindley before she left court yesterday that rumor was not true, madame; and I, myself, was there when he told your husband that the boy was to remain with his mother and his stepfather. I tell you again that Lady Lindley had no reason to murder anyone. The king believes her and all connected with her innocent in this matter."

"We must accept the king's word, my good lady," the clergyman said to Mary Stokes. "James Stuart, though misguided, is a good man."

"But if that terrible woman did not kill my Dickon, Pastor Goodfellowe, then who did?" the widow wailed.

"I cannot answer you, madame, but God knows the miscreant, and will punish him with eternal hellfire! You must leave these matters to those more capable of handling them than you, yourself, madame. Now, you should concentrate on your own salvation, for death comes when we least expect it, as poor Lord Stokes found. You must be ready to meet your maker, Lady Mary," the pastor thundered in stern tones.

A Puritan, George Villiers thought, *and a dangerous one. I wonder if he might be responsible. I was there when Richard Stokes told His Majesty that he had sent his impressionable wife's clergyman packing. Lord Stokes was not a liar. Now he is dead, however, and here is this trouble-making Puritan in his house as quick as a wink, and the body not even cold. Stokes had surely put aside a little something for his old age. Some of it will go to his widow, and wouldn't this Puritan like to get his hands on the widow's mite to further his own purposes. I think I must inform the king, and the new earl of Bartram must come with all haste up from the country to protect his mother.*

Before the day was over Pastor Simon Goodfellowe was arrested and taken to the Tower to be questioned in the matter of the demise of the earl of Bartram. He denied any involvement in Richard Stokes's death, was lightly racked, but continued to proclaim his innocence. His alibi was checked, and indeed he had spent the evening praying with a family whose only son was gravely ill. The child had died at dawn and the clergyman had departed, having been called to the countess of Bartram's side by his servant. It was now obvious that he could not have had any part in the earl's murder.

"Shall we release him?" the captain of the guard asked George Villiers, who was at the Tower at His Majesty's request.

"Not yet," the young man replied. "He's a Puritan for certain. Whip him, keep him on bread and water for a week, whip him again, then let him go. By then the new earl will be in London, and his grieving but susceptible mother will be safe from the likes of Pastor Goodfellowe."

"Yes, m'lord," the captain of the guard replied.

With a nod George Villiers turned away, thinking even as he did that he very much liked the sound of *m'lord*. He must be patient, he knew. The queen said by Christmas, and he knew that she knew. Everything might have been perfect in his life but that Piers St. Denis was trying to weasel his way back into His Majesty's good graces. Villiers knew that the marquis needed a rich wife, and only the king could provide one. The queen, however, was adamant that no decent girl be put in Piers St. Denis's care.

"He is said to have unnatural desires," she told the king. "I am told he even shares his women with that villainous half brother of his, Jamie. You cannot entrust him with some poor young girl."

"But I canna get rid of him unless I gie him a bride," the king complained to his outraged wife.

"Of course you can!" the queen responded. "After all, my lord, you are the king. Is not your word law?"

"I hae favored the laddie, Annie, for months now. If I send him away empty-handed, I will seem mean-spirited, and I will nae be! We must find him a wife."

"A well dowered widow, perhaps?" George Villiers suggested. "One yet young enough to give him an heir, of course; but old enough not to be intimidated by him, or his brother."

"Aye!" the king said enthusiastically. He turned to his wife. "I will leave the choice in yer hands, Annie, but the bride must hae gold and be able to gie him bairns."

"Very well, my lord, I will do as you ask me, but I still think if it were up to me, I should send him away empty-handed," the queen replied. "I do not trust your marquis at all. He is too eager to place the blame for Richard Stokes's death on Jasmine and James Leslie." The queen arose from her chair. "He is too anxious for revenge, and I do believe that he thinks he can still get his hands on our grandson."

"Nah, nah, Annie," the king said. "He's a sensitive lad, is our Piers, but I am certain his heart is good. He is just disappointed over losing Jasmine Lindley."

"He is and has always been too good-hearted," the queen told George Villiers later that evening. "I had thought that St. Denis would be dismissed and sent home by now. How was he able to worm his way back into the king's favor again, Steenie?"

"While I was on His Majesty's business in the matter of the Puritan pastor," George Villiers told the queen. "I think the king feels guilty over the matter of Lady Lindley. He knows it was a mistake to even to have suggested St. Denis court her, and now he is eager to make it up to him that the marquis not think badly of him. St. Denis was so adamant about Glenkirk's possible involvement in Lord Stokes's death, that the king dictated a message to James Leslie and his bride asking them to remain in England until the matter was resolved. Then the marquis took the king's message, and personally had it dispatched to Queen's Malvern. I'm certain it was just the wedding gift the bride and groom were expecting," Villiers concluded.

"Wretched creature!" the queen said, irritated. "I can only imagine what Jemmie and Jasmine must have thought when they received such a message. Well, I hope the matter will be settled before the autumn, when they intend to leave for Scotland."

"When is their wedding?" Villiers asked.

Queen Anne thought a moment, and then she said, "Why, I do believe it is tomorrow, Steenie. Tomorrow is the fifteenth day of June, isn't it, my dear boy?"

"It is," he agreed.

"Then it is tomorrow. Ohh, I hope they will be happy, Steenie! Jasmine has had enough sorrow in her life for any woman. I just want her to be happy. Our Hal would want it too, may God assoil his sweet soul."

"Amen," said George Villiers, who had not known Prince Henry, except by reputation. "And may Lady Lindley and Lord Leslie have a long and happy life together!"

"Amen to that, Steenie," the queen replied.

"A long and happy life, my dears," said Robin Southwood, the earl of Lynmouth, as he raised his goblet to his niece and James Leslie.

She was a wife once again, Jasmine thought, smiling happily as she accepted the toast and good wishes from her family. Standing before the Anglican priest saying her wedding vows for the third time, with a third husband, Jasmine prayed that this marriage would not end in disaster as her previous two had. She was struggling very hard with herself to believe what Jemmie and her grandmother said. That the deaths of Jamal Khan and Rowan Lindley had been mischance, and nothing more. Were they right? She had certainly been happy with both of her previous husbands. Now she was being given a third opportunity. Was three the charm for her? Jasmine Leslie prayed it would be so.

"You are the most beautiful bride I have ever seen," the earl of Glenkirk whispered in her ear.

"I have certainly had enough practice," she teased him with a radiant smile.

They exited the small chapel at Queen's Malvern. Once again, as at her wedding to Rowan Lindley, the four carved oak benches had not been enough to hold all the family, and they had stood about the room and spilled out into the hall. Her wedding to Rowan had been at dawn, and the rising sun had come through the stained-glass windows, casting shadows of color on the marble altar with its Irish lace cloth; reflecting off the gold crucifix and the tall candlesticks. Today, however, the wedding had been celebrated at noon, and outside of the house a soft rain was falling. Some remarked on it, hoping it did not portend any misfortune, but Jasmine laughed away their concerns. Her first two marriages had been held on perfectly beautiful days, and each had ended in violent death. A gray day was the least of her concerns.

The wedding feast, originally scheduled for the lawns, had now been set up in the hall, and the busy servants were dashing back and forth with food and drink. Skye had spared no expense with this celebration. Because it was summer, all her children had come to see their niece married to the earl of Glenkirk. Even Ewan O'Flaherty and his wife, Gwynneth Southwood, had arrived from Ireland. The Master of Ballyhennessey was fifty-nine, a large, ruddy-featured man with iron gray hair. He was a plain Irish country squire and happy to be so. His brother, Murrough, age fifty-eight, was virtually retired from the sea now; and content to remain in Devon, supervising the comings and goings of the O'Malley-Small trading fleet. His wife, Joan Southwood, was glad to have her husband home after all his years at sea; yet despite his comings and goings, Murrough had managed to sire three sons and three daughters on his adoring wife.

Willow, the countess of Alcester, and her husband, James Edwards, had arrived several days earlier with four of their eight children, three in-laws, and several grandchildren. Only their youngest son, William, was yet unmarried, but then he was only twenty. Of all Willow's children, it was William whose looks betrayed his Spanish ancestry. He bore an uncanny resemblance to Willow's father. Just looking at him took Skye back decades in time to when she had been the adored wife of the man known as Khalid el Bey, the Great Whoremaster of Algiers, who was in actuality a renegade Spaniard. Willow, of course, had never been told her father's more colorful history, and believed him to be nothing more than a merchant, who was estranged from his family. Watching her prim and oh-so-proper English daughter attempting to manage everything and fussing at everyone, Skye wickedly considered that one day before she died she must tell Willow of Khalid el Bey. That would certainly take her down a peg or two.

And following the fifty-five-year-old Willow was Robin Southwood, the earl of Lynmouth, now fifty-two, and his still beautiful wife, Angel. Then came Deirdre Burke, age forty-seven, and her husband, Lord Blackthorne; and her brother, Padraic, Lord Burke, forty-six; and his wife, Valentina; and of course, lastly, Velvet de Marisco, the countess of BrocCairn, at forty-two, the youngest of Skye's children, with her husband, Alexander Gordon, the earl of BrocCairn. They had brought with them Jasmine's five half brothers, who ranged in age from twenty-two to fifteen. Sybilla, Jasmine's stepsister, the countess of Kempe, and her husband, Tom Ashburne, had also come to the wedding, along with Jasmine's great-uncle Conn, Lord Bliss, and his wife Aidan. And, of course, Jasmine's devoted servants, Adali, Toramalli, and Rohana, were in attendance.

Willow had fretted privately to her siblings that holding the marriage feast in the hall would bring back unhappy memories for Skye. It would be the first time the family had gathered together since Adam de Marisco's unexpected death five and a half months ago. "She is old, and this could hurt her," Willow said, genuinely concerned for their mother.

"She has planned everything herself, sister," Deirdre ventured, gently. "She wants it this way. She cannot avoid the hall forever because Papa died there, can she, Willow?"

Willow opened her mouth to issue a scathing retort, but her brother, Robert Southwood, spoke first.

"Willow," he said mischievously, yet seriously, "you have never been as young as our mother is, even today."

"As usual, Robin, you speak in riddles," replied Willow.

"You were born an old woman, Willow," he told her bluntly. "Mama will *never* be old but in years. Her heart is young. It always has been, and it always will be. She will not live in the past as so many of her generation do. Adam, God assoil his generous soul, is dead, and gone from us. But Mama is alive, and will continue to live until the day God calls her home to him. I know you mean well, but do not bleat at her about the wedding feast in the hall. Where else can it be held in such weather?"

"Well, I don't know why such an ado is being made anyway," Willow grumbled. "After all, it is Jasmine's third marriage, and we are a house in mourning for our father."

"The *fuss* is being made," said James Edwards, Willow's husband, in a rare show of irritation, "because Adam would have wanted it that way, and my lady Skye knows it. Now, cease your carping, my dear. You grow tiresome to the ear. I shall walk in the gardens now, madame, and you shall accompany me."

"*But it is raining!*" Willow protested.

"Misting is more like it," the earl of Alcester corrected his wife. "It will do your complexion good, madame. Come along," and he took her firmly by the arm, almost shoving her from the room where they had all congregated just prior to the wedding service. "We'll be back before the service begins, my dear." And, of course, they were, Willow chastened.

Now the family came together in the hall of Queen's Malvern to celebrate the marriage that had just taken place. The tables groaned with the bounty of Skye's hospitality. There was a whole side of beef that had been roasted over an open spit; platters of lamb chops; capons in plum sauce, and ducks in orange sauce; a huge country ham; crusty pies of game birds and others of rabbit; whole river trouts on beds of cress; two barrels of oysters in seawater; jellied eel; bowls of new peas; and bowls of tiny carrots in cream sauce; along with dishes of braised lettuces from the kitchen gardens; a wheel of hard cheddar and one of Normandy Brie; stone crocks of sweet butter; and round cottage loaves of freshly baked bread. There was wine, and ale, and cider to drink. And lastly strawberries, clotted cream, and small sugar wafers, which were served with a very sweet marsala wine, an old tradition to wish the bride and groom good fortune.

A number of toasts were drunk to James and Jasmine Leslie, some of them warm and loving; some of them wickedly ribald. Jasmine grew more sentimental with each goblet of wine she consumed. She remembered her wedding to Jamal Khan. She had been decked out in scarlet and gold, in garments covered in diamonds and rubies, as befitted a royal Mughal princess. She had just been thirteen. When she had married Rowan Lindley, the marquis of Westleigh, she had worn the wedding gown both her mother and her grandmother had worn. It had been apple green silk with gold embroidery. She had been sixteen and a half.

Now she was almost twenty-five, and had taken a third husband. Her bridal gown was heavy cream silk brocade. The low square bodice was embroidered with swirls of tiny seed pearls over which was draped a creamy delicate lace collar. The V of underskirt showing was striped with narrow bands of cloth of silver. The skirt was bell-shaped and had a narrow waist. The gown's sleeves were divided by narrow silver ribbons and slashed to show cloth of silver. The cuffs were bands of soft lace. Beneath the ankle-length gown Jasmine wore a beribboned chemise, several layers of silk and lawn petticoats, and silk stockings embroidered with tiny gold bumblebees. Her shoes of creamy brocade were decorated with pearls; and her dark hair, in its chignon, was adorned with pearl-encrusted silk roses, and narrow silver ribbons.

"Are you dreaming?" her husband murmured in her ear. "If you are, I hope it is of me, darling Jasmine." James Leslie took Jasmine's hand in his, turning it over and kissing the palm with passionate lips. It was the happiest day of his life. He well remembered the first time he had met her. He had come to Queen's Malvern with the king, and it was thought that the widowed earl of Glenkirk might make a suitable husband for Sybilla Gordon, Jasmine's stepsister, who fancied herself in love with him. He had been introduced to Jasmine, however, and had fallen in love with her immediately. That had been ten years ago. Now he brought her hand to his lips, nibbling at her fingers. "How much longer must we be polite?" he whispered to her.

"There is to be dancing," she replied softly.

"Oh?"

"And some sort of entertainment, I believe," she told him.

"Could we not provide our own entertainment?" he suggested.

"Jemmie!" she half scolded him. "This wedding means so much to Grandmama. You must learn patience, my lord. It is not as if we have not tasted of sensual delights before." She made an attempt to regain possession of her hand, but he would not release it.

Instead he sucked wickedly on each of her fingers, and, when he had finished, he drew her hand beneath the table with its linen cloth, and pressed it against his groin. "As you can see, madame, I am very hungry. I will wager your grandmother would understand my sentiments."

He was hard as a rock, and Jasmine struggled to keep the blush from her cheeks, yet she could not move her hand away. For a moment she stroked him, squirming slightly in her chair as thoughts of their previous encounters rose up in her head, and then she shuddered with a small release of passion. *"My lord!"* she pleaded softly.

He laughed low. "You are as hot for me as I am for you, my darling Jasmine. Very well then. We shall dance and watch the little entertainments your grandmama has provided for us; but when they are all over, madame, I shall take you to bed and drive from your head all thoughts of anyone, or anything but me!" He then relinquished the slender hand he had held captive.

"You will pay dearly for your wickedness, my lord," she promised him, reluctantly removing her hand from his manhood.

"As shall you, darling Jasmine, for keeping me waiting," he responded threateningly, his green-gold eyes laughing into her turquoise ones. "No matter how many years we are wed, I shall never tire of you."

"A bold promise, but then you are a bold man, Jemmie Leslie," Jasmine told him.

Suddenly the room was filled with a shrill and eerie noise. James Leslie looked quickly up. Into the hall came a man in a green kilt with a narrow red and a narrow white stripe identical to the one which James Leslie wore that day. He was playing the bagpipes as he came, each step measured, and dignified. He stopped before the highboard where the bridal party were seated, playing on, a sweetly melancholy tune. When he had finished, he bowed low to the earl of Glenkirk.

"*Alpin More!*" James Leslie said, a smile upon his face. "How came you here this day? You are a very long way from Glenkirk."

"Yer brothers and sisters thought I should be here this day, my lord, and Lady de Marisco agreed. She arranged for me to be brought south. I hae traveled a long way indeed, but we could nae hae ye wed again wi'out yer piper, my lord. I played for ye when ye wed Lady Isabelle, may God grant her soul peace. Now I hae played for ye and yer new lady, may God bless ye both!" He bowed again.

"Jasmine, this is Alpin More, my piper," James Leslie said to his bride. "Alpin, my wife, Lady Jasmine Leslie."

"I have never heard the pipes played so beautifully, Alpin More," Jasmine said. "I hope you will play for us again soon."

The piper bowed once more to his new mistress. She was far more beautiful than the earl's first wife had been. He hoped she could have children, for his master needed an heir. The bride was not very young, but then neither was she very old, and she had already had children, or so he had been told. "I wish ye long life, and many bairns," he told Jasmine gallantly with a smile.

"What a fine wish, Alpin More!" Jasmine told him. "I would have many sons for my lord, and may you play for them one day as well."

The piper grinned broadly, well pleased by her words, which he would repeat to all when he returned to Glenkirk. Perhaps by the time the earl brought his bride home to Scotland she would already be ripening with the Leslie's heir. That would certainly please everyone.

"Now that you have heard the piper," Skye said softly to the bridal couple, "would you not like to depart the hall?"

"But Grandmama, have you not planned for dancing, and for other entertainments?" Jasmine said, surprised at their dismissal.

"Darling girl, do you really wish to remain here when your new husband is in such a state of lust for you?" her grandmother asked, laughing. "Granted I have more years than anyone else in this room tonight, but my memory is still quite intact. A wedding night, be it the first, or the third—no matter you have been lovers before—is still a wonderful night. I remember all of mine in exquisite detail, even the unhappy ones. While it is true that being June it is still quite light out of doors; and the night when it comes will last but a short time, would you not prefer to spend that time alone with James Leslie? I know that if I were you, I should!"

The earl of Glenkirk arose from the highboard, drawing his countess up with him. He bowed to the countess of Lundy and, taking her hand in his, he said, "Madame, you are a woman of the utmost sensitivity. I salute you!" Then he kissed Skye's hand. "I am content to withdraw with my bride from this magnificent celebration that you have given us." He then released her hand and, bowing again, departed the hall with his blushing bride in tow, the cheers of his new relations ringing in his ears.

Skye watched them go, her Kerry blue eyes misty, a smile of remembrance upon her lips. *Well, old man, are you satisfied now?* she said silently. *I have gotten her safely wed to Lord Leslie, and by this time next year we shall probably have another descendant for me to dote upon. God's boots, I wish you were still here with me, Adam! They say that time softens the pain of death, but I probably miss you more tonight than the night you left me so suddenly. And there is time for me yet before I can join you, Adam. I sense it. I don't know whether to be happy or sad about it.*

She felt an arm go about her shoulders, and smiled up into her son Robin's handsome face. He bent his head and kissed her cheek.

"He would be pleased, Mama. This is what he wanted for Jasmine," the earl of Lynmouth said. "He wanted her safe, and now she is."

"I know," Skye answered her son.

"But?" he queried her.

"I do not know," she said softly. "There is something. I sense it, Robin. Yet I do not know what, and I cannot imagine what."

"Perhaps it is just your fancy, Mama. It has, after all, been a difficult year for you, beginning with Adam's death, and then your travels to France. You are not, after all, as young as you once were."

"You sound like Willow," she accused him.

"God forbid!" the earl of Lynmouth exclaimed.

"Nay, Robin, there is yet some shadow lurking about Jasmine," Skye told him. "It is not the imaginings of an old lady."

"Then when it comes, Mama, we shall, as this family has always done, rally about our own and solve the problem," Robin Southwood said.

Skye smiled up at her third son. "Aye, my dear, I suppose we shall. Until then I intend enjoying the summer with both my daughter and my granddaughter about me. And come the autumn I shall be just as glad to see them return to Scotland, as I was to see them come to Queen's Malvern," she chuckled. "Then Daisy and I shall settle down to a quiet winter, which I know will please my old friend. I was always too much for her, Robin, and I fear she has grown too old to cope with me." Skye chuckled. "She is nearer to eighty than I am."

"Boredom has never pleased you, Mama," he said. "You will find some mischief to get into, I have not a doubt."

Skye O'Malley de Marisco laughed at this observation. "Aye," she agreed with him, "I probably shall, Robin."

SCOTLAND

Autumn 1615–Autumn 1618

Chapter Thirteen

Jasmine Leslie saw Glenkirk Castle for the first time on a sunny late-August afternoon. Of dark gray stone, it was battlemented and had four towers, one at each of the major compass points. It sat upon the crest of a hill, surrounded by forested hills. Its great oak drawbridge was down, welcoming her, and Jasmine Leslie knew in her heart as sure as she had ever known anything that she had come home. It was an incredible revelation for a princess, raised at the Imperial Indian court, who had known far greater palaces than the small stone edifice, topping the uneven green hill. And yet she knew! *Glenkirk was home!* How long had it been waiting for her? Her heart soared, beating just a little faster, and then she heard Adali say but one word.

"*Yes.*"

She turned and saw that he, too, felt the magic, and she smiled at him even as he smiled back.

"What do you think?" her bridegroom asked nervously. "Can you be happy here for almost half a year each year, darling Jasmine?"

Seated upon her stallion she turned her head to him, and nodded. "Aye, Jemmie, I can be happy anywhere as long as I am with you. The castle is beautiful. It's a wonderful place for the children."

"You are seeing it at its best," he told her. "I did warn you that the autumn is Scotland's best time. There is much gray and rain and mist the rest of the year."

"I don't care," she said. "It is the land, the castle, the forest, they all sing to me, my lord. Rain or shine, it will matter not to me. *I have come home.*"

The earl of Glenkirk's handsome face split with a wide smile. He could not have been happier to hear her words. He had always loved his home, but after Isabella and the children had died it had seemed such an empty place and was suddenly unfamiliar. Yet this was where he had been raised with his three younger brothers, and his five younger sisters. It had, for many years, been a warm happy place. Now it would be again with Jasmine and her children and the children they would have together. His spirits rose, and his smile broadened once more.

"There are men-at-arms on the battlements!" young Henry Lindley said in an excited voice. "Oh, Papa, 'tis a grand castle!" His horse danced nervously next to the earl's stallion. "Can I ride ahead, sir?" he asked his stepfather.

"Nay, laddie," Fergus More interposed. "'Tis the first time in many, many years that the earl has been home. 'Tis he who must be first of this party into Glenkirk."

"But I could go ahead, and tell them that we're coming," the boy said hopefully.

"They already know we're coming," Fergus More said, and he pointed in the direction of the castle.

From Glenkirk's courtyard and out over the drawbridge they came, up the road that wound down from the hills and toward the mounted party that rode onward to the castle. Clansmen. Leslie clansmen. Mounted and on foot; banners flying; a troupe of pipers led by Alpin More, who was Fergus's kin, leading them as they came. The savage joy of the music rose on the wind, and instinctively the Scotsmen straightened in their saddles. The earl was dressed today as he had dressed every day since they had crossed over the border, in breeches and high boots, leather jerkin over his linen shirt, a cap with a chieftain's badge on his head. Long gone, it seemed to Jasmine, was the elegant English courtier James Leslie had previously appeared to be.

"See that green-and-white banner, Jasmine," he said, pointing. "Those are the Leslies of Sithean. We all descend from the first earl of Glenkirk, but the second earl's sister managed to obtain Sithean for her son and his descendants. And I see my uncle Patrick riding at the head of his people. And I see my cousin, his heir, with his father. Behind the red, white, and green banner are the Leslies of Glenkirk. My uncles and my brothers will be there." His voice had risen just slightly with his excitement.

"You should have come home long since, Jemmie," Jasmine told him, reaching out to touch his hand.

"I almost did once, but then the king wept that he needed my acumen, with poor Cecil dead, and so I remained to serve James Stuart," the earl told her. "But for our English summers, darling Jasmine, I do not think I shall ever leave Scotland again. My heart is full just looking about me, hearing the pipes welcoming me back."

Now they drew to a halt, allowing the clansmen to come to them, and they did, surrounding the earl's party with shouts of joy to see him back amongst them and for having brought a new countess. They reached out to touch the earl and his wife, and Jasmine, following her husband's lead, reached back, her beautiful hand brushing the rough hands thrust toward her, a smile on her lips, her turquoise eyes dancing with an open delight that plainly told of her pleasure to be among them. When they had heard he had taken an English wife they had expected a haughty milady, a nervous creature who would recoil at their noisy earthiness, but this was no milksop. This was a real woman, and the clansmen were delighted.

The earl of Glenkirk and his party were escorted into the castle courtyard. Before either the earl or Adali could help Jasmine from her mount, she was whisked off it by a large, bushy-bearded clansman, who set her gently on her feet with a courtly bow and a grin.

"And who are you?" Jasmine demanded of him, eyes twinkling.

"Red Hugh More, madame, son and grandson of the same," he said with another bow. "I'm the captain of yer guard."

"The castle's guard," Jasmine said.

"Nay, madame, *yer guard*," was the reply.

"I have my own guard?" Jasmine was surprised.

"As hae every countess of Glenkirk before ye," he said. "This is Scotland, and Scotland is nae always a peaceful place."

"So my husband has told me," Jasmine said, laughing. "Well, Red Hugh More, this is Adali, who has been responsible for my life since I was born. You will cooperate in the matter of my safety, eh?"

Red Hugh More looked over the half-Indian, half-French Adali. It was a swift, but skilled assessment that was returned in kind. "He looks like he can handle himself," was his vocal decision.

"I can garrote a man without his even hearing me enter the room behind him," Adali said softly. "It is a quick, silent death."

A slow smile slid over Red Hugh's features. "We'll get on well," he said. "I like a man who can kill wi'out a lot of blood to clean up." Then, bowing to Jasmine, and with a respectful nod to Adali, he withdrew, allowing them to enter the castle.

James Leslie surprised his wife by picking her up and carrying her into the building. "'Tis an old custom, carrying the bride over the threshold, darling Jasmine," he said, setting her on her feet, then taking her hand and leading her up the wide staircase to the second floor of the castle. The children, Adali, Rohana, and Toramalli, came closely behind them, eyes darting this way and that. The earl led them four steps up into an anteroom, and then four steps down into the Great Hall of Glenkirk Castle.

Jasmine's eyes widened. It was an absolutely marvelous room. Huge fireplaces flanked by tall arched windows were set on each side of the room. Hanging from the hall's rafters were multihued silken banners which had been carried into the many battles that the Leslie clan had fought over the centuries. At the end of the room was the highboard which was set in a T-shape. There were arched windows behind it on either side. Over each fireplace was hung a full-length portrait. The painting on the right was of a handsome male in the full flush of his manhood. The painting on the left was of an exquisitely beautiful young girl with an innocent, yet haunting look about her.

"Who are they?" Jasmine asked her husband, mesmerized.

"He is Patrick Leslie, the first earl of Glenkirk, King James IV's ambassador to the duchy of San Lorenzo. He was my great-great-great-grandfather. She is Lady Janet Leslie, his daughter, my great-great-grandmother. She is dressed in her betrothal gown, for she was to marry the heir to San Lorenzo, but instead was the lady of whom I told you, who was kidnapped and became a sultan's favorite and a sultan's mother. It was her youngest son, Prince Karim, who was smuggled out of the Ottoman Empire as a little boy and became Charles Leslie, the first earl of Sithean."

"She is wonderful!" Jasmine said.

"Aye, I am told she was. My father remembered her, for she did not die until after she had arranged his marriage to my mother, who was just a tiny bairn at the time. She was always arranging everything," he chuckled.

"Something like my own grandmama," Jasmine smiled.

"Aye, I expect Madame Skye and Janet Leslie would have gotten along very well together," he agreed.

"My lord, welcome home!" An elderly man made his way forward.

"Thank you, Will. This is your new mistress, Lady Jasmine Leslie. Jasmine, this is Will Todd, the castle caretaker. He has faithfully looked after Glenkirk since I left it."

"And right glad I am to see yer lordship home," Will Todd said. "Now, with yer lordship's permission, and if I am no longer needed, I can retire to my wee cottage and go fishing for the salmon that hae gotten so fat in yer lordship's absence."

"What?" the earl teased the old man. "There are still salmon left in my streams? I would have thought them all poached by now, Will."

"There are plenty of fine salmon for yer lordship. As to poachers, it is difficult to say as we hae nae ever counted the fishies," the caretaker teased his master back.

"Aye, Will," the earl said, "you may go back to your cottage, and you will lack for nothing for the rest of your days, I promise you; but before you leave me, I would have your help a final time." James Leslie drew Adali forward. "This is Adali, who has been in my wife's service since she was born. He will now take over the running of Glenkirk Castle for us, but he will need your help for the next several months that he know what to do, and where everything is, and who is to be trusted, and who will work hard, and who will not. Will you aid him, Will Todd?"

"Aye, my lord!" the caretaker said, and then he shook Adali's hand, looking him up and down as he did so. "Hae ye ever run a big house, Master Adali? As big as this one, I mean?"

Adali forced back a smile, and said gravely, "Aye, Master Todd, I have. My lady's childhood home was a large household."

"Good! Good! Then ye'll nae hae difficulty in learning our ways, and I'll be fishing all the quicker," he chortled.

"I have never fished, Master Todd," Adali said.

"Will, me name is Will, Master Adali, and I'll be glad to teach ye. Our salmon and our trout are worthy opponents, not to mention verra tasty when cooked over a slow fire," he chuckled.

"I shall look forward to it," Adali said. "And you will call me Adali, Will Todd, for we are equals in this household."

The old man nodded. He liked Adali's good manners and the fact that this stranger did not attempt to lord it over him. It boded well for all the servants that their new master was not just polite, but obviously a kind fellow. Then his eye lit on the children. "Bairns?" For a moment he looked a bit confused, but the earl explained.

"These are my wife's children from her previous marriage. Lord Henry Lindley, and the ladies India and Fortune Lindley, Will. The littlest bairn is a very special child." He nodded to the duke of Lundy's nursemaid, who was carrying him, to come forward. "This wee lad, Will, is Prince Henry's son, Charles Frederick Stuart. We call him Charlie-boy. The king has done me a great honor by giving me his mother to be my wife; and he has put his only grandson under my protection."

"Prince Henry's laddie?" Will Todd's eyes filled with tears. "Ah, 'tis sad, my lord. 'Tis sad, but we'll keep the bairn safe wi us here at Glenkirk. The king hae done us a great honor; but then when did the Leslies nae gie the Stuarts their complete loyalty?"

"Always, Will," James Leslie agreed.

"The children are tired after our long journey, my lord," Jasmine interposed. "I think they must have their supper and go to bed. Tomorrow they can explore, and see all of Glenkirk, but for now I think the day is over for them."

"I'll show ye their quarters, m'lady," Will Todd said eagerly.

"I will go with them," Adali said, "and then return. The journey has been long for you as well, my princess," he finished meaningfully.

She nodded.

"Come, and we'll sit by the fire," the earl said. "Toramalli, there is wine on the sideboard. Bring us each a goblet. Already I can hear the family tramping up the stairs. There will be no rest for us for several hours, darling Jasmine, but we'll take a small respite."

The children and their servants followed Adali and Will Todd from the hall even as a troupe of people began to enter it. It was going to take time to sort out all these new relations, but Jasmine could already recognize the Leslies in the crowd. James Leslie's paternal uncles all came forward. James, the Master of Hay; Adam, who had been closest to the earl's father; Michael, the youngest brother, a big, ruddy man in his middle fifties. There was his father's cousin, the old earl of Sithean, who was married to his father's sister;

and his son, Charles, who was married to James Leslie's sister, Amanda. And, of course, there were his two brothers. Colin, the Master of Greyhaven, and Robert Leslie of Briarmere Moor. They clapped the earl of Glenkirk upon the back and embraced him happily.

"This is my wife, Jasmine," he introduced her, lifting her up onto the highboard so they might all see her.

"Ye've an eye for beauty even as yer father hae," his uncle Adam Leslie declared, with a courtly bow to Jasmine and a twinkle in his amber eyes.

"Aye, she's fair enough, laddie, but can she gie us the next earl of Glenkirk," his elderly cousin of Sithean asked bluntly.

"I gave my second husband a son, and two daughters; and I gave Prince Henry a bonnie son, my lord," Jasmine defended herself.

The men were startled, but then they laughed, and Colin Leslie said admiringly, "Why, Jemmie, she's as bold as our mother."

"Aye," his uncle Adam said, "she's as bold as any Scots-born lassie, I'm thinking. Ye'll hae strong bairns."

"*But when?*" the old earl of Sithean persisted. "Ye wed her several months ago, and if yer like the men in this family, ye've bedded her regularly, cousin. Yer seed should be well planted by now."

"Would late winter be soon enough for you, you old trout?" Jasmine asked him, laughing at the surprised look on their faces, her husband's in particular. "Now, get me down, Glenkirk! Your relations have seen me. Where the hell are the women in this family?"

His brothers began to laugh uproariously, and, their surprise easing, the other men joined in, too.

The earl of Glenkirk lifted his wife gingerly from the table. "Why didn't you tell me?" he whispered to her, unable to keep the grin off his handsome face.

"I was going to, tonight, when we were all tucked up in our marital bed, but when that old man started twitting me, now seemed as good a time as any. I wouldn't want it thought, James Leslie, that you weren't doing your duty by me."

"A chair for the countess," the earl of Sithean called, and his demand was immediately met. "Sit down, me dear," he invited her. "Yer carrying a most precious burden, ye are. Ye must take a care of yerself, lassie," he cautioned Jasmine.

"I've borne four children already, my lord," she reassured him.

"Aye, aye, but yer a wee bit longer in the tooth now, lassie," he said concerned. "Did ye ever miscarry of a bairn?"

"My first," she told him. "'Twas the shock of my first husband's murder that did it. I was fourteen at the time. I've had no difficulties since then, my lord, and this child is planted deeply and firmly."

The old earl smiled. "Aye, he's a Leslie," he said.

"Now, tell me, sir," Jasmine said, "where are the women?"

"They will come tomorrow when yer rested," Adam Leslie said. "All the aunts and yer sisters-in-law are anxious to meet ye, although when the word reaches them of how fair ye are, they may change their minds," he teased her. "My Fiona is quite the beauty," and then he lowered his voice, "but I canna say the same for my brothers' wives. Once they were pretty creatures as the young always are, but they hae nae stood the test of time verra well, but Jemmie's sisters are pretty lasses."

"You are very wicked, aren't you?" Jasmine said mischievously.

"It comes from living wi my Fiona all these years," he told her. "When she and Jemmie's mother were young, they were rivals for a time, but they later became friends. Both were headstrong, difficult lasses, I fear. My Fiona hae softened a bit, and I've grown wicked wi age," he said, chuckling. "Are ye wicked, Jasmine?"

"Sometimes," she said. "Ye must ask Jemmie. He will tell ye, I am certain. I think being wicked is far more fun than being good, Uncle Adam, don't you?" Her eyes twinkled.

"Aye," he agreed with her. "I'm glad ye hae a bit of spunk, lassie. Jemmie's first wife was a sweet child, but about as exciting as a bowl of oat stirabout. Ye look like a lass wi hot blood in her veins, and that's just the sort of wife he needs."

"Are you flirting with my bride, Uncle?" the earl of Glenkirk said.

"Nay, laddie," Adam Leslie declared. "'Tis she who is flirting wi me, the pretty vixen. Yer a lucky man, laddie."

"He's won my heart because he has grandpapa's name," Jasmine replied to her husband. "You know my weakness for men named Adam."

"Perhaps we'll name our son Adam," James Leslie said.

"Nay," Jasmine said. "Our first son will be called Patrick after that handsome devil over the fireplace. Our second son will be Adam, and the third, James, my lord."

"God bless me!" the old earl of Sithean chortled. "The wench is ambitious in her desire to gie the clan sons. I fully approve!" He stamped his gnarled cane upon the floor of the hall enthusiastically.

And afterward, when the Leslie men had all departed, and they sat together at the highboard eating a simple repast of broiled trout and toasted cheese and apples, James Leslie said, "You've made a grand impression upon my brothers, uncles, and cousins, madame. As for the clansmen, they will be devoted to you forever for the way you accepted their rousing greeting, darling Jasmine."

"I often watched my father reach out to his subjects when he would pass through their towns. They were so eager to touch the Mughal. It meant so much to them. Today, when your clansmen came to greet us and surrounded us with such a warm welcome, I did what my father did, reaching out to them as they did to us. I suddenly realized, Jemmie, that here in your highlands you are very much like a little king to your people. Perhaps this is why the Scots have always had such difficulty serving a single king when each chieftain is in reality a king himself within his own holding. It is a very heady experience."

He nodded. "How quick you are to understand us, but no country can survive amid its neighbors without a strong monarch." He took her hand and began to nibble upon her fingers. "We have not had a moment to talk," he said, "since you made your momentous announcement. We had no sooner gotten rid of my relations when Adali and Will Todd were calling us to the highboard to eat." He turned her hand over and kissed the inside of her blue-veined wrist. "When do you plan to produce my son, madame?" His look was intense.

"'Twill be sometime in late winter," she said. "The very end of February, or in early March. It happened that first night when you returned from your silly little trip to Edinburgh." She caught his hand and began to suck upon his fingers.

"I don't want to harm the bairn," he said desperately.

"We don't have to worry about it yet, my lord," she told him. "I can yet ride both my stallions, the two-footed and the four-footed one." She caressed his face. "I have never wanted a man like this, Jemmie. I desire you always, and it took us so long to come from England. We haven't been in a proper bed in weeks. Are you not hungry for me, too?"

Reaching out, he cupped her head in his hand, his mouth brushing suggestively against hers. He could see her nipples pushing against the silk of her shirt, and his lust rose up to almost choke him. *"Aye!"* he managed to grind out, aching to possess her.

"I do not know where to go," she said intensely.

"I do!" he groaned, pulling her up from her chair and practically dragging her through the Great Hall and its antechamber beyond. They reached the wide staircase and, picking her up, he almost leapt the steps to the floor above, where the apartments of the earl and countess of Glenkirk were located. Kicking the door open, he strode in, still holding her in his arms. Then he set her gently down. "Do not keep me waiting long, madame," he said intensely.

"Jesu!" Fergus More whispered to Adali. "He was nae this way with Lady Isabelle. I dinna know if I can get used to all the burning looks between them and this intensity. Why they can scarcely keep their hands off one another."

"Passion between a man and his wife is a good thing," Adali murmured reassuringly. "Have you never had such feelings for a woman?"

The Scotsman shook his head. "Nay," he said, "but I'm thinking I might work up to them wi Mistress Toramalli. Sends a shiver down me back, she does," he admitted. "Do ye think she likes me, Adali?"

"I will ascertain if an advance on your part would be met with favor by Toramalli," Adali told him diplomatically. "Now, you had best attend your impatient master, Fergus More." Then he moved into his lady's bedchamber, where the twin maidservants were helping Jasmine to disrobe. "We have a great deal of work to make the castle habitable again, my princess," he told her. "It has been virtually shut up for most of the years the earl has been in England. Will Todd did his best, but there is a lot more for us to do."

"It isn't as bad as Jamal's place on my wedding night," Jasmine said laughing. "I will never forget that. I gained great satisfaction from selling off those appalling women in his zenana." Naked, she stepped into the tub that had been prepared for her, quickly washing without the help of her servants.

"There is enough wood by the fire for tonight, and for the morning," Adali said. "I have seen that wine was placed on the sideboard in the dayroom, and there is a basin with a supply of love cloths by your bed, my lady. Rohana and Toramalli have made it with our own linens and featherbed. You will be comfortable, and tomorrow we will make it even better. The rooms have a smell of mustiness about them, but it is not surprising considering the circumstances."

"It's a wonderful castle," Jasmine said softly. "We have finally come home, Adali. You knew it too, didn't you?"

He nodded, smiling. "Aye, I did, my princess. I would not have thought this pile of stones in the hills of Scotland would have felt like that to us, but it does." Then his eyes twinkled, and he changed the subject completely. "Would you object, my lady, if Toramalli had a suitor? Fergus More has indicated he would be interested in paying her court, if she would have him do so, and with your permission."

"*Toramalli?*" Jasmine asked her servant. "It is your decision."

"The cheek of the man!" Toramalli, who was hot-tempered began.

"He's a lovely man," her sister Rohana said. "You are very fortunate. And he has asked permission before approaching you. What delicacy of feelings, my sister."

"He probably means you, and can't tell us apart," Toramalli said, grumbling, as she dried her mistress off, but she was smiling,

"If you think so, then let Adali have him approach the lady he would court," Jasmine suggested as Rohana lowered a nightgown over her head, and it slid down to cover her body. It was white silk, with a round neckline and long sleeves.

"An excellent suggestion," Adali said. "Come, ladies, let us take the tub from the room. Together, the trio lugged the small oaken tub from Jasmine's bedchamber.

When they had emptied it down a stone chute in the garderobe, they stored the tub away and returned to the dayroom. Fergus More had just exited the earl's bedchamber. He looked hopefully at Adali.

"Toramalli wonders if you really know the difference between herself and her twin sister, Fergus More," Adali told him. "Do you? If you do, then you have her permission to court Toramalli, she says."

The twins stood side by side, identical in features, but for one difference. Dark-haired and dark-eyed with golden skin, each possessed a flower-shaped birthmark at the corner of her eye. Toramalli's was on the right. Rohana's on the left. Without hesitation Fergus More walked directly to the correct twin and stood before her.

"Of course I know which one ye are, Mistress Toramalli," he said quietly.

"Well," Toramalli answered him pertly, "if you are clever enough to know the difference between Rohana and me, I suppose we could keep company for a while, Fergus More."

"Come to the kitchen with me now, lassie," he invited, "and we'll hae a cup of ale. Yer sister can come to," he added as an afterthought.

"You go," Rohana said. "I'm much too tired, but I thank you for the invitation, Fergus More." She yawned broadly.

The two servants departed from the apartment, Adali remaining just a moment longer to snuff the candles and bank the fire. Rohana found her way back to her bedchamber, which was located within the apartments, bidding Adali good night as she went.

James Leslie had entered his wife's bedchamber by means of the connecting door between their rooms. Jasmine stood silently looking out of the windows across the moonlit hills. Hearing his entrance, she turned, smiling, and held out her arms to him. "My lord," she said softly, and enfolded him within her embrace.

Wordless he caressed her face as if for the very first time. His green-gold eyes adored her. Then his two hands tangled within her hair, and he kissed her deeply, his mouth warm and firm. "I love you," he finally said. "I have from the moment I first laid eyes upon you. I know I have said it before, but I shall say it to you for the rest of our lives that you never think I might grow tired of you. I will always love you, darling Jasmine."

"Ohh, Jemmie," she responded, "you fill me, heart and soul, to overflowing with your love for me. I love you, too. I would have to be the worst bitch created not to love in return the man who loves me so, but your love is so overwhelming that I wonder if I am worthy of it. How happy I am to carry a child created of such love!"

In response he picked her up and laid her upon their bed, coming down next to her, to cradle her in his arms. "Thank you," he said simply, and then he kissed her again. His lips, tender at first, became more demanding as their passions rose. He loosened the ribbons on her gown, sliding his hand beneath the sensuous fabric to fondle her breasts.

She moaned as his fingers brushed her sensitive nipples and, laying her upon her back, lowered his head to suckle upon them.

The touch of his lips upon her susceptible flesh was almost too much to bear. She shivered with pleasure as her nipples tingled almost painfully with the exacting pressure of his mouth drawing so strongly upon them. She caressed his dark hair, fingers twining about the thick tendrils, and here and there she saw a wisp of silver among the ebony. Closing her eyes, she sighed deeply when he removed himself from her breasts. His big hands drew her nightgown from her and stroked her still slim body. Bending, he kissed her belly, sending shivers of excitement down her spine.

"I want to feel you against me," she said softly.

In response, Jemmie pulled his own nightshirt off and drew her back into his arms so that their bodies touched, transferring the warmth between them. Jasmine reached out with her hand to stroke his manroot, petting him with a delicate touch. He was warm and firm beneath her hand. "Make love to me, my Jemmie," she purred at him.

"I don't want to hurt you," he fretted.

In response Jasmine slipped from his embrace and quickly mounted him, letting his solid length slide deeply into her. "We do not have to deny ourselves the pleasure of each other's bodies quite yet, Jemmie, my dearest lover. If we are careful we may have several months of delight. I know what to do, and as I have had more experience in this than you, you must follow my lead. Rowan and I never denied ourselves when I carried his children." She rotated her hips gently into his groin, and he groaned with enjoyment. Reaching up with his hands, he fondled her breasts, watching her through half-closed eyes as she moved upon him. "Does this please you, my lord?" she teased him.

"Witch!" He squeezed the tender flesh of her bosom.

"Ummmmmm," she murmured. God's boots! She was going to peak. He would have no joy of his own, but then she felt his love juices burst forth within her, and she fell sobbing with relief upon his chest.

"Ahhhhhhh!" he groaned. "You are delicious, madame." They lay entwined for a time, and then he pulled himself up, settling the pillows beneath him. Drawing her into his embrace between his legs, his hands reached out to cup her faintly rounded belly.

The warmth of his hands was incredible. He was cradling their unborn child between his big hands. God, how safe she felt! How comforted the baby must be with his father's hands protecting him so tenderly. Jasmine fell asleep, enfolded by her husband's great love; and even more certain now than she had been earlier in the day, that she had at last come home. She would no longer have to run, or be a wanderer upon the face of this earth. *Glenkirk was home. For now. Forever!*

Chapter Fourteen

By midmorning of the following day the earl of Glenkirk's family was pouring into the castle to meet Jasmine. His paternal uncles, James the Master of Hay, and his wife, Ailis; Adam and his wife, Fiona; Michael of Leslie Brae with his Isabelle. The old earl of Sithean came with his women. And, of course, James Leslie's siblings. His sister, Bess, and her husband, Henry Gordon. His two brothers, Colin, the Master of Greyhaven with his wife, Euphemia Hay; and Robert of Briarmere Moor, who was married to Euphemia's sister, Flora. Jemmie's sister, Amanda, was married to the earl of Sithean's heir; and his sister, Morag, was the wife of young Malcom Gordon. They surrounded the earl of Glenkirk, hugging him, and covering him with happy kisses.

Finally, Fiona Leslie cried, "Enough! Enough! We all know our Jemmie. We hae come to see his bride. Come forward, Jasmine Leslie!" And when Jasmine stood before her, she looked her over with a critical eye, and then smiled broadly. "Welcome to Glenkirk, madame." Looking at her nephew, she said, "Yer mother would be pleased, and yer choice..."

"*Fiona!*" her husband warned.

Fiona Leslie glared at her husband. "I was only going to say Jemmie's choice appeared to be as fine a one as his mother made all those years ago." Then she smiled sweetly.

There was relieved laughter. Fiona Leslie had been her sister-in-law's best friend when they had grown up although their earlier relationship had been a rocky one. She was an outspoken woman, and they all knew she had thought Isabelle Gordon a sweet ninny; but since the unfortunate girl's brother was married to Jemmie's sister, no criticism of her would be tolerated publicly.

"I'm glad that I meet with your approval, madame," Jasmine replied, her eyes twinkling mischievously at Fiona, whom she immediately liked. Despite the difference in their ages, they were going to be friends.

"Ye'd meet with Cat's approval, and that's more important. Yer already breeding, I'm told," Fiona said. "Well, ye hae plenty of family about when the bairn is born. Is yer mother back from England yet?"

Jasmine shook her head. "Not yet. She stayed later this year because she thought Grandmama might be lonely now that my grandfather is gone, but I am sure Grandmama wants nothing more than to send Mama back to Dun Broc as quickly as possible so she may have some peace."

"Hah!" Fiona chuckled. "Yer grandmama sounds like a woman after my own heart. Yer mother's a good woman, however, and means well."

"Who is yer mother?" Bess Gordon asked.

"Why 'tis the countess of BrocCairn," Fiona said impatiently to her niece. "Do ye know nothing, Bess?"

"Well, Jemmie hae been in England, and I didna know," Bess said spiritedly. She turned to Jasmine. "No one tells me anything!"

Adali and Will Todd were passing wine to the assembled guests. "I have not had time yet to staff the castle," Jasmine explained.

"Ohh, I hope ye'll bring it back to the way it was when Patrick and Cat and our parents held sway here, James Leslie," the Master of Hay said wistfully.

"Aye!" Fiona enthused. "'Twas so grand then, Jasmine." She looked to her brothers-in-law, her nieces, and her nephews. "Ye'll hae to help Jasmine wi all of this. She canna be overtaxed as she now carries the next earl of Glenkirk wi'in her belly."

"I'm no weakling," Jasmine protested. "I have four children already, and they are quite strong and healthy."

"Aye, ye've four bairns, but not one of them is a Leslie of Glenkirk," Fiona said.

"Aunt, give over," Jemmie interposed. "My wife is not the family's broodmare. We're having a child, and lass or laddie, it will be welcome to Glenkirk, but that is not why I married my darling Jasmine. I wed her because I love her, and I have for many years now. I am grateful that she accepted me as her husband. Now let us all celebrate being together again," the earl of Glenkirk concluded.

"Aye! Aye!" their guests chorused.

Then suddenly there was an uproar toward the rear of the Great Hall. Turning to look, they saw two small boys engaged in a bout of fisticuffs, rolling about on the floor and howling wildly.

"'Tis Connor!" Morag Gordon said, aghast.

"And Henry!" Jasmine cried, looking to her husband.

The earl of Glenkirk stepped forward and forcibly separated his stepson and his nephew, a hand holding tightly to the collar of each boy, who squirmed and struggled in his grip. "What is going on?" Jemmie Leslie demanded of the two miscreants.

"He said I were a savage and talked funny," Connor Gordon declared, glowering at his rival.

"You said I was a sissy!" Henry Lindley defended himself. "I was escorting my sisters into the hall, Papa, when we were accosted by this boy. He insulted India and Fortune."

"What, exactly, did he say, Henry, that you felt it necessary to give battle? By the way, this is my nephew, Connor Cordon."

"He said," Henry declared in a clear voice, "'Look at the wee sissy wi the skinny, yellow-eyed wench and the carrot-topped lassie.' So I hit the little snot-nosed savage. I'll not have my sisters maligned!" He glared furiously at his antagonist, his turquoise eyes blazing.

"Connor," the earl said, "do you know who I am?"

"Aye, m'lord," the boy answered.

"This is my stepson, Henry Lindley, the marquis of Westleigh; and his sisters, Lady India and Lady Fortune. You will apologize to your new cousins for your bad manners." He released his hold on the boy.

Connor Gordon brushed his clothing off and bowed quite nicely. "I hope ye will accept my apologies, Lady India and Lady Fortune. I hae ne'er seen a lass wi yellow eyes before."

"My eyes are golden like my father's," India said grandly.

"And my hair is red-gold, not carrot-colored," Fortune piped up.

Jemmie Leslie loosed his hold on Henry. "Now, gentlemen, shake hands," he commanded the boys. "We are a family, and I will have no squabbling amongst us. Do you both understand?"

The two nodded, Connor holding out a somewhat grimy paw to Henry Lindley, who took it and shook it.

"I hae a pony," Connor said. "Do ye?"

"Aye," Henry answered, suspiciously. "Why?"

"We could ride together," Connor replied. How old are ye?"

"Six and a half," was the reply.

"God's nightshirt!" Connor Gordon said. "I'm eight, and yer every bit as big as me, ye are! And ye weren't afraid! Yer nae a sissy at all, but a braw laddie despite yer English!"

Henry Lindley looked up at his stepfather. "What's *braw?*" *he* said, suspiciously.

"He's complimenting you, Henry. Braw means brave," the earl said.

"Gie us one like that, lassie," the old earl of Sithean said, thumping his cane on the floor. "English or nae, he's a fine laddie."

"Run along and play, you two," Jemmie instructed the two boys. Then, taking India and Fortune by the hand, he led them over to meet his aunts and his sisters, all of whom made a great fuss over the little girls, admiring their beauty, and their intelligence.

"Mama's going to have another baby," Fortune confided to Fiona.

"I know," Fiona replied, smiling at the child. Fiona was childless among all the Leslie women, except for a bastard son born many years earlier when she was wed to her first husband. The baby had been put out to fosterage immediately after his birth. He had lived to age three, then died of a fever one winter. It had been a hard birth, and Fiona could not bear children ever again. Knowing it, Adam Leslie had still married her, for he loved her. "Ye hae hair the color of my great-grandmam," she told Fortune. "She was a verra great lady." She playfully tweaked one of Fortune's curls.

"Mama says I'm a hoyden," Fortune replied.

"So am I," Fiona told the little girl with a wink, and made an immediate friend.

The meal was a simple one, for Jasmine had not yet had time to hire servants, and Will Todd, along with Adali, had done the cooking.

"Dinna fear," Adam Leslie said. "The word is already out that the earl is back, and ye'll hae servants aplenty by week's end. Those that were here before, and are nae too old to work will come, and those who are too old will send their kinfolk to obtain the positions."

His words were prophetic, and within a few days the castle was fully staffed once more. Will Todd remained to aid Adali for the present, helping him to choose the proper people.

"I'll stay the winter," Will Todd said. "The castle is a snug place in the winter, but come the spring I'll be off to my wee cottage wi its pretty stream, and the salmon just asking to be caught." He grinned at Adali. "They already respect ye, which is guid considering yer a foreigner. Ye'll hae nae trouble wi them."

Within days the castle was clean again; the floors swept; the rugs and the tapestries brought from storage to be laid upon the floor and hung upon the walls. The chimneys were cleaned and drew flawlessly. The windows were washed, and sparkled in the beautiful autumn weather. The furniture lost its lackluster look and glowed with polishing. Silver appeared upon the sideboards; scented potpourri filled beautiful porcelain bowls that Adali had found in a storage area in the west tower of the castle. Firewood was stacked by the fireplaces. Crystal decanters of wine sat upon the sideboards in all the rooms. Flowers, a mixture of domesticated and wild, were everywhere throughout the living areas of the castle. Even a schedule had been set for meals, which were now served on time each day.

One of the last remaining monks from Glenkirk Abbey came to tutor the children. Once a well-known house of learning, the abbey had fallen upon hard times. The old faith was practiced secretly or discreetly throughout Scotland. The Presbyterians and the Anglicans now held sway. Religious houses were barely tolerated if at all. At Glenkirk, however, the Leslies, while members of the new religions, practiced tolerance where the abbey and its inhabitants were concerned. The last abbot had been one of their cousins. Now but a scant dozen monks remained, the majority elderly, and three in their middle years. Once there had been a school at the abbey. It no longer existed for lack of students. The monks were pleased to send one of their own to teach the earl's stepchildren.

Jasmine, who had been educated by a priest, told Adali, "See that the abbey is sent a deer to hang in their larder; and since Will Todd enjoys his fishing, have him do some for the monks. And send bread when we bake at least once a week, and a wheel of cheese, and a basket each of apples and pears."

He nodded. "Brother Duncan will be pleased."

The autumn deepened, and the trees began to turn on the bens, which Jasmine learned was the Scots for mountains. The red oaks mingled with the golden aspen and birch and the deep green of the pines. Red whortleberry, hazel, bog myrtle, and holly with their rose, yellow, shiny green leaves and bright red berries brightened the woodlands. There was heather in bloom on the hillsides. The nights had become cool and crisp, and never had Jasmine seen such stars in the sky as she saw from the battlements of Glenkirk Castle. Her husband had not lied when he said that autumn was the most beautiful time of year in Scotland.

Jasmine's mother and stepfather and half brothers returned in mid-October from England. The countess of BrocCairn brought rather disturbing news. The king, it seemed, had sent to the earl and countess of Glenkirk to invite them to his Christmas court. "I wasn't there when the messenger came," Velvet Gordon told her daughter. "We were over at Blackthorne Hall, saying good-bye to Deirdre and John."

"How strange," the earl of Glenkirk remarked. "Jamie knew we intended returning north in late summer."

"Grandmama will have taken care of it," Jasmine said confidently.

And indeed Skye O'Malley de Marisco, who had hoped for a little peace and quiet now that she had seen Jasmine safely remarried and her youngest daughter and her family returned to Scotland, found herself in the midst of a situation worthy of her younger days. She had sent the king's messenger back to Winchester, the royal autumn residence, with a note to the king saying that her granddaughter and her husband had already returned to Scotland for the autumn and winter months. Her surprise was great, therefore, when several weeks later the most beautiful young man she had seen since her third husband, Geoffrey Southwood, appeared upon her doorstep and was ushered into her library where she sat reading by her fire. She arose as he came forward.

The young man bowed with great elegance, and once again she was reminded of Geoffrey. "Viscount Villiers at your service, madame."

"So you are George Villiers," Skye said. "My granddaughter has nothing but kind things to say about you. Sit down.

Will you have wine?" She was already pouring him a goblet of her best as she spoke. Handing it to him, she asked, "To what do I owe the honor of your visit, my lord? Surely you know that Jasmine and Jemmie are at Glenkirk."

"But why did they go when the king expressly forbade it until the matter of Lord Stokes's murder was cleared up?" George Villiers said. "The king is furious with them, and that wretched Piers St. Denis is egging His Majesty into issuing a warrant for the earl and countess of Glenkirk. The queen has, so far, been able to prevent her husband from doing so. She sent me to you to learn if you know of any reason for the Leslie's disobedience so she may defend them against the marquis of Hartsfield's accusations. He says they have fled because they know that their guilt in Lord Stokes's murder will soon be discovered."

"When did the king order Jasmine and Jemmie to remain in England, my lord? They said nothing of it to me. James Leslie has always been a loyal adherent of the Stuarts. He would not flout the king's authority under any circumstances. It is not in his nature. Besides, I thought the king was convinced that neither Jasmine nor Jemmie had anything to do with that poor man's murder," Skye said.

"St. Denis convinced the king to send a messenger here to Queen's Malvern before your granddaughter's marriage, instructing Glenkirk and his bride to remain in England. St. Denis still believes he can still somehow revenge himself on them and obtain the custody of the little duke of Lundy. The king cannot rid himself of St. Denis until a wife is found for him, and the queen cannot bring herself to give St. Denis some innocent young heiress because of his reputation for deviant passion. The queen, I believe, hopes St. Denis will just go away, but of course he will not. And the king is too kindhearted to send him away because he fears he would hurt his friend, and he, himself, would look like an ingrate. So Piers St. Denis remains at court, making difficulties for all," young Viscount Villiers concluded.

"No messenger came to Queen's Malvern from the king either before or after my granddaughter's marriage. In fact it has been a most uneventful summer with one exception. Jasmine is to have a child in late winter," Skye told George Villiers. "If a messenger had come, the Leslies would have remained here, but none did, and they followed their plans to return to Scotland."

George Villiers sipped at his wine thoughtfully, pulling himself back to the day that the marquis of Hartsfield had convinced the king to keep the earl and countess of Glenkirk in England. He had offered to carry the king's missive to one of the royal messengers for dispatch himself, and had hurried off clutching the packet. *"But he didn't deliver it!"* the viscount said aloud. He looked to Skye. "St. Denis offered to take the message to one of the royal messengers, madame. Obviously he did not do so, knowing that Jasmine and Jemmie would return north as they had planned. It was his idea to bring them back to court for the Christmas festivities in December, too! He has planned it all, the clever devil, and I underestimated him! I thought we had him beaten! What a fool I am, and Jasmine warned me, too," Villiers cried despairingly.

"Not so much a fool, my lord," Skye soothed the young man. "You are not experienced enough in court intrigue to know that a desperate man will resort to rash measures to ensure his survival." She looked past him to the darkening sky beyond her windows. "It is too late for you to begin your return journey today, George Villiers. You will stay the night, and then tomorrow *we* will return to court to explain to the king that his messenger never arrived. We will make no accusations, however, for we have no proof; but you will immediately upon your return seek out the head royal messenger and learn if any of them have left the royal service since last June. If not, you will ask each messenger if he was entrusted with the royal missive. If you are right, then none will admit to it," Skye told him, "and then you have your proof of St. Denis's dishonesty, and the vitriol he harbors toward my granddaughter."

"But what if a messenger has left the royal service since last June?" Villiers asked her.

"Then," said Skye, "we have no proof against St. Denis. We can plan no further until we know everything we need to know, dear boy, or St. Denis makes a foolish move."

"Mad as hatter, you are!" Daisy Kelly told her mistress when informed that Skye would be leaving for Winchester in the morning. "Since the master has died, you've been your troublesome old self again, and we just ain't young enough anymore for your wicked ruses!"

"Speak for yourself, you old fool!" Skye snapped at her. "Do you think I can allow this St. Denis fellow to ruin my darling girl's life? Besides, you aren't coming to Winchester with me."

"*What?*" Daisy squawked indignantly.

"I'm taking Bramwell's daughter, Nora, with me. I need you to stay here and pack up what we'll need to spend the winter in Scotland," Skye said calmly. "Now I won't need much for tomorrow. Just some traveling clothes and one decent gown for my audience with the king."

For once in the over sixty years of their association, Daisy was rendered speechless. Muttering beneath her breath, she set about to do her mistress's bidding, thoroughly disapproving of it all.

In the morning as she bid Skye farewell, she asked, "When do we leave for the north?" Her tone was sharp, and her lips twitched with acute annoyance.

"I'll want a full day's rest when I return," Skye told her, "but the day after that we'll go. We've never been to Scotland, Daisy," she cajoled her faithful servant. "You'll get to see Pansy and her family. Don't you want to see them?"

"Saw me daughter all summer long," Daisy replied sourly.

"I'll be back as quickly as possible," Skye told her, climbing into her big, comfortable traveling coach.

"I don't doubt it," Daisy said.

George Villiers was amazed that the coach was able to keep up with him on their journey south, and old Lady de Marisco was an intrepid traveler it appeared. They traveled until dark. She ate a hearty meal, then returned to her bed; up and ready to go first light. They traveled directly from Queen's Malvern, which was located near Worcester, through Glouster, Swindon, and Andover, directly into Winchester. There had been no need to come near London at all. The king and queen liked to hunt in the autumn in the nearby New Forest.

"They'll not be in the town itself," Villiers told Skye, "but in their hunting lodge outside of it. They enjoy the informality of it much better, but it's a bit hard on the courtiers who don't have houses here, or aren't able to rent houses. Many end up sleeping in barns and in haystacks," he chuckled, "and washing in icy streams."

"The price of following the court," Skye said dryly. "Can you find this old lady a place to lay her head, my handsome lad?"

"Madame, you may have my cubicle in the royal lodge," he said gallantly. "It's terribly tiny, but you will be able to change your garments and get a decent night's sleep."

"If I were twenty years younger, my lad, you wouldn't have to give up your bed at all, just share it," she teased him.

"It is the first time I have ever regretted my youth," he told her, and Skye laughed aloud, delighted by his quick tongue and the charming compliment he had just paid her.

"You are more dangerous than St. Denis, I think," she said.

His dark eyes flashed a moment, then he said, "I think that you praise me too highly, madame."

"Nay, Villiers, I think you are greatly underestimated, but they will learn it in time," Skye told him quietly with a small smile. What a charming rogue he was, she thought, and very ambitious, but there was no harm in ambition. She had had it herself in her youth, when life was so wonderfully intense, and she could scarcely wait for one day to end so another could begin.

She wore black for her audience with the king. She was, after all, in mourning for her beloved Adam. Her dark hair with its two silver side wings was affixed in its familiar chignon. "Give me a bit of color for my cheeks," she asked Nora, the maidservant who had traveled with her.

"Let me do it," Nora said. "You have beautiful skin for any woman, let alone an old woman, my lady. We want the merest touch of color. Too much, and you lose the proper effect." She dabbed the color on ever so slightly, smoothing it until Skye's cheeks showed just the faintest touch of rose. "Perfect," she announced, and held up the small traveling glass for her mistress to see.

Skye looked into the mirror. She was astounded. She did look frail. An elegant, fragile old woman stared back at her. *Who is she?* Skye wondered. *I don't feel old in my head. Just my joints. No wonder Bess never allowed mirrors about her in her later years. Still, she had lived longer than Elizabeth Tudor, and dammit, she did look better!*

The king stared at the woman before him. She was garbed in the height of fashion, and her jewelry was incredible to behold, especially the diamonds and pearls she wore. Blue eyes met his for just a fraction of a second before she curtsied, back straight as a poker, head lowered just the proper amount. Then she rose and awaited permission to speak.

"Steenie tells me ye treated him verra well, madame," the king began. "He hae pleaded wi me to listen to ye, and so I will. What excuse can the Leslies of Glenkirk possibly hae for disobeying me, madame?" The king glared at the elegant old woman before him. Despite her age, she was still a great beauty, and he somehow thought it indecent that she should be. "Well, madame?" he barked.

"Viscount Villiers tells me that Your Majesty sent a message to my granddaughter and her husband at Queen's Malvern, but no messenger at all arrived at my home during the summer. They departed for Glenkirk as they had planned in late August. Your Majesty knows that if James Leslie had received your instructions, I should not be here today to speak for him, or for my granddaugher," Skye said firmly.

"Dinna receive my message? Are ye saying, madame, that no royal messenger arrived? Am I to understand that is the reason for this disobedience?" The king looked confused.

"No messenger arrived," Skye repeated.

"This is verra strange," the king puzzled.

"Perhaps Lady de Marisco was not aware of a messenger's arrival," Piers St. Denis said, confusing the king further.

Skye's head swiveled just slightly, and she pierced the marquis of Hartsfield with a strong look. "I do not know you, sir," she said icily, "but rest assured that *nothing happens* with regard to my household of which I am not fully aware. If I say no royal messenger arrived at Queen's Malvern, then no royal messenger arrived. To question me further on the matter would be to imply that I am lying. Is that what you are implying, sir?" Her beautiful face was stony.

"Madame, at your age," he began, only to be cut off.

"*My age?* Sir, you do indeed presume!" Skye told him. "My age has nothing to do with the matter at hand. *Who are you?*"

"I am the marquis of Hartsfield," he told her, but she had already known it.

"And I, my lord, am the dowager countess of Lynmouth and Lundy, *and* the dowager duchess of Beaumont de Jaspre. How dare you impugn my honor! Were we not in the royal presence, I should call you out myself. I am quite an excellent swordswoman, and I do believe it would give me great pleasure to slit your gullet, you arrogant puppy! I am not surprised my granddaughter chose Glenkirk over you. It is the difference between water and rich wine." She turned to the king. "My lord, you know that I have the utmost respect for Your Majesty, but must I remain here to be insulted by this *person?*"

It was a magnificent performance. The queen caught Viscount Villier's eye and saw that he was close to losing his vaunted composure. The marquis of Hartsfield looked stunned by the attack he had just encountered at the skilled hands of Skye O'Malley de Marisco. The king, mindful of Lady de Marisco's age, was distressed that she should feel under attack in his presence, and when she swayed just slightly before him, or at least he thought she did, he cried out, "A chair for Madame Skye!" using the appellation he had heard her family use for her. A footman ran forward with a small chair, which he slipped behind her.

Skye sank with apparent gratitude into the seat. "Thank you, Your Majesty," she murmured weakly, her hand upon her chest.

"Wine!" shouted the king, and it was brought.

She sipped slowly, smiling weakly at the monarch, and nodding her thanks.

"My dear Madame Skye," the king began, "I dinna want ye to feel that yer family is threatened, for it is nae so. If ye tell me that my messenger dinna arrive, then I accept yer guid word, for in all that I hae heard about ye, I hae nae heard it said that ye were a liar. Indeed, 'tis said about ye that if gie yer word, it is yer bond."

"Aye, Your Majesty," Skye said quietly. This was too damned easy. Bess Tudor would have never been gulled so easily, she thought, and yet James Stuart was a sweet man. Seated, she was better able to study Piers St. Denis. He was slowly recovering from the drubbing she had just given him, and even now she could see him considering his next move. "If Your Majesty wishes, I will send to Glenkirk, and the Leslies will return; but Your Majesty should know that my granddaughter is with child. James Leslie will at last have an heir again after *all* these years." *There!* That would prevent St. Denis from demanding their return. The king was softhearted, and would not endanger the Leslie infant.

"Nah! Nah!" James Stuart said, even as she had silently predicted. "We canna allow any harm to come to Jemmie's bairn, madame. I accept yer word in the matter, and it is now closed."

"Thank you, Your Majesty," Skye said sweetly, pleased to see that the marquis of Hartsfield had been neatly checked. She arose from her seat, handing her goblet to a page, curtsying once again to the king. "Your Majesty will excuse me, I hope. I have traveled far and am quite tired. I must start back in the morning."

"Aye, Madame Skye, ye hae our permission to retire. Go wi our blessing, and when ye write to yer granddaughter, tell her we are verra pleased to learn of her coming bairn. Steenie! Escort the lady!"

Viscount Villiers stepped forward and offered his arm to Skye. Accepting it, she moved with stately grace across the room to the door. There, however, the marquis of Hartsfield stood blocking their way. He glared at Skye, openly angry, and she laughed.

"You have not the skill to play my game, my lord," she told him mockingly. "I learned from Bess Tudor herself."

"She is dead now," he said menacingly.

"*I am not,*" replied Skye boldly, and she passed from the room with George Villiers. When they were in the hallway beyond, Skye said to him, "I would not be surprised if Lord Stokes met his end at the hands of Piers St. Denis. He is dangerous and desperate enough."

"Do you truly think so, madame?" Of course! Why hadn't he thought of it himself. St. Denis was the logical culprit, having the most to gain, or so he believed.

"I do. See if you can link him to the crime, and the king's troubles will be over, my ambitious young lord," Skye told him. "The poor queen will not have to find him a bride, and the king can imprison him and thereby be free of his irritating company.

"But how?" Villiers was thinking aloud. "He has no friends."

"There must be someone," Skye told him.

"Only his half brother," came the reply.

"Can he be suborned, my little viscount?" They were now standing in an alcove.

George Villiers shook his head. "I do not believe so."

"There must be *something* this man wants that he does not have," Skye said. "Every one of us has a weakness, my young friend."

"What is yours?" he asked her, smiling.

She chuckled. "I am past temptation now, George Villiers. I have wealth, health, children, grandchildren, and great-grandchildren. I look far better for my years than I ought to, or so my eldest daughter tells me—and she does not lie. The only thing I lack no one can give me. I want my Adam back! I have never missed anyone as I miss him. It seems as if he was always there in my life. But we are not conspiring here over me. It is St. Denis we must bring down. Younger brothers always envy the elder, and this one, I expect, is no exception."

"He is not the younger, but the elder by a few hours," said the viscount. "He is the bastard, and Piers St. Denis the legitimate heir. But he is loyal to a fault and would not betray his brother."

"What if he could be legitimized, and made the marquis in place of his brother?" she suggested. "He is human, this bastard, and while he may appear to have accepted his fate gracefully, I believe he would leap at the opportunity to change it. Particularly if a lovely and wealthy young wife went along with it, eh? Consider it, sir. Only an accident of birth has prevented this man from being the marquis of Hartsfield. You think, in the dark of the night, he does not consider it?"

"You are diabolical, madame," George Villiers said admiringly.

"I am a practical woman, dear boy," she told him. "When I want something that is perhaps thought unattainable, I seek a way to get it. Get the marquis's brother to tell the truth of the matter regarding Lord Stokes, and you will have what you want. A clear field with the king, and a path strewn with riches and titles—*which is what you want.*"

"Jasmine did tell you about me," he chuckled. "Your advice is sound, Madame Skye, and I shall follow it to the letter."

"I have no doubt that you will triumph," she told him.

"Tell Jasmine I shall write to her," he said. "I did promise."

It was the last she was to see of George Villiers for the time being. The following morning Skye set off back to Queen's Malvern, where Daisy awaited her, still fuming ten days after the fact about their trip.

"If the king accepts yer excuse, then why are we going?" she demanded of her mistress, having heard the tale of Skye's latest adventure.

"The king is not the problem," came the reply. "It is the marquis of Hartsfield that I fear. He is not ready to give up, and probably won't be until he is in hell. He appears to have given up any attempt to win Jasmine, but he wants the power that having the wardship of Charlie-boy would give him. He has already managed to remove one rival and escape justice. Now he will come after Jasmine and Jemmie, and I must warn them," Skye concluded as she climbed into bed.

"Why not just send a messenger?" Daisy suggested.

"Just remember, my girl, that the king's messenger never arrived here," Skye told her. "It is far easier to remove a messenger than it will be to remove me. No! Tomorrow I rest, and the day after we go! If you want to remain behind, dearest Daisy, you may. I'll not force you to make a journey you do not want to make."

Daisy sighed deeply. "You'll not leave me behind," she said, resigned. "Haven't I always been with you, my lady? But the truth of the matter is that I feel my age more than you do. We'll take Nora along also to give me a bit of a hand."

"What a fine idea!" Skye said enthusiastically, not daring to tell her old servant that she had already told Nora that she would be traveling with them to help Daisy.

"Good!" Daisy replied. "Then it's settled. Now you get some rest, my lady. We'll be traveling hard, I suspect, for you'll not want to let that marquis of Hartsfield get ahead of us, eh?"

Nothing felt better than one's own bed, Skye thought, as she snuggled down into her featherbed. "Aye," she agreed with Daisy. "I don't know what he plans next, but he is not beaten yet," she said. "He's up to some mischief. I can sense it in my bones."

And, as always, Skye's instincts were sharp. Piers St. Denis knew that he was unwelcome at court now, yet he remained, for the king was not able to bring himself to dismiss him and send him home. The queen, supposedly in charge of finding him a suitable wife, dallied interminably over a possible selection of eligible women and girls. And Villiers, now elevated to the rank of viscount, was unbearably obnoxious to him.

"You'd think he was a royal duke, and not just a pimple on the king's arse," he groused to his half brother.

"Unless he makes a serious mistake, he will be a duke one day," Kipp said thoughtfully. While Villiers was indeed scornful of Piers, he had been nothing but distantly polite to the Hartsfield bastard, as Kipp was known about the court. In a strange way Kipp admired George Villiers. He allowed nothing to stand in his path, and his unflagging charm had won him many supporters among the powerful, unlike Piers, whose arrogance far overrode his charm of late. Piers hated to lose, and he played only to the king. Villiers was more clever, and played to the whole court, and it was certainly paying off for him. Kipp wished his brother would be more like him. Of late Piers's hunger for revenge and for power was overwhelming his charm and his common sense. Kipp had attempted to warn him.

"I need no advice from you on how to behave," Piers snarled. "I have the means by which to win this game in my hands even now. Pack our things. We are leaving for Scotland."

"What have you got?" Kipp asked him, curious.

Piers St. Denis smiled cruelly and, reaching into his doublet, offered his half brother a rolled parchment. "This," he said.

Kipp unrolled the parchment, and read it. He was astounded. "How did you get the king to do this?" he asked.

"The arrest warrant was already made out but for the names, but the king had signed it. I stole it off his secretary's desk. I shall decide when we get to Scotland whether it shall be both Jasmine, and her husband, or just James Leslie. I somehow fancy the lady becoming my possession and my toy while she bargains for her husband's life," he said cruelly. "Then I shall see James Leslie hanged in the king's name, after which I shall marry his widow immediately, thereby gaining both her wealth and her children. It is a foolproof plan, Kipp. The king's warrant will be accepted by the Scots, who have no real knowledge of what is happening here in England. Old king fool may weep and protest after the fact, but there will be no denying his signature at the bottom of that warrant." He laughed coldly. "I said she was mine, and she is, even if I must wait a bit longer to attain the prize. And that old woman who is her grandmother will not stop me either!"

"Piers, Piers," his brother cautioned. "This is a very dangerous game you are attempting to play. The Leslies are not without influence in Scotland. You have already committed one murder. Do not, I beg you, attempt another. You will surely be caught!"

"I had to kill Stokes," St. Denis said. "You would not, you weakling! It was the first time in your life that you ever disobeyed me, but I have forgiven you, Kipp. Because of your mother's peasant blood, you are not as strong as I am, and that you cannot help. I will not be caught, big brother. Remember? *I never get caught!* How many beatings did you take for my sins when we were growing up?" he laughed.

"You cannot always be fortunate, Piers," Kipp warned him.

"Why not?" the marquis of Hartsfield demanded. "Perhaps I shall not marry her. Perhaps I shall have her hanged also, but *after* you and I have taken our pleasure of her and taught her the delights of pain. I can still control her wealth and her children. Mayhap I shall take her eldest daughter for a wife. *Yes!* We can raise the little bitch to suit ourselves, and she will complain at me that I killed her husband. 'Tis a much better plan, Kipp! Eh?"

"I think it too dangerous," Kipp replied bluntly; and he did. It was *all* becoming too dangerous, and Piers had the look of a fanatic about him these days. Seducing highborn ladies, and raping peasant girls was a lark, but when Piers had suggested murder, he had thought him simply struggling with the frustration of losing for the first time in his life. His brother enjoyed holding power over people, and hence his passion for whipping his conquests with a variety of implements until they begged and pleaded with him for mercy. That seemed to arouse Piers far more than just a beautiful, exciting woman eager to share his passion.

But murder? When it had first been brought up he didn't believe Piers would ever follow through with such a plan, and so as he had always done, Kipp followed along. Then Piers had instructed him to kill Stokes, and he couldn't do it, but Piers had, making him come along to witness the deed. He would never forget the surprised look in Richard Stokes's eyes when he realized he had been killed. Piers had obviously enjoyed driving the slender dagger deep into his victim, twisting it slowly to inflict pain as well as death. Kipp had turned away, vomiting into the underbrush with both shock and guilt. But Piers had felt no guilt. He had removed a rival, and he was elated.

Now his brother was contemplating another murder, nay, two murders. How could he betray him, although he knew he should go to the king and beg mercy for Piers. He was obviously as mad as his mother had become after several years of marriage to their father. Piers might mock Kipp's mother, but it was she who had the major burden of raising her lover's two sons, and caring for his delicate wife as she slipped in and out of reality until her death at the age of thirty.

Kipp sighed. He would have to go to Scotland with Piers. He knew what he was going to do. He would steal the royal warrant from his brother so he could not use it to commit additional murders. *I should be the marquis,* Kipp considered, as he had often secretly and guiltily thought. *I am far more responsible than my brother.* Then he sighed again. He must be loyal to Piers. It had been their father's dying wish of him, *and he had promised.*

Chapter Fifteen

The de Marisco's traveling coach had rumbled into the courtyard of Glenkirk Castle in midafternoon on St. Andrew's Day, which was the last day of November. The sun was already setting in a blaze of glory over the western mountains. It had taken over three weeks from Queen's Malvern, and the weather had been foul most of the trip. Thistlewood, sitting up on his box, had never been happier in his life to see the end of a journey, especially knowing he wouldn't have to make the return trip until the late springtime or early summer. As Daisy so pithily remarked constantly on their journey, they wasn't getting any younger, any of them. Then she would look pointedly at Skye, who just ignored her, and determinedly encouraged them all onward. But they could all see that she was tired, nay exhausted, Thistlewood the coachman amended.

"Get the earl," he called down to a footman as he drew the horse to a halt, and in short order James Leslie exited his house.

Recognizing the coach, he hurried to its door and, pulling it open, was surprised to find Jasmine's grandmother dozing in a corner of the carriage. "Madame Skye?" He was astounded to see her.

She opened her blue eyes, smiled, and said, "Thank goodness we're finally here, Jemmie!"

"She's fair wore out," came Daisy's voice from the dim interior of the vehicle. "Wouldn't travel at a reasonable pace. Nay! Not her!"

The earl of Glenkirk reached into the coach and, wrapping his strong arms about Skye, lifted her out, calling to Daisy to follow along. Then he tenderly carried Jasmine's grandmother into the castle, directly up the staircase, and into the Great Hall, where he set her down in a chair by one of the roaring fireplaces. She made absolutely no protest, which indicated to him her weakened condition. Going over to the sideboard, he poured her a full goblet of rich red wine, and then pressed it into her hand. "It's from Archambault," he said. "Drink it down," he gently commanded her. Then seeing Adali, he said, "Fetch your mistress immediately. Tell her that her grandmother has arrived." He turned back to Skye, who was gratefully drinking down the wine.

When she had finished it she looked at him, and said, "Whiskey would have been better. Don't tell me you don't have your own still about, for I am certain you do, dear boy."

He laughed. "You'll live," he said, but he was concerned by the faint purple shadows beneath her eyes. She had come with a purpose, and she had come quickly, for she had not sent ahead any warning of her arrival. It did not portend anything good, but he would wait for her to tell him, for when she regained her strength she would. He took her hand in his, and kissed it. "Jasmine will be so happy to see you." Then he simply sat by her side, holding that elegant hand in his, willing the warmth back into her slender body, realizing that if he loved Jasmine, he loved this old woman as well, and her indominable spirit which he hoped would be passed on to his children.

"*Grandmama!*" She flew into the hall, hurrying to Skye's side.

"My darling girl," Skye said, holding out her arms to Jasmine who, kneeling next to her grandmother, was wrapped in her embrace.

"Why on earth have you made such a long journey in such chancy weather?" Jasmine asked her, now sitting upon the floor by her grandmother's knee and looking up at her. "Why didn't you tell us you were coming?"

"There was no time," Skye said. "I had to reach you before that scoundrel St. Denis makes more mischief, darling girl."

"The marquis of Hartsfield?" Jasmine said. "What on earth has he to do with anything?"

"More wine?" the earl asked her.

Skye looked at him quizzically.

"Whiskey?" he said, smothering a laugh.

She nodded, and, when she had drunk a bit of the amber liquid, she began her tale even as Daisy and Nora were telling it to Adali. Adali listened to the two women. He was pleased to see that Madame Skye had added Nora to her personal staff to be of help to Daisy. The girl was the daughter of the Queen's Malvern housekeeper and majordomo, the Bramwells. She was no slattern, and could be trusted. They were going to need all the cool heads they could muster, Adali thought, until this business with the marquis of Hartsfield was settled once and for all.

Skye settled into Glenkirk Castle. Adali housed her in the west tower apartments, which had once been used by the fabled Janet Leslie. It consisted of three floors. On the first was an anteroom, and two small bedrooms which would house Daisy and Nora. On the second floor was a dining room with a pantry, and a lovely dayroom that had once been used for preparing food for m'lady Janet. On the top floor was a lovely airy bedchamber and a garderobe. All the rooms but the garderobe had fireplaces. It took several days to make these rooms habitable again. The draperies and the bed hangings had to be found, brushed, and hung. The dust sheets were removed from the lovely old oak furniture, which was then polished up. Wonderful oriental carpets were brought from the castle storerooms and laid upon the floors. They had belonged to the lady Janet, and when she had moved to her own newly built castle of Sithean, they had somehow been left behind. Skye's clothing was stored in the garderobe. Her featherbed, pillows, and personal linens were used to make the bed, and the remainder of the linens put in a cedar-lined oak trunk. Silver candlesticks and shining brass lamps were brought to illuminate the rooms; wood was stacked by the fireplaces, to be replenished each morning and afternoon. A crystal decanter of wine and one of whiskey along, with four silver goblets, appeared upon the sideboard in the dayroom, along with a bowl of spicy potpourri.

"I am amazed that she would leave Queen's Malvern," the earl of Glenkirk said to his wife as they lay contentedly in their bed. Outside the northwest winds howled, and an icy rain pelted against the windows.

"I am not," Jasmine said quietly, and snuggled against her husband's shoulder. "She doesn't want to be at Queen's Malvern for the holidays this year, Jemmie. Can you understand that? And she would not go to any of my aunts, or uncles, for they will make a long face of it and her heart will break all over again. I am the only one who wasn't there, and so she has come to me. I am glad! I have never had a baby without Grandmama nearby to watch over me."

He put his hand upon her belly, feeling the child stir beneath his touch. "He's a strong bairn, Jasmine."

"You're certain that it's a lad," she teased him.

"Aye," he answered her with great certainty.

"So am I," she said softly, and she put her hand over his. "Patrick, sixth earl of Glenkirk. He will follow a proud tradition of Leslies, Jemmie, won't he? And he'll be a grand man."

"Like our other lads," her husband answered her. "With you for a mother, he cannot help it, Jasmine, my darling Jasmine!" and he kissed her tenderly. He would not make love to her now, for her condition prevented it, but he enjoyed stroking her and kissing her, as did she. Her breasts were large and decorated with slender blue veins now. He found it very exciting to think that those beautiful breasts would shortly nourish his bairn. A wetnurse had also been found for the coming child.

The children had all settled well into Glenkirk, making friends easily with the castle and village children. India, who would be eight in March, and Henry who would be seven in April, were, along with little Fortune, receiving lessons daily from Brother Duncan. Little Charles Frederick Stuart, at age three and a half, was considered too young, but he was intelligent, and Brother Duncan said that perhaps next autumn, after the bairn's fourth birthday, they might begin to teach him his letters. The little not-so-royal Stuart did not seem to mind waiting.

"He's all Stuart," the earl said of his stepson and ward. "Charm just like his father, and a smile that would break an angel's heart."

On the twelfth of December the Leslies celebrated Skye's seventy-sixth birthday with a family gathering, now that Jasmine's grandmother was well rested, and recovered from her long journey. This was the Leslies' first opportunity to meet Skye, and she was warmly welcomed amongst them and quickly liked. The pipes, which Skye had known in Ireland as a child, were the entertainment, along with the men of the clan, who danced for her, much to her delight.

"I do like a man with good legs," she remarked, "and you Leslies seem to be all well endowed with handsome limbs."

"And other parts," a female voice said pithily, to ensuing laughter from the women members of the clan.

India Lindley, her dark ringlets shining, cast her golden eyes up at her great-grandmother, and asked, "Are you *very* old, Grandmam?"

Skye nodded. "I am very old, India."

"Was Grandsire Adam very old, too?"

"He was eighty-four, India," Skye said softly. Damn! She missed him, she thought sadly.

"Will you live to be as old as Grandsire Adam, Grandmam?" India persisted. "I do not like it that he has gone away from us."

"I do not like it either, India," Skye told the child. "And as for how long I shall live? That, child, is in God's hands."

"I hope God will let you live forever, Grandmam!" India told her.

"Thank you, child, but I do not. One is born to die, India. It is our fate, and no one lives forever, nor would they want to. When I die I shall be reunited with all those whom I have loved and who have gone through that door we call death into the next life. I shall not be sad about it."

"I will," India said forlornly.

Skye laughed. "You will have your memories of me, child, and you will know, because I have told you so this night, that I am happy because I will be with my Adam again. But enough, India! This is a celebration of my birth, and I am here with you to enjoy it! Fetch me another piece of that apple tart with cream!"

"She's a grand old lassie," the elderly earl of Sithean remarked to his nephew of Glenkirk. "Is she here to stay?"

"I don't know," James Leslie said. "For the winter and the spring, at least. And I'm certain since she is here, BrocCairn will want her to visit them. She has never been to Scotland in all the years Velvet has been wed to Alex. They are coming for Christmas if it does not snow too heavily. And Uncle Adam and Aunt Fiona are coming up from their house in Edinburgh. We will have a full house indeed."

And on the twentieth of December the Gordons of BrocCairn arrived with four of their five sons. Sandy, the eldest, had remained at Dun Broc with his pregnant wife and her family. Jasmine's favorite half brother, Charlie, now twenty, lifted her up, and gently swung her around, while the twins, Rob and Henry, age eighteen, and Neddie, now fifteen, cheered his efforts.

"Put me down this instant, you loon!" she scolded him, but Jasmine was laughing even as she upbraided Charlie Gordon.

He set her gently upon her feet. "Yer as big as a year-old heifer," he teased her. "How's my namesake?"

"He's named for Prince Charles, too," Jasmine reminded her sibling. Then she drew forth the little duke of Lundy, who was peeping from behind her skirts at these four big fellows his mama said were his uncles. "Say hallo to your Uncle Charlie, Charlie-boy," she encouraged him.

"Charlie is *my* name," the duke of Lundy said truculently, looking up at the laughing man.

"*It was my name first,*" Charlie Gordon replied, swooping the youngster up in his arms and tickling him. "Shall we share it?"

"I gots an Uncle Charles," the little boy persisted, giggling.

"Aye, laddie, ye do. Royal Charles, who will someday be our king, God bless him! But I'm nae *Charles*. Like you I'm just plain Charlie, and I'm happy to share my name wi ye, laddie," Charlie Gordon concluded, his eyes twinkling at his little nephew.

"I'm nae plain," Charlie-boy responded. "I'm a duke."

"What's that?" his uncle asked mischievously.

The child shook his head. "I dinna know," he said to the laughter of his family.

"Ah, well then," his uncle told him, "there is plenty of time for ye to learn all about being a duke, laddie. For now I think ye would far enjoy just being a wee lad, eh. Hae ye a puppy?"

Charlie-boy shook his head again. "Nay," he said. "We all share Mama's Feathers, but she's a silly old thing."

Charlie turned to his youngest brother. "Neddie, where's the gift we brought for our wee nephew."

Reaching into his doublet, Neddie Gordon drew forth a small black-and-gold puppy, handing it to his elder sibling.

"'Tis for you, Charlie-boy," Charlie Gordon said, handing the puppy over to the wide-eyed child. "'Tis a Gordon setter, and will be a good hunting dog when it is grown." And when his nephew had taken the puppy gently into his arms, his uncle set him down on the floor again with his prize. Turning to his brother, he said, "Neddie?" and a second puppy was drawn forth from the younger Gordon's doublet and handed to Henry Lindley, who had been looking slightly crestfallen at his little brother's good fortune. "We'd nae forget ye, Henry," Charlie said to his now delighted older nephew.

"What about us?" Fortune demanded boldly.

Robert and Henry Gordon brought forth puppies from their doublets, and handed them over to their very pleased nieces.

"That's the whole litter," Charlie Gordon told his half sister.

She sighed. "'Twas kind of you," she said, weakly watching as India squealed when her puppy peed on her bodice; and her own spaniel, Feathers, growled menacingly from behind her skirts at these unruly intruders onto her territory; and the three older puppies, hastily placed upon the floor chased after her two elderly cats, Fou-Fou and Jiin, who, with amazing agility, leapt atop the sideboard, hissing while her beautiful blue-and-gold parrot, Hiraman, screeched wildly, "*Robbers! Rubbers!*" while flapping upon his perch by the fireplace.

The children, of course, giggled and ran after their puppies, gleefully tumbling over one another, while the adults began to laugh.

"'Tis certainly a well-ordered household," Velvet Gordon teased her daughter.

"'Twas your sons who brought chaos into it," Jasmine said spiritedly. "'Twas all calm until you came, Mama."

"What's for dinner?" her stepfather, the earl of BrocCairn, asked, grinning. "'Twas a damned long, cold ride over from Dun Broc. There's a good storm coming in another day or two. I can feel it in the air. We're in for a wicked hard winter."

"I hope Uncle Adam and Aunt Fiona get here safely before the storm breaks," James Leslie said.

"I wanted Mama to come over to Dun Broc, and stay with us," Velvet said. "Alec and I have been married for over a quarter of a century, and you've never seen my home, Mama."

"In the spring," Skye promised. "I've done all the traveling about I intend to do for a while."

"Thank God for that!" Daisy muttered gratefully from her seat by her mistress.

"Why, Daisy," Velvet teased her mother's companion. "You haven't had so much fun in years now, admit it! Your life was in a rut."

"I like me rut very well, Mistress Velvet," Daisy responded.

"Well, you're out of it now," Skye said, "and I vow you're looking younger than you have in twenty years."

On the twenty-second of December Adam and Fiona Leslie arrived from Edinburgh in the gray late morning. By noon the snow had begun to fall, and by dusk it was piling up upon the hillsides, in the forest, and upon the battlements and windowsills of the castle. Outside there was not a sound to be heard as the snow fell softly, showing absolutely no signs of letting up.

In the hall that night Adam Leslie delivered some rather unsettling news to his nephew. "Before we left I met Gordie MacFie in the High Street. He told me that he hae heard there was an Englishman nosing about the city seeking ye out. Said the fellow claimed to hae an arrest warrant for ye, signed by the king himself, Gordie said."

"St. Denis!" Jasmine cried, turning pale.

"Did MacFie see this Englishman, learn his name, or even see the alleged warrant?" the earl of Glenkirk asked his uncle.

Adam shook his head. "Nay. I asked."

"It is St. Denis!" Jasmine repeated. "What is the matter with him that he will not give up his futile pursuit? And did the king not give us his word, and to Grandmama, too, that we were free of the marquis of Hartsfield and his machinations? How can Piers St. Denis have an arrest warrant for you, Jemmie? *How?*"

"It is a forgery, darling Jasmine," he reassured her.

"How do you know that?" she demanded of him. "The king, it would appear, blows this way and that where St. Denis is concerned."

"We are safe here at Glenkirk," the earl told his wife.

"How can you be certain?" Jasmine cried, fearfully, her hands going to her belly as if to protect her child.

"Lassie, lassie," Adam said, kneeling by her side. "Jemmie is telling ye the truth. The winter hae begun, and nae man can travel wi' in these Highlands until the spring. The snows hae already begun to clog what few roads we hae. Fiona and I were fortunate to get here at all, and we'll nae be going home to Edinburgh until the spring comes, and the roads are open again. If this Englishman didna leave Edinburgh, and arrive here before we did, then he is nae getting here until the spring. And if he got here, what could he do? This is Leslie and Gordon territory. Do ye think we would allow him to harm the earl of Glenkirk, or his family. I dinna hear this fellow hae an army wi him. He is alone. We hae two clans' worth of lads ready to defend yer man. Dinna fear, lassie. Ye and yers are safe at Glenkirk."

"I will not run!" Jasmine said fiercely. *"Not this time!"*

"Ye dinna hae to run, lassie," Adam said quietly. "We Leslies hold what is our own, and we willna allow our earl to be taken unfairly."

The snow finally stopped falling on Christmas Eve, and they attended midnight services in the castle chapel. The Anglican mass was said by Ian Leslie, a middle-aged cousin who had been given his living by the earl. The Anglicans had made a small inroad in Scotland despite the Presbyterians and the Covenanters. The earl of Glenkirk would not have ministers of either of those factions in his house, for he held them responsible for the murder of his first wife and sons.

The Great Hall was hung with holly and other greens. A huge Yule log was dragged in, the children all accompanying it, followed by their yapping puppies. There was hot cider and mulled wine to drink, and a roast boar with an apple in its mouth that arrived upon an enormous silver salver carried by six clansmen. The children were given little bags of sugared sweets and raisins for a treat. They played games such as Hide-and-Seek, and Find-the-Slipper, while their elders sat back, well filled with bread and meat, and cheese, and wine.

The piper came into the hall that night and was given the gift of a silver piece after he had played for them. The men had, as they had on Skye's birthday feast, danced, their Leslie and Gordon kilts swaying in time with the music, their handsome faces flushed with whiskey and high spirits.

On January 1 the family exchanged gifts. The children all received ponies, which, the earl informed them, they would have to personally care for, even little Charlie-boy. Henry Lindley was told that he would have to help his brother until the duke of Lundy got a little bigger.

"When you own something," the earl of Glenkirk told his four stepchildren, "you have a responsibility for it. It will be the same with your estates and with your families. You will be responsible for its lands and its people, *your* people. And you lassies, when you are wed one day you will have the responsibility for your household, and its servants. You will have to see to their health and their wellbeing. It will be easier for you when that time comes if you begin with the small responsibility of a pony now."

"He's a good father," the earl of BrocCairn remarked to his wife about their son-in-law. "And our grandchildren will be the better for it, I dinna doubt. Ye canna let the bairns run wild."

James Leslie had a special gift for his wife. He gave her the deed to *A-Cuil*, a small lodge in the hills above Loch Sithean, which had belonged to his mother. "It isn't much, not like MacGuire's Ford, with its little castle and lands. It's just a wee stone house on a hill. We'll go there in the spring so you can see it, and after that it is your private place for when you seek to be alone."

"Wasn't that once Gordon land," Velvet said to her husband.

"Jemmie's great-grandmother was a Gordon," he remarked. "She left it to Cat. When the marriage was arranged between her, and Jemmie's father, Cat's father included *A-Cuil* in his daughter's dowry. Cat refused to wed her intended until he returned *A-Cuil* legally to her sole possession, which, I am told, he did on the very day that Jemmie was born. He knows the story better than I thought," the earl of BrocCairn told his wife.

On Twelfth Night Skye kept to her apartment in the West Tower of the castle. She could not face the celebration, but she did not want to spoil it for the children. Her daughter and granddaughter joined her in the afternoon, and together they wept for Adam de Marisco, gone from them a full year now.

"When Willow's father died," Skye told them, "I thought I would die, too, but for Willow's sake I had to be brave. When Geoffrey Southwood died I mourned him and our son John almost to my own death. It was Adam who pulled me back. Then I lost Niall Burke, but by that time I had become hardened to death, and there was Adam once more. I swore I would not marry again. I had buried five husbands by then. He insisted that that was because he was the only husband for me. He promised me he would live forever by my side; that he would not leave me as the others had done." She sighed deeply. "But we don't live forever, my darling girls, do we? And I had over forty years with that wonderful man. Now all that is left for me is to await death."

"Mama! Do not say such a thing!" Velvet implored her mother.

"If you are yet here, Grandmama," Jasmine said quietly, "perhaps it is because God still has things for you to do. Have you not always scolded me about fighting my fate? Do not fight yours, whatever it is."

A small smile touched Skye's lips. "How clever of you, Jasmine, to use my own logic against me," she told her granddaughter.

"Never *against* you, Grandmama," Jasmine replied. "I need you!" She took her grandmother's hand and placed it upon her distended belly. "And Patrick Leslie needs you. And the babies that will come after him. I can't have babies without you by my side, Grandmama. Do not return to Queen's Malvern except in the summers, when Mama and I will go. Stay here in Scotland at Glenkirk with me."

"Glenkirk is your home, Jasmine," Skye told her. "Queen's Malvern is mine. I will return to it in the spring, and I will not leave it once I am safely home again. I will die there as my Adam did, and you will bury me next to him on that hillside."

Velvet began to weep piteously. "Do not talk so, Mama."

Skye shook her head irritably, her eyes meeting those of her granddaughter. Jasmine understood her and would one day see that her wishes were carried out. Poor Velvet. There had been but one adventure in her life. How could she possibly understand? And yet from that adventure had come this magnificent granddaughter. Reaching out, she took Jasmine's hand in hers and squeezed it. Jasmine smiled back.

A few days after Twelfth Night there was a brief thaw, and the Gordons of BrocCairn took the opportunity to make their way the few miles separating Glenkirk from Dun Broc.

"I doubt I'll be able to come back until spring," Velvet told her daughter. "You don't need me to have babies, Jasmine. You seem to do quite well all by yourself, and besides, Mama is here with you." She was snuggled down between several fox and wolf pelts within the heavy sledge that had brought them across the hills in time for Christmas. Three of Jasmine's half brothers were settled about their mother, and Charlie was up on the bench seat with his father to help with the driving.

"I will try and send word of some kind," James Leslie told his in-laws. "I'll light a fire on the beacon hill for you to see when Jasmine has delivered the bairn. If it burns two nights running, then you will know it's a lad. One night for a lass."

"It's a laddie," Jasmine said stubbornly.

Now only Adam and Fiona Leslie remained at Glenkirk with them, and Jasmine was glad for the company of Jemmie's aunt, who was set in years between Jasmine and Skye. She was a clever, wickedly funny woman, and through her Jasmine learned all about her husband's mother. She was sorry that she could not know Cat.

"She would like you even if you are the exact opposite of the wife she picked for Jemmie. She did her best, though, aligning him to the more powerful branch of the Gordon Clan. Isabelle, however, hae all the common sense of a peahen," Fiona declared bluntly. "Only a fool would hae gone to St. Margaret's Convent that day. The Covenanters had been swaggering all about the area, rooting out the poor hapless priests of the old kirk and their adherents. It was a particularly vicious band that had already committed several atrocities in the name of God, crucifying priests upside down, looting and burning. Jemmie told her nae to go, but she insisted, saying that the nuns had finished some linens for her, and she must hae them. So she went, taking her laddies wi her, and ye know the rest." Fiona crossed herself. "God hae mercy on their guid souls," she said.

"And they never found them?" Skye asked.

Fiona shook her head. "By the time the mischief was done, they were long gone back to whatever hell hold they had climbed out from," she said.

"I do not understand this business of people believing one religion is superior to another, but then I was raised in my father's court, and he was a very open-minded man," Jasmine told Fiona.

The winter deepened, and reached its midpoint. The snows were piled high, blocking all travel. Some nights they could hear the wolves howling high upon the bens. Only the gentle lengthening of the days indicated that the winter would eventually leave the land. January passed. Then February. The life they led was peaceful and ordinary. Jasmine oversaw the household with Adali's help. The children took their lessons with Brother Duncan in the mornings and early afternoons, and played with their puppies, who were growing by leaps and bounds, in the later afternoon. They rode their ponies about the courtyard of the castle, which was kept shoveled, and Jasmine could not ever remember seeing her children so happy. At last they had a normal life, and James Leslie was responsible for it.

In midmorning of the fifth day of March Jasmine told her grandmother and Fiona that she might be going into labor. By late afternoon she was absolutely certain she was in labor. The birthing table was brought from the castle attics and set up in the dayroom of the Glenkirk's apartments. Rohana, Toramalli, Adali, and the two older women stood in attendance.

"What can I do?" the earl asked of his wife, kissing her moist brow. "I know how hard birthing can be. I well remember Isabelle's travails when she bore Jamie and George." It was the first time Jasmine could ever remember hearing him speak of his dead sons by name.

"You and Uncle Adam keep the children amused," she told him, drawing his head to hers, and kissing him lightly. "I have shamefully easy births when compared to most women, or so Grandmama says."

"'Tis true but for Fortune, who decided to be born wrong-way around. We were in Ireland, as you know, Jemmie, and had not my late sister, Eibhlinn, come from her convent and turned the babe about, it would have been an even worse situation. Both Jasmine and the baby might have died. Of course Fortune was born a healthy infant, thank God! This child is positioned quite properly," Skye quickly reassured him.

"And will be born before much longer," Jasmine assured her husband with a grin. Then she winced as a pain swept over her. "The little devil is anxious enough, my lord. Another determined Leslie for the world to contend with, I'll vow."

Patrick Leslie, destined to be the sixth earl of Glenkirk, was born three minutes after midnight on the sixth of March. He was his father's image, with a headful of dark hair and eyes that, while a baby blue, already showed signs of darkening to green-gold in future. Cleaned and swaddled, he was put to his mother's breast and suckled strongly from the start, causing his mother to declare him a little beast of a bairn. When she said it the infant stopped sucking for a moment and regarded his maternal parent with strangely intelligent eyes for a long minute, then turned back to the nourishing nipple.

"God's nightshirt!" Jasmine said softly.

Her husband chuckled. "He's a Leslie all right. He reminded me of my father just then, the little devil!"

"Strange," Jasmine replied, "he reminded me of mine."

Since the new heir to Glenkirk was to be named Patrick, he was baptized on the seventeenth day of March, the Feast of St. Patrick. Jasmine asked Skye to stand as Patrick's godmother, and young Henry Lindley would be his half brother's godfather. The baby shrieked properly as the water was poured gently over his head, indicating to all that the devil had flown out of him.

By mid-April young Patrick was in the care of his wetnurse, chosen by Adali, as all Jasmine's wetnurses had been. Adali seemed to know everything that went on around them wherever they went. When Jasmine teased him about it, he smiled.

"If I am to protect you and yours, I must know *everything*," he told her. "Mary Todd is Will's niece by marriage. Her husband died soon after her child was born. Will brought her to Glenkirk to look after himself. I knew her child would be weaned by the time your new babe was born. Her milk is rich and plentiful. She's a good, healthy girl, and is content to reside here in the castle until your lord Patrick is himself weaned from her breast. *And* you, my princess, do not have to be separated from your son. A most perfect arrangement, eh?"

"You are, too, Adali," Jasmine said laughing. "I could not do without you, my old friend."

"I pray God, my princess, that you will never have to," he replied seriously.

By mid-April the snows were melting off the bens, and Adam and Fiona decided to return to Edinburgh.

"Find out if Piers St. Denis is still lurking about," Jasmine said.

"If it was St. Denis," James Leslie murmured.

"You know it was!" Jasmine said angrily. Then she said, "I am sending a Glenkirk man with you, Uncle Adam. He carries a letter to my friend, George Villiers, who is at court. Steenie will know what is going on if no one else does. See he gets safely out of Edinburgh and on the road to England."

Adam Leslie nodded. "I will, lassie. Best we *all* be reassured should we hae to defend ourselves from this Englishman."

Spring began to evince itself on the hillsides which were now green with new growth. The roads were open, and Skye began to consider a visit to Dun Broc to see her daughter, Velvet.

"I will remain with Velvet a few weeks," she announced to them, "and then we can all travel south to Queen's Malvern for your English summer. It will be good to get home again."

She was, Jasmine considered, finally recovered from the shock of Adam de Marisco's death. Skye would mourn him for the rest of her life, her granddaughter knew, but the worst was over now, and she would finally get on with the business of living once again, Jasmine thought. It was a relief, for now she could get on with *her* life, too. She did not know if she would always make the summer trip south into England because Glenkirk had gained a serious hold on her heart, but while Skye lived, Jasmine knew she would go.

But before Skye's servants could even pack her trunks for a departure from Glenkirk, a messenger arrived from Adam Leslie in Edinburgh. Piers St. Denis, the marquis of Hartsfield, was indeed in the city; and Adam, himself, had seen the royal warrant he possessed with the king's signature, calling for the arrest of the earl and countess of Glenkirk on a charge of treason.

"*Treason?*" James Leslie was astounded. "What treason?"

"The warrant don't say," the messenger said, "but Master Adam says this Englishman is coming north to Glenkirk, and he's got a troop of men in his pay wi him."

"It's a fraudulent warrant," the earl said, "but we'll have to run until we can get it straightened out."

"That's what Master Adam suggests," the messenger said. "He told me to tell her ladyship that her messenger got off safely to England and is already across the border, well on his way south."

"*I will not run!*" Jasmine told her husband. "*Not this time.*"

"The hell you won't!" he answered. "Do you realize the danger we're in, Jasmine? St. Denis is a madman, but he somehow got the king's signature on that damned document, or forged the king's signature. It doesn't matter. He appears to have the law on his side for now. I don't intend to wait here at Glenkirk for him to come and get us."

"This castle is strong enough to withstand a siege," she said.

"Aye, if we could get the drawbridge up," he told her. "It's been down for so many years now I doubt the mechanism works anymore. Besides, even if we holed up in the castle, it's the wrong time of year for a siege. There are no crops in yet to feed us. We're practically out of our winter stores. And what of my people? I don't intend leaving them vulnerable to St. Denis and his mercenaries. Mercenaries, in a temper, could destroy the fields and slaughter my cattle and sheep. I won't have it! There is no other choice open to us but to run."

"We can't leave the children," she protested, "and we can't take them on the run, especially the baby. Do you think St. Denis will not use them against us? I know he will!"

"Only the Glenkirk heir and your not-so-royal Stuart are of any real value to him," Skye spoke up. "Secrete them at the abbey with Mary Todd and Adali. Your little Lindleys can come with me to Dun Broc. They will be safe there with their grandparents. This will leave you and Jemmie free to play hide-and-seek with St. Denis. He's at a great disadvantage here in your Highlands."

"Aye," the earl said. "He could bring an army and still never find us. My family is large, and we can visit with each one of them. St. Denis doesn't know who is who, and there are none who will tell him once we get the word out that he is an enemy."

"But won't his mercenaries pillage and burn if we are not found?" Jasmine worried.

The earl of Glenkirk shook his head. "It's very unlikely, darling Jasmine," he reassured her. "While he is free to look for us, and even free to take us into custody should he find us," James Leslie told his wife, "if he attempts to ravage the land in a temper, or allows his men to thieve from our people, he is quite apt to find himself in serious difficulties. Besides, he isn't here for spoils. He's come for us. Horses stolen. Throats cut in the darkness of night. No food available. Even with his little band of men to back up his perfidy, we can exercise some control over him, sweetheart."

"I'll go south into England with Velvet and her family when they make their annual pilgrimage," Skye told them. "The Lindleys must spend the summer in their father's house, and all must appear as if 'tis normal."

"Tell my brother, Charlie, I want him with the children when they are at Cadby. They must not be unprotected," Jasmine said.

Skye cast an indignant look. "Indeed," she said.

"Ohh, Grandmama, I am sorry," Jasmine cried. "Of course you wouldn't leave the children unprotected."

"I have played this little game many times before you, darling girl," her grandmother said. "You must remember one thing, however. At no time can you allow yourself to be afraid. St. Denis is playing at a great and dangerous deception in his forlorn effort to gain power and wealth. His chicanery is doomed to failure, for the king has no part in it, and the king is all-powerful. St. Denis will be exposed for the dishonest and dangerous trickster he is. The children will be safe. Glenkirk Abbey is in an even remoter area than this castle. No one will think to look for Charlie-boy and little Patrick there even if they learn of the abbey. Henry, India, and Fortune will be safe with me. Even if St. Denis learns where they are, what can he do? He has no rights over your children," Skye said. "And to keep his mind off your children, it will be up to you two to play cat and mouse with the villain. At no time should you appear to be hiding from him. You will be here, then there, and gone again by the time he reaches where he thinks you are. It should really be quite amusing, darling girl. From all previous indications, the marquis of Hartsfield is not a very patient man, nor a good loser. When a man is angry, he makes mistakes, forgets to be clever and careful. You, however, will be clever and careful. Your only obligation is to each other and your safety. And most important of all. Do not believe any rumors bruited about, Jasmine. St. Denis will eventually attempt to frighten you by claiming to have your children in custody. Do not believe him, darling girl. It will be a lie, like all the other lies he has told and is telling. Unless you hear from me to the contrary, your children are safe, whatever the circumstances otherwise that you may believe, or that may be presented to you as fact. *Do you understand me?*"

Jasmine nodded. "Yes, Grandmama."

"Very good," Skye said. Her mind was racing. She could feel the blood surging through her veins. It was just like the old days!

"I knows that look," Daisy whispered to Nora. "We're in for a time of it, I can tell you, girl! I've been by her side almost my whole life, and that look bodes no good, I can promise you."

"What does it mean?" Nora whispered back. "That look of hers?"

"It means she's ready to do battle, and she don't go into battle to lose, I can tell you."

"But we're going back to England," Nora said.

"Hah!" Daisy said. "But before we gets there, girl. That's what I'm worried about. *Before we gets there!*"

"What are you two mumbling about?" Skye snapped.

"I was just telling Nora it seemed like the old days," Daisy said.

"Aye, doesn't it," Skye O'Malley de Marisco said, and she smiled mischievously.

Chapter Sixteen

Adali watched from the battlements of Glenkirk Castle as Piers St. Denis, the marquis of Hartsfield; his brother, Kipp, by his side; and a party of twenty men made their way down the hill road that led to the castle. Other than St. Denis, and his brother, the riders were poorly equipped and poorly mounted. Dregs from the alleys of Edinburgh, Adali thought scornfully. They had been bought with the promise of whiskey and coin and could be subverted by anyone with more whiskey and more silver. Nonetheless, St. Denis was a dangerous man, and Adali would not underestimate him. As the first clop-clop of horses' hooves hit the solid oak of the drawbridge Adali hurried from the castle's heights so he might be in the courtyard to greet their visitors.

Piers St. Denis's bright blue eyes missed nothing as they entered Glenkirk. The castle was old but in excellent condition. The men on the battlements were alert and appeared hardened. This Leslie earl obviously had plenty of gold and silver of his own. The marquis let his mind wander for a moment to the possibility of controlling two fortunes—Jasmine's and her husband's. And Rowan Lindley had not been impoverished either. *Three fortunes!* And if some of the children did not reach adulthood, well, could those fortunes not be his? And whatever happened, the king would surely forgive him. After all, despite the queen and that arrogant snake, Villiers, Piers St. Denis could still command a place by the king's side. James Stuart loved him. Despite his apparent indifference and apathy toward the marquis of Hartsfield of late, the king still had an affection for him. He would be forgiven whatever he did despite what Kipp had said to the contrary.

Of late he had begun to mistrust his brother's loyalty to him. Kipp had developed a rather unpleasant habit of questioning his every move, and attempting to anticipate him. He hadn't liked the men Piers had recruited in Edinburgh, claiming they were too rough, and would run at the first sign of danger. He had even disputed his brother's giving these alley rats part of their pay in advance, but the marquis knew he could have never gotten his little band put together without a show of coin.

"Honest men would trust you," Kipp said.

"I don't want honest men," Piers responded. "Honest men have a conscience. I want none of that. These creatures will obey me for no other reason than to obtain the rest of their silver."

"They could as easily slit your throat for it one night," Kipp remarked dryly. "You've wasted your money, Piers. All we had to do was remain in Edinburgh and command the earl of Glenkirk to come to you in the king's name. If he didn't, the Scots government would have then sent out their own men to capture him. They would have known how to handle the situation. You have marched into James Leslie's own territory with twenty men of dubious report, and you believe you can take him? The local authorities would have acted had you but shown them the king's signature on your warrant."

"I could not take the chance that someone here would see that signature," the marquis of Hartsfield told his brother. "What if someone knows the king's hand, Kipp?"

Kipp St. Denis was shocked by his half brother's words. "You told me the king signed that warrant, but just left out the names," he said. "Are you now saying the king didn't sign the warrant?"

"I asked him to, but he never seemed to have the time," came the startling answer. "I know his hand well enough, and so I signed it for him, smudging it slightly. Then I took his seal and stamped partly over it in the sealing wax." Piers St. Denis laughed, almost childishly. "Do you think he will be angry at me, Kipp? Old king fool always forgives me when I'm naughty. He likes me to be naughty, so he can correct me with his *wisdom.*"

The impact of what his half brother had done slammed into Kipp St. Denis with an almost physical force. He had forged the king's name to a document that would allow him to murder two innocent people. This was treason! Didn't Piers understand this? Nay. He didn't. All he understood was that he wanted something, and he would have it at all costs because he always got whatever it was he sought. *And he always escaped punishment for his sins.* But not this time, Kipp thought. God help him. This time his brother had gone too far, and there would be no escape.

"When it is discovered the king's signature is a forgery," he said to Piers, "you will be charged with treason, and if you have harmed the Leslies of Glenkirk, with the crime of murder as well."

"Who is there to discover it?" Piers said.

"You cannot kill the earl and countess of Glenkirk and expect the king not to avenge them. In the name of God, Piers, James Leslie is related to the king! His clan will march into Whitehall itself to demand revenge. You have lost this game. *It is over.*

"Jasmine de Marisco Lindley chose James Leslie for her husband and has by now delivered a child sired by him. *It is finished.* Let us return to England before it is too late. No one need know about the warrant. We will say it was merely a rumor, and we will burn the damned document today before anyone can steal it off of us and prove otherwise. If you make up to the queen as Villiers has done, she will relent and find you a wife. She is a vain woman, but well-meaning. You will keep your favor with the king. Do not throw everything you have gained away in this passion you have for revenge. It is not worth it, Piers. *You will lose all!* You must come to your senses, brother, I beg of you!"

"You grow tiresome, Kipp," the marquis replied wearily. "Ahh, look! There is her Indian, Adali, awaiting us."

Adali noted Kipp's urgent conversation as the two men approached. He wished he knew what was being said. The marquis's faithful dog, Kipp, looked mightily distressed. Interesting. They came to a halt before the staircase leading up to the castle door. "Welcome, my lord," Adali said in a pleasant voice. "Welcome to Glenkirk Castle. Your men will be shown to their quarters by our own men-at-arms. Dougie, lad, take the gentlemen's horses to the stable," he instructed a stableboy. "And if you will follow me, please." He led them into the Great Hall, clapping his hands as he entered the room and telling the servant who hurried forward, "Wine, for my lord St. Denis, and our other guest. Please to sit by the fire, sirs. A gray day always seems colder." Taking the tray from the servant, he personally offered them the silver goblets of red wine.

The marquis of Hartsfield sniffed appreciatively. "Ahhhh," he said, "Archambault wine. It is the finest!"

"It is, my lord," Adali agreed pleasantly, and remained standing attentively as they drank. When they had put their cups down, he said, "And how may I be of service to your lordship?"

"You may inform the earl and his wife that I have arrived," the marquis of Hartsfield said.

"I am afraid I cannot do that, my lord. You see, the earl of Glenkirk and his countess are not here right now."

"Where are they? When will they return?" demanded Piers St. Denis

"I cannot be certain where they are right now, my lord," Adali said in a noncommittal tone, "and as for when they will return, I have absolutely no idea. Glenkirk is always in readiness for them, of course, whenever they do come home, and generally they send a messenger ahead so I may have meals prepared, but the messenger only arrives a few hours before my master and mistress do."

"How long have they been gone?" the marquis said.

"This time? Several days, I believe. It is so peaceful here that one day rolls into the next, and I forget the time myself," he said.

"I do not understand why it is, you, who are so careful of your mistress's safety, don't know where she is," Piers St. Denis said skeptically.

"I have no fear for my lady's safety when she is with her husband," Adali replied. "And as for where they are, the earl has not been home in several years. He has, I have discovered, an enormous family, and a large clan, many of whom are also distantly related to him. We arrived here last autumn, and then a short time later the winter set in so that the roads were blocked with ice and snow until recently. The earl wished to begin visiting his family and clansmen and women—to introduce his wife to them and to renew old acquaintances and loyalties."

"Where are the children?" St. Denis asked suspiciously.

"They, too, are visiting the family," Adali said smoothly.

"I have a royal warrant for the arrest of the earl and the countess of Glenkirk," the marquis of Hartsfield said. "If you do not tell me where they are, I will have you taken on a charge of obstructing the king's justice, Adali!"

"My lord, I have told you the truth. I have no idea where they are. I am a stranger in this land and know little of it, or of the earl's relations. I have not had the time to learn yet. However, like my mistress, I respect the king. The old man who was steward here before me lives in a cottage nearby. Perhaps he can tell you some of the places you might look to find my lord and my lady. Come, I will take you to him."

Adali led them from the Great Hall and out into the courtyard again.

"Where are my men?" Piers St. Denis inquired nervously.

"They have been housed in a barracks and are being fed," Adali told him cordially, as they passed beneath the castle's iron portcullis and out across the drawbridge, off the main track and into the woods, picking out a barely discernible track to follow.

"Why are we going this way?" St. Denis queried Adali.

Adali stopped. "This is the way to Will Todd's cottage, my lord. He lives near a mountain stream, and will probably be fishing when we get there. There is nothing to be fearful of, my lord."

"I am not *fearful,* I was just curious," the marquis snapped.

Adali smiled to himself and continued onward. Actually, there was an easier path to Will's cottage, but he chose the more roundabout way in order to confuse the two men with him. It was a rocky path that led up a hill, and down again, through sharp brambles, and thick gorse bushes. He could hear the men behind him cursing as their clothing caught on the briars, but he moved with such fluidity that neither his white pants nor his white coat was shredded or torn. Finally, they could hear the water of a stream ahead of them as it tumbled over the rocks in its bed, but it was not Will's water, Adali told them, leaping from stone to stone as he quickly crossed it. Again he could hear cursing behind him as his companions unsuccessfully followed him, splashing their way through the stream. He chuckled softly to himself.

At last they exited the wood and crossed over a meadow filled with shaggy, big-horned cattle. "Mind your feet," Adali warned them as he tiptoed through the clumps of cow manure, almost laughing aloud at the marquis of Hartsfield's yelp of dismay.

"How much farther is it?" Kipp called to him.

"We're almost there," Adali replied calmly.

And then they saw the cottage on the far side of the meadow, heard the swiftly flowing water beside it. As they approached it they could see a figure, almost hip-deep in the stream, fishing rod in hand.

"Hello, the house!" Adali called loudly. "'Tis Adali, Will Todd, and I've brought visitors."

The figure turned slowly, openly annoyed to be disturbed at his pastime. Then, reluctantly, he moved nearer the bank, but did not come from the water or cease his activity. "What 'tis it ye seek?" he asked, his local accent thick to the ears of the two Englishmen.

"Good morrow, Will Todd," Adali said cheerfully. "These two gentlemen are seeking his lordship. I would not know where to tell them to look, but I am certain you can help them."

"Here," Will Todd moved nearer the bank, and thrust his fishing pole at Adali. "Dinna drop it, mon! I canna chatter wi it in hand." He pierced the two strangers with a sharp glance. "So yer seeking his lordship, eh? Weel, I canna rightly say where he maught be, but hae ye sought at Sithean for him? He maught be there. Or he and his lassie could hae gone to Hay Hoos or Greyhaven. Or mayhap he's at Briarmere Moor or Leslie Brae. Hae ye looked in any of these places, sir?"

"What is he saying?" St. Denis demanded tightly. He could hardly make out a word the old man was uttering.

"I thought he was quite clear," Adali replied, "but then I've been listening to these people for several months now, and I do have a rather good ear for accents."

"Yes! Yes!" St. Denis almost shouted, "But what the hell did he say? It sounded like gibberish to me."

"Will Todd said that the earl of Glenkirk and his wife might be over at Sithean visiting the earl of Sithean, who is Lord Leslie's uncle. Or he could be at Hay House or Leslie Brae, visiting with his uncles, or he might be at Greyhaven or Briarmere Moor, with his brothers."

"Or the Gordons," Will Todd spoke up again. "He maught be wi the Gordons, fer our Morag is wed wi a Gordon."

"He could also be visiting with the Gordons, his late wife's family. Their youngest son is wed to the earl's youngest sister," Adali translated quickly.

"Or the games," Will Todd added. "He maught hae gone to the games, but then there be several this summer. Two, or three, I dinna remember." He took his fishing rod back from Adali and stepped back out into the swiftly flowing stream. "'Tis all I can tell ye," he said with a firm air of finality.

"*Games?*" The marquis of Hartsfield was puzzled.

"Because the winters are so long and so harsh," Adali explained, "the Scots like to hold games of athletic prowess in the summer months. It allows the clans to gather together, the men to exhibit their skill at things like tossing the caber, it's a log, my lord; or throwing big round stones a distance. The women come to gossip. They dance, and there are bards and the pipes. Will is right, however. There are several sets of games this summer, and the earl could have gone to any of them, for he is related to many people through his Stuart connections."

"How barbaric," St. Denis sneered.

"Let us return to Edinburgh," Kipp said. "Seeking out Glenkirk here will be like looking for a needle in a haystack. If you send for him in the king's name, he must come or risk treason."

"Oh, I'm certain you can find the earl if you really want him," Adali lightly taunted the marquis of Hartsfield to see what he would do when torn between his brother's suggestion and that of Adali.

"Edinburgh is our best bet," Kipp St. Denis insisted.

"*No!*" the marquis said. "We are here, and surely it cannot be too difficult to find these places the old man has named."

"And do not forget the games, my lord," Adali helpfully volunteered, causing Kipp St. Denis to stare hard at him.

"Do you know where they are being held?" the marquis asked.

"Well, I believe there are some at Inverness, and others at Nairn, and I had heard of some being held at Loch Lomond, my lord."

"You will write it all down, and give us directions," the marquis of Hartsfield said. "We will stay the night and start off again in the morning." Piers St. Denis was too excited to contemplate Adali's cooperation, but Kipp St. Denis was not.

"What are you up to?" he asked the castle steward when they were finally alone in the Great Hall, the marquis having been shown to a guest chamber.

Adali turned a bland face to him. "Master St. Denis?" he said.

"You know what I mean," Kipp said. "Why are you being so helpful to my brother? Your loyalty to your mistress is legendary."

Adali smiled a small smile. "Why, sir, your master carries a royal warrant from the king. For me to disobey would be treason, wouldn't it now? As my mistress respects the divine right of kings, so do I also. I cannot disobey King James, even for my mistress."

Kipp was not content with the answer. "You are up to *something*," he said suspiciously. "You would not betray your mistress, I know it!"

Again Adali smiled. "If, sir, I believed your brother had any chance of catching up with my lord, and my lady..." He allowed the rest of the sentence to hang.

"They knew he was coming!" Kipp gasped.

"They knew he was in Edinburgh all winter long," Adali replied. "It would seem that Scotland is a very small country, sir, and once more I remind you that the earl of Glenkirk is related to many people throughout it. We had word before Christmas, but immediately the first storm of the season came, and the roads were to be blocked for the next few months. We were told, however, that when the roads were open again, the marquis of Hartsfield would be paying us a visit. Unfortunately, the earl and his wife could not wait, for they have many visits themselves to make this summer."

"He will hunt them into hell and back," Kipp said despairingly.

"By the time he catches up with them, *if he can catch up with them,*" Adali told his companion, "there will no longer be any danger for my master and my mistress, sir, but I fear there may be great danger for your half brother."

"They have sent to the king!" Kipp whispered.

"The king is an honorable man," Adali told him. "He would not take back his word to the earl and countess of Glenkirk."

"I warned him," Kipp almost whispered to himself. *"I warned him!"*

"Then you are surely wiser than your brother," Adali told him. Then he said, softly, "There is yet time for you to save yourself, sir."

"I swore to our father on his deathbed that I would watch over Piers," Kipp said, his defenses down, his mood desperate.

"You have tried to prevent your brother from his folly, have you not?" Adali asked him softly. "I have seen it myself."

"For many years," Kipp confided in Adali, "I have followed along in my brother's wake. He was simply ambitious, and I saw no harm in his actions when he caught the king's attention. And over the years I kept him from much wickedness, although I have not always been successful in my attempts; but the women he so enjoyed abusing, I made certain they were, for the most part, experienced in the amatory arts. Only three or four times did he misuse an innocent; but they were girls of no import, and afterward I was kind to them and paid them not to complain to the authorities."

"You joined him in his deviant practices, I am told," Adali said quietly, not willing to let Kipp escape his censure.

"I did," Kipp admitted, "but by doing so I kept many women from greater harm at my brother's hand. I accept my shame, Adali. Our father encouraged us as young men to such wickedness, for as he grew older it seemed more difficult for him to enjoy a woman without hurting her. I remember telling my mother. It was she who warned me for my own sake I must play my part or risk losing my father's favor."

"But your father is long dead," Adali reminded him. "Your brother has now strayed completely into evil's dominion. There is no going back for him, Kipp St. Denis, but you have not yet crossed completely over into the darkness. You have a conscience, and you now have the chance to save yourself as you will not be able to save your brother. Would your father want to lose *both* of his sons, if he were here to make the decision? Would he want to see his proud old name wiped from the face of the earth?"

"I am his bastard," Kipp said simply.

"But he gave you his name, and he raised you in his house, and favored you as well as he did his legitimate heir," Adali argued. "I believe your father loved you, too."

"If I do not stay with Piers," Kipp said, "he will continue on to worse mischief, Adali."

"He will continue on anyway," Adali replied. "You are not responsible for his behavior. *Save yourself while you have the opportunity!* You have lived your whole life through Piers St. Denis. Now live your life for yourself. If you asked the king for his mercy, I know he would give it to you. King James has a large and a kind heart. He might even reward your timely behavior."

An accident of birth. It was only an accident of birth that had kept him from being the marquis of Hartsfield, Kipp thought silently. Did he dare to hope he might change that? Was it possible? Could he betray Piers? Was it really a betrayal? Aye, he had promised their father he would look after his younger half brother; but Piers no longer wanted looking after. *He has never really listened to my good counsel,* Kipp said silently to himself, *and by following him, I have been dragged down in the gutter with him. He will be caught in this attempt to revenge himself upon the Leslies and in his endeavor to steal the fortunes belonging to them.*

And whatever made Piers believe that the king would give him custody of all those children? The queen despised him so openly she could not even bring herself to pick a wife for him! She would hardly allow her only grandson or the other children to come under Piers St. Denis's control. Indeed Kipp believed the queen would kill him herself before she would see those children in Hartsfield House.

And what of the Leslies of Glenkirk? And the old and powerful countess of Lundy? Would they allow their children to be put into the hands of a man like Piers St. Denis? It was madness even to consider it, and yet his brother had not only considered it, he assumed it would be because he wanted it to be. *But it wouldn't.* Suddenly Kipp St. Denis realized that if he did not act now to save himself, he would be as doomed as his brother, and he didn't want to be. Why should he share Piers's fate? How many beatings had he taken for Piers when they were children, and Piers had found it so amusing, but it had not been amusing. Sometimes Piers even did bad things just so he could see his brother punished.

"I have no coin of my own, nor powerful friends to intercede for me," he told Adali, and then waited to see what Adali would say to him.

"I will give you the silver you need," Adali replied softly. "And as for allies, sir, go to the king and tell him the truth of this matter, and you will have friends a-plenty, not only at court, for your brother has made many enemies there who will befriend you, but among my mistress's family. A word in the king's ear, and you could have a reward greater than any you could possibly anticipate, Kipp St. Denis."

"How can I be certain of what you say?" Kipp asked.

Adali drew himself up, and said sternly, "I am Adali, confidant and friend of the royal Mughal princess you know as Jasmine Leslie. I do not lie, nor do I offer my favor or aid lightly. If I tell you it will be so, then it will be so! Make your decision before it is too late, Kipp St. Denis, or suffer your brother's eventual bad end." Then, turning on his heel, he began to walk from the hall.

"*Wait!*"

Adali turned.

"If I go, I *must* have coin," Kipp reiterated.

Adali reached into a hidden pocket within his white coat and drew out a small leather bag. "There is both gold and silver in it," he said quietly, handing it to Kipp. "More than enough to get you to England and then some."

Kipp slowly took the bag from Adali. "If I change my mind," he promised, "I will return the bag to you, Adali. What of my horse?"

"When you desire your mount it will be available to you," Adali told him. "I will see you are not followed, but ride swiftly."

The two men parted. It was interesting, Adali mused to himself, that Kipp St. Denis had offered to return the bag of coins if he did not leave his brother. *He does indeed have a conscience,* the steward thought, *but is his loyalty to the marquis greater than his sense of self-preservation, I wonder? We shall see. We shall see.*

Adali hurried down to the kitchens to make certain that the dinner would be of the finest quality. The marquis of Hartsfield must be well fed and filled with rich wine, the last few cups of which would be spiked with a sleeping draught that would have him sleeping through into the following afternoon. Next Adali moved on to the stables, and instructed the head groom to make certain that Kipp St. Denis's horse was rested and fed and available to his master on request.

"He's got a loose shoe, Master Adali," the head groom told the steward. "Wouldn't take much to fix it. Blacksmith be working today."

"Have him replace all four of the horses's shoes," Adali said, "and Dugald, this will be our wee secret, eh?"

"Aye, Master Adali," Dugald said, winking broadly.

"The horses belonging to the marquis and his other men," Adali continued, "I think they might be taken to the high pasture to graze until they are needed."

"Aye, Master Adali," the head groom said with a grin. The earl's new steward might not be a Scot, but he thought like one, Dugald decided. At least where the English were concerned.

Piers St. Denis enjoyed sitting at the head of the highboard in the Great Hall that night. He let his eye wander to the banners hanging from the rafters, banners which indicated the many battles in which the Leslies had fought, and to the beautiful tapestries hanging upon the walls that their women had created. He admired the heavy and copious amount of silver upon the sideboard, the two magnificent portraits hanging over the fireplaces, and noted that the lamps burned only the purest scented oil and that the candles were of beeswax, not tallow.

The meal served him was exquisite. There was a fat duck in plum sauce, a small trout poached in white wine and set upon a bed of fresh cress on its silver platter, another silver platter of lamb-chops, artichokes steamed in wine and served with drawn butter, bread still warm from the ovens, and an excellent cheese. For afters an apple tart with thick, clotted cream was offered. Adali had inquired solicitously if his lordship would have wine, ale, or cider. The marquis had, of course, chosen the fine wine that Jasmine had always served. He had eaten alone, but for his brother, Kipp, who was oddly silent.

Now, however, as the evening drew in, he began to feel sleepy. It was not surprising, considering the long journey up from Edinburgh. Yawning, he pulled himself to his feet, but fell back again into his chair, his legs weak beneath him. Piers St. Denis laughed drunkenly.

"Let me help you," Kipp said, coming to his aid.

"Les take a serving wench with us, Kipp, and have some fun," the marquis muttered. "I like the one over there with the big titties and the big bottom. Looks like a squealer, eh? We can fill 'er at both ends, brother." He laughed again, collapsing against his sibling.

"Perhaps later, Piers, when you have rested," Kipp said.

"Wanna whip 'er hard," the marquis said, "just like I'm going to do to Jasmine. Whip 'em and fuck 'em, eh, Kipp? Thas how to treat a woman. How old's 'er daughter, Kipp? We'll whip 'er, too, and teach 'er how to suck. She's too little to fuck right now, but we can teach 'er other things."

Kipp helped his brother to his bedchamber and, pulling his doublet and boots off as he had so often done, put him to bed. He had been drugged. Of that Kipp had no doubt. Now it was up to him to decide. Piers was out of control, he knew. The talk of debauching little India Lindley had disgusted him. They had *never* harmed a child, but he knew if his brother said he would do it, he would. *I cannot countenance it,* Kipp thought, *and if I remain, I cannot prevent it. Only by going can I save myself, and mayhap in the end, my brother.* He once again sought out Adali.

"You drugged Piers's wine," he said.

"He will sleep until tomorrow afternoon," Adali said matter-of-factly, not denying it. "You have decided then."

"Will you see that I am awakened so that I may leave at first light?" Kipp said. "I have such a long journey ahead."

Adali nodded. "What made you decide?" he asked curious.

"He speaks of seducing and debasing Lady Jasmine's eldest daughter," Kipp said. "The very idea revolts me. I can no longer be of help to a brother who considers such perversions as brutalizing a child."

"He will not harm her," Adali said tightly, "or my mistress, or any of her family. I would kill him myself this night, but that the earl has insisted we resolve this matter within the tenets of the king's law. Best the marquis of Hartsfield be exposed for all to see as the corrupt creature he is, Kipp St. Denis. You are wise to escape him now while you have the opportunity."

In the hour before dawn Adali himself awakened Kipp, took him to the kitchens, fed him, and gave him a supply of oat cakes, cheese, salted meat, and wine to aid him in his travels. He also instructed him in a shortcut over the mountains known only to the local folk. It would cut two days off his journey south. Then, leading him to the stable, he helped him to saddle his horse.

"I have seen to his shoeing," he told the surprised Kipp. "You will travel better for it. Do not fear that any of your brother's men will see you leave. Like their master, they will sleep well this day." He laughed softly as he led the horse from the stables.

Beneath the portcullis Kipp St. Denis mounted his animal. Looking down at Adali, he said, "I am sad, Adali, but I know I have made the right decision, hard as it was. My brother is lost to me."

"One door closes, another is opened wide," Adali said wisely. "God watch over you in your travels, Kipp St. Denis." Then, reaching into his coat, he drew forth a small sealed parchment. "Deliver this to Viscount Villiers, if you will, and your safety is assured." Then Adali slapped the rump of the horse and watched as Kipp rode forth from Glenkirk Castle. "You have seen nothing," he said quietly to the man-at-arms on watch.

"Aye, Master Adali," the soldier replied.

The night faded away, and the day began at Glenkirk as it always did. A messenger was dispatched to the earl informing him of St. Denis's arrival and Adali's success at subverting Kipp, who had obviously, according to Adali, been considering a departure from his brother's service for some time. In midafternoon the marquis of Hartsfield stumbled into the Great Hall, shouting for his brother, for Adali, for someone.

"Ahhh, my lord, you are awake at last," Adali said coming forth. "Are you hungry? How may I serve you?"

"Where the hell is my brother?" St. Denis demanded.

"Your brother?" Adali looked puzzled. "Is he not with you, my lord? I thought he was always with you."

"No! He isn't with me, or I wouldn't be asking," snapped the marquis. "Bring me some wine! My mouth tastes like a whore's cunt!"

"The last I saw of your brother was last night when he put your lordship to bed. This traveling is hard on you, I can see as you are not used to it. Life at court ill prepares one for such travel as yours, my lord." He poured St. Denis a large goblet of wine and handed it to him. "Your wine, my lord."

The marquis drained the goblet swiftly. "What time is it?"

"Almost four o'clock of the afternoon," Adali said cheerfully.

"Where are my men?"

"Like you, my lord, they slept like the dead," Adali replied.

"Find my brother!" the marquis ordered Adali, who bowed in a servile manner and left the hall. He returned within the half hour to inform Pier St. Denis, "Your brother seems to have left the castle, my lord, for his horse is gone from its place in the stables. It must have been early, for the stable lad did not see him go. I suspect he left during the time when the night watch and the day watch were exchanging places. The night watch thinks he saw a rider leave, but he is not certain, and the day watch saw nothing. I regret I can tell you no more." Adali bowed.

"If you have harmed him..." Piers St. Denis began, but Adali cut him short.

"My lord," he said angrily, "you are under the protection of the earl of Glenkirk. No one would harm you or yours while you are here. If we wished you harm, you, your brother, and your men would have all been slain in your beds last night, and already buried in a pit upon the ben, even as I speak. No one here has harmed or injured your brother in any way. I do not know where he has gone, or why. Now, my lord, would you like something to eat?"

"He'll be back," the marquis muttered almost to himself. He felt headachy and out of sorts. He ate alone, served by men servants. There were no women in sight at all. Finally he called to Adali, and said, "I want a woman, dammit! Fetch me that serving wench who was in the hall last night. The red-haired wench with the big tits!"

"I regret, my lord, that we have no whores at Glenkirk for our guests," Adali replied quietly, his tone firm.

St. Denis stamped from the hall and found his bedchamber. While he did not feel sleepy, he did sleep, awakening again just at dawn. Dressing himself, he returned to the hall. "I will be leaving this morning," he told Adali. "Have you written down the names of the places the earl and Jasmine might be? And the directions to these places?"

"I have, my lord," Adali reassured him, serving the marquis himself. There were no other servants in the hall to be seen at all this morning. Adali placed a bowl of oat stirabout before the marquis with a chunk of bread and cheese and a goblet of cider.

When Piers St. Denis had eaten, he took the parchment with the listings and the map from Adali and strode out into the courtyard, where his men stood milling about. "Have any of you seen my brother?" he demanded of them, but they all shook their heads no. His horse was brought, and the marquis mounted it, looking about him. "Where are my men's horses, Adali?"

"We could not stable so many, my lord, and so we sent them up to the high pasture to graze," was the helpful reply. "It is on your way to Sithean, my lord. If your men carry their saddles and packs up to the meadows on the ben, they can round up their horses, and you will be quickly on your way. To send up for them ourselves would mean the loss of another day for you, and I know that you do not want to lose another day in your search for my master and my mistress." He smiled.

Piers St. Denis cursed under his breath. He suspected that Adali's polite manner masked a successful effort to thwart him in his pursuit of the earl and countess of Glenkirk. Yet Adali had been very cooperative. There was nothing the marquis of Hartsfield could put his finger on to justify his suspicions even if his instinct told him otherwise. "If my brother should return," he began, "you will tell him where we have gone, Adali, will you not?"

"Of course, my lord. If you follow my list as I have written it for you—Sithean to Greyhaven to Hay House, to Leslie Brae to Briarmere Moor and thus on the Huntley, the stronghold of the Gordons—I will know exactly where you are at all times. I shall be able to send Master St. Denis directly to you when he returns."

"But what of those places where the games are held?" the marquis asked Adali.

"My lord, you should catch up to my master and mistress long before then. If you do not, I can only say, Inverness, Loch Lomond, or Nairn. I do not know which they shall attend, nor when. You will have to find that out for yourself."

Piers St. Denis yanked at his horse's head and, without even a simple farewell or thanks, motioned to his men to follow him and rode out of Glenkirk Castle.

"Good riddance!" Will Todd murmured to Adali, coming from the shadows.

"A fool, 'tis true," Adali said, "but a dangerous fool, Will. What report do you have of Kipp St. Denis? Is he long gone?"

"He is riding like the devil himself is after him," the old man said. "The watch upon the heights have all reported back. He was off Leslie lands by late yesterday. I believe he will be in Edinburgh wi'in a few days. Master Adam's pigeon will inform us when he reaches the city, and he will see that young St. Denis gets safely over the border into England. Where is the earl now?"

"At Dun Broc visiting his in-laws for a brief time," Adali replied. "Where he goes next will depend upon our marquis and his patience. If he is clever, he will send parties of men out to check at all the places I have said the earl might be. It would save him time. By denying him his brother, we have removed his only real ally. Those alley rats of his look neither loyal nor resourceful, just greedy."

"Our clansmen will be watching them every step of the way, Adali. We'll be ahead of them, I promise ye. When do you think we will hear from Jamie Stuart himself?"

"Our messenger must have surely reached the king by now," Adali said. "And when Kipp St. Denis arrives, the king, who is prone to indecision, will finally, it is hoped, have to do something, Will. Then his decision must be made known in Scotland, and St. Denis caught and held for king's justice."

"So 'tis cat and mouse until then," Will noted.

"Aye," Adali agreed.

"Ahh, 'tis guid to have the earl home again," Will replied. "'Twas verra boring at Glenkirk while he was gone."

"'Tis *nae* boring now," Adali chuckled.

"Aye," Will said, his weathered face wreathed in smiles. "'Tis just like the old days."

"The old days?" Adali looked puzzled.

"Aye," Will replied. "When the current earl was but a bairn, and his mother, Mistress Catriona, was loved by her husband, and the earl of Bothwell, and lusted after by the same Jamie Stuart now on the throne. Ahh, what a time we have then, although we clansmen folk weren't meant to know it, but we did. There was comings and goings, and the king wanted the current earl's mother for his mistress, and her husband was lost at sea, and she, so in love wi the earl of Bothwell, who was the king's cousin. They called him the *Uncrowned King of Scotland*, and Jamie Stuart was so afraid of him that he had him put to the horn and accused of witchcraft; but it dinna get him Mistress Cat. She did her duty by the clan, matching her children up, and then she fled to her true love. Those were the days, Adali! These would seem to be verra much like them. The Leslies of Glenkirk are nae a quiet clan."

Adali laughed. "So it would seem, Will Todd, but then my mistress has never been what one would call a *biddable lass*. I would say the earl and his wife are more than well matched where trouble is concerned."

"Aye, which is all the more reason we'll keep them safe from this Englishman. We have lost one Leslie countess to perfidy, but we will nae lose another, Adali. We'll nae lose another!"

Chapter Seventeen

Adali had not given the marquis of Hartsfield a straight routing. While Sithean lay near to Glenkirk, his next destination of Greyhaven would take him to a distant point, and then back again, and then to another distant point. Not being familiar with the countryside, however, Piers St. Denis did not realize the deception. He missed his brother's company and felt unsafe with these Edinburgh cutthroats. Now he had to deal with them. There was no Kipp to stand between them. Where had he gone? *He should be here looking after me as he promised our father, dammit,* the marquis thought angrily, not considering the possibility his brother was gone for good.

At Sithean he was again greeted with cordiality by the old earl and his wife. He was well fed and comfortably housed, and his men and horses were nicely cared for, but James Leslie and his wife were not at Sithean. Had they been?

"Oh, aye," the old earl replied. "'Twas several weeks ago now, it was, my lord. Was it nae, my dear?" He turned to his wife.

"Aye," she replied, dourly.

"A loovely lass, the new countess. Are ye acquainted wi her?" Sithean smiled pleasantly at Piers St. Denis.

"I have a royal warrant for your nephew's arrest, and his wife's as well," the marquis of Hartsfield said irritably. "Do you not understand that I am on the king's business?"

"Oh, aye, aye," the old earl said. "How is Jamie Stuart, my lord? He is always getting in some sort of fret and ordering arrests. He was such an unruly and nervous bairn. He doesna love his homeland."

There is obviously nothing here, the marquis thought peevishly. "I will be leaving in the morning," he told his hosts.

James and Jasmine Leslie watched their enemy as he departed Sithean. They had come up into the hills above Sithean to A-Cuil. They had traveled without the trappings of their station. Adali had remained to watch over Glenkirk and coordinate their stream of information. Rohana was at the abbey with Mary Todd, Charlie-boy, and wee Patrick. Toramalli had gone with Skye and the children to Dun Broc. Only Fergus More and Red Hugh remained with them, which was providential, as Jasmine did not cook. Fortunately Red Hugh did.

A-Cuil was not a large lodge. Set in the hills above Loch Sithean, it had been constructed of stone, with a slate roof. Its first floor consisted of a tiny parlor and a kitchen. There was a single bedroom beneath the eaves on the second floor. Surrounded by a pine forest and set upon a cliff, A-Cuil had a panoramic view of Glenkirk, Sithean, and the countryside surrounding them. The lodge itself, however, blended into the landscape, and was rarely seen by passersby below. Jasmine liked it here, and even with the presence of Red Hugh and Fergus More, she found it romantic. The valet and the man-at-arms slept in two small loft rooms in the little stable belonging to A-Cuil.

"I could live here forever," Jasmine told Jemmie.

He laughed. "Where would we put the children, not to mention Adali and the twins, madame?"

"If we lived here we wouldn't have children, or servants," she replied with what she believed was perfect logic.

"You would learn to cook?" he teased her. "These dainty beringed fingers would knead bread and peel carrots?" He caught her hands in his and kissed them, nibbling playfully upon her fingertips.

"Beast!" She snatched her hands away. "I could learn to cook if I wanted to learn to cook," she told him.

James Leslie laughed. "Jasmine, my darling Jasmine, you have absolutely no talent for the culinary arts, but where the amatory arts are concerned, now there you are most facile." He pulled her down into his lap, kissing her mouth and enjoying the breathless flush he brought to her cheeks. Pulling open the ties on her shirt, he slid his hand beneath the silk and fondled a deliciously plump breast.

"I didn't know you peeled carrots," she murmured, nuzzling his neck, then licking it.

He slid his tongue into her mouth, his thumb and his forefinger twiddling with her nipple. "Ummmmm," he replied, his mouth working feverishly against hers.

The door to the lodge sprang open, and the earl of Glenkirk almost dumped his wife most unceremoniously onto the floor as Red Hugh, grinning from ear to ear, stomped in with a brace of rabbits.

"Dinner," he said, swallowing his chortles. "Maybe I should skin 'em out back, my lord." He moved through into the kitchen.

Jasmine, however, couldn't control her fit of giggles as she laced up her shirt again. "Maybe living here forever isn't such a good idea, Jemmie," she said. "We don't have much privacy, do we?"

"Nay, we don't," he grumbled. Dammit, he was hot for her! A-Cuil would be nice for a few days' respite if they were alone, but he really wanted to be home at Glenkirk. His in-laws would have already departed for England and Queen's Malvern; but they would be forced to run from here to there all summer long just because of that damned fool, Piers St. Denis.

"Why don't we go home?" Jasmine said suddenly, as if reading his thoughts.

"To Glenkirk? We can't," he said.

"Why not?" Jasmine responded. "St. Denis has already been there, and is now off on a fool's chase about the countryside. We are having him watched, and will know when he comes our way again, Jemmie. But I don't want to bring the children home. Not until this matter has been settled. It is easy enough, however, for you and me to flee again if the marquis of Hartsfield comes in our direction once more."

He considered it and thought that she was right. "We'll spend one more night here, madame," he told her, "but I shall send Fergus More and Red Hugh back to Glenkirk to advise Adali of our change of plans."

"Not until after supper," she chuckled, and he laughed, agreeing.

And when they had had their supper of broiled rabbit, oatcakes, cheese, and cider, they sent Fergus and Red Hugh back to Glenkirk with a message for Adali. Then they sat together on the edge of the hillside, watching the sun set in the west.

Jasmine sighed happily within her husband's embrace. "The sunsets are so different here than in India," she said. "In India the colors are lush and exotic, but not so vibrant and rich as here in Scotland. I love our Scots sunsets, Jemmie. I love Scotland. I have seen it at its best, and at its worst, and I love it! *It is home!* It is home as no place has been since I left India."

"And yet so different," he replied.

"Aye," she said, but did not elaborate further. There was no need for her to do so.

They remained lying in the grass, listening to the small night creatures chirping and singing as the light from the sunset faded, and the skies above them were filled with a plethora of stars. They watched the moon rise.

"'Tis a border moon," Jemmie said softly.

"A *border moon?*" Jasmine was puzzled. "What does that mean?"

"It's large and full, and 'tis what the border Scots call it. They always went raiding with a border moon to light their way. My stepfather was a borderer. He took my mother raiding with him once."

"Did she enjoy it?" Jasmine asked.

"Aye," he admitted.

"I think I would, too," Jasmine told her husband.

A wildcat, hunting its dinner, shrieked in the forest behind them, and the earl of Glenkirk rose, drawing his wife up with him. "Come," he said, "let us go to bed, darling Jasmine."

Together they made certain that the stable door was secure so that the horses would be safe from the marauding beast. They laid the heavy oaken bar across the front door of the lodge and, banking the fires in the parlor and the kitchen, climbed the narrow staircase to their bedchamber. The room was flooded with moonlight. James Leslie threw another log on the fire in the small fireplace near the doorway.

To the left of the doorway was a bank of casement windows. Jasmine opened them a crack. To the right of the door was a small single round window, beneath which was a little table. On the bit of wall space by the fireplace was a mirror, and a chair was set next the hearth. The curtained bed and the clothes chest were the only serious pieces of furniture within the bedchamber. They pulled off their clothing and slipped beneath the coverlet, their bodies immediately intertwined.

He cradled her, his big hand stroking her face. "Have you any idea how much I love you?" he asked her softly.

"At least as much as I love you," she replied, slipping her arms about him.

He began to kiss her face. Slowly, tenderly. His lips grazed lightly across her cheekbones, brushed her eyelids, skimmed over her forehead, and finally found her lips. The sweet pleasure between their two mouths increased as their passions rose and soared. Her breasts flattened as he pulled her hard against his furred chest.

She was dizzy with his kisses. She ran the tip of her tongue across his sensuous lips teasingly. They parted, and she pushed within the cavity of his warm mouth to play, moaning into his throat, for her breasts felt swollen, and were aching with her desire and becoming irritated rubbing against his chest.

He eased her back slightly, his free hand caressing her bosom. Jasmine's body arched up to meet his touch, and she sighed as her head fell away from his. "Beautiful! Beautiful!" he murmured, and she sighed. His dark head dropped to feast upon her round, silken flesh.

"Ahhh, Jemmie, my love!" she cried softly.

When he finally lifted his head from her breasts, his green-gold eyes passion-glazed, she squirmed away from him, rolling, and then pushing him onto his back. A slow smile lit his handsome face.

"'Tis my turn, my lord," she said softly to him. Then, seated upon her heels, she began to unplait the single braid into which her hair was fashioned. She moved deliberately and meticulously, unwinding the three thick strands until they were completely free of one another, and with her fingers she combed her hair. When it hung again in a single curtain of ebony, Jasmine lowered her head and began to stroke his body with sensuous movements of her long hair. Sometimes she would bend so low that she could kiss and lick at his torso with a hot, little tongue that darted here and there across his body, teasing at him, taunting his navel with its wicked point. Lower and lower she moved until she had grasped his manhood in her hand. Drawing the foreskin back she said, "Is this how I peel a carrot, my lord husband?" Then the tip of her tongue encircled beneath the ruby head of it before she took him into her mouth to suckle upon him.

His body arched beneath her wicked ministrations. His big hand fastened into her dark head, at first encouraging her in her actions, then finally forcing her to break off before he exploded in a frenzy of wild desire. Their eyes met, and her look was so lustfully primitive, her mouth wet with her unsatisfied hunger for him, that he lifted her up and lowered her slowly upon his raging rod, their eyes never breaking off contact. Only when she sheathed him completely did Jasmine's eyes close, and, leaning back, she sighed deeply, contracting her inner love muscles about him, causing him to groan with utter pleasure.

She moved slowly on him and with great deliberation, stoking their fires carefully so they might have greater satisfaction of each other. Finally, however, he rolled her beneath him, never breaking off the contact between them, pushing her legs back so he might drive deeper into her. Her teeth sank into his shoulder as he began to piston her faster and faster. Her rounded nails raked at his back.

"Jemmie! Jemmie!" she gasped. "You're killing me!" Yet he forced her higher up the mountain, and she could already feel the coming wave. Her nails dug deeper into him.

"Bitch!" He slapped her lightly, forcing her arms back so she do him no further damage. His buttocks contracted fiercely as he drove hard into her. His lust for her was uncontrollable. He groaned with frustration, not quite able yet to satisfy them, and desperate to do so. Jasmine was the most exciting woman he had ever known, and he wanted her delight in their conjunction to be every bit as wonderful as his was.

"*Ohhhh! Ahhhh!*" The wave was almost there. Stars began to explode behind her eyelids. "*Jemmmmmie!*" The wave had reached her. It burst over her, and she spiraled upward, then down into a swirling eddy of warmth and fulfillment. "*Ahhhhhhhhh!*"

"Ah, God! Ahhhhh! *Oh! Oh! Oh!*" he sobbed, his own desire cresting just behind hers. He collapsed atop her, panting. "Jesu, woman, you have nigh killed me!" Then, kissing her, he rolled off of her, clutching her hand in his. "I love you, my darling Jasmine," he told her, kissing her fingertips passionately.

"I love you, Jemmie Leslie," she responded. "Don't you dare get murdered like poor Jamal and Rowan! And no dying suddenly either like my sweet Hal! I absolutely forbid it!"

He laughed low. "You have made your bed with me, madame, and you will have to lie in it for always. I will never leave you, my darling wife. It will take more than that fool, St. Denis, to part us. He has seriously begun to annoy me, disrupting our lives in this manner. I shall probably have to kill him eventually."

"Good!" she told him. "I'll help!"

"You are already a good Highland wife," he teased her.

Jasmine slid easily into the curve of his arm. "Your Aunt Fiona says that Leslie women are every bit as hard and fierce as Leslie men," she told him. "Besides, St. Denis really does deserve to be severely punished for being such a poor loser and so damnably troublesome."

"I agree," her husband said, "but we will probably just let the king decide the marquis's fate, unless, of course, we are given no other choice than to protect ourselves. I believe, however, that we can probably just stay out of his way for the present."

The following morning they rode back down from the hills to Glenkirk and took up residence once again. Word of their antagonists's whereabouts was brought to them on a regular basis. He visited all the homes that Adali had listed and, unsuccessful, finally headed even farther north to the Huntley, to the Gordons. The summer bloomed about Glenkirk, and they had it all to themselves.

"Let us go down to Edinburgh," the earl suggested one day. "There is but one road to travel, and if we do not meet our messenger returning from England, we will wait there for him."

"I think, perhaps, that we should," Jasmine agreed. "It will be better to resolve this matter most publicly, and thus put an end to it, Jemmie. I almost feel sorry for St. Denis. What will he do when he no longer has us to stalk and to hate? He will never be welcomed at court again, and it was his life. And no decent family will give him a female relation to marry. He might as well be dead."

"His hate will eventually devour him," James Leslie said fatalistically.

They departed for Edinburgh the following morning, arriving several days later. Adali accompanied them, along with a young servant, Maggie, Fergus More, and Red Hugh. There were two houses in Edinburgh that belonged to the Leslies of Glenkirk. Leslie House had been inherited by the earl's aunt Fiona. She and his uncle Adam lived there when they were not visiting their various relations in the north. The other residence, Glenkirk House, had belonged to James Leslie's mother, a gift from his father, the previous earl. Unlike Leslie House, which was set off the High Street, Glenkirk House was off Cannongate near Holyrood Palace.

Of brick, it stood five stories high and had a deep basement, where the kitchens, pantry, stillroom, storeroom, washroom, servants' hall, and servants' quarters were located. It possessed its own stables and was set amid its own gardens, both kitchen and flower. Unlike many town houses in Edinburgh, Glenkirk House had its own indoor sanitary facilities. They settled into it quite nicely and waited for something to happen. Most of the great families who lived in the city were gone to the north or to their homes in the borders, as it was deep summer. The weather was wet and mild, but the mists clung to the hills beyond the city and wreathed about the battlements of Edinburgh Castle.

Farther south, at Queen's Malvern, Skye was pleased to be home again. Her grandson, Charles Gordon, had taken the Lindley children to young Henry's seat at Cadby and was watching over them closely. The earl of BrocCairn, impatient, had ridden off to court to see whether the king had sent to Scotland to prevent any further mischief on the part of the marquis of Hartsfield. Only Velvet and her three youngest sons remained with Skye. Her daughter was so busy with her rambunctious offspring that she left her mother much to her own devices. Skye spent many hours seated upon a small stone bench she had instructed placed by Adam's grave on the hillside. It was peaceful there, and she felt comforted despite the turmoil going on just beyond the fringes of her own life.

"I can no longer make everything all right for everyone, Adam. Am I getting old at last?" she said aloud to the stone marking his grave. She sighed deeply. "Our darling girl is in danger, and the king is obviously still dragging his feet. Ahh, Adam! Bess would have never tolerated such goings-on, even among her favorites, except for Dudley, of course. Dudley could do anything, and he did. We can but pray our son-in-law can move poor old Jamie Stuart to action before it is too late."

The earl of BrocCairn found the king in his hunting lodge near Winchester and had hurried to gain an audience with him. As he stood among the petitioning courtiers, George Villiers spotted him and wondered who the tall distinguished man in the kilt could possibly be. He asked the queen, with whom he was walking.

Queen Anne turned, and her eyes lit up. "Why that is the king's cousin, the earl of BrocCairn. I wonder what he is doing here." Catching his eye, the queen waved at BrocCairn and beckoned him over.

He came and, bowing to her, kissed her hand. "Madame, I am pleased to see you once again."

"Alex, what are you doing here of all places? I would think you at Dun Broc; nay, 'tis summer so it would be Queen's Malvern to visit your wife's family. Oh! I am rude!

This is George, Viscount Villiers, but we call him Steenie, for he has the face of an angel."

The earl of BrocCairn bowed politely to Villiers, and then he said, "I hae come to importune the king, madame, for the marquis of Hartsfield is in Scotland causing much trouble. Can ye gain me my cousin's ear, madame? And yer influence upon him would also be much appreciated by our family."

Villiers was fascinated. He followed along as the queen bustled into her husband's privy chamber, saying as she came, "Here is your cousin of BrocCairn, Jamie, and he brings wicked news. You must hear him at once!"

Viscount Villiers melted back against a paneled wall to listen.

"Alex!" The king came forward slowly. His joints were stiff from the damp weather they had been having. It was almost like being home in Scotland again, he considered irritably. "What news, mon? Ye dinna come to court anymore but rarely. It must be verra serious to bring ye so far south, eh laddie?"

Alexander Gordon bowed low before the king, kissing his cousin's outstretched hand. "It is verra serious, Jamie," he said.

"Sit! Sit!" the king invited him, and they sat together on a bench by the fire. "Now, laddie, tell me what troubles ye?"

"The marquis of Hartsfield hae been in Scotland since early last winter. He hae a royal warrant wi yer signature, Jamie. It is for the arrest of my stepdaughter and her husband on a charge of treason. Now, I dinna believe ye signed such a document, nor hae any unkind intent toward the Leslies of Glenkirk, but St. Denis would appear to hae yer permission in this evil unless ye say otherwise. If he can capture Jasmine and her Jemmie, the law will seem to be on his side."

"Ohhh, the wicked devil!" the queen cried. "Jamie, ye must do something this very minute! Poor Jasmine and Jemmie. Have they not had enough troubles these past few years?"

"I dinna sign any warrant," the king said slowly. "Piers did surely importune me to do so many, many times, but I dinna."

"Nonetheless who is to say in Scotland that it is nae yer signature, Jamie?" BrocCairn replied to the king. "Did ye nae get Glenkirk's message? A man was sent south weeks ago, and we know he got as far as Queen's Malvern in safety. The rest of the journey would have been surely easy. And he knew where to find ye."

"Steenie, fetch Barclay to me," the king said, then turned to his cousin. "He is my secretary, and will know what messages came, but since Stokes was killed, the workings of my royal office are nae so efficient, Alex."

When the king's secretary entered he was immediately questioned as to the arrival of a message from the earl of Glenkirk.

"From Scodand?" Barclay sniffed. "One of my assistants would have seen to it. Was there to be a reply? If there was, the messenger would have been told to wait at the court."

"Find that message at once!" the king thundered in a rare show of spirit. "How dare ye keep it from me! 'Tis a matter of life and death, Barclay. This willna do, mon. This inefficiency willna do at all." And when Barclay had run off to find the message, the king muttered ominously, "There will hae to be changes made, I can see that."

"My lord?"

"Aye, Steenie, my sweet love," the king answered.

"A day ago Kipp St. Denis sought an audience with me," Viscount Villiers said. "Do you think it might have something to do with this matter? I did not see him, fearing to offend you, but I know he is about the court, my lord. Shall I find him for you?" His handsome face looked anxious, as if he feared he had done something wrong.

The king nodded. "What can my poor Piers hope to gain by arresting the Leslies of Glenkirk?" the king wondered aloud.

"He means to murder them, cousin," BrocCairn said bluntly. "He believes he can gain our wee grandson and thus hae power over ye, the damned fool! And, he hae nae forgiven Jasmine for choosing Glenkirk. What on earth ever made ye even offer her to him, cousin?"

"Because he's a meddlesome old fool!" the queen snapped.

The king shrugged helplessly, seeming to agree with his wife's sharp assessment. "'Tis past now," he said.

"Nae for the marquis of Hartsfield," BrocCairn replied. "Jasmine was forced to be parted from her bairns, Jamie. We brought the little Lindleys to Cadby, and my Charlie is wi them. As for our mutual grandson, and the infant heir to Glenkirk, he hae to hide them at Glenkirk Abbey for fear of St. Denis. They should nae be parted from their mother, cousin, but we could do nae else gien the situation. Ye maun stop St. Denis before he does a serious damage to our family."

The king's secretary, Barclay, returned, and sheepishly handed the king an unopened message from Glenkirk. Glaring at him, James Stuart broke the seal on the missive and, opening it, read it through. He had no sooner finished than his favorite returned, Kipp St. Denis in tow.

St. Denis knelt before the king, head bowed.

"Speak," said the monarch.

"I ask your pardon, my liege," Kipp St. Denis said quietly, and he raised his eyes to the king. "I am nothing more than my father's bastard, but he gave me his name and raised me with his heir. I promised my father, when he lay dying that I would always look after Piers. Now I have no choice but to break that vow, my liege, for my poor brother is surely mad to have done what he has done. Have mercy on him."

"And what hae he done?" the king said softly.

"When we went into Scotland I did not know that the signature upon the royal warrant was forged, my liege. It was at Glenkirk that my brother admitted it to me. His desire to revenge himself upon the Leslies is so overwhelming it has certainly rendered him demented. He took the warrant off your secretary's desk, signed it, added the names of James and Jasmine Leslie, and then sealed it with your seal. I did not know this when I went to Scotland with him. I only went to protect him, as I have always tried to protect him from himself.

"We were caught in Edinburgh over the winter, and I thought to dissuade him during that time, but I could not. He hired a group of cutthroats to take with him, and when the roads opened in the spring we marched north. When we arrived at Glenkirk, and found the Leslies gone, I realized we should never find them unless they chose to be found. The summer, I thought, and my brother would grow bored, and seek to return to court; but Piers's talk became more wicked, more evil, and when he spoke of hanging the Leslies, and making little Lady India Lindley his wife, and that perhaps her brother would not reach his manhood and he would then control his fortune, I knew I could no longer influence him; that he had become crazed and evil beyond all.

"I went to Master Adali, the castle steward for help, and he saw that I was able to reach Your Majesty safely. You must not allow my brother to continue on along his wicked path, my liege. *You mustn't!*"

"Ahhhh, my puir Piers laddie," the king mourned, "but I think ye are overfearful of yer brother's actions. I nae ere saw that much wickedness wi'in him, Kipp St. Denis. I dinna believe my sweet laddie would murder, even if his puir heart was broken."

"My liege," Kipp St. Denis said quietly, "my brother, Piers, murdered the earl of Bartram with his own hand. He lured him outside of his gates and drove a dagger into his heart because he feared that you might grant Lord Stokes custody of your grandson, Charles Frederick Stuart. He coldly removed his rival, then he attempted to place the blame upon the Leslies of Glenkirk. Fortunately Your Majesty was too wise to believe such ill of them. Then he made certain that the message telling the Leslies to remain in England, which Your Majesty sent to the Leslies, was never dispatched. That is why they were gone from England when Your Majesty, again at my brother's suggestion, I would remind you, invited them back to court."

"Ohh, the wicked devil!" the queen cried.

George Villiers, however, listened, not without some admiration for the marquis of Hartsfield's machinations. No one, except the clever old Madame Skye, had considered him the culprit in Stokes's murder. He would have gotten away with it, too, had not his brother confessed. He might have gotten away with it all had he not been so impatient for his revenge. It was a lesson to be learned. Sometimes revenge must wait, even if it meant a very long time.

"Cousin," the earl of BrocCairn said, "ye must do something else Jasmine and Jemmie be killed at St. Denis's hand!"

"Ye must write to your governor in Edinburgh that the Leslies are innocent of any crime and that it is the marquis of Hartsfield who is the traitor," the queen insisted.

"And I will carry the message myself for Your Majesty," George Villiers said. "This matter requires a bit more authority than a plain royal messenger, my dearest lord."

"I will accompany him," Alexander Gordon added. "They dinna know yer pretty favorite in Edinburgh, Jamie, but they know me."

"Barclay!" the king snapped. "Where are ye, mon?"

"Here, my lord!" the secretary said, stepping quickly forward.

"Ye hae heard," the king told him. "Write it down, but keep it simple, for my Scots are simple people. Do it now, and then bring it back to me wi my seal to sign." He slumped against his cousin. "I am weary, Alex. I canna take this excitement any longer. My years tell upon me, I fear." He looked at the still kneeling Kipp St. Denis. "Ye may rise, mon. I know how hard it was for ye to come to me, but giving yer loyalty to yer king first was the proper thing to do. Ye will nae suffer for it, laddie."

"I only ask mercy for Piers, my liege," Kipp said. "Let me take him home and look after him. His mother was frail of mind, and I fear he has inherited her tendencies." He brushed his knees off.

"We will see," the king responded. "We will see. For now I would hae ye remain here at court, Master St. Denis, where I can speak wi ye when I need to again. Answer me one question before ye go. Why did ye nae kill Lord Stokes for yer brother?"

Kipp St. Denis almost recoiled at the query. "I could not harm an innocent being, my liege," he said. "I vomited afterward, for Piers insisted that I accompany him. I shall never forget the look in the earl of Bartram's eyes when he realized what had happened." He hung his head in shame.

"God forgive me that I could not prevent my brother from his wickedness."

The king nodded his head. "Ye may go now," he dismissed the man. "Does he tell the truth, I wonder?" he said after Kipp had gone.

"I have heard it said," Viscount Villiers noted, "that it was Kipp to whom the ladies were often drawn, and not Piers. I have heard it said that he is a decent man, but for his brother. What a pity he was not the legitimate son, my dearest lord. How sad that the house of St. Denis will die out now. It is, I have been told, an old name." Then, pouring a goblet of wine from a sideboard tray, he gave it to the king. "Drink, my dear lord, and be strengthened," he said sweetly. Then he turned his attention to the queen, while the king and his cousin of BrocCairn talked together.

"What plot do you have in your head, Steenie?" the queen inquired.

The viscount's fine dark eyes glittered, and he brushed the errant lock of chestnut hair from his forehead. "St. Denis may or may not be mad, madame, but I will wager he will never forget his position. Yet it is unlikely that he will ever have a wife, and the name will die with him and his brother."

"*Unless?*" The queen smiled, light blue eyes twinkling. "What scheme are you contemplating, my fine young coxcomb?"

"Kipp St. Denis was born first, madame, and someone only recently suggested to me that there might be something he desired above all things, but he did not think he would ever have."

"He is a bastard sprig," the queen said softly.

"So is your grandson, Charles Frederick Stuart," Villiers said daringly, "and yet Prince Henry saw that he was ennobled, and had him created a duke. Do you not think Kipp St. Denis has contemplated his accident of birth many times? He would have to be a saint not to have thought about it, and I do not think he is a saint, madame."

"You are suggesting that the king take away Piers St. Denis's title and inheritance, and give it to his half brother?"

"The marquis is mad, and a danger to himself and everyone else about one who offends the king. He must be confined or executed, madame. The king will have no choice but those two."

"Aye," Queen Anne agreed. "There is no other choice but death or imprisonment for Piers St. Denis."

"But what of Kipp, madame? If the king creates him marquis of Hartsfield, the family need not die out. I even have a possible bride for him. Margaret Grey, the widowed countess of Holme. She is just nineteen, has a modest inheritance from her late husband which would serve as a dowry, as well as a two-year-old daughter, proving that she is capable of childbearing."

"Such generosity of heart, my dear Steenie," the queen murmured. "Why do you care what happens to Kipp St. Denis or their family name?"

"Because, madame," Viscount Villiers said, "I can think of no greater revenge upon Piers St. Denis for all his arrogance and unkindness to my dear lord than to have him aware that his titles, his inheritance, his estate, and indeed even the bride he thought you would choose for him, have been ripped away and given to his bastard half brother."

"If he is mad, will he understand?" the queen wondered.

"Mad, he may be, madame, but he is not insensible to what will go on about him," George Villiers said. "It will eat into him each day as the years go by, and he will be incapable of doing anything to relieve his suffering or to regain his former status. It is the worst thing that could happen to him, madame. Execute him, and it is over for Piers St. Denis. Take and give what was his to Kipp St. Denis, and you will inflict upon him a punishment of the subtlest kind, one that will burn into his very soul."

"You are cruel," the queen said.

"Aye," he agreed, not denying it.

"I will think on it," the queen told him.

"Convince our dear lord, and the new marquis will be his devoted servant forever," Viscount Villiers cleverly pointed out.

At that point in their conversation Barclay returned and presented the king with a document to sign. George Villiers was at once on the alert. The king read the parchment slowly, carefully, and then, taking the quill from his secretary, signed it. Barclay then spread it firmly, and the king dripped the dark red wax upon it, and then pressed first the royal seal, and secondly his own signet ring into the cooling wax. Waiting a moment for the wax to harden, Barclay then rolled the parchment up upon the table and sealed it a second time with wax. The royal seal was again imprinted upon it, and the secretary, looking up, handed the document to Viscount Villiers.

"There's time to ride out yet today," the earl of BrocCairn said to the young Englishman, "if yer up to it, laddie."

Villiers nodded. "Just give me a half of an hour to get ready," he said. Then he knelt and kissed the king's hand.

James Stuart reached out and stroked the young man's silky hair. "Ahh, Steenie," he said, "must ye go? Can my cousin of BrocCairn nae take it alone? What will I do wi'out my bonnie laddie?"

"I promised the Leslies my friendship," George Villiers said. "It would be a poor promise if I did not help them now when I could, my dearest lord. I will not linger in your Scotland, and I will return to you as soon as I can." He kissed the royal hand again and, rising, departed the king's privy chamber.

"He's a wee bit too pretty for my taste," BrocCairn said bluntly, "but Jasmine and Jemmie say he's a good man. Now tell me, cousin, how is young Charles? Is there a chance I might pay my respects before I leave ye today?"

"Are ye thinking of the future, Alex?" the king teased him.

Alex Gordon looked startled at the king's comment, then he laughed. "I suppose I am," he said. "Sandy's married, ye know, but my own Charlie is going to need some kind of living eventually. A place wi yer son might be just the thing for him. Besides, now that ye Stuarts are in England, I fear our great and extended family will begin to separate. We share a grandfather, Jamie, though my name be Gordon. For my family's sake I dinna want to lose our wee prestige wi the royal Stuarts. I need a son in England, and God knows there is little for Charlie in Scotland. His brother's wife hae already birthed an heir for us."

"Honest as ever," the king replied with a smile. "There's time for ye to renew yer acquaintance wi royal Charles before ye must set out for Edinburgh. Annie, will ye take our cousin to the prince? And dinna worry, Alex. We'll find something for yer laddie before the summer's end. Farewell now, and God bless ye." The king extended his hand.

The earl of BrocCairn took it and kissed it fervently. "Farewell, cousin," he told the king, "and God bless ye! Hae it not been for yer timely intervention, a great injustice would hae been done in yer name."

Chapter Eighteen

Clan Bruce was hosting a small summer games on the other side of the Firth of Forth from Edinburgh. As late summer approached the weather had turned sunny and warm.

"We'll go," Jemmie Leslie decided. "You've seen all that Edinburgh has to offer, darling Jasmine. You've seen the castle, and blessed Queen Margaret's chapel. You've visited the markets, and the King's Cross, where my stepfather, Francis Stewart-Hepburn, Lord Bothwell, was sadly 'put to the horn,' outlawed by his cousin, our own King James. We'll go across the water to the Bruce games, then return to Edinburgh to pack up and go back to Glenkirk."

"But what about St. Denis?" Jasmine asked him. "We have had no word from England yet, Jemmie. Is it wise for us to go home yet?"

"St. Denis is in the north, chasing shadows," her husband said. "We have naught to fear from him, sweetheart. As for our messenger, he will more than likely go to Glenkirk when he finds we are not here."

They sailed across the Forth with the earl's aunt and uncle.

"Adam still loves the games," Fiona said. "'Tis he who taught Jemmie how to toss the caber. He generally wins, despite his age, when he competes. You'll enjoy the games. They'll run about four or five days."

The servants had already gone ahead to prepare the tents that would house them. The Leslie griffin flew from their tops and made their lodging easily visible. Fiona had instructed Jasmine how to dress so she would not appear unusual to the clannish Scots who were gathered. All the men wore lengths of plaid wrapped about them, and linen shirts, knit hose, and wide leather belts along with leather shoes upon their feet. The women wore ankle-length skirts and white shirts with plaid shawls, their clan badges in full view, and knitted stockings and leather shoes upon their legs and their feet. It was simple, comfortable clothing.

Their lodging was equally modest, but comfortable. There were wood and leather camp beds set up, covered with feather mattresses, and comforters. There were braziers to heat each tent. Outside the tent beneath the awning were two chairs. The servants had pallets which were placed at their lord's discretion, either inside or outside the tents. The earl of Glenkirk did not think it wise that his wife's female servant sleep out-of-doors, where she would be prey to lechers and drunkards. Maggie would be inside while Fergus and Red Hugh would be just outside the tent's entry, where they might also serve to guard their master and their mistress.

Jasmine had never experienced anything like the games, and the only time in her entire life she had slept in a tent was during the weeks in which she made her way from her father's court to Cambay on the coast. It had been a dangerous adventure then. Now, she decided, it was fun. Their hosts, the Bruces, were providing both food and drink for their guests. Great cook fires burned night and day. The fare was simple. Hot oat stirabout, oatcakes, and cider in the morning. Mutton, oatcakes, and ale in the afternoon. Many of the guests at the games supplemented this rather spartan fare. The Leslies had brought a half a wheel of cheese, fresh bread, a fat, cooked capon, wine, apples, and pears.

"All those oats give me the wind," Adam Leslie complained. "After five days if we all turn our arses to the sea, we'll create enough of a blow to send the French fleet back to Normandy."

Jasmine had never seen anything like the games. There were footraces. The men stripped off their shirts and ran the different courses. There was wrestling. The man to beat was the Erskine champion, a tall, bare-chested beefy fellow in his red-and-green tartan. Young men of the Bruce, MacDuff, and Lindsay clans tried, but failed. Black Ewen Erskine remained champion for these games. There was the stone pitch, in which heavy, smooth round stones were pitched with one hand down the length of a field. Happily the host clan won that contest. Then came the tossing of the caber. Logs of even length had been hewn, and now each contestant lifted up his log in turn, ran a few steps, and heaved the heavy timber as far as he could. Adam Leslie, considered almost an old man by the young clansmen, pitched his caber farther than any of the younger men. There was one contestant left. His nephew, the earl of Glenkirk. His dark hairy chest straining and wet with his effort, James Leslie launched his caber with a fierce grunt. It soared through the clear air with what seemed exquisite grace, passing the log thrown only moments earlier by Adam Leslie.

"I declare James Leslie winner of tossing the caber," said Jock Bruce, the master of the games.

The earl grinned. "At least it's still in the family," he teased his uncle.

"Ye'll hae to beat me three times running, laddie, before I'll gie over to ye," Adam said, laughing. "'Twas a lucky throw, I'll vow, Jemmie. There are games at Sithean next month. We'll see then."

"One of these days yer going to pull something important if ye keep on like this," Fiona muttered ominously.

Adam Leslie slid his arm about his wife. "Naught for ye to worry about, darlin'," he said gallantly.

James Leslie had also entered the archery contest. Jasmine stood by his side, fidgeting. Her father and her brothers had taught her to shoot. "Why can't women enter the games?" she demanded of her husband. "I'm as good an archer as any man, dammit!"

"Women don't come to the games to compete," the earl said.

"Well I wouldn't want to in most of your sports," Jasmine responded. "They're much too rough, but women hunt, too. They know how to use a bow. I think women should be allowed to compete in archery."

"Next she'll be wanting to join the dancing," Adam Leslie snickered. "Lassie, lassie, keep to yer place."

"*My place?*" Jasmine's turquoise eyes flashed, and in that moment her husband caught a glimpse of the Mughal's daughter. "And, what, pray, good uncle, is *my place?*"

Adam Leslie had also in the same moment as his nephew seen something so fierce and so royal in his nephew's wife that he had almost been frightened. Drawing a deep breath he said, further compounding his blunder, "Why, lassie, 'tis yer place to be a good and obedient wife to Jemmie Leslie and gie the family healthy bairns."

Fiona began to giggle. The earl groaned.

"In other words, Uncle, I should keep silent, bow to my lord's wishes, and spend my life up on the *ben enciente!*" She snatched her husband's longbow and notched an arrow into it. Drawing the string back, she let the missile fly. It hit the target dead center. Pulling another arrow from its holder she fitted it into the bow, and loosed it. It split the first arrow in the target. Shoving the bow back at her husband, Jasmine said scathingly, "Any man who can match that shot will have five gold pieces from me. Is there any man here who would try?" She looked about the dumbstruck men. "No one?" Jasmine Leslie turned her back on the astounded men and walked away.

"Jesu!" Jock Bruce said admiringly. "She's even more woman than yer mother was, Jemmie Leslie! Where the hell did she ever learn to shoot like that? And why would a woman want to shoot?"

"She was her father's youngest child, born in his old age, and he doted upon her as did her eldest brother. They taught her so she could hunt with them," the earl of Glenkirk said.

"What a braw lassie! Ye'll get strong sons off of her," the host of the games said, "and she'd be mighty handy in a siege, too."

His remark broke the tension left by Jasmine's anger, and the men laughed heartily, but the earl of Glenkirk was not amused. His wife had embarrassed him publicly not just by her actions, which had been spectacular to say the least, but by her sharp words, heard by all. He turned and stamped back to their tent. There he found Jasmine calmly drinking a cup of wine. "Do wives in India shame their husbands publicly, madame?" he demanded of her.

"This is not India," she said calmly.

"Nay, madame, it is not. *It is Scotland!* And in Scotland women do not discomfit their men before a crowd," he told her.

"You are just angry because I am a better shot with the longbow than you are," she said airily. Jasmine was feeling much better now.

"Aye, you are," he agreed, "but your words were far sharper than your arrows, and wives here do not openly speak to their husbands as you spoke to me back at the archery trial."

"'Twas not you with whom I was irritated," Jasmine replied. "'Twas your uncle Adam. He thinks all women should be humble, meek, and barefoot wi bairns," she **gently mocked** Adam's accent.

"My uncle is of the old school," the earl told his wife. "He believes that a woman should defer to her lord."

"Like your Aunt Fiona?" Jasmine replied scathingly. "She leads him by the nose, Jemmie!"

"Aye, she does, but he doesn't know it," the earl said. "I will tell you something that few people know, or remember. My Aunt Fiona was a wild creature in her youth. They say her wifely ardor put her first husband into an early grave, but he was a weak creature. Widowed, she set her sights upon my father, and why not? She was every bit his equal in breeding, being an earl's daughter. My father entered his bedchamber one evening to find Fiona there, naked upon his bed, for she sought to compromise him before he could wed my mother. Uncle Adam was with my father. He had always desired Fiona, and so my father slept in his brother's room that night while Adam tamed his Fiona. In the early days of their marriage Fiona was his slave, but then one day she realized he needed her every bit as much as she needed him. From that moment on my aunt has manipulated my uncle, but she does it in such a way that he believes nothing has ever changed and that he is still the master of his house. Fiona is very clever, darling Jasmine."

Jasmine put her silver cup down. "Are you suggesting that I *manipulate* you, my lord?" She smiled wickedly.

He laughed in spite of himself. "Be serious, madame," he scolded her. "My uncle is of a different time and sees women as all men saw them forty years ago. As most men in Scotland today still see their women. This is not England, with its more liberal appreciation of the fair sex, darling Jasmine. What is between us is private, but in public I do not believe I am asking too much when I ask you to yield before my manly superiority." His green-gold eyes were twinkling as he said these last words. "And you must find a way to make your peace with my uncle, sweetheart." He took her hand in his and kissed it.

She poured him his own cup of wine, and handed it to him. "What am I to say to him?" she asked. "That I might be breeding again?"

"Aren't you?" he said knowingly.

"Perhaps," she said. "I am not certain yet. *How did you know?"*

Pulling her from her seat, he sat down in it, drawing her into his lap and cuddling her. "Because there is nothing about you, darling Jasmine, that I do now know; no nuance of which I am not acutely aware. You are the breath I breathe; the very beating of my heart; a part of my soul." He kissed her slowly, deeply, lingeringly; his big hand cupping her dark head, his fingers kneading her scalp.

She sighed, molding herself close against him. "Jemmie! Jemmie!" she murmured breathlessly, pulling away from him. "The whole encampment will see us! We are not alone. What will they say?"

"They will say the earl of Glenkirk is a fool for his beautiful wife, who talks far too much for her own good," he replied, kissing her again, "and that the earl of Glenkirk should beat his beautiful wife occasionally to keep her docile and amenable to his will."

"You would never beat me," Jasmine said, dismissing his words.

"Nay, I would not," he agreed, "but if you do not behave yourself while we are here at the games, I may be tempted to give your pretty bottom a smack, madame!"

She jumped from his lap. "You would not dare!"

James Leslie eyed her lazily from his camp chair and, reaching out, pulled her back into his lap, kissing her soundly. "A woman who says *you would not dare,* when she knows damn well that I would, is either asking to be spanked or is foolish. Are you asking to be spanked, madame," he murmured, nuzzling her soft neck.

"No!" She giggled helplessly as he nibbled at her flesh.

"Then you are foolish, darling Jasmine," he teased. His fingers were unlacing her shirt as he spoke, and now he slipped a big hand into the garment to cup her breast. It fit into his palm like a nesting dove.

"I am not!" she protested. Oh God! Her breasts were so very sensitive now. She was surely breeding again. He rubbed the nipped insistently, teasing at it until it was hard with longing. *"Jemmie!"* she cried out softly as he laid her back against his arm, and then, lowering his head, began to suckle upon her breast. "Someone will come! Someone will see us! Ohhh, God!" She could feel the wetness between her legs.

Raising his head, he tipped her from his lap and pushed her into the tent. There were no words for the moment between them. They both knew what they wanted. Sliding to her knees upon the grassy floor of the tent, Jasmine waited but a moment for her husband to join her. Kneeling behind her, he pushed up her skirts, gazing admiringly upon the twin moons of her bottom. He loosened his own clothing and moved himself into position, pushing himself slowly into her hot, throbbing passage, groaning with pleasure as she tightened herself about him. Completely sheathed within her, he let himself enjoy the sweetness for a long moment. Then he withdrew himself very slowly before thrusting himself back hard into her quivering body. Her back arced itself concave as she ground her buttocks into his belly.

"Oh, witch!" he groaned, his hands fastening themselves strongly about her hips as he began to piston her fiercely. If she were not already with child, she soon would be, he thought randily.

Her body was bent in a posture of complete submission, and yet she did not feel as if she had surrendered, Jasmine thought. They had suddenly wanted each other, and it was she who had chosen the path that they would take. She who had knelt and offered herself to him. She was gaining every bit as much pleasure from this mad encounter as he was. His love rod was so strong. It pierced her to her heart. She could feel every one of his fingers, single and individual, as it pressed into the soft flesh of her hips. She would be marked for several days, for her creamy skin was very fine.

The heat of his body was burning her. He drove himself deeply into her, withdrew, and propelled his length hard once more. The walls of her passage clutched hungrily at him, seeking to capture him. "Don't stop," she begged shamelessly. "Ohh, Jemmie, don't stop!"

He sought to please her, please himself, *please them*. Back and forth he slid his manhood, back and forth, until he could suddenly feel himself expanding, feel the tremors of excitement from Jasmine as she began to slide over the edge into the white hot pleasure, and, unable to restrain himself any longer, he let his love juices burst forth with a loud groan. *"Ahhhhh! Ahhhhhhhh! Ah! Ah! Ahhhhhhh!"* Falling away from her, he rolled onto his back as she collapsed facedown into the soft green grass.

They lay panting for a short time, and then Jasmine said weakly, "You will not control me with your passion, my lord."

James Leslie burst out laughing. "And here I thought you sought to cajole me with yours," he teased her.

"Oh beast!" she cried, and pretended to smack at him.

Defending himself, he pulled her into his arms and kissed her once again. "Madame! Madame! 'Tis not fit you beat your husband."

She lay contentedly in his arms. "You are the most aggravating of men, Jemmie Leslie, and always were. You are only fortunate in that I love you to distraction, and above all others, else I think I should kill you." Rubbing her face against his silken covered chest, she kissed it.

He stroked her dark head, entwining her thick plait about his hand and arm. "I have never needed a woman before, my precious, darling Jasmine, but I need you," he admitted. "Until I set eyes upon you for the first time, I did not know what happiness could be. I am jealous of any man who gazes at you. I resent the years we have not spent together. My love is for you alone."

"Oh, Jemmie! Sometimes I think I am not worthy of such a love from such a man. I am very spoilt and imperious, and I hurt without meaning to hurt; but I love you, my darling husband!" Jasmine declared passionately to him, and she kissed him hungrily.

"Ah, here ye two are," they suddenly heard Adam Leslie's voice, and he entered their tent as the earl scrambled up, pulling his wife with him. Adam's eyes twinkled mischievously.

"Uncle," Jasmine brushed the grass from her skirts, and attempted to smooth her hair, "I would apologize for my outburst earlier."

"Och, lassie, 'tis naught," he replied graciously. "Yer breeding again, I expect, and a breeding woman is apt to be testy and a wee bit skittish. Yer forgiven. Now come gie us a kiss to seal the peace between us, eh?" He held out his arms to her.

Laughing, Jasmine went into them and kissed his cheek. "Is nothing a secret in Scotland, Uncle?" she asked him.

"Verra little," he said, and he chuckled.

In the evening the men danced to the wailing of the bagpipes beneath the August full moon, the light from the fires casting wild shadows over everything in their path. Jemmie pointed out to her the distinctive plaids worn by the different clans. The Bruce tartan was red with white lines separating the red into boxes, and in the center of each square was a smaller green box separated by red lines. The MacDuffs had worn their hunting colors—a plaid of dark blue, green, medium blue, and red. The Erskines' tartan was red with black; the Lindsays' a similar design but in red and green. Jasmine's shawl was the Leslies' hunting colors—boxes of medium blue and green with broad bands of dark blue, and narrow bands of red and yellow.

On the last night of the games Jasmine stood with Fiona Leslie watching the men as they danced. Gracefully they stepped between the crossed swords, never once moving the blades with their feet. The pipes played with fierce intensity. A soft wind brought the fragrance of heather from the hillsides. The flames from the fires leapt as madly as did the dancers. There was something wonderfully wild and primitive about it, and that part of Jasmine that was Celtic was moved and touched.

When the dawn came, however, the skies, bright for several days, had lowered, and rain threatened. The encampment began to break up, and Bruce's meadow began to look like one again as they packed their belongings and prepared to return to Edinburgh.

"Ye can save yerselves a day if ye leave directly from here," Adam Leslie suggested to his nephew. "We'll follow in a few days' time and bring yer steward, Adali. He can close up Glenkirk House. Ye'll be home all the quicker wi'out the baggage carts."

The earl turned to his wife. "Jasmine?"

"It would be easier, but I have to go back to town, my lord. I have business with my bankers, the Kiras, that I must conduct in person."

They crossed the Firth of Forth once more and rode back into the town. James Leslie went directly to his home, but his wife went to her bankers, in Goldsmith Alley, off the High Street, so that they might leave the city all the sooner, and return home to Glenkirk. Stepping back out into the street, her business complete, Jasmine suddenly found herself surrounded by a party of rather nasty-looking men. A familiar voice greeted her sneeringly.

"So, madame, we meet again," Piers St. Denis, the marquis of Hartsfield, said. "I have a warrant for your arrest. Take her and put her on the horse," he commanded his men.

Maggie, behind her mistress, and unseen, pressed herself back into the shadows of the doorway. To her surprise, a hand caught at her arm and slowly eased her back into the building. Startled, she turned about to see David Kira, a finger to his lips, warning her to silence as he quietly closed the door behind them. He drew her back down the hallway of the building, and into a side room.

"Why did ye nae help my mistress," Maggie demanded.

"One man, and a Jew? It would have been worth my life, mistress. You, however, I have saved. I will let you out the back door, and you must run to your master and tell him what happened. Your horse will be returned to Glenkirk House by nightfall," he said. Then, opening a small door in the room's outer wall, he beckoned her through. "Go down the alley, lassie, and you'll find yourself back on the High Street. You know your way from there, do you not?"

Maggie nodded. "Thank ye, sir," she said, finally, remembering her manners, and giving him a smile.

"Hurry!" he told her. "I expect there is a need for urgency."

The door closed behind her, and Maggie did just as the banker had advised her. She ran. Down the alley and out onto the High Street, but she did not go directly to Glenkirk House, which was located off the Cannongate. Instead she ran to Leslie House, which was set on a small street that bisected the High Street. It was nearer, and Master Adam would have a horse to get her to Glenkirk House all the quicker. Maggie ran on, praying that she would remember the right street. Then she recognized it, and, turning, she dashed down it, swiftly reaching the door of Leslie House, and pounding upon it with all her strength.

The servant answered looking askance at the disheveled Maggie. "Yes?" he said loftily.

Maggie pushed past him. "Master Adam! Master Adam!" she called urgently, and Adam and Fiona Leslie came forth from the library. "'Tis my mistress," Maggie gasped, her breath coming in desperate gasps. "She's been taken!" and Maggie began to cry.

Fiona took the girl by the arm, and drew her into the library. Adam poured a small whiskey and shoved it at the servant.

"Drink it, lassie. Ye canna hae a fit of hysterics now. Drink it down and tell us what hae happened," he said.

Maggie coughed and sputtered, but she managed to get the potent amber liquid down. She stood silent for a moment as if gathering her strength, then, taking a deep breath, said, "We went to Master Kira's, and when we were coming out this man with a strange accent, he was nae a Scot, even a Sassenach like these southerners are, said my mistress was under arrest, and his men put her on her horse and rode away. They dinna see me, for I was behind her, and then Master Kira pulled me back into the building and let me out the back to come and tell my master, but 'tis a long walk to Glenkirk House from here, and ye were nearer, and I need a horse for mine was left behind, and Master Kira said he would hae it back to us by nightfall, but I need one now!" She stopped as if to catch her breath.

"God's foot!" Adam Leslie swore. "'Tis that damned Englishman, and why the hell dinna we know he was back in Edinburgh?"

Maggie began to cry in earnest now, tears streaming down her face, her sobs loud and most pitiful to hear.

"Cease yer caterwauling, lassie!" Adam Leslie roared. "I need to think, damnit."

"Ye need to get Jemmie," Fiona said, and she put her arms about the weeping Maggie. "There, there, lassie. Ye did absolutely the right thing coming here first." She turned back to her husband. "Adam, dammit! Get on yer horse, and find the earl!"

James Leslie thought his head would explode so great was his anger when he learned that his wife had been taken by Piers St. Denis. Still, he forced himself to remain calm, mainly with the help of Adali, who laced the earl's tea with whiskey and made him quiet himself as he drank it.

"Breathe slowly, my lord, as I have taught you," Adali said. "Anger will but create a confusion inside your mind. You must not allow your wrath to produce chaos within your thoughts. We are dealing with a madman who is both clever and, to my great surprise, resourceful."

James Leslie nodded and drank the hot tea.

"What blather is this?" Adam Leslie demanded impatiently. "We need to gather up our men and find the bastard, so we may slaughter him for his incredible presumption in laying hands on a countess of Glenkirk!"

"Nay," the earl said quietly. "We need to outfox this madman, Uncle, before he can harm Jasmine. I have lost one wife to insanity, and I will not lose another."

"Where could the marquis have taken my lady?" Adali asked.

"If he still hae that damned warrant, he may hae gone to the castle. We're in luck if he hae, for I know the governor. He's a sensible man and will nae act hastily unless he is entirely certain of himself," Adam Leslie said. "I'll go up the hill, but ye are to remain here. That warrant has both yer names, laddie. Why the hell hasn't our messenger returned from England? He should be here by now!"

Adam Leslie went "up the hill," as he had so colorfully put it to his nephew, to Edinburgh Castle. There he sought out his friend, Robert Chrighton, who was currently the castle governor, but the governor had not seen Piers St. Denis since the spring. He was shocked by Adam's tale.

"He did hae a warrant as I recall," the governor said.

"A forgery," Adam Leslie said bluntly. "His half brother admitted it to the steward at Glenkirk before he deserted the marquis. Ye know the king's signature, Robbie."

"Time hae past since Jamie was here," the governor said. "He hae grown older, and his hand may nae be as steady."

"So," Adam Leslie said triumphantly, "ye were suspicious!"

"The seal was genuine," the governor hastily told his guest.

"But the signature was nae! Dinna fret, Robbie. We sent a messenger down into England to tell the king what was happening. He'll be back soon wi the truth. If St. Denis brings the countess of Glenkirk to the castle, ye'll send word, will ye nae?"

"Aye, and I'll keep her ladyship comfortable, and safe."

"Ye'll gie her back!" Adam said sharply.

"I canna until this matter of the warrant is straightened out, Adam," his friend said.

Before Adam Leslie might protest, however, there was a knock upon the governor's door, and a servant entered to announce, "The earl of BrocCairn and Viscount Villiers, my lord."

"God's boot!" Adam Leslie chortled. "Here is yer answer in the nick of time, Robbie. BrocCairn, 'tis good to see ye. Do ye hae some paper wi ye saying this Englishman is a liar and a traitor? He hae just this day snatched Jasmine from the streets of the town."

"Jesu, I am glad Velvet isn't here to learn that," Alexander Gordon said. "My lord governor, Adam Leslie, may I present Viscount George Villiers, who carries a warrant from the king himself for the arrest of the marquis of Hartsfield. The forgery that Hartsfield carries attempting to cause harm to the Leslies of Glenkirk is not valid, and never has been, my lord governor."

George Villiers handed the rolled parchment to Robert Chrighton. "You will find a personal message from His Majesty as well within the roll, my lord," he said bowing.

Adam Leslie was staring at George Villiers in amazement. Never before had he seen such a beautiful young man. He was tall, and very manly in appearance, with his flashing dark eyes and wavy chestnut hair. His clothing was the height of fashion, and certainly did not have the look of a man who had ridden hard. It was unwrinkled, and every bow and furbelow was in place. "So yer the king's new love of whom we hae heard," he said frankly.

George Villiers burst out laughing. "I am most fortunate to have His Majesty's favor and affection," he told the craggy Highlander.

"His great-great-grandfather liked the laddies, too," Adam Leslie said matter-of-factly. "Can ye use a sword, laddie?"

"I can," Villiers replied, and then he said mischievously, "His Majesty's great-great-grandfather must have liked the ladies equally as well, else His Majesty not be here today."

"Aye, he did, just like our Jamie," Adam replied, not in the least nonplussed by the angelic-looking Englishman.

"Where is Jasmine?" the earl of BrocCairn asked.

"We dinna know," Adam replied. "I came up the hill because I thought he might hae brought her here wi his forged warrant, but Robbie says he hae nae seen the bastard since the spring."

"Where is Glenkirk?" BrocCairn demanded.

"At his house," Adam said. "I didna want him out where this Englishman might catch him as he did Jasmine."

"This is a crown matter now, Sir Robert," Alexander Gordon said. "Ye must send out men to seek the countess of Glenkirk, who hae been kidnapped by this man. He is treacherous, but the felons wi him will quickly gie way to yer authority. We can waste nae time. This man is dangerous."

"I imagine," said George Villiers, "that he did not bring Jasmine here to the castle for fear the truth is out by now. I do not think he expected it would take him almost a year to run her to ground. He could not take the chance that Sir Robert had received word from the king that St. Denis is on a mission of revenge, and not on royal business. Lord Gordon is correct when he states that the marquis of Hartsfield is dangerous. We have only recently learned from his half brother that he personally murdered Lord Stokes."

"God's blood!" Adam Leslie swore.

"He will seek to leave Edinburgh," Lord Gordon said. "We must learn in which direction he hae gone as he will have Jasmine wi him."

"How do we do that?" Villiers asked.

"First we will return to Kira, the banker's residence, in Goldsmith Alley. He will tell us what he can, and we will speak wi his neighbors to learn if they saw anything. Someone will hae seen *something*," Lord Gordon replied. "It was broad daylight." He turned to Adam Leslie. "When we hae seen Kira ye will go back to Glenkirk House and tell my son-in-law what we are doing. We will go to him immediately when we hae learned anything. Then we will follow this St. Denis, and we will nae cease until we hae regained our Jasmine." He turned again. "Sir Robert, ye will gie us men to aid us in this search?"

"Aye," the governor said slowly, wondering what it would cost him to send out his men. Part of his living was made from what he could save from the subsidy allocated the royal treasury for Edinburgh Castle.

"The king shall know of your eager cooperation, my lord," Viscount Villiers said with a charming smile. His own instinct had told him the direction of the castle governor's thoughts. "I shall personally inform him of your generous aid." He bowed to Sir Robert with a flourish.

The three men withdrew from the governor's privy chamber, and Adam Leslie said with his characteristic bluntness, "Yer nae such a silly puppy as ye look, sir, are ye?"

"Nay, sir, I am not," George Villiers replied with a small grin. Then he asked the older Scotsman, "Are you always so frank, sir?"

"'Tis the only way I know to be," Adam answered him candidly.

George Villiers shook his head. "In a way I envy you, sir," he told Adam, "but you would never succeed at court with such an attitude."

"*That cesspit?*" Adam said scornfully. "Never! I hae enough of the king's court when Jamie was here in Scotland. When he hurried himself south with such undisguised enthusiasm, I watched as the hand and arse kissing, ambitious members of my race dashed after him in their eagerness to share his good fortune. It is said that many were younger sons, and but sought their fortune, but I was a younger son. I hae a fine wife, a small house in Edinburgh, and Glenkirk Castle will always be my home in the Highlands. I am nae a rich man, but what I hae is more than enough, for I am here in my homeland. I was born a Scot, and I will die one, my fine young lordling. Nay. I am nae a courtier, but each man must choose his own path through life. This is mine."

The trio departed Edinburgh Castle and rode down the High Street to Goldsmith Alley. David Kira was awaiting them. He ushered them into his library, and George Villiers was surprised at the richness of the interior of what seemed from the exterior to be a poor man's house.

"I have been expecting ye," the banker said quietly. Then, "A serving girl saw the entire thing from the upstairs window. There were eight men with the lord. They rode back out onto the High Street with the countess, but she could not see from her vantage point in which direction they turned. The lord, however, was leading her ladyship's horse, and they had tied her hands to the pommel of the saddle so she could not escape them, but also so no bystander would notice that she was captive. It was cleverly done."

"Why did she nae cry out?" Adam Leslie wondered aloud.

"Because, Master Leslie, a small silk handkerchief was stuffed into her mouth, and tied with a bit of cord. Then they covered her head with her shawl so it would not be noticed," David Kira said.

"Thank ye, Master Kira," Lord Gordon said, rising with his companions. "We'll ask out on the High Street to see if anyone noticed this party of men and a woman."

Out on the High Street they eventually discovered a beggar who had indeed seen nine men and a woman. "Took the Leith Road, my good lords," he said, his grimy hand outstretched.

The earl of BrocCairn dropped a silver piece into the upturned palm. "Dinna drink it all," he advised, before riding on with his fellow travelers. He turned to Adam Leslie. "Go to Glenkirk House now and tell Jemmie we're on the Leith Road. Tell Sir Robert as well. Villiers and I will continue on to the port, although why the hell he is headed there, I'll never know."

"Probably because it is the one place you wouldn't think to look for him," Viscount Villiers opined to Lord Gordon, as Adam Leslie turned back toward Glenkirk House. "He did not trust to go to Sir Robert, for he suspects the game is up. There is no place in Scotland where he will be safe with a kidnapped countess of Glenkirk. Most men in his position would head for the borders with Jasmine. He, however, is not most men. He will try and get on a ship for England, thereby avoiding anyone in pursuit, or so he thinks." George Villiers chuckled. "He'll have some time attempting to force Jasmine upon a vessel, if indeed he can do it at all."

Alexander Gordon chortled. "Aye, she's like her mother, and hae a verra hot temper; although Velvet claims her temper is more like Jasmine's father's, the Mughal's. I'm afraid Piers St. Denis hae bitten off far more than he can chew, which he'll shortly discover to his dismay."

And, laughing, the two men continued on down the short distance that separated Edinburgh from its port town of Leith.

Chapter Nineteen

They had taken her completely unawares as she had stepped forth into Goldsmith Alley from David Kira's house. A small cloth was stuffed into her mouth before she might scream or utter any sort of protest. A narrow string was tied about her head to prevent her from spitting out the gag. They boosted her onto her mount so quickly and lashed her hands to the pommel of the saddle that there was simply no opportunity to fight them. Her shawl was drawn down over her head and she was led away.

Jasmine knew instantly who her captor was, and if it had been possible to wreak havoc upon him, she would have gladly done so. She had been very careful as they were gagging and binding her not to glance back at Master Kira's house. Maggie had been but a step behind her, but a quick surreptitious peep at the door from which she had just exited revealed that Maggie was no longer there. Clever girl, Jasmine thought, relieved. If they had both been captured, who would there be to tell Jemmie? But Maggie would have to hurry, or the trail would be lost!

They had ridden out onto the High Street. After a few moments they turned onto another road. Leith, the signpost had said, Jasmine noted. Leith? Of course! It was the port for Edinburgh, but where in the name of heaven was he taking her from Leith? Back to England? It couldn't be

England. By now Piers St. Denis's deception was well-known at court, and the king would have put a stop to it. Where then? None of her questions would be answered until they stopped, and she got this damned gag out of her mouth. She pushed at it with her tongue. It wasn't lodged too tightly, but her mouth was becoming exceedingly dry. Jasmine concentrated on her breathing in an attempt to calm herself. She wasn't so much afraid as she was angry.

They had not traveled a great way down the Leith Road when they came to an inn and stopped. It was a rather disreputable-looking place. Jasmine could hear the drunken shouts from within the building. The men accompanying them dismounted, stretching and scratching. Tying their rather scruffy mounts to a hitching post, they looked to the marquis.

"We leave you here," he said. "I give you your horses. Do what you will with them."

"And our silver?" a tall ruffian demanded. "Ye promised us silver, too, for our services, m'lord. We ain't letting ye and the lady go wi'out our silver," he finished menacingly.

Piers St. Denis pulled a bag from his doublet, and tossed it scornfully to the man. "Here," he said with a sneer.

"It ain't enough!" the man complained, weighing it in his palm. "Ye've shorted us, Englishman. Why should we expect any less from one of old King Jamie's pretty boys?" He moved forward threateningly.

The marquis of Hartsfield's hand slid to his sword. Yanking it from its scabbard, he moved his horse slightly forward and ran the man through. As his victim pitched headfirst to the ground, he withdrew the sword from the surprised man's chest, wiped it on his victim's clothing, and returned it to its place. "Does anyone else wish to debate the point with me?" he demanded coldly. Then, turning his horse, he departed the inn yard, leading Jasmine's mount behind him, as the seven remaining ruffians flung themselves on the dead man, grasping for the money pouch and arguing over the disposition of his horse.

"Ummm! Mmmmm!" Jasmine noised to get his attention.

He turned back to her, smiling. "Would you like me to remove the gag from your mouth, my sweet?" he asked her solicitously.

She nodded eagerly.

"Do you promise me that you will not scream, cry out, or make any attempt to attract the attentions of anyone?"

Again she nodded. "Mmmmm! Mmmmmm!"

"No," he said coldly. "This is your first lesson in obedience, my sweet. I do not like recalcitrant women. With me as your master you will finally learn your place. You really should have chosen me, Jasmine. Now I must punish you and James Leslie for the public insult you have done me. I could have you both hanged, you know, for I possess a royal warrant, but first I shall use you to draw the earl of Glenkirk to me. Tonight you shall write a letter telling him that you have made a mistake and that you wish to be with me. How he will suffer. He will, of course, come for you to see if it is true. Then I shall kill him, and you will belong to me forever! I told you that you would be mine one day, and you will." His bright blue eyes glittered with his words.

He is totally mad, Jasmine thought. Completely and utterly insane, which made him even more dangerous, she considered. She must take the first opportunity to flee him. Certainly Jemmie knew by now what had happened to her, but how could he possibly know where to look for her? He couldn't, and therefore it was up to her to escape Piers St. Denis, the marquis of Hartsfield, before he killed them both. She could smell the sea as they approached the port, but he did not go into the town. Instead, he turned off on an almost invisible dirt path that led up a small hillock. At the top was what appeared to be a deserted cottage. It was there that he stopped, dismounting from his own horse and lifting her down off her own mount. Below them was Leith, and beyond the Firth of Forth and the sea. He pulled her by her bonds into the cottage, even as she resisted him now, digging her heels into the earth, and struggling.

To her shock he slapped her. "I will have no defiance from you, madame!" he said. "You are here to learn obedience, and you will not leave this poor place until you do." He yanked her into the small house.

Once inside, however, he undid the cord binding the gag and pulled the rag from her mouth. *"Bastard!"* Jasmine managed to gasp. "You have almost choked me with that thing!"

Piers St. Denis slapped her again. "Thank me for my generosity in removing it, you bitch, or I'll stuff it back in your mouth again!" he snarled at her. "Only that I long to hear the sound of your voice once more overrules my common sense, but if you continue to speak to me with such disrespect, you will be gagged until you learn to speak to me with a gentle tongue." His hand fastened itself into her dark hair, and he forced her face up to his. "Do you understand me, Jasmine?"

"You are hurting me, my lord," she replied through gritted teeth.

"Do you understand?" he repeated.

"Aye, I understand," she told him, forcing her anger back. He was, she realized, perfectly capable of killing her.

"Good," he almost purred, and then he passed his hand over her heaving bosom. "I want you naked," he told her. "I have never seen you as nature fashioned you, and I am most anxious to do so, my sweet."

She shuddered with revulsion at his words, but he mistook her gesture for fear, and was very pleased. "What do you think to gain by this, my lord?" she asked him. "You have violated the king's trust, and he will certainly see you chastened for it."

Piers St. Denis laughed. "Nay, he will forgive me. Old king fool always forgives me, for he loves me, you see. I am never chastened for my wrongs. I never have been. When we were children it was Kipp who was always beaten for my sins. Since I loved my brother, our father thought I would be better behaved if it was Kipp who was punished and not me, but I enjoyed it when Father laid the birch on Kipp's rump. Once I even beat my brother myself just to see how it felt, and it felt powerful, my sweet. I never was allowed to beat the king, of course, but he did let me scold him now and then. He would weep at my words when I would upbraid him. I believe that secretly the king longs to be mastered as I will master you, my sweet." He fondled her again, and, when she attempted to pull away from him, his hand in her hair tightened and he pinched one of her nipples hard.

She winced, crying out in pain, and to her disgust he smiled.

"Have you ever been strapped?" he asked her. "The Scots have a lovely instrument called a tawse. It is a piece of leather about six inches in width, and one end of it is divided into half-inch fingers four to six inches in length each knotted several times. Laid expertly across the bottom it brings a fine pink sheen to the buttocks and a warmth to the skin such as you have never experienced. In my tender care you will become quite familiar with the tawse. You will learn to enjoy the heat and the pain it gives you." He put his face next to hers. "Open your mouth for me, Jasmine, and receive my tongue," he commanded her.

She spat at him fiercely.

The marquis of Hartsfield's face darkened with his displeasure for a brief moment as he wiped her spittle from his cheek, then he smiled slowly. "You are going to give me much pleasure," he told her. "You will not yield to me easily, and that is to the good." He pinched her nipple again cruelly until she finally was forced to cry out in protest.

Jasmine had attempted to control her temper, but this was just too much. "You fool!" she hissed at him. "Do you really believe that you can bully me into some sort of a submission to you? And if you think the king will forgive you for what you have convinced yourself is a mere peccadillo, you are very much mistaken. My husband and my stepfather both are related to King James by blood ties. The king is a Scot for all he is now England's king, too. Blood ties, I have learned, are of paramount importance to the Scots. Release me while you have the opportunity, my lord, and then flee for your very life! If the king does not catch you, and execute you, my husband and his family will hunt you into the ground and kill you where they find you!"

His answer was to wrap his arms about her skirts, and lift her up to where a hook had been screwed into the cottage's ceiling beam. There he hung her by the ropes fastened about her wrists to the hook. Her feet were but two or three inches off the floor, but she was quite helpless. "There," he said. "Now we may begin, my sweet." Grasping at one of her feet he pulled the leather shoe from it, ducking the other foot, which kicked out at him, then grabbing it and yanking the shoe from it as well. Taking up the length of rope that had kept the gag in place, St. Denis lashed her ankles together so she could not harm him. "Why are you garbed like a peasant?" he asked her.

"I have been at the games given by Lord Bruce across the Forth," she said. "Even noblewomen dress like this at the games, you ignoramus!"

"How convenient for me," he mocked her. "Your simple clothing makes it easier for me to strip you." Reaching up, he undid the tapes holding her skirt, and then those that fastened her petticoats. Pulling them off, he tossed them onto the single chair within the cottage. Walking around her, he viewed the graceful line of her back and the round curve of her buttocks. His hand smoothed the bow of her flesh, fondling it lightly. His heart was hammering in his excitement as he feasted his eyes on the creamy expanse. He could almost hear the satisfying smack of the tawse as the thick leather met soft skin. Piers St. Denis smiled wolfishly to himself and licked his lips.

Walking back before her, he knelt and removed the garters from each of her legs. Then he slowly rolled the dark knit stocking down her right leg, slipping the wool underneath the light bonds about her ankles. He then followed suit with the stockings on her left leg. Loosening her leg bonds, he retied but one leg, fastening it to a small nail in the nearby wall, leaving a single leg free. His hands moved up that leg, squeezing lightly, feeling it. His breath was harsh.

Jasmine had the sensation that her skin was crawling as his fingers brushed the inside of her thigh. It was all she could do to keep from crying out with her revulsion and distaste. She did not, however, because she knew he would take it as a cry of fear, and he wanted her to be afraid. God! How he reminded her of her half brother, Salim, with his soft hands and his softer voice; but she was no longer a bedazzled and confused child of thirteen.

"Do you like this?" he asked her, his fingers tickling at her nether lips provocatively.

"You are disgusting," she answered him coldly.

"Your aversion but excites me further," he told her, and he loosened his clothing, for his manhood was straining against it almost painfully. Then, standing, he reached out to rip open her blouse and her chemise, baring her bosom to his hot eyes. He filled his hands with her soft flesh, almost whimpering in his excitement. "Dear God, you are so beautiful!" he groaned. "I can scarce contain myself, and that has never before happened to me, my sweet. You are indeed a rare prize, and you belong to me!"

"I belong to no one, you loathsome, pathetic creature!" she told him. "I am James Leslie's wife, but not his possession, any more than he is my possession."

"I will kill your husband," Piers St. Denis said, his hands crushing her breasts in his excitement. "How can you deny me, my sweet?" He drew a fully engorged manhood from his clothing for her to see. "But look at what the simple thought of possessing you has done to me?"

She laughed scornfully at him. "You are no better than a mere and untried boy," she told him. "You will spill your seed upon the ground before you will slop it in me, *my lord.*" And she laughed again, despite her great discomfort as she hung just above the floor.

"Don't say that!" he almost shrieked at her. "You do not know me! I will fuck you until you are insensible before I lose my juices, you proud bitch!" Then he slapped her once again.

Jasmine laughed all the harder at him. "Look! The dew pearls upon the tip of your lance. The flood is near, pitiful weakling! You cannot hold it back for you are so unnatural a man you know not how!"

"*Bitch!*" he half sobbed at her, as she prophesied his defeat, and his juices spurted forth onto the barren dirt of the cottage floor.

Jasmine heaved a soft sigh of relief. She had prevented her rape for the moment. Now she had to get him to let her down from this very uncomfortable position. "My arms are going numb," she complained at him. "*I am going to die! If you kill me, you will die a most painful death when the Leslies catch up with you!*"

Looking down at his shriveled manhood, Piers St. Denis felt anger, not to mention a sense of great frustration. She had tricked him into an embarrassing and callow act of release of his lust. She was stronger than he had anticipated. Usually the mere sight of his manhood was enough to set his victim sobbing and begging for mercy. "You will hang there until it pleases me to release you, bitch!" he told her, and, going behind her, he bound her two ankles together again. Picking up the tawse, he said coldly, "You will be punished now, my sweet, for your nasty behavior. You will learn not to goad me in future." The leather flicked out, meeting her buttocks with a noisy smack, several of the narrow fingers separating, and inflicting their own damage. A second time. A third and fourth.

When he had uttered the word *punished* Jasmine had known what was to come. She had taken a deep breath and bitten down hard upon her lip to prevent any cry from escaping her. The leather strap hurt with the first blow, and with each additional blow she felt her flesh growing warm. The tiny knotted fingers of leather stung terribly, but she did not cry out. "*Bitch!*" she heard him mutter beneath his breath as a fifth and sixth blow followed the first four. He was quite obviously determined to make her cry out, Jasmine realized, and if she did, then perhaps he would be satisfied, and let her down from this hook from which he had her suspended like the carcass of a doe in a larder. Her arms really were growing numb, and, after all, her only interest was in surviving his bestiality. Jasmine opened her mouth and shrieked a release of the pain he was inflicting upon her.

The tawse fell on her buttocks a seventh and an eighth time, the marquis of Hartsfield grunting with his exertions. "That's it, you proud vixen, beg me for mercy!" His arm delivered a ninth and a tenth blow. Jasmine's pitiful cries began to restore his good humor, and a smile touched his lips. *"Beg me to cease, you bitch!" he* said.

"Stop!" she appeared to sob. "Oh, please stop! I am burning!"

The tawse fell an eleventh and twelfth time, then she heard it drop to the floor, and he was in front of her once again. Jasmine squeezed out several tears from beneath her eyelids. He loosed her ankles from the rope, and she restrained herself from kicking him wherever she could. She couldn't get down from this damned hook by herself.

"Ohhh, please let me down, my lord!" she whimpered to him.

To her shock, however, he instead knelt before her, his hands forcing her legs apart, and holding them firm as he leaned forward, he pushed past her nether lips with his tongue to find with unerring aim the sensitive jewel of her sex. His tongue began to tease it, but while he was able to arouse it so that her body gave him a libation of love dew, Jasmine herself was repulsed by his actions. Still, Jasmine knew that he would expect some show of emotion from her. "Ohhh!" she cried out at him. "Do not! Do not!"

He laughed, drawing away from her, and looking up at her with wild eyes. "That's it, bitch," he whispered. *"Beg!* But you do not fool me, my sweet! You are born a whore like all women. Like my mother who sold herself to the highest bidder, and like Kipp's mother, who simply sold herself to her master so she could live like a lady. At least they disliked being mounted. You, I suspect, enjoy a man between your legs." He rose and walked away from her.

"Aye," Jasmine answered him boldly, "I do."

He turned, looking at her surprised. He had never before heard a woman admit to enjoying *it*. All the women he had ever known whined, and complained, and made excuses. "You like being fucked?" he said, intrigued.

"Of course," Jasmine told him. "Most women do if you approach them properly. Let me down now, my lord. You may keep me bound, but I can no longer feel my arms, and I don't think that good. It really isn't necessary to abuse a woman in order to enjoy her favors, you know. Just the sight of me naked aroused you today, did it not?"

It had! For the first time in his life he had swollen with lust just looking at a woman. He hadn't had to whip her. He had done that afterward in his disappointment, and while he had enjoyed it, he realized he was not now aroused at all by his viciousness. It gave him pause.

"Let me down," Jasmine repeated once more.

Wordlessly Piers St. Denis lifted her from the hook. Leading her to a wall he reached down and, lifting up a wide leather collar, fastened it about her neck. There was a chain attached to the collar which was also fastened to the wall. Then he unbound her hands. "Sit down," he commanded her, pulling her skirt and petticoats from the table and tossing them to the dirt floor

Jasmine gingerly lowered herself to the pile of clothing. Her bottom was sore, and, touching it with tentative fingers, she could feel the weals that he had raised with his strap. She began to rub her arms in an effort to regain some sensation in them. "I am cold," she told him. "Light a fire, if you know how, or are you useless in there also?"

"No fire!" he snapped at her. "This cottage is thought to be deserted, and a fire might bring a search party to my door, seeking you, my sweet. That would be most unfortunate, would it not?"

"Then at least let me put my clothing on, or I shall die of an ague. You know how sensitive I am to the damp and cold." She sneezed as if to emphasize her point. "You will get little enjoyment out of a sick woman, my lord, will you now?"

He acquiesced, although not particularly gracefully. "Very well," he said, gathering up her stockings, and tossing them to her. "But no shoes, madame. I cannot have you running away, can I?" He smiled mockingly at her.

Jasmine quickly drew her wool stockings on, fastening them with their ribbon garters. Then she yanked her petticoats and skirt on, thankful that two of her undergarments were flannel. She attempted to draw her chemise and blouse together, but they were badly torn. "Let me have my shawl," she asked him. "If the ague attacks my chest, I shall expire, and you will suffer an even more horrible death than the Leslies have planned for you for just kidnapping me."

He flung her the shawl with an ill-concealed grace. "What makes you think your Leslies will ever find you before I have seen to James Leslie's death and returned with you to England, where the king will then be forced to give you to me to wed?"

"They will find us," Jasmine said firmly. "And how many times must I explain to you, my lord, that King James will *never* give me in marriage to you. My family would not allow it, and I should kill myself before I would ever allow you dominion of any kind over me!"

"I have already gained control over you, my pet," he told her. "Did your love juices not sweeten my tongue just moments ago, and did you not cry out with your pleasure?" He laughed. "You are a far grander conquest than I ever anticipated, for I have discovered that I do not need to strap you to become excited by your charms. Still, I will probably continue to do it for my mere amusement. And when we return to England my brother, Kipp, shall also be well entertained between your milky thighs while I billet my cock in one of your other two orifices. Have you ever accommodated two lusty stallions at one time, my pet? It is, I have been told, an unforgettable experience for all three people involved." He came now and sat himself beside her for a moment. "You are such a strong woman, my pet. I am strong, too, but Kipp is weak. I shall teach you how to wield the tawse and the birch on him. You will tease him with your sensuous body and mouth, and then we shall complete the torture by coupling before him until he is weeping with his own desire. If he can restrain himself from release, then perhaps I shall let him have the pleasure of your body, too. As I am your master, my pet, so shall I allow you to be mistress over Kipp. Like me, he has a fine, big cock, and shall give you much pleasure." He began to stroke her eagerly.

Jasmine looked past him to the window. It had become dark while they had been there. Glancing back at her captor, she could hardly see his handsome and dissolute face. The dark, however, did not seem to disturb him at all. "I am hungry," she said, "and thirsty."

"I am hungry, too," he murmured, pushing her back and beginning to kiss and suck upon her breasts.

Angrily she pushed him away. "Is it your intent to starve me, my lord?" she snapped at him. "Is this how you show me your affection?"

"I will have to go down into the town to get us food and drink," he said pettishly.

"Then do so!" Jasmine ordered him imperiously. "And afterward, if you have pleased me with a good dinner, who knows what will transpire between us, my lord marquis." Her tone was now a purr of suggestion.

"Bitch!" he snarled suddenly, drawing away from her and standing. "Do you think to gull me with your suggestive words? If you would have me believe you, you must give me a little pleasure now," he told her.

"What would you have me do?" she asked him, wondering what wickedness he had in mind for her. Was he going to use that damned tawse on her again? She didn't think him recovered enough yet to mount her, but she could not be certain.

"On your knees," he ordered sternly. Then he pulled his limp manhood from his clothing. "Not enough to unman me," he warned her, "but skillfully enough to give me a frisson of pleasure so that my trip into Leith will be a happy one." His hand fastened into her hair, and he forced her head forward. "Open your mouth, my pet, and show me just how truthful your words are. Or are they false, and you seek to lull me into a stupor?"

Jasmine blanked her emotions and took him into her mouth. For a moment she was unable to act, but then she began to suckle hard upon him, her tongue teasing at him, her teeth grazing him just enough to arouse him. If this was the worst, she thought, then it would be worth it. She drew fiercely upon him, and he began to moan, his fingers kneading into her scalp, pressing her nearer and nearer to his groin. Jesu, she thought! Would he never let her stop. In a moment he would surely burst in her mouth, and she didn't believe that she could bear that sort of torture.

"*Enough!*" he finally ground out, and allowed her to fall back upon her heels. He looked down at his organ, and was amazed. It was larger than he had ever known it to be. "You are a sorceress," he said low. "I have never known a woman who could please a man so well."

"I have kept my part of the bargain," she said. "Now go and fetch us some food and wine, my lord marquis, before I expire both of hunger and of cold."

"Very well," he said, and, bending he retied her hands. "I do not want you getting into any kind of mischief while I am gone," he told her with a chuckle.

"Go," she said stonily. "I am growing fainter by the minute."

He left her alone in the darkness, no fire, no candle for light. Her last glimpse of him was of the marquis outlined in the door as he went through it. Then he was gone, the door closing behind him. Immediately Jasmine began to work her wrists together in an effort to loosen the rope with which he had bound her. Outside she heard the muffled clop of his horse's hooves as Piers St. Denis rode off down the hill. She had no idea how long he would be gone, how much time she had to escape him. The rope began to ease its grip. Jasmine breathed deeply and slowly, calming her beating heart, clearing her mind so she might act expeditiously and not lose this chance. Finally, she was able to slip one wrist free of its bonds. Quickly she pulled the rope from her other wrist, rubbing them both to ease the chafing they had taken this afternoon between being bound to the pommel of a horse, then hung from a hook. The skin was raw with the abuse she had suffered.

With gentle fingers she felt all around the leather collar he had put about her throat. It was fastened in the back of her neck by an iron padlock that was attached to a chain which was affixed into the wall of the cottage. It would be impossible to remove it without either the key to the lock or a knife with which to cut the leather. Her only option, therefore, was to somehow get the chain out of the wall. Turning about so that she faced the wall she felt it. Stone, worse luck. Jasmine almost cried with her frustration, but then she began to run her fingers slowly over the wall, seeking the ring that held the chain. Finding it she felt around it, and a slow smile lit her features. The ring's bolt had been set into the mortar holding the stones. The mortar was dry and old, and crumbled beneath her very touch. She pulled at the ring, but while it wriggled about, it held fast.

I need something to help me loosen the mortar, she thought, and was immediately discouraged. If there was anything useful within the cottage, she couldn't see it, and besides, the chain allowed her no latitude farther than a few feet. There was nothing within her reach. She shivered, yanking her shawl about her shoulders. As she did, her hand made contact with the clan badge Jemmie had given her, which was pinned to the Leslie tartan of her shawl. She almost cried aloud with relief.

Quickly she undid the badge and, with the pin, began to chip away at the crumbling mortar. She had to force herself to work carefully, for the badge was her only weapon. The town was at least two miles away. By the time Piers St. Denis rode down into Leith, found an inn, obtained food and wine, and rode back again, it would be at least two or more hours. There was time, provided she did not panic and damage the pin. Jasmine chipped, and chipped, stopping every now and then to wriggle the ring. The sound of the pin scraping against the mortar seemed at times very loud, for there was not another sound to be heard but her anxious breathing. She had to get away from St. Denis. This was likely to be her only chance, Jasmine sensed. If he violated her further, she would never again be able to face Jemmie. And what if, by his brutality, the marquis harmed the child she was now carrying?

And then, when she thought she would never be able to free herself in time, the ring slid loose from the mortar in the wall, and the chain fell with a noisy clank onto the floor. Jasmine scrambled to her feet, legs trembling with her excitement, gathering up the links as best she could. *Her shoes? Where were her shoes?* She moved carefully about the small room, seeking, feeling. Then she found them, first one, then the other. She eased her way until she reached the single chair and, sitting down, pulled her footwear on quickly. Standing, she considered her next move. She must leave the cottage, of course, but where was she to go? Down to the Leith Road? And once there, what? To Leith or back to Edinburgh?

The first thing was to get out of the cottage, and so, gathering up the chain, Jasmine went to the door, opened it, and moved through. Her horse was unsaddled beneath a small shed at the rear of the cottage, but she would not take him. It would be the first thing that the marquis would notice when he returned. Jasmine hurried off down the path that led back to the road. Once there, she briefly hesitated. If she went toward the port, she was likely to run into Piers St. Denis returning from his mission, but if he returned to the cottage and found her missing, he would probably think she was on the road toward Edinburgh and go in that direction to seek her out and bring her back.

Jasmine turned toward Leith. If she heard a horseman coming, she would hide in the ditch beside the road. There was no moon, and it was a dark, misty night. It was very unlikely she would be seen. She could surely gain the town and obtain help. The first thing she wanted was to have this damned collar off her neck. It was rubbing her delicate skin most. She walked swiftly, and, as she did, she contemplated how she would kill Piers St. Denis, for she knew now for certain that she would never again be safe unless he were dead and in his grave.

What a pity this wasn't India. She would have had him thrown into a pit with a dozen cobras to be stung to death. She contemplated what terror would look like on his handsome face. But she wasn't in India. Perhaps they could return him to England and have him dragged along behind one of her grandmother's trading vessels as it made its way out to sea. It would be a most terrifying and slow death. Quite fitting, she thought, for the presumptuous creature who had brutalized the Mughal's daughter. The Leslies, however, would probably just hang the bastard as she had hanged the man who had murdered her second husband, Rowan Lindley, she finally decided.

The lights of the town were drawing nearer, and she had to consider what she was going to do next. She would make an odd sight, leather collar about her neck, chain still attached to it, as she walked about the streets. She stopped a moment and pinned her blouse together as best as she could. Then she wrapped the chain about her waist, tucking the end into her skirt, and drew her shawl up over her head to hide the leather collar about her neck. It might not have done in the daylight, but in the dim, poorly lit streets of Leith, it would do quite well. Coming into the town itself, she stopped a woman selling herbs and asked her for directions to the harbor.

"East-Street, mistress," the herb woman said, pointing.

Jasmine hurried onto the narrow street. It had suddenly occurred to her that there might be an O'Malley-Small ship in port, and if there was, she was safe. She gained the docks and, outside the harbormaster's office, was a large slate board upon which were chalked the names of the ships at dock. Jasmine stopped, and ran her finger down the board. She was almost weeping with nervousness, and disappointment until she reached the last name on the board. *Lord Adam!* The little coastal freighter her grandmother had named after her grandfather, for he would have no great vessel called by his name. Adam de Marisco had thought it presumption. Noting the location, Jasmine made her way down the docks to where the small boat sat bobbing at its mooring. Who was the freighter's captain? She didn't know. Jasmine picked her way up the gangplank. There was only a single lad on watch, but there was a light in the captain's cabin. Seeing her, the lad on watch came forward.

"We don't allow no women on board, mistress," he said firmly.

"I am Jasmine de Marisco Leslie, the countess of Glenkirk," Jasmine said. "Where is your captain? I must see him at once!"

The lad looked at Jasmine critically. "You don't look like no countess to me, mistress," he said boldly.

"Nevertheless I am," Jasmine replied, drawing herself up proudly. "Now take me to your captain before I box your ears, presumptuous boy! Your manners are wanting, and I shall tell him. And you will address me as *my lady*, not mistress. Do you understand me?"

"Aye, mis... my lady," the boy said. "If you will follow me." Well, it wouldn't be his fault if she was some town whore, he thought. The captain could deal with her, the uppity bitch.

Jasmine followed the lad across the deck. He flung open the door to the cabin house, and motioned her through. She stepped into the cabin, and relief washed over her so hard that her legs buckled, and she had to grab on to the table in the room's center. *"Geoff!"* she managed to say. "Thank God it's you!"

Captain Geoffrey O'Flaherty turned at the sound of her voice. His eyes widened in surprise. *"Jasmine?* Jesu! It is you!" Then, seeing her obvious state, he put his arms about her. "Cousin, what is it? Why are you here? What has happened? What the hell is this thing about your neck? Ewan," he called to the boy. "Fetch some wine for her ladyship." He settled her in a chair and waited while she recovered herself. "Now, tell me, cousin," he said when she had quaffed the goblet the cabin boy had given her, "but first let me cut that leather from your neck." Carefully he sliced through it with his knife, and, pulling it off flung it, chain and all onto the floor.

Jasmine took a deep breath. What on earth had happened to her? She had been so strong up until the moment she had seen her cousin. "I thought you were on the East Indies run," she began, rubbing her neck gingerly.

"I am," he replied, "but the captain of this vessel fell and broke his leg. I was in port with not another run scheduled for the *Cardiff Rose* for several weeks. We didn't have another captain, and mother would not let father take *Lord Adam* up the coast, so I did. This is my son, Ewan. It's his first voyage, and if he likes it, he'll come out the Indies with me in another year. But you did not come to visit, cousin. Tell me what has happened."

"What do you know of my return from France?" she asked him.

"Precious little," he answered her. "I returned to learn that you had come back, and you had married Lord Leslie. What else is there, cousin?"

Jasmine told him. She told him of the king's foolishness and of Piers St. Denis's refusal to accept defeat, which had led to betrayal and murder. "Jemmie and I have spent the entire summer traveling about Scotland just to avoid him until our messenger could return from England. We have spent the last few days across the Forth at Lord Bruce's games and planned to leave Edinburgh tomorrow for Glenkirk. I had to go to David Kira before we left, however, and, as I was leaving his house, I was set upon by the marquis and his cutthroats," Jasmine told him. Then she went on to tell him of her kidnapping, leaving out the more unpleasant details, for she was, she found, uncomfortable even thinking of them.

"Jemmie must be frantic," Geoffrey O'Flaherty said.

"Maggie, my maid, was with me. They didn't see her, and I know she hurried right to my husband."

"But how did St. Denis know where to find you?"

"I think simply bad luck on my part," Jasmine said. "Just mere chance that I was leaving Goldsmith Alley as St. Denis was passing by it. I don't know what I would have done, Geoff, if one of Grandmama's ships hadn't been in port. I took a chance, and this time my luck was better. Not only a ship, but a cousin who knows me."

"You will be safe here," he told her, "for I doubt that this marquis would even consider that you had found such a safe refuge. And you are right, I expect, that finding you gone, he would assume you would attempt to get back to Edinburgh. Where do you think your husband is, Jasmine?"

"Possibly in Edinburgh, Geoff. He could not know that St. Denis had brought me to Leith. The Leslies will probably think we are headed for the borders. They will have alerted their friends there."

"I want to remain here with you," Geoff O'Flaherty said, "but Ewan is an excellent horseman and can ride to Edinburgh to alert the earl as to your whereabouts and that

St. Denis is still in Leith, if, indeed, he has not fled, being unable to find you."

"I am so tired," Jasmine said, and indeed her eyelids were drooping.

He settled her into his bunk, and said quietly to his son, "Go to the harbormaster and tell him that Captain O'Flaherty needs a horse. Then get directions to the Leith-Edinburgh Road. It is not a great distance to ride."

"How will I know where to find the earl when I get there?" young Ewan asked.

"Ask for Glenkirk House," Jasmine said sleepily. "It's on a side street as you go toward the Cannongate." Her dark head fell back upon the pillow once again.

Obeying his father, Ewan O'Flaherty went to the harbormaster and asked for the loan of a horse. "I must ride to Edinburgh, and fetch the earl of Glenkirk," he told the harbormaster self-importantly.

"Ye'll nae find his lordship in the town," the harbormaster said. "He is here in Leith, laddie, for he sent to me this very evening asking if any vessels were leaving tonight, or on the morrow. Then he and his men came down to these very docks and searched the two ships going out on this evening's tide just before they sailed," the older man finished.

"Oh, sir," Ewan said excitedly, "can you please tell me where the earl is now? It is very important that I find him!"

"Why, laddie, ye'll find him at the Mermaid, which sits just off the docks," the harbormaster said, pointing a gnarled finger.

"Thank you, sir!" Ewan said, and he set off at a run for the Mermaid tavern and inn. Dashing into the taproom the boy called out, "I am seeking the earl of Glenkirk. Is he here?"

James Leslie arose from the table, where he had been sitting with his father-in-law, his uncle, and several other men. "I am he, lad," he said. "What is it you want?"

Ewan O'Flaherty hurried over to the table, and bowed as his mother had taught him. "My father, Captain O'Flaherty, would speak with you, my lord, on a matter of import to your lordship."

"And who is Captain O'Flaherty that he would speak with me?" the earl asked the boy. "I do not know him."

"He is my great-grandmother's grandson," the boy replied, "and you are well acquainted with my great-grandmother."

"Who is your great-grandmother?" the earl asked, smiling slightly.

"Lady de Marisco," Ewan said, jumping back, frightened, as the earl leapt to his feet.

"Jesu, lad! Why did you nae say so in the first place?" He pushed Ewan gently. "Lead on then, laddie, and take me to your father."

"We'll go wi ye in case this is some sort of trap," Adam Leslie said, standing up and beckoning to his companions.

The men, led by the boy, trooped from the Mermaid, and onto the docks, following Ewan to where the *Lord Adam* was moored. As the sound of their booted feet hit the deck of the small ship, Geoffrey O'Flaherty emerged from the cabin, sword in hand.

"Nay, father," the boy cried. "This is the earl of Glenkirk. He was here, and the harbormaster told me where to look!"

Geoffrey O'Flaherty sheathed his weapon and held out his hand to James Leslie. "Jasmine is in my cabin," he said without further explanation, for he knew that was what the earl wanted to know.

The earl nodded, and, moving past the captain, entered the cabin. Jasmine lay sleeping upon the captain's bunk. He went to her and, kneeling down, kissed her cheek softly. "Darling Jasmine," he murmured low. "I have come to take you home."

The turquoise eyes opened slowly and filled with recognition. Jasmine smiled. "Jemmie! I knew that you would find me!"

Chapter Twenty

They returned to Glenkirk Castle, and it was as if Piers St. Denis, the marquis of Hartsfield, had disappeared off the face of the earth. He was nowhere to be found either in England or Scotland. BrocCairn and Adam Leslie had gone back to the cottage where Jasmine had briefly been held captive. It was as empty as when she had left it but for a jug of wine, a stale loaf of bread, and a bit of cheese lying upon the table. The wine carafe was full, and neither the bread or the cheese had been eaten. St. Denis had obviously returned to find Jasmine gone, deposited their meal upon the table, and sought after her. Not finding her, he had himself vanished.

George Villiers returned to England, his mission for the king successfully completed, and his only rival for James Stuart's attention vanquished. Shortly after the new year the king, with the urging of the queen, created Villiers the earl of Buckingham. The king then pronounced Kipp St. Denis legitimate by virtue of his father's public affection for him and the fact that his father had allowed his eldest son the benefit of his name. Kipp was then made marquis of Hartsfield, as he had been firstborn of the previous marquis's sons.

The queen, who had made Kipp her especial pet, for Kipp, following Villiers's lead had given Her Majesty much time, respect, and attention, found him a suitable wife. Kipp had, the queen was fond of saying, a good heart, and he had endured much under his brother's wicked domain. The bride, a beloved bastard daughter of one of the favorite courtiers, came with a suitable dowry. She was delighted with her good fortune and devoted to her husband, who was equally pleased with her.

The king spent the winter months personally making plans for his return to Scotland in the summer to come, for his family and advisors were resisting the idea. He sent orders that Holyrood Palace was to be completely refurbished for the visit and sent word to Glenkirk that he would expect to see both James and Jasmine Leslie there to greet him when he arrived in Edinburgh. It was to be a full state visit with both the queen and Prince Charles in attendance.

"When is he coming?" Jasmine asked.

"I expect he will arrive in mid-July," her husband answered. "If I know Their Majesties, they will want to remain to hunt in August and September. They will begin their progress, however, in early June."

"And every family in their path will both dread and anticipate their coming," Jasmine laughed. "Particularly as they will travel with the entire court. It is outrageously expensive to entertain royalty, even for a meal, or a single night. Grandmama said it was months before the lawns at Queen's Malvern were back to normal after the old queen came those many years ago; but when the king came after Charlie-boy's birth, he and the queen came alone, with only a few attendants."

"I am relieved to say we will nae have to entertain the royal Stuarts," Jemmie said. His speech had begun to slip back now and then into the dialect of the land. "He'll nae venture into the Highlands."

"But where will he hunt?" Jasmine asked her husband.

"He'll keep to the pack at Holyrood. 'Tis safer for him." Jemmie chuckled. He took her hand and kissed it. "You are lovely when you are full wi my bairns," he told her.

"Only at Holyrood?" Jasmine persisted.

"Probably at Falklands and in Perth," he replied. "Is it another son, darling Jasmine? It seems I recall you did promise me at least three sons." He put his hand upon her belly, which was only now beginning to swell with the new life she sheltered within her.

"It will be as God wills," she teased him, "but I will admit it is already behaving like a boy, and he will come before the king comes, which will give me time to regain my figure for the new gowns you're going to buy me so I won't embarrass you before the court."

"I thought you didn't want to go to court," he said.

"I don't want to live at court in England," she told him, "but the king has asked us to join him in Edinburgh, and I do not see any reason why we cannot go for a short time."

"It will mean you lose your English summer," he told her.

"So will Mama and BrocCairn," she replied. "We will invite Grandmama to Glenkirk. She likes it here, and you like her."

"I do," he admitted. Then he teased, "You have it all figured out, madame, don't you? Tell me, will these gowns be expensive?"

"Verra expensive," she teased back, and when he pulled her into his arms, kissing her soundly, Jasmine thought she had never been happier. She had had nightmares for several weeks after her escape from St. Denis. At first she had been unable to tell Jemmie what had happened to her other than to reassure him that she had not been raped. She knew she was not to blame for St. Denis's wicked behavior, but she was frankly embarrassed by the dreadful humiliations she had suffered at his hands. The welts and weals upon her body had healed quickly, but the injury to her pride was greater than the blows he had inflicted upon her.

Finally, she told him, leaving out but a single detail. Jasmine would not tell her husband of how St. Denis had made her kneel before him and take his member into her mouth. James Leslie need never know it had happened; and if they ever again found themselves face-to-face with the villain, and he taunted Jemmie with the knowledge, she would deny it. James Leslie would, she knew, believe her before he would believe St. Denis. She had done what she had to do to save her life, but would Jemmie fully understand that? She dared not take the chance and spoil the greatest happiness she had ever known.

Adam John Leslie was born on the fourteenth day of May in the year 1617. He had his parents' dark hair and eyes that promised to remain a smoky blue. Named for both sides of his family, he was a fat, cheerful infant who happily moved from his mother's breast at the age of one month to the breast of the plump farm wife who was his wet nurse. His sisters, now nine and seven; and his brothers, who were eight, five, and a year, seemed content with their new sibling. As for James Leslie, he was ecstatic at the birth of another son.

Jasmine had born her sixth child with the same ease as she had most of her children.

"You have grown content and lost your restlessness," Adali remarked. "You are like your mother, I think."

"Which one?" Jasmine asked him, a small smile teasing at the corners of her mouth. "Rugaiya Begum or Lady Gordon?"

"Both," he told her. "How happy the begum would be to see you now, my princess."

"She sees us, Adali," Jasmine responded. "She and my father both." They had learned late in the previous year of the death of Jasmine's Indian foster mother, the princess wife of Akbar, Jasmine's father.

Adali nodded, his brown eyes just slightly teary. Then, catching himself, he said, "We must concentrate on your new wardrobe, my princess. The king is even now on the move north."

And he was, although his English advisors had pleaded with James Stuart to avoid this additional extravagance to his overspent budget. While their advice was good, the truth was they dreaded this long trip to Scotland, and then back to England again. Even Villiers, now Buckingham, had suggested that perhaps such an indulgent trip was not particularly wise.

"What then, Steenie?" the king snarled at his favorite. "Do ye fear such an expense to my treasury will mean less wee gifties to ye? Dinna be selfish! I am like a salmon who must spawn back to its breeding grounds one more time. Dinna fret me again about it, and tell the others I will nae hear any more about it. We leave on June 1!" Then the king did something he had never done. He flung a vase at his favorite in a temper, and the Earl of Buckingham beat a hasty retreat.

A royal visit to Scotland was a huge undertaking. A route had to be decided upon, and it depended on the great houses in its path where the king might stay a night or two. The court would have to fend for itself, which meant finding inns, or barns, or packing tents which, on occasion, even the king would billet himself in for lack of better accommodation. The king's bed was brought complete with its mattress, featherbed, down coverlet, pillows, and linens. It had to be set up each night with its heavy draperies for His Majesty to sleep in unless there was a suitable bed offered by the royal host. Tapestries, beeswax candles, fine porcelain, linens, and silver were packed for Their Majesties' comfort. As the king had a great love of soft fruit, cherries, peaches, apricots, grapes, and melons were also sent north posthaste as they became available.

The king, who had gladly and swiftly vacated Scotland upon his ascension in order to escape his contentious Scots nobles, now waxed very sentimental with each mile they traveled. The queen rolled her mild blue eyes in exasperation. The courtiers grumbled excessively at the inconvenience and the expense involved in this great landward voyage northward. Finally, they crossed the border. A host of the great border families came to greet them. Armstrongs, Douglases, Eliots, Hamiltons, Hays, Johnsons, Lindsays, Homeses, and Hepburns came forth, banners flying, pipes playing wildly and joyfully as they welcomed their king home again. The English courtiers in their satins and laces looked askance at the bare-legged Scots in their kilts and caps.

William Drummond of Hawthornden stepped forward, bowing to the king. There had been two Drummond queens of Scotland. David II's wife, Margaret; and Annabella Drummond, wife of Robert III, and the mother of James I. The Drummonds were ever loyal to the Stuarts. The Drummond of Hawthornden offered James Stuart a special greeting.

And why should Isis only see thee shine?
Is not the Forth as well as Isis thine?
Though Isis vaunt she hath more wealth in store
Let it suffice thy Forth doth love thee more.

"What does it mean?" Prince Charles asked softly.

"Isis is England, the Forth, Scotland," Villiers, who was now the prince's good friend, replied. "And he's saying that Scotland loves your father more than England. It is quite clever, Your Highness."

"Aye," the queen said. "The Scots are clever, but they are also stubborn. Wait. It will not be long before they are arguing with your father over something, my son. Mark them well, for you shall one day have to deal with them, and they are a proud and difficult people. And you may be certain that the Presbyterians will give him trouble."

The king, however, was delighted to be back. He was flattered by the many delegations greeting him with kind words and by the fine statue of himself that had been raised at the Nether Bow. His reign from England had already brought new prosperity to his native land. Best of all, the peace and order he had struggled so hard to bring to Scotland while he was still only its king was still fairly secure and in place.

The court was to stay at Holyrood, a mile down the Cannongate from Edinburgh Castle. Originally an abbey built in the twelfth century, it took its name from a piece of the true cross, or rood, which was its most prized possession. The abbey guesthouse had become a favorite lodging of the Scots kings. Marriages, funerals, births, and other state occasions took place at the abbey. Finally, James IV decided that the guesthouse should become a royal palace. Of course it was necessary that the new palace be enlarged and its appointments enhanced.

James IV built a large northwest tower with pointed turrets and a crenellated parapet that reminded Jasmine of the châteaux in the Loire near Archambault, and Belle Fleurs. He then added a south wing to the tower that had its main door flanked by two semicircular towers with witches' caps roofs. Holyrood had a distinct elegance to it. It was surrounded by lovely gardens and set within a large forested park overseen by one Thomas Fentoun, the royal keeper of the park, and of the king's beasts, which included a lion, a tiger, several lynx, and a vast number of game birds. Deer roamed freely.

The royal suite was in the northwest tower. The queen was housed on the second floor, in rooms that had belonged to her late and never known mother-in-law, Mary, Queen of Scots. There was a Presence Chamber hung with black velvet with the arms of Marie de Guise, who had been James's French grandmother, emblazoned upon the ceiling. Off of this chamber was the queen's bedchamber. There were two other small rooms, one for dressing and one for dining, which was draped in crimson and green. A narrow private staircase, which opened into the queen's bedchamber, connected the queen's apartments with the king's, which were directly below it. Those rooms had belonged to the king's father, Lord Darnley. Prince Charles and the earl of Buckingham were housed near the king's apartments.

As the royal party entered the park of Holyrood, they found awaiting them a number of the Highland families, including the Leslies of Glenkirk. Jasmine and Jemmie had arrived earlier and, finding the palace steward, had been informed a bedchamber had been set aside for them, for the king had expressly sent orders that they were to stay at Holyrood while he was there.

"We have a house just several streets away," the earl told the king's steward. "Give our chamber to another."

"I am sorry, my lord, but I have my orders. His Majesty wishes you to be near him during this visit," the steward said firmly.

"How kind of him," Jasmine chimed in smiling. "And what an honor, my lord, to stay in the king's house."

James Leslie heard the warning in his wife's voice. "Very well, darling Jasmine," he said. "I but thought only to help the royal steward, who must find housing for the entire court, not to mention many of those who have come down from the Highlands."

"Your lordship is most thoughtful," the royal steward replied. "Tell your servants they may sleep in the servants' hall."

They were directed to the appointed chamber in the south wing. It was very tiny, with a south window and a corner fireplace. Its only piece of furniture was an oaken bedstead.

"Where on earth are we to put the trunks?" Jasmine wailed.

"What an honor to stay in the king's house," he mocked her.

"It did not occur to me that the king would have such tiny guest chambers," Jasmine grumbled. Then she said, "If we push the bedstead against the window wall, we can just fit in two small chests of clothes along the opposite wall. There is no place to hang my clothing. Toramalli and Rohana will have to fetch my gowns from Glenkirk House each day, and they can sleep there, too." She turned and bumped into Red Hugh.

"Sorry, m'lady," he said.

"Red Hugh, you must stop chasing at my heels," she scolded him. "It wasn't your fault, dammit! How many times must I say it?"

"I was derelict in my duty, m'lady." he told her. "If I hae been wi ye that day, that English bugger would nae hae caught ye. Praise God ye were nae harmed, but ye could hae been, and 'twas my fault, for I let ye send me away instead of remaining wi ye. I'll nae do it again!"

"I am safe with my husband," Jasmine said. "Now go back to Glenkirk House and tell Adali that we will need curtains, linens, and bedding. Then come back with him and show him this chamber. Can you not hear the crowds cheering already? The king has entered Edinburgh. He will soon be here, and my lord and I must be among the first to greet him, Red Hugh. Now go, and after you have shown Adali this room, you may come and find us, and dog my heels once more," she concluded, gently teasing the big Highlander. He really had been very upset by her brief kidnapping.

They left the palace and, mounting their horses, rode back into the park, mingling with the other Highland families awaiting the royal party. Finally they arrived, all a-horse, the cheers of the Edinburghers filling the air. The king looked a trifle tired with his long journey, but extremely pleased to be in Scotland. Spotting the Leslies of Glenkirk, he leaned over, first to the queen, and then the prince. Then, making eye contact with his cousins, the monarch nodded his greeting, and the queen waved brightly.

The Scots nobility joined in with the English nobility and rode through the park to the palace, where scores of groomsmen were waiting to take their horses. The king had already gone inside with his personal party by the time the Leslies reached the courtyard. They had no sooner dismounted, however, when the earl of Buckingham hurried over to them. He bowed to them with a flourish.

"Steenie, our congratulations," Jasmine said. "One more step up the ladder, eh?" Then she laughed.

George Villiers raised an amused eyebrow in agreement and kissed Jasmine's hand. "You are ravishing as always, madame. Living in the wilds of Scotland has not diminished your beauty one whit. You are a mother again, I am told. How many is that now, madame, six? And yet you keep your figure." He eyed her lasciviously, waggling his eyebrows, and then he laughed. "May my sweet Kate be as fortunate."

"You are not married then yet?" the earl said.

"Her father says I must climb a bit higher," George Villiers said low. "He fears I shall lose the king's favor if I marry his daughter too soon. He desires that Kate marry higher than an earl." Villiers lowered his voice even more. "I shall be a marquis next year." He linked his arms through theirs. "Come now and let us go in. What a lovely place this is. I shall enjoy exploring it, and I am relieved to know we shall not have to travel again for a while. The king has invited you to a private supper in his apartment tonight. The round of state banquets will begin tomorrow, but tonight the king says is for old friends."

And it was a most intimate party, much to Jasmine's surprise. The great families were left to fend for themselves while the king ate a simple supper of salmon and rabbit pie, surrounded by his immediate family and a few cousins, among whom were the earl of Glenkirk, and his father-in-law of BrocCairn. The queen looked weary, and admitted to it.

"Heaven only knows that I love to ride," she said, "but I have ridden all the way from England, and my bottom is worn out." She sipped listlessly at her wine cup.

"We will put a sheepskin on your saddle, madame, like we do in the northeast," the earl of Glenkirk said with a smile. "You will not want to miss the hunting season, for I know how much you love to hunt, and you will remember how good a season we have here in Scotland. Soon the deer and the grouse will be ripe for the picking, eh?"

The queen favored him with a smile. "I do, indeed, remember hunting in Scotland. Holyrood Palace will not be enough for us once we have rested up. We will want to go to Falklands and into Perthshire as well."

"Oh sweet Jesu," Buckingham moaned low. "More traveling."

The queen ignored him. "Will we get to see our grandson?" she asked Jasmine. "How is little Charlie?"

"He flourishes, madame, and is extremely pleased not to be the baby in the family anymore. He reveals in his role as big brother to Patrick and Adam. When we know exactly when you plan to go to Falklands, we shall send to Glenkirk for the children so you may see them all," Jasmine concluded.

The next day the round of entertainments began. The king received the heads of the clans, who had come from the Highlands and the borders to greet him. He hunted in the park about the palace, and in the evening he presided over state banquets, and the queen gave several elegant masques in which the English court took part, and the Scots court watched open-mouthed, for the queen had never given anything like these masques when she was their queen alone. The exquisite costumes, the painted and gilded sets that moved, the tinkling music, all was as amazement to them, and they were not certain that they approved such frippery and expensive lavishness.

James Stuart had wanted to come home for sentimental reasons, but he had another agenda as well, which was the de-Puritanization of the Scottish church. As he wanted one Great Britain, a plan defeated by the English themselves, he wanted one state church both in England and in Scotland. Five articles were to be incorporated into the Scottish church that would bring them in line with England's church. They were simple things, such as kneeling at communion and the celebration of Christian holidays, but the Presbyterian element were set firmly against them. The king spoke openly with his Scots courtiers about the five articles. Some of them were violently opposed; and of those in opposition, there were those who considered it just another English intrusion on Scottish nationalism; and others who considered it a throwback to the Roman Catholic Church, which but a hundred years earlier had held sway in Scotland, and of which they had, in the main, rid themselves. Fights broke out to the amusement of the English and the aggravation of the queen.

"Did I not tell you?" she said to her son. "Your father will have his way in this. He has forgotten that the Scots will argue him into the ground unlike the English, who respect his divine right. Observe and learn from this display, Charles."

After several weeks the king moved on to Falkland Palace, which had been built beneath the Lomond Hills. James had made Falklands over to the queen on their marriage, and they had frequently hunted there. It had been his own mother's favorite palace. The forests around the palace were famous for hunting and filled with game and game birds. It was here that Charles Frederick Stuart celebrated his fifth birthday, in the presence of his royal grandparents. He had arrived dressed as the little Scot he was, in his Hunting Stuart tartan kilt, white silk shirt, and doeskin doublet, with its buttons of silver and stags horn. Sweeping his feathered black velvet cap from his auburn curls, he bowed first to James, then to Anne, and lastly to his uncle, Prince Charles

"I am happy to see Yer Majesties looking so braw," he said, and then, "Ha ye brought me a wee giftie, mayhap?"

"*Charlie!*" Jasmine was mortified.

The king, however, chuckled indulgently. "Gie over, madame, for he's just a little laddie. What would ye like, Charlie?"

The child thought a moment, and then he said, "Something belonging to him who sired me, so I may always remember him, my liege."

The king looked astounded, and the queen gave a little gasp. She looked to Jasmine, but Jasmine shook her head, her look equally surprised. The king could not speak, and his mind was benumbed for a long moment. Then Prince Charles stepped forward, and, as he did, he pulled a ring from his finger and handed it to the child. It was gold, and carved into the ruby set into it were the arms of Henry Stuart along with his motto, *Virescit Vulnere Virtus.*

"This ring belonged to him who sired you, nephew," the prince told Charles Frederick Stuart. "Do you know what the motto says, or have you not yet begun your studies."

"*Courage grows strong at a wound,*" the child translated. "I began my studies last year, Your Highness. Thank you." He bowed.

"Very good!" the prince approved. "Someday you will have to come and serve me, nephew." He looked to Jasmine. "You have done well, madame, and you also, my cousin of Glenkirk. He is a studious, well-mannered child. I most highly approve." The prince then stepped back next to his father.

The king had now recovered, and he said, "Ye hae been wed two years now, and we nae ever gave ye a wedding gift, James Leslie."

"Sire, when ye gave me Jasmine, ye gave me the greatest gift any man could have," the earl of Glenkirk said gallantly.

"Verra pretty, verra pretty indeed," the king replied, a small smile touching his lips, "but ye must hae a wee giftie of us. Since I canna allow that a man of lesser rank than the duke of Lundy raise my grandson, James Leslie, I am creating ye first duke of Glenkirk. 'Tis a fine gift for ye, and 'twill cost me naught as ye already hae the lands and the castle," he finished with a chuckle.

"Oh my!" Jasmine said, quite surprised by their elevation in rank.

"Aye, madame, ye married beneath ye, but now I hae righted that too, eh? Yer the duchess of Glenkirk!" the king said, smiling at her.

James Leslie was dumbstruck. *He was the duke of Glenkirk! My God, how proud his mother would be, and his father, too!* He fell to his knees before the king and, taking the royal hands up, kissed them. To his great surprise there were tears in his eyes. *The duke of Glenkirk!* He had never, ever considered such an honor. "Thank ye, Jamie," he said low, so that only the king heard, and then, louder, "Thank ye, Yer Majesty." He arose, bowing low as Jasmine, by his side, curtsied.

And afterward his father-in-law of BrocCairn, and his uncles and brothers gathered about him, congratulating him, and clapping him upon the back. His mind was awhirl. His eldest son, Patrick, would one day be the second duke of Glenkirk, and God willing his line would continue on down through the centuries even as the line of Patrick, the first earl, had descended down from that day when King James IV had made a simple Highland laird an earl.

The Leslies of Glenkirk took their leave of the king at Falklands and returned home several days later. Jasmine could hardly wait to write to her grandmother to tell her of the honor given Jemmie. She had wanted Skye to come to

Scotland that summer, but her grandmother had refused, saying that she had enough of travel. Jasmine had missed seeing Skye. Her grandmother was in truth her best friend, and she had so much to share with her.

"I will not miss my English summer again," she told her husband.

The king and the court returned to England in late autumn. Winter set in. One year ended, and another began. At last the spring came, the snows melting off the bens, and Jasmine traveled south to England and Queen's Malvern with her family. She was very relieved to see that her grandmother, at age seventy-eight, looked hale and hearty as they approached her home. Jasmine jumped from her horse and flew into Skye's open arms.

"Well, well, my darling girl," Skye said happily, "I am as glad to see you as you are to see me." She hugged her granddaughter hard and, releasing her, turned to James Leslie. "Come, my lord duke, and give me a kiss. The last duke to kiss me, as I recall, was my most unfortunate fifth husband, God assoil his poor soul."

"You had five husbands, Mam?" Lady India Lindley, age ten, said incredulously.

"I had six, child, and several charming lovers as well," Skye told the girl. "I know that you will remember me, India, as naught but an old lady, but once I was as ripe and lovely as your mother."

"I think that you are still beautiful, Mam," India said.

"Why, bless you, child, I thank you." Skye laughed. "You surely have your great-grandfather's charm. But come into the house, my dears," she invited them. "It is starting to rain, and I want a good look at these babies of yours, Jasmine. Gracious! Is that Patrick? He is going to be a big boy." She peered at the two-year-old in his nursemaid's arms. "How do you do, Patrick Leslie," Skye said. "I am your great-grandmother, and I helped to birth you. Where is the other laddie? The one named after my Adam. Ahhh," she said with a satisfied smile when he was presented to her in the front hallway of her house. "He has *his* eyes, doesn't he?"

"From the moment of his birth, Grandmama," Jasmine said.

"Tomorrow, when the rain is over, you will come and see the monument we have set over his grave," Skye said.

They settled into Queen's Malvern for the summer. In a few weeks Henry Lindley and his two sisters would be departing for his seat at Cadby. Adali would accompany the children and remain with them until the summer's end, when they would return to Queen's Malvern, and thence to Glenkirk. Their Gordon grandparents would also remain with them. James Leslie, however, insisted upon personally taking his stepchildren across the countryside to Cadby.

"At last we have time together," Skye said to Jasmine when they had gone. It was evening, and they sat together in the family hall before a fire that took the chill off the early June evening. The young Leslies were safe asleep in their cots. Charlie-boy, who did not like being separated from his elder siblings, had been allowed to ride over with the duke's party. He felt very grown-up. "You are happy, of course," Skye said, "and that makes me happy, darling girl. Will there be more babies?" She sipped at her wine cup, then nibbled on a sweetmeat.

"I did promise Jemmie three sons," Jasmine said with a smile "and I should like another daughter, God willing."

"You take the potion I gave you?"

Jasmine nodded. "Two sons in two years was enough for the present. I wanted a rest else I be worn out like so many women."

"Good, good," the old woman nodded. "I did the same after I birthed Ewan and Murrough. His son rescued you last year, I was told."

"I went to the docks in Leith, hoping to find one of your ships in port, and I did. Fortunately, it was Geoffrey O'Flaherty captaining. Heaven knows if a stranger to me would have believed such an outlandish tale; his little son certainly thought I was mad, or a whore sneaking aboard to find business. I was dressed like a simple Scotswoman, as we had just come from the games hosted by Clan Bruce."

"They have never found Piers St. Denis?" Skye asked.

Jasmine shook her head. "I still fear he may come back some day to try and take me away from my family. He is quite mad, Grandmama."

"You need have no fears, darling girl. Put them behind you, for he has undoubtedly fled the country," Skye said.

"But fear, madame, is an excellent goad when dealing with recalcitrant women," a familiar voice said, and Piers St. Denis stepped from the shadows of the room. He was badly dressed in the simple garb of a citizen of the merchant class, a small white ruff about his neck relieving the severity of his black clothing.

"*Oh, God!*" Jasmine whispered, and her heart began to beat very quickly at the thought of having to contend once more with the madman.

"How did you get into my house?" Skye demanded, not in the least afraid. He was mad, of that she had not a doubt, but he also reminded her of her first husband, Dom O'Flaherty, and she had never been really afraid of Dom, who had been nothing more than a bully.

"The front door was open, madame, and there were no servants about to stop me. Tsk. Tsk. Such carelessness," came the mocking reply.

"*Get out!*" Skye told him firmly.

Piers St. Denis laughed, genuinely amused. Too bad she was so old and dried up. If rumor had it correct, she had been a marvelous fuck in her youth. Her granddaughter, however, promised equal delights.

"How did you know I was here?" Jasmine had finally found her voice, and now that the shock of his arrival was over, she found her fear had gone also. She was very angry.

"It is well-known that you and your mother like to return here to Queen's Malvern in the summer. You did not come last year, of course, because the king went to Scotland; but I knew you would be here this summer. I had but to wait until your parents and husband took the young Lindleys off to Cadby. I am a most patient man, my pet, and you are a very clever woman. I shall not underestimate you again. I was very surprised to return to our little love nest to find you gone. And how quick-witted of you to go to Leith, knowing I would believe you were trying to escape back to Edinburgh. It was adroitly done, my pet."

"What do you want here?" Skye demanded of him.

"Why, madame, I would have thought that was obvious. I am going to kill you both, and then I shall slay your two Leslie children, who are within this house. My only regret is that I cannot destroy your little Stuart bastard, and break old king fool's heart as he has broken mine. You see, madame, I have given up all hope of your ever being mine; but it is due to you that I have lost everything. If you had not led me on only to reject me, I should yet today be marquis of Hartsfield, with a rich wife chosen by the queen and the king still my friend. You, and you alone, are responsible for my misfortunes, and you will pay for your treachery."

"*No!*" Jasmine almost shouted at him. "*You* are responsible for your own bad fortune, sir. I told you from the beginning that I was in love with James Leslie, and pledged to him, and him alone. You would not listen! You kept insisting despite everything I said that I would be yours. You even followed me to Scotland after my marriage, and after the birth of my first Leslie son, and had the temerity to kidnap me. It is your stubborn nature that has caused you to lose everything, not I. Now go away while you yet have the opportunity, or I shall call the servants, and they shall hold you for the local sheriff. There is a price on your head, and many who would gladly have it."

He moved across the room until he stood directly before the two women. "I will not be deterred in my purpose this time, madame," he said. "Know this, and be afraid of my power. My traitorous half-brother is this day a widower. Had he not been up in London when I arrived at Hartsfield Hall, I would have killed him, too. His wife was quite a lovely woman. I whipped her until her back was raw, and she was begging for mercy. Then I forced her as I did you, but her mouth and tongue were not nearly as skillful as yours, my pet. And when she had finished, I had my way with her. How she screamed, but more so when I plundered her temple of Sodom, for it would seem my brother had never been that way. And when I had my fill of her ripe charms, I slit her throat and left her dying in a pool of her own bright red blood. My final act before leaving my home was to strangle her infant son. I will not allow my half-brother's bastard line to defile the house of St. Denis."

"And where were the servants when you were doing all of this, sir?" Skye demanded, not certain that she believed him.

"At a fair in the village," he said. "She had allowed all of them to go, the silly, softhearted creature. But I have wasted far too much time here tonight. I must complete my revenge, then disappear for good this time. The jewelry that you are wearing, Madame Skye, will keep me comfortable for quite some time." He smiled and, moving closer, reached out to take the heavy gold necklace with is sapphire pendant from her.

Jasmine was in a half daze from listening to the story Piers St. Denis had just told them. She heard her grandmother speak.

"I told you once, sir, that you were not skilled enough to play my game," Skye said, and her hand moved so swiftly that Jasmine could not believe what she was witnessing. The dagger appeared from nowhere and plunged straight into Piers St. Denis's heart muscle. Skye smiled into his face as she twisted her weapon in order to inflict the most damage and ensure his very swift death. "I will not allow you to ruin my darling girl's life ever again," Skye said firmly, then she stepped back a pace.

He crumpled to the floor, a look of incredulous surprise upon his very dissolute face. Then the light fled from his bright blue eyes, and Piers St. Denis breathed his last. He was quite dead.

Jasmine's breath escaped her in an audible whoosh. "*Grandmama!*" was all that she could say.

Red Hugh ran into the hall and, seeing the body, swore. "Jesu! Why is it, m'lady, that whenever yer in danger from that fellow, I am nae where to be found? Is he dead?" He knelt for a moment by the body.

"He's dead," Skye said. "He got in because the door was open for the breeze, and there was no servant in the front hall. From now on there must always be someone there." She sat down heavily. "Get me some wine, man. I've just killed the devil's own son."

He arose. "Whiskey would be better, madame," he said, pouring her out a dram. "Here! Drink it down, and I'll gie ye another."

Skye followed his orders. She was weak with relief.

He took the dram jigger and poured her a second libation. "One more," he said. The old lady looked pale. "Ye did a fine job of it, madame," he told her. "He dinna hae a chance once ye stuck him wi yer blade. I dinna know that ye carried any weapon."

"Old habits are hard to break," Skye remarked. "I have always, since my girlhood in Ireland, carried a dagger." She looked dispassionately at the body of Piers St. Denis. "Get rid of that, Red Hugh. Take it to the parson in the village and have it buried in unhallowed ground. He was an evil man, and while God may forgive him, none of us will." She pulled herself up. "Come, my darling girl, and help me upstairs. I have had quite enough excitement for one day. Will there ever come a day when my life is completely at peace? Nay. I know the answer to that, and I can even hear your grandfather laughing at my foolishness. There will be no peace for Skye O'Malley until she is dead and buried."

"Are you certain you will find peace even then?" Jasmine teased her grandmother, as they made their way up the staircase.

"Probably not, my dear duchess, probably not," Skye said, and then she laughed along with her darling Jasmine.

Queen's Malvern

Midsummer's Eve 1623

Epilogue

The old woman was dying. They had not said it to her, of course, but why else had all her children gathered here together at Queen's Malvern with their spouses, offspring, and grandchildren? Even her eldest child, her son, Ewan, now in his sixty-seventh year, had made the trip from Ireland to bid her a proper farewell. God's boots! Was it that long ago she had given birth to Ewan in that draughty tower house that the O'Flahertys called home? Her sister, Eibhlin, had been there to help her, and again ten months later when Murrough had been born.

So many years gone by. So many wonderful adventures. She outlived them all. Her husbands. Her lovers. Bess Tudor. What a great friend to her the queen had been. And what a bitter enemy. She had, she decided, absolutely no regrets at all. She had lived her life to the fullest; raised her children well; founded a commercial enterprise that had made them all wealthy. *And she had loved.* From her innocent first love for Niall Burke, Deirdre and Padraic's father, to her last love, Adam de Marisco. Aye! She had loved well, and been well loved by them all.

The curtains about her bed had been drawn back at her request so she might gaze out the open windows. Willow, of course, had wanted the curtains drawn and the windows shut, but Skye would not have it; and Robin, her dearest Robin, had overruled his eldest sister, which gave their other siblings the courage to side with him. Willow was growing sallow as she aged. *I have not told her the truth about her father,* the old woman thought, *but I think I shall spare her the knowledge that the "respectable Spanish merchant" in North Africa whom she believes sired her was, in truth, a renegade who took the name Khalid el Bey, and was known as the Great Whoremaster of Algiers.* A bubble of laughter choked the old woman for a brief moment. Such a knowledge would destroy poor proper Willow, and she did not want *that* on her conscience as she went to meet her Maker. *There is no harm in my daughter's ignorance, and after all, I have kept this secret for sixty-three years. Even my dearest Daisy did not know.*

Daisy Kelly, her faithful tiring woman and dearest confidante and friend. She had died suddenly just over a year ago, and nothing had been the same ever since. Just gone to bed one evening and never awakened in the morning. Young Nora had been a great comfort to the old woman, but it was not the same. Nora had not been young with her mistress, nor shared her many adventures or her secrets. No. It hadn't been the same, nor would it ever be again. Her time was long past. Her eyes strayed to the windows beyond. It was almost sunset now. The sky was slowly becoming streaked with gold, lavender, pink, scarlet, and orange. It was, she thought, the most beautiful sunset she had ever seen. Soon the midsummer fires would begin leaping from the hillsides. It was a most magical night.

"Grandmama?" Jasmine placed a kiss on her forehead. "How do you feel?"

"Tired," she answered the young woman. *Jasmine.* Darling Jasmine, her husband called her. Her favorite grandchild, although she had certainly never had a favorite until Jasmine had come into her life. She felt no shame at all in loving Jasmine best of all of them. She had arrived a month ago for her English summer, with her beloved Jemmie, and her eight children. India, who at fifteen, was already a great beauty; Henry, now fourteen, and his father's image; Fortune, at thirteen outgrowing her coltishness, and promising to rival India shortly; Charlie, the not-so-royal Stuart, now eleven, and, like his elder brother, every inch *his* father's son. And the four little Leslies; Patrick, Adam, Duncan, and the old woman's youngest descendant, Janet Skye, who had been born just over six months ago on her own eighty-second birthday.

She turned toward the windows again, and it was then that she saw them as they came walking toward her out of the sunset. Niall Burke as she had first known him, his smoothly shaven face tanned by the outdoors, his short-cropped hair as midnight dark as her own. Her father, and Eibhlin, who was smiling at her. And Khalid el Bey, with his long oval face, with its well-barbered black beard and those melting amber eyes fringed in the outrageously thick lashes she had always envied. And here was Geoffrey Southwood, lean, blond, and arrogantly handsome, his lime green eyes laughing at her surprise. *And her darling Daisy!* Not old and wizened as she had been but a year ago, but apple-cheeked, and gap-toothed, and young again. The old woman strained to see them all, yet something was missing.

"*Come, little girl, it is time for us to go now.*" Her eyes widened, and he was there before her, holding out his hand for her to take.

"*Adam!*" she said, reaching for his hand, and Jasmine gazed anxiously at her.

Skye rose from her sickbed, gazing long and lovingly at each of them; her smile was as bright as the morning. Her heart was filled to overflowing with the deep, pure happiness she felt. She would miss her children and grandchildren, of course, but one day they would meet again. For now another door was opening. Another wonderful adventure was beckoning to her. Never fearful of a new venture, she eagerly accepted their invitation. *"Gentlemen, lead on!"* she cried; and then, linking her arms with those of Adam de Marisco and Geoffrey Southwood, she hurried off toward the sunset and down the road to forever, without so much as a regret or a backward glance.

"Jemmie!" Jasmine's hand went to her heart as she felt the pain of the separation. She looked up at her husband, stricken.

"Aye, she is gone, darling Jasmine," he said gently, putting his arms about her. "She is gone from us for now. Do not weep, sweeting. She would not want it. She would want you to be brave as she was brave."

"They say I am like her," Jasmine said brokenly, "and I wish it were so, but it is not. There will never be a woman like Skye O'Malley ever again, Jemmie. *Never again!*"

James Leslie, the duke of Glenkirk, leaned over, and gently closed the old woman's now sightless Kerry blue eyes, but upon her face he saw there was a tiny smile. She had been glad to go, he thought. *No.* There would never ever be a woman like Skye O'Malley. *Godspeed, Skye,* he said silently. *Godspeed until we meet again!*

About the Author

Bertrice Small (1937–2015), was an American *New York Times* and *USA Today* bestselling author of over fifty historical, contemporary, fantasy and erotic romance novels. She lived on Long Island, New York. Her first novel, *The Kadin*, was published in 1978. She was a member of The Authors Guild and Romance Writers of America, and in 2004 received a Lifetime Achievement Award from *Romantic Times* for her contributions to the romance genre.

About the Publisher

This book is published on behalf of the author by the Ethan Ellenberg Literary Agency.
https://ethanellenberg.com
Email: agent@ethanellenberg.com
Facebook: https://www.facebook.com/EthanEllenbergLiteraryAgency/

Made in United States
Cleveland, OH
10 March 2025

15045091R00262